# HARLEM RAIDERS

## A Novel Based on a True Story

By

## Peter J. Pranzo, Ret. Lt., NYPD

Printed in the United States of America

First Printing October 2019

For information Righter's Mill Press, LLC
475 Wall Street
Princeton, NJ 08540

Library of Congress Cataloging-in-Publication Data
TXu1-915-534 July 8, 2014
Pranzo, Peter J.
HARLEM RAIDERS/Peter J. Pranzo 7-9-1946
ISBN: 978-1-948460-03-3

First Edition

Jacket Designed by Brian Hailes
Visit our Web Site at http://www.rightersmillpress.com

# DEDICATION

*I dedicate this book to the men and women in law enforcement agencies across America, many, who in their daily assignments, have concluded their tour of duty by serious injury or death. These heroic officers have sacrificed their own existence in order that others may live and work in peace.*

# ACKNOWLEDGMENTS

*This writing gig is a world opposite the realm of grunt work in law enforcement throughout busy police precincts. To enter either one is a privilege. I thank the folks at Three Corners Entertainment for the writing opportunity; Richard Sand and Karen Venable for their guidance, writing tips, and patience, and Jeffrey Batoff and Al Longden for their acceptance of this old, retired street cop.*

*None of us accomplishes anything worthwhile by ourselves. That, of course, includes me, especially as it relates to my family, friends, and my extended family—the NYPD. As such, I wish to take this opportunity to thank all those who supported me and those who literally kept me alive so I could help others and do what had to be done. I begin with the hundreds of police officers I worked with during my 21-year career, from Brooklyn to Harlem to the elite city-wide Street Crime Unit, and in my heart remember those who are no longer with us, and cherish the time we served together.*

*I must highlight the heroic men and women who worked in Harlem's 32nd Precinct, from patrol to all the specialized teams. It is within this historic community where the basis for the story, "Harlem Raiders," takes place. A special thank you to the guys in my unit, the toughest and best of the best, who never hesitated to put their lives on the line for me and those they swore to protect. Woven into the soul of the Three-Two was the surrounding neighborhood of dedicated people and community leaders who stood up to the most fearsome drug lords. Also, I would be remiss not to acknowledge the NYPD's*

Organized Crime Control Bureau and the DEA in their strive to eradicate drugs. Working alongside has always been a privilege.

Finally, and most importantly, a special thank you to Rachela, my wife of over 50 years. A woman of strength who stood by my side through an era of American history that was amidst a narcotics and murder epidemic never seen before. Despite the threats to our family, Rachela cared for our two children and guided us through the side effects of violence by her courage, love, and support. Later, she transcribed my chicken scratch into typed prose for "Harlem Raiders," and is the only one who never rejected my work or me.

# CONTENTS

# PREFACE

Three decades in American History that defined turmoil were the 1960's-70's-80's.

There were three high profile assassinations; a US President, a National Civil Rights Leader, and a US Senator. Another president resigned amidst political chaos. Racial divisiveness and an unpopular war lead to mass demonstrations and violence. The proliferation of crime and narcotics completed the perfect storm.

Minority communities within major cities were held hostage by organized crime, mostly by the Sicilian Mafia. Narcotics were the hot commodity. New York City, and in particular, Harlem became the murder and heroin capital of America. It led the way to a forgotten people, and the sanctity of life itself. Drug addicts littered the landscape. Thousands of 'users' concealed themselves in abandoned buildings, awaiting death. Homicides, not including overdoses, ran into the thousands, annually. Shootings tripled that. Poverty, crime, and hopelessness, enhanced the separation of the police and a community they had sworn to protect.

Only a handful of community leaders dared to break down the racial barriers that enabled small units of law enforcement to enter their violent neighborhoods, effect thousands of arrests, remove guns, drugs, and criminals, and restore freedom.

The story of the *Harlem Raiders* highlights one of the most successful police teams, who, at their own peril, partnered with a historic American community and freed its people from the clutches of organized crime.

# INTRODUCTION

*Deep within the underworld of narcotics, the role I played on the street was not a pleasant one, but necessary to accomplish my mission. A work assignment turned into a personal fight for survival. Defying death became a daily ritual. I worked alone, day and night. No bulletproof vest, no gun.*

*Witnessing the exploitation of human beings within a historic American community broke my heart, but not my spirit. I would seek justice, the kind relegated to rogue behavior.*

*Being one of the first women in the DEA was difficult enough. Being one of the first women of color—double it. It was this contrast that made me who I was undercover and who I am today.*

*My name is Yono. This is my story.*

## CHAPTER 1

# 'H' RETURNS

"I'm not sure about this."

Brianna looks at her friend in the strange glow of the flashlight. A torn blanket does little to keep the cold out, as it slices across the Harlem River. She can't believe Lina is doubtful now. It had been her idea.

"Why?"

"It might hurt."

Brianna gives her a small, friendly smile. "Yes, but only for a second. And then . . . ecstasy."

Moments before, the two climbed to their rooftop hideout between an ancient stairwell and a rotting brick cornice. Once at the top, Brianna and Lina huddled together in their red-and-gold cheerleader uniforms underneath hoodies and sweatpants.

A half-empty glassine envelope stamped, 'Loco' rests upon Brianna's lap.

Lina still isn't convinced.

"Remember the promise we made to each other at my Sweet Sixteen?" Brianna says. "We'd do something special."

Lina takes a deep breath, nods.

"My cousin loaded the syringe and showed me how to use it," Brianna whispers. "Push up your sleeve. I need to tie this piece of rubber tubing around your arm in a tight knot to find a vein. You'll do the same for me with the other piece. Then all we do is stick in the needle and push down the plunger.I'll do it to you first, then you jab me. We'll each take half." She smiles reassuringly.

Lina shudders and frowns. The doubt returning. "Are you sure? Maybe . . . just you."

Brianna bristles with anger. "We agreed we'd try it together, remember? Just once."

A sharp gust of wind slashes through the blanket and across the youngsters' faces. The girls shiver. "I'm freezin'," Lina says. "It's late, my Mom's gonna' be looking for me."

"Look, Li, it'll be quick. The high is supposed to be great and only lasts an hour. Besides, everyone's doin' it."

"Not everyone."

"Everyone who matters."

Lina hesitates. "I'm scared."

"You wanna' do me first?"

Lina closes her eyes for a moment. "No." She shakes her head as if shaking off a chill, holds out her arm and pulls up the sleeve.

Brianna slips the band over Lina's upper arm, tightening it with a yank.

"Ow!" Lina yells.

"Ssshhh. That's the worst part."

"Really?"

"My cousin said it makes your arm go numb, so you don't feel the needle."

Lina looks doubtful again but relaxes as she slips the band around her friend's upper arm.

"Tighten the knot, Lina. Pull harder! . . . Okay, okay. That's good. Look, I can see a spot to push the needle in. Let me see your arm." She aims the flashlight.

Their inexperience shows as Brianna repeatedly tries to push the needle into the skin of Lina's upper forearm. Multiple test jabs leave tiny droplets of blood puddling across her arm.

Lina flinches. "I can feel that! Your cousin lied!"

"Hold still! It'll just take a second."

Finally, Brianna completes the injection, immediately followed by Lina's jittery hands taking control of the hypo and puncturing Brianna's bulging vein. She pushes down on the plunger.

There is a pause as the two youngsters gaze into each other's eyes awaiting the anticipated feeling of euphoria.

"I don't feel good, Bri. I don't think it's working right. Something's wrong."

One girl moans in pain followed by the other. Eventually, the sounds become muted as their makeshift fort plunges into darkness.

---

An NYPD helicopter hovers in the morning's sunrise, its occupants peering down onto ice-covered rooftops. The aircraft's low altitude, and the *whomp-whomp* sound of the blades, cut through the quietness of the New York City neighborhood. An observation is made. They see two girls lying face up, just feet from the edge of the roof. An ice-laden blanket partially covers them.

The co-pilot stoically rattles off a radio transmission.

"AV-1 to AV-Central," the co-pilot says. "AV-1 to AV-Central." He points towards the roof. The pilot nods as he maneuvers the craft for a closer look.

"This is AV-Central," the voice on the radio squawks. "Come in AV-1."

The copilot presses the talk button again. "Be advised, we have the missing subjects in view. Location, rooftop, S/W, C/O West 141st Street and Lenox Avenue. No movement detected, Central. Alert units below. We'll remain in place."

"Central to AV-1. Message received—ground units alerted and on their way."

"AV-1, 10-4."

The copilot sets the mic in his lap as his partner points towards the street. Police vehicles and medical emergency response vans are swarming in front of the building. Car doors burst open as dozens of figures begin spilling out. Moments later, officers and emergency personnel explode across the rooftop, flooding the scene.

_____

They find the young victims with the rubber tubing still in place. A syringe dangles from one of the girl's arms. Dry tracks of blood lay clotted in the subfreezing temperature.

Two uniformed officers begin cordoning off the area with yellow crime scene tape. Within minutes, two well-seasoned Homicide Detectives arrive. The sea of on-scene blue 'uniforms' parts, as the two meander towards the children's lifeless bodies. One detective leans over and points his flashlight directly into the half-opened eyes of one girl, muttering to his partner.

"Jesus Christ. These are just kids. A couple of more OD's."

The other detective responds in a louder voice, "Or murders. What's the difference being killed by a gun or 'smack?' It's all the same. Let's make sure we bag up that 'Loco-H.' Maybe we can track down the packers and pushers."

"Got it. Don't worry, we're gonna' get these scumbags."

Crime Scene photographers begin snapping away.

The gruesome scene of the children breaks the hearts of first responders and distraught parents. As the cops hurry to secure the site, two teams of paramedics hustle a pair of covered stretchers preparing to carry down the bodies of Brianna Tefon and Lina Ferez.

Later that morning, reporters set up their equipment and get to work as the pair of 'uniforms' watches over them, protecting the scene.

The men and women with microphones sound strangely distant as they broadcast the demise of two teenagers on West 141st Street in Harlem. One commentator points to the icy blanket, which is all that remains of the original tragedy. The camera zooms in for a closer shot.

"This is all that is left of the two young cheerleaders from Central Harlem High. This is where they came to experiment with something that, according to friends and neighbors who knew them best, neither girl had any experience with. This is where they spent their final night on Earth."

The camera zooms back to the reporter's face as a plume of white steam escapes his mouth.

"This is Michael Flannery, News Today."

In the studio, the sharply dressed anchorwoman shakes her head, sighing. It takes several moments for her to gain her composure before continuing.

"Police believe the overdose of the two girls is the direct result of a local chapter of the MS-13 Gang, who push lethal Mexican heroin on behalf of the Sinaloa Cartel. The street-cut drug is unstable and impure. And, as we now know, deadly."

And, at home, the girls' mothers wail and cry for their losses that have no end.

---

Ramone heads up the three flights of shaky stairs with his trio of well-armed bangers, pissed enough to take out the city block. Fortunately, unlike some, he can think clearly enough to see the big picture. He didn't help put the MS-13 where it was by thinking small.

He taps lightly on a new, fortified steel door. Several seconds later, the peephole opens and a pair of dark eyes checks him out. The locks begin to disengage one at a time until the door opens to a large room, formerly an apartment.

Ramone, wearing his trademark blue bandana and skintight muscle shirt, walks brazenly to the center of the room. No one needs to be told to pay attention. He's the most vicious of the drug lords. The better part of his face, neck, and upper body are covered in black-inked *Mara Salvatrucha*—spider-webbing blending with a bold *XIII* and three triangles denoting Honduras, El Salvador, and Guatemala. Dozens of workers cease their cutting, mixing, and packaging operation as they gather around with subordinate gang members.

Ramone glares at each person, finishing with the focus of his rage.

"Miguel, ya' fucked-up man! *Whad'ya mezcle con nuestro 'Loco H?'* "

Miguel responds, but tries to sound more conciliatory. "Just a taste of fentanyl, man. Gives that extra boost."

"You're a fucking fool!" Ramone snaps. "Two kids OD'd. Two school kids dead, man. The pigs will be all over us now. You were supposed to keep things smooth—no problems. All we asked for was straight Mexicana shit right to the Americana Harlem streets."

Miguel puts his hands up as if to say, *What's the big deal?* "I increased sales, man."

Ramone's rage flares in his eyes. "We lose customers that way, dick-head. You've jeopardized our whole operation." He pauses for a moment, then shouts, "You're done! Ricardo, you're in charge now."

"But, boss . . ." Before Miguel can get the next word out, Ramone pulls out one of his 9mm semi-autos and fires two rounds into the neck of his foreman.

Miguel thrusts his arms forward in a feeble attempt to block the incoming bullets. He stumbles, falling onto the worn, planked floor where he bleeds out.

The workers stand for several moments, shocked. The smell of gunfire lingers in the air as they watch a man die.

"Wrap him up and get him out of here," Ramone says to the new plant leader. "Put him in that garbage pail. Make some holes in it, seal it up, weigh it down, and drop him into the river later tonight. Understand?"

"Yes, sir," Ricardo answers, and then turns to his crew. Ramone stops him and orders, "And remember—pure product only."

Ricardo's eyes widen. "Of course." He spins around, yelling out to everyone, "You heard. Genuine product only! Back to work."

## CHAPTER 2

# A HARLEM STORY

This morning is supposed to be another average school day for hundreds of teenagers. Instead, masses of high schoolers are ushered into the quiet school auditorium. Rumors and news recycling account for the buzz between parents and their loved ones. Reporters stand with rolling cameras on the sidewalks out front. Uniformed patrols protect the innocence within the building.

Father Ingal, church patriarch for over four decades, steps forward on stage and begins to pray to the assemblage.

"Lord Thy God, please watch over our children sent to you this day. We can't ask you why. We can only beg for your grace and mercy for Brianna and Lina."

Father Ingal lowers his head and tone.

"Please everyone, pray with me.............................."

Principal John Cafira steps forward to the mic, pauses, and speaks with compassion, "Thank you, Father Ingal, for leading this morning's service. Students, parents, faculty....., I wish we were not here for this today and that Brianna Tefon and Lina Ferez were sitting amongst us. They were your classmates and deserve to be honored."

He gestures to the packed auditorium.

"The pinks and purples decorating this hall honor their absence. The oversized photos remind us of the beauty and potential of a pair of sixteen-year-olds, who brought life into their friends and the cheer squad they loved."

He pauses, gathering his thoughts.

"Whether we lose a loved one to illness, accident, or violence, days like today are never easy. Perhaps Brianna and Lina thought using heroin would be fun and exciting. However, they made the wrong choice. Now, it's not my intention to frighten you, but the reality is they did not experience exhilaration or joy, only suffering and death. We can only pray they have found peace."

He pauses again, focusing on the Ferez and Tifon families, who are stunned by the loss of their children. "The truth is, heroin kills, and it's not just happening here in Harlem, but in neighborhoods across America. I have experienced this type of tragedy before, many years ago. Never in my wildest nightmares would I envision this curse returning here. Now, I would like to bring forward our guest speaker for today's service. Please, I ask for your undivided attention."

An old woman, tall in stature, pushes and slides her walker across the large stage.

"Good morning, my beautiful children."

The seventy-year-old stands before the assembly in the high school auditorium, wears metal leg braces, puts her walker off to the side, and sits in a large, soft chair. Her dark blue dress flows around a slight and frail silhouette, while her silver-streaked black hair is pulled back and tied in a bun, which shows off a face that does not represent her age. She is of African-American/Hispanic descent and is one of the senior members of the community. Some in the audience recognize her, most do not.

She hesitates and looks about slowly.

"My name is Yono. I've come to grieve with you over the loss of Brianna and Lina and also to share a story with all of you. A history lesson of sorts. It is an uplifting Harlem story of life and hope."

Behind her, black and white photos of an old Harlem, dating back from 1920 to 1950, are displayed on a large screen at the rear of the stage. They show a historic community of jazz clubs, unique restaurants, theaters, an opera house, upscale boutiques, and many ornate churches.

"Many years ago, long before you were born, I was a child myself and didn't need this silly, metal contraption." She points to the walker. "Central Harlem was once a vibrant community, where hard working and culturally active people lived for decades. Its fame did not come from violence, but from the famous individuals who lived and entertained here."

She purposely raises her voice, tinged with anger.

"The 1970's version of Central Harlem was an entirely different era. This chapter of a radically changing neighborhood was one that succumbed to the infiltration of a destructive and evil force, narcotics. This deadly plague came to our home and took thousands of our children. They were all about your age back then and were taken violently and needlessly. It is a story of two Harlems, one likened to a piece of New York prestige and the other nicknamed by the police themselves, Dodge City."

The students appear wide-eyed as they take this in.

"In New York City, over seventy years ago, two children were born. One, a White child in Queens, and the other, a Black child in Harlem. They, along with their parents, were as different as night and day. No one realized these two young people growing up in completely different environments would one day work together. They would become an unstoppable force giving you the freedoms you enjoy today. The ability to live, worship, play, go to school, and prosper right here in our community."

She catches her breath before continuing. A photo appears on the screen behind her.

"The woman you see is Renee Jons. She is an adult here, but as a child, she had long, striking, black locks of hair, only surpassed by large oval-shaped eyes imitating pools of dark mountain lakes. She double-dutched, played with dolls, had many young friends, went to school, and excelled. This young girl enjoyed a life unequaled in color, diversity, imagination, and talent. She was full of exuberance and hope. She became a single mom to five children, a social worker, and earned a Doctorate Degree. Her life would ultimately change a community, a city, and a way of communication amongst people of all races and religions. Mayors, Governors, religious leaders of all faiths, a President's wife, and even a Pope, would come to see her in Harlem. It would become Renee's Harlem."

Renee's photo is replaced by that of a man in a police uniform. Yono looks out at the audience and sees she has their complete attention.

"The child from Queens was named, Paul Pasano. He grew up in the suburbs, played sports, and dreamed one day of becoming a New York Police Officer. He would do that and much more. Aside from marrying and raising a family of his own, he would eventually become one of the most decorated Superior Officers in the history of the NYPD."

The photo on the screen fades away.

"Together, this community leader and police Sergeant would challenge the largest and most ruthless Mafia organizations in the world. Paul and Renee faced death many times but never gave up. Now, I know most of you are on the verge of adulthood, and I will treat you in that light. However, I do have to warn you, some of this is graphic."

Yono pauses as every eye is watching her.

"You see, what has been happening is not the beginning . . . No, it started long ago, in a place far away………

## CHAPTER 3

# BLOODFIELDS

*The First Wave—1970*
*Central Turkey*

Majestic hilltops and tranquil valleys, filled with thousands of acres of red and golden poppy plants, glisten under a bright morning sunrise. Once the beautiful flower petals fall off, a sac is revealed containing the raw, gummy opiate that is refined into pure heroin.

A tiny parcel of land is carved out of the surrounding foliage. Three peasant farmers, standing in shallow graves they dug themselves, plead for their lives.

*"Lütfen, bayım, bizi öldürme. Lütfen, Hayır! Hayır!"*

No more than a slight nod by a Capo leader and the three farmers are gunned down. Their bodies are riddled with quarter-sized bullet holes from head to foot. The sounds of gunfire echo throughout the valley as a warning to others.

A tractor pushes the fertile, dark soil over the mutilated bodies as the Mafia Capo shouts out in Sicilian dialect, *"Nero mani sfiorano il prodotto non verrra tollerato e il risultato sara lo stresso destino!"* ("Skimming the Black-Hand's product will not be tolerated and will result in any or all of you the same fate!")

The large crowd of meagerly paid Turkish workers begins to slowly disperse, returning to their assigned crop chores. Their weathered faces express no emotion.

If seen from above, the countryside would show dozens of similar gravesites. The peasant farmers call these 'Bloodfields.'

———————

*Palermo, Sicily*

Members of the three most powerful families in the Mafia sit in a stone farmhouse.

"I understand the Turkish poppy fields have been secured," Enrico Seteola says in Sicilian. "That's the easy part, but how does the product get to the states?"

Sonny Inzarita refills his coffee cup. He knows he must be careful partnering with the two other Mafioso families, the Seteolas and Giadanas. He has to be especially careful with Enrico, who sports a six-inch facial scar and is by far the most unstable.

"The Turkish poppy fields will be overseen by the Seteolas," Sonny says. "You, Enrico, will monitor the harvesting by local farmers. Have it bundled and brought by railway to the port of Mersin. There it will be loaded onto cargo vessels and shipped to the port here in Palermo. I'll have it trucked up to our farmhouse labs. We'll refine and brick it, then send it to my cousin, Carlos Giadana in New York, by ocean freighters. He'll truck it to the Bronx, where it will be cut and packaged for sale. The Giadanas and associates will distribute to the local dealers in Harlem, the center point of the operation. Understand?"

It is abundantly clear, at least in Italy, that Sonny Inzarita is the organized crime leader of this unholy trinity that forms a single, vicious alliance. The representatives of each family nod in agreement with the Capo's plans to corner the heroin production and buyers' market.

The stocky, bent-nosed Inzarita takes a sip of his coffee, then asks for any input or questions.

Enrico Seteola is still skeptical. "Just who will be cutting and selling in New York? How will our product be safeguarded and marketed? And what kind of person would defile themselves to use such a devil's mix?"

Sonny's dark eyes lock onto Seteola. "Carlos Giadana, my cousin, has already put his market plans to work in Harlem. He is doing well but needs more of the pure product. He makes hundreds of young American drug addicts every day. The White ones have the money, but Carlos uses the Harlem dark ones, the unfortunates, to sell. It turns out they make both good salespeople and product users. He has one of their own who thinks he's in charge. They call him 'the flashy colored one.'"

Sonny looks at each man, ending with Enrico. "Those who have *nothing* will do *anything* to have *something*. Their stupidity and greed surpass their common sense. Remember this, trust no one outside our families."

The other Mafiosos grin and laugh as Sonny Inzarita raises a glass of wine and proposes a toast, *"Salute per fortuna!"*

———————

*East Harlem, New York*

At a private table in the basement of an Italian restaurant, Carlos Giadana gives orders to a dozen of his underlings.

Speaking in Italian, he methodically goes over the list for the proper etiquette of cutting, diluting, and packaging into $10 dime and $25 quarter bags of heroin. The attending reps' can then forward the protocols to their Harlem street overseers and dealers.

In a deep, raspy voice, Carlos speaks quietly, but intently.

"Listen carefully. These Harlem 'moolies' are hungry, but never give too much power to any one of them. Keep them satisfied. Well off, but not rich. If they use, that's okay. It gives them more incentive to sell. You provide them with the tools, guns, start-up money, and plenty of product. Make sure you distance yourself from the actual street sales. If you can, have them cut and package in the Bronx, and sell in Central Harlem. As it spreads, you spread with it. *Capisce?*"

The gang of young Italian subordinates soak in every word.

One of those is DEA undercover, Nick Scalia, who checks his watch. He will have to report in soon. He was already late. But, his bosses will understand. Better to be late than blow his cover. The damning information he gathered and passed along to the DEA/NYPD Task Force over the past two years would not be enough to bring the Italian organization down. Every day, the case against them grows stronger. However, while the scope of their deviousness becomes wider, it will not ensure convictions of those pulling the strings.

Giadana slaps the table with his hand. "Now eat!"

The others repeat in unison. *"Mangia!"*

Nick smiles as he takes a sip of wine.

## CHAPTER 4

# DODGE CITY

It is a sullen, rainy day in a dead zone enveloping the urban drug and crime infested neighborhood of Central Harlem on W. 154th Street. It's a striking reversal from the once vibrant lives, which thrived just one decade before. New York streets and sidewalks are filled with litter and stained with blood from previous shootings. The remnants from years of organized crime control are exposed in gory detail as dozens of heroin addicts line up in a rear alleyway. They wait their turn to cop a daily fix of multiple dime bags of potent 'smack.'

One junkie says to another, "This the place for a hit, bro?"

"What the fuck you think, doper? I'm waiting here for ice cream?"

Ten to twelve-year-old lookouts are strategically placed at corners of nearby intersections, standing ready to call out '5-0' on the first sighting of local cops from the 35th Precinct. This is the most violent square mile in America. It is labeled, 'The Murder and Drug Capital of the U.S.' A gun packing, multi-tattooed bull adjusts the weapon in his waistband as he oversees the entire operation to protect buyers, sellers, lookouts, and the 'stash.' Money holders are secreted in doorways counting their take. In a matter of minutes, the large crowd of those hooked quickly assembles. They buy their 'skag' and scurry back to their local drug dens.

The Mafioso's plan is in full bloom. Millions of dollars are made weekly within the confines of this single, urban, ghetto battlefield.

Harlem is the epicenter of turbulent times across American cities. Anti-war, anti-government, and anti-police protests fill the streets. A wall of racial disharmony and distrust between the police and the communities they swore to protect, grows to epidemic proportions. A lack of understanding and communication blossoms into hatred and contempt on both sides. As the racial divide, crime, narcotics abuse, and poverty increase, there is a yearning for leadership and an outcry for resolution.

———————

Renee Jons holds tightly onto two of her five young children, as she meanders around discarded syringes and the junkies who claim this community is theirs.

She murmurs at what lies before her. "God Almighty. A disgrace."

Renee's former life of freedom, promise, and hope is vanishing.

Police sirens are heard in the background as the young lookouts scream out, "5-0! 5-0!" The hundreds of junkie bystanders, buyers, sellers, and the gun-toting thug scamper like roaches, heading for the nearest broken cinder block building entranceways. This mad exodus repeats itself day and night.

The onslaught of overworked Harlem cops race down W. 154th Street from 7th Avenue in a four-car caravan. They come to a screeching halt in the middle of the block.

"Hold it, you motha' fuckas'," they yell while bolting out with guns drawn to begin chasing down the slowest of the pack. A few are tackled, rolled, and cuffed. Three of the 35th Precinct's finest chase others up a broken stairway to the third floor of a 'shooting gallery.' They kick in a crudely boarded-up door located in a graffiti-covered, dilapidated apartment. There are dozens of fecal covered mattresses laid out in long rows occupied by grossly swollen individuals, who are too sick to run, and plead with the bluecoats to leave them be. The stench overcomes even the most tenured professionals with the strongest resistance.

The pursuing cops are not interested in what lays before them. They are searching for the drug holders. The sickly group is searched by the glove-wearing officers. This portion of their raid is a failure, as the sizeable 'stash,' currency, and guns they were looking for, are not found. As the disappointed cops begin to leave with their meager catch, the stench of rotting human flesh and blood from people barely alive, lingers with them.

The remaining addicts begin to shuffle away. One lags behind.

"Please, officers, let me hang. I ain't hurtin' nobody." The cops down at street level hear the plea. They recognize the voice of a local, light-skinned junkie named, Corisa. She has become the leader of the unfortunate, begging the other officers to be left alone. Her long straggly hair and torn clothes reek from filth. She is sickly and barely able to stand.

One of the precinct's toughest senior cops, John Calvoy, knows of her plight and tells the others, "Let her be. She's too far gone." The blue-coats leave, taking with them a handful of arrests for simple possession.

As the patrol cars leave the block, Corisa is out front kneeling along-side one of her youngest and weakest comrades, lending aid. "Look, Gina, you're a mess. Let's get you cleaned up, honey." Arm-in-arm the two tread slowly up to the drug den where Corisa gently lays the teen down on one of the makeshift beds.

Several patrol cars head back to the station house to process a few of the users. In one car, John Calvoy looks over at his longtime part-ner. "Hey, Will, you know this is fucked-up. We're not even making a dent here."

Will Fennar returns with his own version of dejection. "John, whatta' ya' want to do? We're alone out here and nobody gives a God-damn. Those no-balls brass and 'suits' down at Headquarters don't have a clue of what's going on up here. As long as it's contained and there are no riots, they couldn't give a fuck. Let's process these mopes, get down to court, and back to our families. Deal?"

---

The sun is setting and the cold overtakes any residual warmth generated by the daylight. Most of the addicts have completed their last hit of 'smack' for the day, while a few of the capable ones light the candles strewn about.

As she covers Gina with a blanket, Corisa makes a plea. "Why are you so stubborn? You're burning up with fever. I'll call an ambulance and get you to the hospital and with a couple of days of treatment you'll at least be able to care for yourself."

"No! Leave me alone. They hate me there. All they do is load me up with methadone, and I throw up all day. I just want to stay here. And why do you care anyway?"

Corisa, losing patience, pauses….then sighs in disgust. "Fine, suit yourself," as she glances around, hoping the other addicts don't see her take a crumpled sandwich from her inside pocket and offer it to Gina. "Here, take a few bites."

"I don't want anything from you," as she pushes the food away.

"You have to eat. You can't live on drugs alone."

"Leave me be and go look at yourself in the mirror. You're a 'junkie-ho' just like me, even worse. You go to the hospital and get fixed, then you can talk."

After some hesitation, Corisa delivers a quiet response, "I'm weaning myself off on my own, and maybe you can do the same."

"Yeah, sure."

Corisa pulls the blanket up to Gina's chin and places the food alongside her. She stands, and before walking away, gives a final instruction. "Eat and stay warm. I'll check on the others, then I have to go."

"Go where? Buy more 'skag?'"

"No, I have things to do." Then says in a more compassionate tone, "I'll see you tomorrow."

———————————

On a warm morning, Renee Jons and her five children are dressed in their Sunday best. They are heading to church, walking among all the addicts hanging out on her block.

Renee shouts to the loiterers, "Get off my block. Go to Harlem Hospital and get on a program, but get out of my neighborhood." Some curse words are slammed back at her, but she continues on her way.

Inside the ornate cathedral, the local minister gives a stirring speech to over 500 people, requesting all to pray to send help for his community. At the end of his speech, he asks for feedback.

Renee causes a stir as she calls out to all in attendance, "God isn't going to come down off that cross and move out the drug problem. We have to do it. You, hear? We have to do it ourselves."

An old man yells back, "Miss Renee, we're no match for the guns out there!"

Renee responds, "More of our children are dying every day. Our bathtubs are supposed to be used for bathing, not for laying our young ones in every time we hear gunshots outside. Do you understand? They're killing our babies! We have to get the police to act. We have to get the Mayor involved. We have to demand help. God says to help ourselves." The crowd of parishioners agrees quietly, but the expression on their faces is fear. "We need to do God's work," Renee tells them.

---

In the fall of 1977, Harlem's drug kingpin, Tayne Fortel, is arrested. At NYPD Headquarters, the Police Commissioner is briefed at a meeting of the Chiefs and Commanding Officers of the Harlem precincts. The discussion is about the flamboyant Tayne Fortel's arrest and the destabilization of Harlem's drug trade, which is going from bad to worse, as the rival factions fight over Fortel's territory.

The Chief of the Organized Crime Control Bureau explains to all present, "Yes, we did good in removing Tayne Fortel. He led the Council of Black Drug Gangs that controlled the Harlem streets and is connected to the Giadana crime family. But, the void in leadership can be problematic. The mobsters are concerned by the arrest of Fortel for two reasons. He has the potential to flip and there is the possibility that large orders of raw heroin already placed from their overseas operation will be canceled. Our main concern is that Harlem will become open territory. Murders will increase, and there will be more fear and harm to the residents of Central Harlem. I tell you all, be prepared for the worst!"

An upset Commissioner interjects, "I've heard the crime stats and the projection for Harlem murders to be over one thousand this year. New York City, and in particular, Harlem, has become known as the murder and heroin capital of America. That sickens me. I've got stacks of letters from residents fearing for their lives. They're locked in their apartments, too afraid to step out onto their local streets. I just got off the phone with the Mayor who is demanding resolution. I understand one of the community leaders, Renee Jons, is getting together with residents and forming demonstrations to be held at the local precincts. This woman calls my office and the Mayor's office every day demanding we take action. Tell me, what do you need to get the job done?"

The 35th Precinct Commanding Officer, Victor Deteo, cuts in. "Look, Commissioner, just give us the right personnel. We need young, tough, narcotics and specialized unit cops. We need street bosses that don't mind getting dirty, leading teams that will make the necessary arrests. We can't stand by and obsess about the brutality complaints. Let's take back the streets, boss."

The Commissioner concludes, "Set up a Narcotics Task Force. Find and send in a leader and cops with high arrest records." He then raises his voice, bangs on the large table with his fist and shouts out, "This stops now! We won't lose Harlem or New York City. If we do lose this city, all of us, including the Mayor, will be looking for a new job and a safer place to live!"

---

Two days after the meeting at NYPD Headquarters, the multi-million dollar drug trade continues in high gear. There are localized 'red star' and '3-D' dealers scattered up and down the avenue covering over twenty blocks. This is their territory. It was assigned by Tayne Fortel and carefully monitored. Fortel is facing decades in prison. 'Black Sunday,' led by Vic Ferris, is the most vicious and first to test the waters in a takeover attempt of Central Harlem. Two carloads of hitmen armed with Mac-10s come up Bradhurst Avenue, with Ferris onboard giving commands, "Kill all these fucks!"

On every corner, they empty full clips of large caliber gunfire into the heads and torsos of the dealers and associates. The noise is deafening. Hundreds of residents hug the sidewalks and streets. Drug buyers and innocent bystanders are collateral damage. Bullet holes and fragments litter the ground. Sidewalks are layered with pools of blood, finding pathways off curbs into roadway storm drains, blending with an ever-present supply of garbage. Within three minutes, twenty blocks are attacked by the killers. Twelve dealers are dead. Three bystanders also killed. One woman and two children seriously wounded. 911 calls pour in.

Heavily armed police and Detectives swarm the neighborhood, which now resembles a war zone. They're too late. The Bradhurst Avenue bloodbath comes and goes.

Ambulance and medical personnel arrive and set up roadside triage attempting to save lives. Newspaper coverage and broadcasts are off the charts. 'Black Sunday' made its mark. With no overall steward, the Harlem drug business is out of control and has become open territory for the dozens of other small gangs fighting for their piece. Fears have been realized. Even the Giadana crime syndicate has not counted on this sequence of events. This disruption of drug service will not be tolerated.

———————

Late Monday, following the Bradhurst massacre, Carlos Giadana meets with his local henchmen in the basement of their small Italian restaurant in East Harlem. Each has been responsible for an area of Harlem turf. Giadana is in the midst of a Sicilian tantrum, smashing wine bottles and glasses, and overturning heavy, wooden tables. Curse words in Sicilian dialect flow loosely. The subordinates remain silent as their chief is having a breakdown. He's a crazed man. And a well-armed one with a lot of power.

He orders, "Bring me 'Black Sunday's' Vic Ferris. I want him here now. Fucking dead or alive. Go get him!"

Within twelve hours, there is a quiet meet with Giadana's 1st lieutenant, Vito Tiafona, and Ferris. Tiafona is concerned that if they let Giadana meet with Ferris, he'll kill him. This would destabilize the whole operation even further. Tiafona decides to work Ferris in smoothly, so his boss will accept the arrangement. Amazingly, despite Giadana's reluctance and skepticism, 'Black Sunday' is given full charge over Central Harlem's street operations.

———————————

The cartel's takeover scheme worked. Vic Ferris has taken Tayne Fortel's place. That quickly, Central Harlem's heroin operation is back up and running. All street dealers and their cohorts are made aware of the arrangement, including DEA undercover, Nick Scalia.

## CHAPTER 5

# 'SARGE'

At NYPD Headquarters on November 23, 1977, Paul Pasano is being promoted to the rank of Sergeant. One hundred officers are sitting before the Mayor and Police Commissioner. With families present, the officers' names are called one by one, as they walk onto the stage to receive the gold colored shield.

Paul is pensive as he waits his turn. Although his upcoming status of boss opens a new world, this seasoned cop already walks and talks with swagger, personifying an old NYPD adage; 'sleep well, I'm out here to protect you.' He has a gritty style conforming to nothing or no one.

After years in plainclothes, he feels awkward in his dress blues and unhappy about having to cut his hair and shave off his beard. Realizing how far he's come and the violence he has experienced, his mind races to dark places....... *long flashes and loud bangs. Two cops ambushed and gunned down in West Harlem. He sees the murderers and empties his gun. They escape. After putting the wounded officers in his patrol car, his partner speeds off to the hospital. He sits in the back seat with one of them shouting, "Stay with me!" He puts his fingers into the bullet holes to stop the profuse bleeding—it doesn't work. Newspaper clips with headlines read, 'Open Season on Cop Killings - Black Liberation Army takes the lives of twelve NYPD officers in one year.' Pasano remembers his comrades' funerals, hunting down the BLA ringleaders, and his nightmares that followed.*

*He remembers his transfer to Brooklyn South and how he saved a nurse from being raped and murdered. Thoughts of him and his partner, Bobby Stewart, running down a dark alleyway and going head to head with a perp who shot and killed two elderly store owners. Pasano targets him, aims his gun, and shoots him dead......*

"Sergeant Paul Pasano." The sound of his name being called brings him back.

The new boss steps forward and shakes hands with both the Mayor and the PC.

During the speeches, reference is made to the rising crime rate in New York City. The Commissioner announces a new commitment. "We need smarter and tougher leadership in our law enforcement efforts. I need you to carry it out. It's 'all in or die trying.' The city's existence lies in the balance."

There is applause and emotional meetings with families immediately following. Paul, his wife, Rachel, and their two small children, are brimming with pride.

"I'm proud of you, Paul," Rachel whispers into her husband's ear as she reaches up and hugs him.

It all comes with a newfound hope that maybe this young Sergeant would lighten his load from tough day-to-day crime fighting to more of a supervisory position. This is not to be.

---

At home, a phone call comes in that evening from the Chief of Patrol's office.

"Captain Levin, Sarge. I'm sorry for this last minute change of plans, but your assignment to the 6-9, Canarsie, Brooklyn, has been rescinded. You're going to Central Harlem's 35th Precinct instead. Your strength, and leadership are needed to help stem the tide of narcotics and murders."

The truth is, Paul's a collar guy without a "hook." He has a high number of arrests but has no connections Downtown.

The phone is hung up. Paul whispers to his young wife, "I'm heading back to Harlem."

Rachel cuts in, "You were there already. Why again?"

"This is the NYPD," Paul says. "It's just part of the job. This time, it's Central Harlem." He sarcastically continues, "You know that little drug and murder problem they got. But, not to worry. It'll all work itself out. I'll be okay. We'll be okay. I'm sure it will be a short stint anyway."

Paul wraps his arms around Rachel. The expression on his face, unseen by his wife, is one of concern.

----

Sergeant Pasano is driving his red Volkswagen packed with police equipment, uniforms, and gear across the Triborough Bridge and down onto W. 145th Street towards the 35th Precinct. The roads are laden with potholes and lined with broken sidewalks. Abandoned buildings still stand, blackened from previous fires, with no windows, and sheet metal where doors once hung. The remnants of broken cars with missing wheels laying on cinder blocks complete the view. Just one block from the precinct, all traffic is stopped. There's a demonstration ahead with scores of people carrying hand written-signs reading, *'NYPD, Do your job!' 'Give us back our streets!' 'Stop drugs!'* There is almost an equal number of police on hand to keep the peace.

Pasano comes to a stop at a police barricade and mutters to himself, "Goddamn. They should be out locking up scumbags, not watching the good people." He flashes his new Sergeant's shield to one of the young bluecoats on the street and is waved through. He flashes his shield again to an older cop standing security as he carries his first load of gear into an old police garage next to the Three-Five station house under renovation. Although well decorated himself, Pasano does a double take at the rack of medals above this senior officer's shield. A piece of it is covered by a black stretch mourning band, in memory of a police officer recently killed. The officer salutes Pasano, and it's promptly returned as the two shake hands and exchange greetings.

"John Calvoy, Sarge. Welcome aboard."

Staring at the officer's medals, Pasano remarks, "Thanks, John. Congrats on your accomplishments, buddy."

Calvoy seems taken aback. No one has mentioned that to him in a long time.

With that, the tenured Harlem cop asks, "Hey, Sarge, you want some help? I'm just hangin' here."

"It's Paul, John. Nah', three trips in and I'm done, but thanks."

He heads into the makeshift precinct. After pushing in a small door, hand-cut within a massive, green wooden overhead garage door, he catches an eyeful. A few steps in, he finds himself stepping across large cracks in a cold cement floor, bordered by unpainted sheetrock walls.

The dimly lit garage is dotted with oil stains where cars once parked. He thinks to himself, *'Guess this city is in the financial shitter.'* This is the home of the 35th Precinct cops, a house of heroes. Some of them grew old here. Seen a lot. Done a lot. Probably too much.

Pasano stops to shake a few hands and keeps moving towards the bosses' locker room. On the way, he pauses at the only neatly painted wall in the building. It's out of nowhere. The wall holds the fifteen plaques of the police officers killed in this one precinct encompassing one square mile. Pasano's eyes well up, and he gets a lump in his throat, and for a moment, remains silent. He continues slowly down the unpainted hallway into the locker room. After finding an empty locker, he gives the inside a fast wipe down and stows his gear.

The first thing on the agenda is a sit-down with the Commanding Officer, Deputy Inspector Victor Deteo, a middle-aged guy, tough Italian Brooklyn cop, who has been on the job for years. He knows he must gain Pasano's confidence to utilize and channel this young Sergeant's energy and street expertise. This is vital to lead cops on a mission to remove the drug empire that has overtaken his precinct.

"Congrats on your promotion, Paul. Well deserved. Welcome to the Three-Five. I apologize for these working conditions. The main building is undergoing a complete reno' and we should be back in shortly. I guess you kinda' guessed why you're here."

"Yeah, boss," Pasano quips. "I've got no hook and the Irish Police Commissioner hates Italians. That's why we're both here."

The CO breaks out into laughter. "I see you come with a little edge to ya'. That's good. You'll need it."

Paul grins. "Just trying to lighten the mood. I appreciate the opportunity to work among all these hero cops. It's an honor. Speaking of that, what's the deal with John Calvoy? I met him out front doing security. Seems respectful and motivated and has a rack of medals that could choke a horse. It's a waste for him to be doing security, no?"

Inspector Deteo answers, "You've got good eyes. You're right about John Calvoy. He's one of the most likable and matured men in the precinct. But, of late, he's been a little down, a little burnt-out. Maybe he's had enough."

"I understand."

Deteo continues, "As long as you're in this precinct, you'll have my complete support. You know our mission, to take back the streets. I'd like you to take the first month backfilling with the existing units, Robbery-Burglary, Special Narcotics Enforcement, Anti-Crime, and various patrol teams.

You saw those demonstrations out front. That's Renee Jons. She's 'juiced' right to the Mayor's office. Meet with her first thing. Explain to her your intentions and what's to come. We need her support to accomplish this because there's no way we can go into a Black community and arrest thousands of people without their support. Team selection has to be done carefully. After about thirty days, we'll begin setting up the Narcotics Task Force. You know that's the real reason you're here."

Paul responds with confidence, "I'm ready for it. When we put the Narc Task Force together, I'd like to consider John and talk with him. I'll need some good, tough, but fair and well-adjusted cops of all backgrounds. They'll balance out the craziness of what we're about to do. I know how to work the streets, but you know I come with some baggage; civilian complaints, IAD investigations, and a couple of 'iffy' incidents." Laughing a bit, Pasano continues, "But, aside from that, Inspector, I'll work harder than anyone to accomplish what has to be done here."

The two shake hands.

## CHAPTER 6

# TEEN REBELLION

Inside Renee Jons' apartment, an argument ensues with her oldest daughter, Olivia. She's a strikingly beautiful fifteen-year-old with long brown hair braided to the side. Carrying an attitude and wearing overly applied lipstick and eyeshadow to disguise her age, Olivia's obsession with older boys and adventure typifies a young girl's quest for individuality. The disagreement is over her involvement with a young man who is a known drug dealer in the community.

"Liv', how well do you know this boy? He's already dropped out of school. I hear things."

The teenager snaps back. "You know nothing and hate all my friends."

"That's not true. I'm afraid for you, for your safety. Promise me you'll not do anything foolish. You're my heart. I want you to go to college and make a better life for yourself."

"Mamma, I'm fifteen. I want to have fun, that's all I want right now."

"Promise me, please."

"Yes, mamma, I promise." She walks from the kitchen.

Minutes later, Renee is leaving the apartment and instructs her daughter, "Now, honey, I'm leaving for work. I'll be at Harlem Hospital. If you need anything, the number is on the kitchen table. Please do your homework and look out for your little sisters. Okay?"

"Yes, mom."

"Love you always, Liv'."

"Yes, Mamma. Me too."

Renee heads out the door, down the three flights of stairs, and into her car parked out front. The teen is looking out the front window and sees her mom drive off. Richard, Renee's oldest son, comes home from school and enters their apartment.

His sister greets him. "Hey, Rich, want to do me solid?"

"What's up, Liv'?"

"I want to go see my friend for an hour. Will you watch the girls for me? Please?"

"Why you always lying, Liv'? Even mom knows what you're up to. Everyone knows you're hangin' out with that Darrel guy. He's bad news. Nothin' but trouble."

She pleads with her brother, "Please, don't meddle in my life. I want to go out for just an hour and meet up with my friends. C'mon, Rich, I'll be right back."

"You better be, 'cause I'm tired of covering your butt."

"Good, I owe you one." She hustles out the door and is gone in seconds.

———————

There's a sizeable chill in the air despite the time of year, and most of the junkies are concealed within their drug dens at W. 138th Street, just off Lenox Avenue. The unmistakable stench leaks out from the building entrance. Olivia makes quick glances left and right, then ducks into the condemned building. She disappears and finds her way to the person her family has the most fear of, Darrel Cahill. He's a low-level dope pusher, who mixes and beats down 'Red Star's' heroin, enabling him to make some extra bags for himself to use or sell. This skimming operation is dangerous. Paying addicts expect a quality product. They won't accept less. A poor hit generates a negative reputation. This drives away the repeat customer, necessary for a growing operation. If word gets back to Darrel's overseer, 'Black Sunday's' Vic Ferris, death is the cartel's only recourse. It's a gamble, but greed usually trumps fear.

Olivia walks up to Cahill's apartment and raps lightly four times on a reinforced metal door.

"It's me, Darrel, Olivia."

After looking through a peephole, Darrel disengages all the latches and crossbar. He opens the door and allows her in.

"What's up, girl?"

Darrel is in his late teens and the age disparity between him and Olivia is apparent and concerning. He's a bad one with a long rap sheet, but a young female can be blinded by the bling and excitement of a pusher. Olivia is taken in by it all and is even contemplating a trial hit of 'smack.' Inside Cahill's apartment, there's the usual scattering of product, bundled, stamped, and ready for street distribution. An older, armed 'muscle' is present, along with a couple of low-life junkie 'yoers,' who work for product only. Cahill, in showoff mode, manhandles Olivia by forcibly kissing her.

Olivia doesn't like the rough treatment and tells him to stop. He ignores her and kisses her again.

"Please, Darrel. I wanna' leave now."

"What's the matter, slut? Thought you liked that."

As she tries to leave, Cahill blocks her path. He grabs her by the throat and pushes her against the steel door. Her head slams with a force that echoes out into the hallway.

Cahill shouts into Olivia's face. "What's the matter, I ain't good enough for ya'? I know Renee Jons is your bitch momma. Means nuttin' to me. Here, take this with you." He reaches into his pocket, pulls out two glassines of 'Red Star' heroin, and jams them down her pants.

Cahill tells her, "Now, when you grow up and are ready for a real man, you come back, and I'll show you a good time, hear?"

Olivia chokes trying to catch her breath. She begs. "Please just let me go home."

There is a loud knock at the door, with a sickly, female voice on the other side. It's Corisa, the disheveled neighborhood junkie on the hunt for a fresh hit of 'smack.' "One bag, man! Just one bag!" The door opens and Corisa reaches in with a $10 bill. Darrel snatches it and throws a glassine of 'H' at her. He spits out, "Here, you fuckin' animal." He grabs Olivia by her hair, throwing her out into the hallway colliding into Corisa. He and his associates break out in loud laughter as Olivia and Corisa fall together, rolling onto one another. The door slams shut behind them and more laughter can be heard from inside.

Corisa's getting worse. Her daily fix has doubled in just a month. Track marks are scattered across her swollen limbs and neck, but she manages to get herself off the floor and help Olivia up. The younger girl cringes at the touch of the scarred, emaciated woman, recoiling from her.

Corisa reaches out and grabs her by her shirt, pulling her face close to hers, and speaks in a hoarse whisper, "Look at me! Do you want to be me? Do you? You don't belong here! Get the fuck out of here!" Olivia turns and runs down the steps. Corisa straightens herself up, tucks her glassine of 'Red Star' in her front pocket, turns and stares at the closed apartment door with a fierce look on her face. She turns and walks down the stairway.

## CHAPTER 7

# THE TEAM

Sergeant Pasano is present at multiple roll calls making a pitch for volunteers to join the Narcotics Task Force being formed.

He describes the nature of what is to be accomplished. "We will be making thousands of arrests inside buildings and out on the streets. It's tough, dirty work. Dangerous work. Drug dealers, users, guns, money, and drug carriers will be taken."

Pasano continues, "Everyone goes. Whatever it takes. This comes directly from the Mayor's office, and the P.C. wants it implemented forthwith. People are dying. Every day we waste, more children are succumbing to heroin. Seniors are locked within their apartments. Residents are afraid to walk to church.

Submit your name. The CO and I will review your past performance. I'll be talking to your immediate supervisors. Remember, once we start, there's no turning back. There are over three hundred of you in this command. You're the toughest and bravest of the NYPD. I don't have to tell you that. But, I can only choose about eight or ten of you. The team will have to be diverse. It's our only way for community acceptance, but we will work together like one big, blue machine. So, I ask, whoever gets selected to put aside any negative racial feelings that you may harbor. This can destroy the unit. And, remember one thing,

I'll be out there with you. I'll never ask you to do anything I am not doing, and I'll back you up one hundred percent."

Pasano knows from the past that arresting thousands of people from their own community, especially Harlem, always a tinderbox, will not be easy. It has never been done before on the scale he is planning, but the cancer must be removed.

For two days, Pasano reviews the records of over one hundred volunteers. It's tedious work. He conducts just as many one-on-one interviews. It's a difficult task, especially when you don't want to offend anyone. He needs a blend of Black, White, and Hispanic cops, all professionals, who will understand the unit's goals. From the upper brass there is apprehension, skepticism, and some fear. Fear of a repeat of the 1964 race riots.

Pasano receives a phone call from the Borough Commander, Chief Machik. He knows Paul is making his final team selections and offers the young Sergeant some advice and a warning.

"Look, Sarge, Central Harlem was, and still is, a flashpoint. One serious mistake and the entire city will pay. One cop making one misjudgment, and there goes New York. Yes, good tough cops are needed, but they must have a good balance of right and wrong. They must be able to make a commitment to carry out an assignment that might take years to complete. Do you understand?"

Pasano, respectfully responds, "Yes, sir. I understand completely." Paul thinks to himself, '*Am I in over my head?*'

––––––––––––

A week later, the selection process is complete. Pasano runs it by the CO.

"Inspector, these guys are the best of the best. I would trust any one of them with my life."

He explains every choice and expresses complete confidence in the final eight. His diverse team consists of three Black officers—John

Calvoy, Jim Kellig, Will Fennar, three Whites—Gary Ritone, Don Sels, Rob McTerren, and two Hispanics—Al Viega, Rico Lorez.

Inspector Deteo agrees. "Paul, after looking them over carefully, you're right."

"Yeah, boss. They're a good mix of ex-'Narcs,' military, and martial arts experts. All are active cops, respectful, and know the Harlem streets like nobody else in the city. They all have balls of steel and are loyal to a fault. Those traits are needed, Inspector. Above all, they're team players."

"Okay, Paul. But, now comes the hard part. Your mission is to break the stranglehold of Mafia control and take back these streets to return them to the good people who call Harlem their home."

"It will be done. I promise you."

The only complication with the team selection is a slight disagreement with Inspector Deteo who wants a female in the unit and questions Pasano. "Paul, I know women are new to the NYPD and to this point, most have limited experience, but Kana Marterez's name came up. Two uniformed patrol Sergeants who she rolls with, say she is the best of them and is street tough. The only drawback is—just two years on the job."

"Look Inspector, she's from the South Bronx, all well and good. But she's young and has no narc experience. Also, the guys might have to overcompensate their attention looking out for her."

Inspector Deteo responds, "I know controversial feelings are held by a lot of the men. They question if women can handle the rigors of law enforcement, especially in arrest or combat situations."

"True, boss. I maintain those same feelings."

The compromise between Pasano and Deteo is maybe later on. Maybe.

———————

Pasano backfills as a supervisor within other precinct arrest units; Plainclothes-Anti-Crime, Robbery-Burglary, and Special Narcotics Enforcement. He picks up valuable knowledge and expertise since he's learning from the best. He spends many hours gathering intelligence and detailing work methods for his 'Narcs.'

––––––––––––

Three weeks later, he heads a team meeting with his Narcotics Task Force. They are deeply involved in going over arrest tactics and sharing intelligence. The Sarge is meticulous with his unit's battle plans. "Besides what we already know about the major street dealers and locations, we will also have the community residents on our side giving us tips through a confidential hotline. We will begin with the high drug volume streets targeting block-by-block, building-by-building. We seal them off and go in. One of our major support teams is the Special Narcotics Enforcement Unit, (SNEU.) They will use their expertise in setting up their equipment in abandoned buildings nearby overlooking the target locations, do the observations and photography, and transmit the details to us on the streets. We collar up buyers and dealers, with guns being priority one. Narcotics and currency next. And listen up. We all have to be on the same page involving the use of force. You know these scumbags in the drug world don't go easy. Force will have to be used, and when necessary, deadly force."

Lives are at stake. They're ready.

––––––––––––

At the Central Harlem High School gym, a large community meeting is taking place where Renee Jons is the guest speaker. It's an open forum with over three hundred community residents seated in metal folding chairs. Renee outlines her journey, beginning when she first organized the tenants' association in her own building.

"I demanded and got repairs and services to the residents at the W. 154th Street dwelling. With success there, I continued my crusade in organizing a local block association, where the streets would be observed by local residents for drug dealers, users, and gun carriers. Members of the block association would forward the information to the 35th Precinct."

Renee continues, "I began to feel empowered. I felt there was strength in numbers. I saw progress. Today I am here to seek your help to spread block associations across the entirety of Harlem. I do this for you. I do this for me. I do this for the children. Now I want all of you present to participate and spread the word. We will not be a forgotten people.

"We shall overcome adversity and use the powers of the Mayor's and Police Commissioner's office. We must break down that wall of racial disharmony and distrust between the police and residents of Harlem. We will instill a new birth of confidence, communication, and understanding. I know many of you are afraid. I was. I am. But, so help us all, we will succeed. We will take back our communities, our lives."

## CHAPTER 8

# MEETING—MYSTERY—MURDER

The next afternoon, Renee Jons is en route to her first meeting with Sergeant Pasano and his narcotics team. She enters the partially renovated precinct and walks up to the front desk announcing herself to the acting Lieutenant in charge. "I'm here for a meeting with Sergeant Pasano."

The Desk Lieutenant immediately recognizes her and realizes the seriousness of this visit. He alerts Pasano's office and the CO, Victor Deteo, and respectfully responds, "Sergeant Pasano is waiting for you upstairs, Ms. Jons. Third floor."

Inside his office, Pasano meets Renee Jons, a person almost as well known as the Mayor, with probably as much political clout. The two shake hands, exchange short pleasantries, and get straight to the point.

Renee quietly asks, "Sergeant Pasano, can you help me? Can you help my community?"

Paul responds with a more pronounced tone, "That's what we're here for. It will be done, Ms. Jons, you have my word. Understand, when I target in on a mission, especially one as serious as this, I don't fail. I assure you, we will break organized crime's grip on this community."

"I appreciate your commitment, Sergeant." Then she speaks in a softer tone with a serious look, "We've been waiting and pleading for help for years."

Pasano cuts in and proudly announces, "Now, I want you to meet the team of a specially selected Narcotics Task Force. These are the highly trained men who will return your streets and your Harlem community back to you."

The team members begin filing in the small office. Their mere size and presence overshadow the room. Renee appears surprised by the team's diversity and smiles with acceptance.

"Also Ms. Jons, we'll have access to the Special Narcotics Enforcement Unit, Anti-Crime and Robbery Teams, and the NYPD's Narcotics Intelligent Unit at Headquarters. And, we'll have hundreds of tough and dedicated uniformed Harlem cops backing us up."

He begins introducing his new unit members one by one, giving a short, verbal bio of their accomplishments. "First, our team's senior man, Detective John Calvoy," as Pasano shakes the Black officer's hand. "Don't let that touch of gray on top and soft demeanor fool you. He's all grit and a Fordham graduate. Those medals are the real deal. Next, Detective Will Fennar, our runner, a college track star, former Army Ranger and Harlem cop who can chase down anyone." The tall, trim, younger Black officer smiles.........Now, Detective Jim Kellig. Our decorated Marine and Karate expert. We call him 'Cool Breeze' 'cause of his good looks. But, underneath is a decorated Vietnam Vet and one of the finest cops in the Three-Five. These three guys have been hitting the Harlem streets for years." The Sarge moves closer to the next three team members, all White, with medals to their chin........ "Detective Gary Ritone. All Army. Was an undercover narc for years, city-wide, until he settled into the Three-Five. He's one of our NYPD hockey players. He skates on the ice and runs on the street." Gary openly laughs.......Pasano moves down the line......"Detectives Don Sels and Rob McTerren—well seasoned and decorated officers, but are relatively new arrivals at the Three-Five. Their background, Brooklyn plainclothes. Also from the Army Special Forces. These two Green Berets come highly recommended." The Sarge sports a big smile, "Last but not least, our Puerto Rican reps' by way of the South Bronx, where they cleaned up the worst of the worst for almost a decade. The medals they wear and their experience earned them a spot at the Three-Five in our unit." The two Detectives, Rico Lorez and Al Viega, high-five with the Sarge. "And finally, Ms. Jons, me. By way of Brooklyn. A hot-headed Italian, ready to fight the fight."

Renee pauses for the moment and seems overwhelmed by the quality of the men standing before her. She states her approval. "Gentlemen, I am humbled and impressed. I thank you for your dedication and what you're about to accomplish." She closes in on the crew with tears in her eyes. Her voice cracks as she pleas, "Can you do this for the children?"

The nine men simultaneously agree, "Yes," as they each give Renee a handshake and personal commitment. Standing outside the office looking in is Commanding Officer Victor Deteo. He catches Pasano's eye, and they nod to each other.

---

Sergeant Pasano holds a meeting with the final eight. He explains the tactics to be used for street enforcement and building raids. He is frank, explaining that Carlos Giadana and his Cosa Nostra are behind the hundreds of million-dollar drug business, with the heroin connection from Sicily to Harlem. Ending the meeting, Pasano has one final thing to say, "They have to be eliminated, one way or another."

---

Renee's coming home from a late shift at Harlem Hospital. With the lack of parking spaces available on her street, the exhausted social worker must walk two blocks to her apartment. It's cold and dark. The street lights have been broken for years. A biting wind whips up and down the empty streets whistling through the alleyways. Discarded paper bags, cups, and newspapers, rise, fall, and spin, swirling with the dust.

Squinting her eyes, Renee looks ahead and sees an older man lying on the sidewalk, moaning in pain.

Corisa is attending to his swollen, ulcerated leg that is rotting from gangrene. She dabs his grossly deformed calf using an old bottle of alcohol and a damp cloth. The moans are from the soul of a man with little life remaining.

As Renee reaches the two, she offers some help. "Mister, that leg definitely needs medical attention. I'll be home in a couple of minutes and will send an ambulance for you." She bends down next to Corisa and helps wrap the man's calf with a scarf taken from her pocketbook.

Renee, in sympathetic tones, asks the man, "What's your name? Where do you live?"

The sick man replies, "I know who you are. Ms. Renee, right?"

"Yes."

"Thank you, Ms. Renee, but both of you, please just let me be. Help me up. I stay right here."

Renee cuts in, "Here in this abandoned building? You shouldn't be in there. No heat or water. That's no way to live."

"He's got no other choice," Corisa says. "There's no place for him to go."

Groaning, the elder reaches out his arms. "Just get me up, and I'll be on my way."

The two ladies help him to his feet and he hobbles into the dilapidated apartment house.

An unmarked car pulls up at rapid pace and comes to a screeching halt. Two officers in plainclothes, with NYPD shields hanging by chains around their necks, make a quick exit and confront the two women. It's Sgt. Paul Pasano and Det. John Calvoy.

Pasano, as usual, speaks first in a commanding tone.

"What's going on folks? A radio run came over the air of a man down. You guys alright?"

Renee responds, "Sergeant Pasano, we're fine, and just finished helping a sick addict."

"Renee?" Pasano is caught off guard. "I didn't realize it was you. Anybody giving you some hassle?"

Corisa cuts in with some snarky words. "You're that new Sergeant everyone's buzzing about. You come to lock up sick people?"

Pasano snaps back. "Lighten up, lady. We came to help."

Corisa murmurs under her breath, "Yeah, right........."

"Hey, shake the attitude. You'll live longer."

"Is that a threat, Sergeant?"

Pasano waves his hand dismissively. "We're outta' here, John. Call for an ambulance and a sector car to this location."

John Calvoy, fast to answer his Sergeant, "Got it, boss."

Pasano calls out to Renee. "You have my number, call if need be."

"Okay, Sergeant. Thank you."

Pasano and Calvoy enter their car and pull away.

Renee glances over at Corisa, who has a scowl adorning her face. She manages to force out some appreciative words. "Thanks for your help."

Renee responds with concern, "You're welcome, young lady. I promise I'm working on getting some decent housing for local folks, especially the sick ones. We're expanding the outpatient Drug and Rehab Center at Harlem Hospital. Speaking of that, you seem to help everyone else around here, but not yourself. You should get yourself into a treatment program."

Corisa snaps back, "You mind your own business, woman. Don't pity me. Pity your daughter." She turns and walks into the abandoned building. Renee is shocked and silent. She hurries home to her family. Renee has a sleepless night. She can't shake Corisa's words.

Early morning, her eldest daughter, Olivia, leaves for school. Renee is in Olivia's bedroom straightening up, changing her sheets and pillowcases. She's also searching for some clue that ties her daughter to what Corisa said. As she pulls the sheets from under the mattress, two glassines of heroin with a red star stamped across them fall to the floor. Renee drops to her knees and cries out, "Oh God, no, please, no, not my little girl!"

---

8 AM and Harlem is already wide awake with the sounds of police sirens wailing through the narrow streets. This latest excursion takes them to W. 138th Street, two buildings in from Lenox Avenue on the third floor. Three bodies lie face down in puddles of dark blood. Darrell Cahill and two associates are cluttered with large caliber bullet holes. There are no mourners for this self-described bully as he is rolled over by one senior Detective, disclosing his two eyes shot out at close range and multiple glassines of 'Red Star' stuffed down his throat. His two comrades incurred the same fate.

With zero compassion in his gruff voice, the old Detective comments to a couple of 'uniforms' standing nearby. "I know these scumbags. Local punks selling beat shit. Attrition by murder."

One older uniformed cop sarcastically remarks, "Yeah, all part of spring pruning."

Word spreads throughout the community of the assassinations. Rumors of drug and gang-related violence fill conversations had by residents and dope hackers. A message has been sent. Those in the business understand.

---

A pair of black-gloved hands, covered partially by frayed, dark green sleeves of a military-style jacket, opens a combo-locked steel safe. Inside are multiple guns, one is a scoped sniper rifle. A .45 caliber semi-auto splattered with blood is taken from a waistband and wiped down with a soft cloth. A partially empty clip is ejected and a fully loaded one is slammed into place before the weapon is carefully placed on a shelf inside. There is a brief pause with a person taking deep breaths. A hard punch to the metal cabinet follows before it is closed and locked.

---

Olivia comes home from school and walks into the apartment where Renee is sitting at the kitchen table, with two bags of heroin on top. Renee is stone-faced. Olivia sees the display before her and gulps for a breath. For a moment there is silence.

Renee quietly speaks. "The drugs are bad, but the lying is worse. Did you hear, that boy you know was found dead this morning? I love you, Liv'. That's why, at the end of this school year, I'm sending you to live with my Aunt Bay in Antigua. It's just too dangerous for you here now. I don't want to lose you."

Olivia sobs. "Oh, Mamma, please don't send me away. I'm so sorry."

With tears in her eyes, Renee tells her, "I know, honey, and so am I. When things are better here, I will bring you home."

Frantic, Olivia begs her Mother, "Mamma, please, no! I won't do it again."

Knowing what's best for her daughter, Renee says, "As hurtful as this is to me, I must do what is necessary to keep you safe. Someday, sweetheart, you will thank me and thank God also." They hug, weeping in each other's arms.

---

Sergeant Pasano sits in the office of the Manhattan Special Narcotics Prosecutor, Leonard Muller, and his assistant, James Horith. The Sarge is giving detailed info on his Narc Task Force mission. Both the D.A. and assistant listen intently as Pasano goes over a list of narc prone locations scattered throughout Harlem, based upon prior narc arrests, homicides, and related narcotics activity. There is input from the three men, as this meeting outlines the guidelines for how the thousands of arrests are to be effected by Pasano's strike team at the specific locations.

Pasano clarifying, "DA Muller, we'll do observations and photos first, and keep the evidence tight and well documented."

There is agreement the arrests will be prosecuted accordingly, and the DA Special Prosecutor gives his commitment to the mission but adds something more. In a matter-of-fact voice, he clarifies, "Look, Sarge, I know what lies ahead for your team, but you have to stay within the boundaries of the law. I've been around a long time and know how high-crime cops work."

"Of course, sir," Pasano quickly agrees, thinking to himself, *'aggressive cops always cross the line, otherwise nothing gets done. But, with these people, play the game.'*

———————————

After the meeting, in a darkened room, there's a man on the phone talking to another with a heavy Italian accent. "Hello, this is Horith. I have the information you need. Yes, yes, on Pasano and his plans to knock out the Harlem drug trade."

The Italian man on the other end answers, "Good work my friend. We'll be in touch, and you will be rewarded. Buona Sera."

## CHAPTER 9

# TAKE BACK THE STREETS

The first large-scale drug raid takes place on W. 154th Street, Renee Jons' block. It's a cool spring evening in 1978, zero hour for the newly formed Narcotics Task Force. The day's target—'Black Sunday' cartel. Radio transmissions are given by the Special Narcotics Enforcement Unit, secreted within high-rise projects, using cameras and binoculars with high-powered lenses. The observation posts (OPs) are two blocks away from the target location. They begin radio transmissions on vital information to the go-teams about to strike; descriptions of dealers, armed bodyguards, money holders, 'stash' locations, and lookouts.

"OP-1 to all units, be advised. We have four dealers on the street holding their own 'stash.' 154-7th to 8th. #1—south side 154—male Black—white shirt—dungs. #2—south side 154—male Hispanic—twenties—stocky—orange shirt. #3—south side—male Black—twenties—green shirt. #4—north side—male Black—teens—black jacket. Multiple buyers. Long lines. Photos completed. All clear to go."

Sarge responds, "10-4. All units, it's a go."

Sergeant Pasano and his eight covertly enter W. 154th Street, just west of 7th Avenue. Other marked radio cars block off the intersections at 154th Street—7th and 8th Avenues. Unmarked trucks enter with shotgun-carrying Anti-Crime cops, who specialize in gun arrests. More backup plainclothes members and uniformed personnel file in.

The four sellers and throng of drug buyers are caught off guard. Gary Ritone and Don Sels, leading a group of uniformed officers, overtake them at gunpoint and cuff them. Some scramble into the abandoned buildings but are chased down and are overtaken by Calvoy and Fennar and a contingent of backups.

Rico Lorez shouts out to Al Viega, "Let's do the roof and work our way down." The two head up the stairways with a unit of patrol teams. Viega orders, "Guys. We do a room-by-room. Nobody stays behind, everyone goes."

Jim Kellig, the narc unit's lead cop, is on the run. He points and hollers out to his boss. "Sarge—gun—gun! Black male."

"With ya', Jim," as they pursue a gun-packing bodyguard down an alley just off 7th Avenue. The perp stops short, turns, and lets off six rounds from a semi-automatic. The shots are deafening as they echo through the streets. The dark, confined alleyway lights up from muzzle flashes as Pasano and Kellig return fire, killing him instantly. He lies face up, blood oozing from his neck and chest.

"Narc Sarge to Central."

"Go, Sarge."

"We got one perp down—DOA. Shot by members of the service. No MOS injured. Notify the Duty Captain for me."

"10-4."

In less than two minutes, two hundred perps line the buildings, leaning against walls, hand-to-hand, from 7th to 8th Avenues. They're held at bay by the small army of bluecoats. Calvoy delivers some loud and clear instructions, "Cut out the sick ones, and use your zip ties to cuff the rest."

Pasano joins the group and orders, "Good clean tosses for everyone. Call if you come up with a gun. Don't unload them on the street. Put the evidence for each perp in an envelope with their name and description and give them to me. Remember, guys, safety first! Bring in the ambulances and patrol wagons."

The first strike is a positive one, with no injuries to the officers. One hundred seventy-five arrests to Central Booking, and twenty-five sick ones to Harlem Hospital. Thousands of glassines full of heroin, five guns, and thousands of dollars in currency are confiscated.

For the first time in a decade, W. 154th Street is void of drug activity.

There is cheering from the windows by neighborhood residents. Renee Jons and members of her community come onto the streets and personally thank all the police involved, including Sergeant Pasano.

"I can't believe this, Paul. You're doing it! Actually doing it." She reaches out to her cop friend. "Paul, you have blood all over you!"

"It's not mine."

Renee pauses with a confused look.

"Renee, this is only the beginning."

"It's been so long for our community, Paul,"

"I know. Please take your people back inside. We've got a lot of cleanup here." He grabs a walkie-talkie and puts over the air, "All Three-Five units—job well done."

One of the young 'uniforms' walks over to Pasano. "Hey, Sarge, can I talk to you for a sec'?"

"Sure, what's up?"

"One of the junkies we swept up in the abandoned building told me she was an undercover."

"Where is she?"

"I cut her loose. While I was bringing her out in cuffs, her backup walked over, pulled me aside, and reaffirmed her story. Both were wearing the day's color."

"She holding?"

"No, sir."

"How'd she look?"

"Fucked-up."

"Okay, so she's good at what she does."

"Did you take her off the set and out of sight before you uncuffed her?"

"I did. They walked away, got into a dark van and left."

"Get the plate number?"

"No sir, sorry."

"It's a little unusual her being in a 'shooting gallery,' but, no problem. In the future, pull people like that aside and come get me. A lot of phonies out there purporting to be cops, fireman, nurses, whatever. I always like to make sure they're who they say they are."

"Sorry, boss. It won't happen again."

"No-no. You did good."

———————

The first major blow is dealt to the 'Black Sunday,' one of the Mafia controlled local drug cartels. The word quickly spreads up and down the streets. It didn't take long for Pasano's team to earn a nickname—'The Harlem Raiders.'

Down in the basement of their East Harlem Italian restaurant where the Giadanas are camped, the capos are unnerved over this enforcement maneuver.

Sitting around a table with his underlings, a red-faced Carlos Giadana vows retaliation. "Today they win. Tomorrow they die. All of them. Lessons must be learned. Get my cousin, Sonny, on the phone."

The war on drugs has officially begun.

## CHAPTER 10

# A FAMILY TORN

The school year comes to a close for Olivia and there is sadness within the Jons' family.

Renee affectionately places her arms around her daughter as they exchange heartfelt goodbyes. The two are crying as an announcement comes over the loudspeaker, *'Last call for boarding for Antigua, Flight #760.'*

An emotional Renee instructs her daughter, "Call me as soon as you arrive. Write to me every week."

As Olivia holds her mother tightly, she says, "I will, Mom." She walks through boarding and turns to Renee, "I'm sorry, Mamma. I love you."

"I love you, child."

---

In a brightly colored airport reception area on the Island of Antigua, an elderly, attractive woman walks with her arm around Olivia. She holds her close and says in a soulful voice, "C'mon honey, come keep an old lady company. I have lots to tell you and want to learn all about you and New York City."

Olivia speaks remorsefully, "Aunt Bay, I haven't been good to my mom."

"Oh, sweetie," says Aunt Bay, "Your mother was also a handful in her teenage years."

"She was?"

"Oh, sure, dear, and I was a smart aleck to my mother when I was your age. She used to tan my fanny." Olivia laughs. Aunt Bay continues, "That's part of growing up. Now let's go have some fun. I can't wait to show you my beautiful Island. The sunsets are breathtaking. When you start school in September, gym class is at the beach. All the kids swim and surf. It'll be a great experience, and you'll make new friends. You're going to fall in love, ya' know."

"Thank you, Aunt Bay. Thank you for letting me stay with you."

In a soft tone, Aunt Bay responds, "You have your mother's eyes."

"It's nice and warm here," Olivia says, as she walks out into the sun.

"Yes, it is, dear."

---

Renee is preparing dinner for her children. It's the first night without Olivia, and everyone feels her absence. Richard and his younger brother, Cavon, still manage to crack some jokes and tease their little twin sisters, Aretha and Kalin. The phone rings. Renee answers.

A man on the other end speaks with a heavy, Italian accent. "Yes, Ms. Jons, this is a courtesy call, a fair warning. Calm down with your anti-drug push. The people using drugs don't give a shit. They're animals anyway. Now, everyone is making money. Even you can make money. I can fix things so you'll never have to work again, or I can fix things that you'll never walk again. That's if I let you and your kids live. I think you understand. We'll be talking."

The caller hangs up. Renee is traumatized. She tells Richard, "Watch the young ones and stay put," as she leaves her apartment and hustles to see her friend, Mrs. James. She takes a few steps down the unpainted, cement stairway and is yoked around her neck and a large ice pick is placed against her throat. She loses her breath and is about to pass out.

The man with the Italian accent whispers to her, "You see how easy it is? This is just a warning," as he lightly pierces her skin, drawing a small amount of blood. "Now, what about those beautiful children upstairs?" He throws her down the stairway, hard, and heads down and out. Renee grabs her neck, and runs back upstairs to her apartment. The door is open. The children are inside hysterical. On the kitchen table is their family cat, dead, its throat cut.

"Mom, Mom! Are you okay?" Richard asks in a panicked voice. "A man came, knocked, and shouted through the door that he found our cat. When we opened the door, he walked in with a knife in his hand and threw the cat onto the table. He turned and walked out."

Renee slams the door shut. She tells the kids, in a shaky voice, "Stay calm!"

She calls 911 and the precinct. Pasano and teammates are processing a collection of drug perps. The Sarge is promptly notified of Renee's encounter. He leaves one of his men behind to watch over the prisoners as he and seven unit members jump in their unmarked cars and speed off to Renee Jons' apartment. Two Homicide Detectives follow behind and two marked patrol cars also respond. Within minutes, the area is flooded with law enforcement personnel. They find the distraught mother with her frightened children. Spreading out, they search the surrounding buildings, streets, and alleyways, with negative results.

Later that evening, Commanding Officer Victor Deteo, Sergeant Pasano, and the Lieutenant Detective lay out plans to provide security for Renee and her children.

Early the next morning, the Deputy Mayor and one high-ranking rep' from the P.C.'s office voice their displeasure over the incident and reinforce the contemplation of added security for Renee and her family.

––––––––––––

Jimmy Kellig, a former marine, a karate expert, and toughest guy in the unit, meets privately with Sergeant Pasano in his office.

"Sarge, I feel sorry for Renee and her kids."

"I know. I do too. I feel we are partly responsible for how deep we've gotten her into this whole fucking mess."

Kellig continues, "I want to help on a personal level."

"Look, Jim, we are arranging for individual attention visits by 'uniforms' around the clock, 24-7."

"Not enough, boss."

"What do you suggest?"

"I'll stay over with her and the kids for a couple of days until things calm down."

"That's going beyond. I'd rather you not get personally tangled up with Renee. For now anyway, until all this comes to an end one way or another."

"Boss, I read you, but it's something I feel obliged to do."

The Sarge concedes, "I get it. I'll clear it with Downtown. You'll make your own hours and go out with the unit like always. I appreciate you stepping up. Renee is the main cog in the whole campaign. We lose her and her support, and we're done. The Mayor and P.C. might shit-can the whole Goddamn operation. But, please, Jim, be on alert at all times."

"Hey boss, I've been doing this the better part of my life. If we do it under the radar, Giadana's flunkies might attempt another hit, and I'll be waiting for them. I'll make quick work of it. Done and done."

"I know. Didn't mean to undercut you. I don't want to lose you, that's all. You know, Jim, when the mob wants somebody, they almost always succeed."

"Not this time, boss," as the black belt Detective reaches into his jacket, pulls out his ever-present Shuriken Japanese throwing star and flips it into one of the office bulletin boards, slicing into a head photo of Carlos Giadana.

## CHAPTER 11

# CHAMELEONS

Just two days following the assault on Renee Jons and the fallout continues to generate within the NYPD. Sergeant Pasano enters the Three-Five at 7 AM to start his tour. His guys are already there, vested-up and ready to go. He does a morning greet, and on his way to the locker room to equip himself, he is stopped by the CO, Inspector Deteo.

"Paul, we've got some news about Ms. Jons' attacker. Please, in my office."

The CO closes the door behind them. Inside there are two 'suits.' One from the NYPD Narc Intelligence and the other from the DEA Intel. Pasano assumes this meet is a serious one. It is. The DEA Supervising Agent goes into detail.

"Sarge, we've heard from one of our Harlem undercover field ops. His street name is Nick Scalia. He's one of our best undercovers, a former Navy Seal, and has some valuable info about the violent attack and threats to the Harlem community leader. He's set up a meet tonight at 2300 hours, under the Brooklyn Bridge. He'll be in an old, black Pontiac sedan. You'll be using one of our nondescript cars, a blue, Chrysler sedan. Backup will be limited, so take precautions. Do a couple of turnarounds to make sure you're not followed. The 'color of the day' is red to recognize and identify all plainclothes officers. Be sure to display yours. We want no accidents and an open line of communication. Is all this clear?"

"Yes, sir. 2300 hours, Brooklyn Bridge, Nick Scalia, black sedan, C.O.D. is red."

"Good, and by the way, you're hurting them. The Giadanas are concerned. We have credible Intel that they're talking about having you killed. So, you know they'll be coming for you."

"Yes, sir. I understand completely."

"One other thing. No one outside this room knows of the meeting. Don't say anything to your guys. I don't care if the Mayor himself asks you, not a whisper. It's too dangerous for the undercover and you. But for safety's sake, we felt you two should meet. You're both working towards the same goal but from different angles. All agreed?"

All present nod in the affirmative. They file out one at a time. Paul is last.

As soon as he walks over to his teammates, he is questioned by Jim Kellig. "What gives, boss?"

Pasano responds, "Just Narc Intel giving some updates about W. 154th Street and who will make a new attempt to re-enter the market after our major hit. I'll get vested-up, and we'll do some scouting."

The team's always level-headed John Calvoy answers, "Ready to fly."

---

Under the Brooklyn Bridge, just before 11 PM, Nick Scalia pulls up in a black beater and dumps it alongside a row of abandoned vehicle carcasses. He steps out, walking past a few homeless folks, then sits down against one of the huge bridge abutments laden with faded graffiti. There's eye contact between him and his backup, disguised as a scruffy hangout. Scalia blends well, wearing a ripped, red sweatshirt and jeans. It's a rainy night, and overflowing drains from the above roadway are cascading polluted water down on the filth below. Scalia's getting drenched but maintains his location. Sergeant Pasano, wearing a red headband, leaves his department nondescript car two blocks from the bridge and walks to his assigned meet. It's dark and wet. Puddles in the mud and broken concrete deepen. The local scavengers run for cover. Pasano spots Scalia propped against an old stone column. He slowly walks to the same column and sits on the adjacent side within earshot of his law enforcement associate. There's a one-minute pause. About fifty yards away, a backup, disguised as an older homeless, presses a transmitter button and speaks to his DEA comrades.

"Be advised, all is clear. MOS in place."

Sergeant Pasano speaks first, "The color of the day is red."

DEA Agent Scalia responds, "And so it is. I've heard good things, Paul."

"Likewise, Nick. When this is over," Paul answers, "we'll have a cold one together."

"Deal. Now listen carefully. I know who roughed up and threatened your friend, Renee Jons. It was one of Giadana's lieutenants, Ralph Patasini, a loose cannon and very dangerous."

Pasano loses his cool. "That's all I need to know. I'll track him down myself and do what has to be done."

Scalia cuts in just as forceful, "No. You can't. It'll fuck up my whole operation. They'll know there's a rat amongst them. They're already looking at me. So, please, let me get my job done, and we can deal with him together."

The DEA undercover backup overseeing the meet and receiving the transmissions turns his point-to-point radio off so no one else hears the conversation. The DEA and NYPD will not condone rogue behavior.

Scalia continues, "I need more time. In New York, Giadana's gonna' go down easy. I've got his whole network laid out. But, I still need his cutting and packing locations in the Bronx. The one I want is his cousin, Sonny Inzarita, in Sicily. I need his poppy farm sites in Turkey, lab and packing areas in Sicily, and his shipping routes. Once I have all that, we can take everyone down. It has to be a coordinated effort. You and your men can wipe out 'Black Sunday.' Finally, Paul, you've heard it before, and I'm here to tell you again myself. They're coming for you."

"So I've been told."

"Be alert. You have a family. Think about them, protect them. Be cautious."

"You do the same."

Scalia stands up. "I have to go. I'm here too long. Wait thirty minutes and then leave. My backups are in color."

Nick Scalia walks away, passes his homeless undercover, and disappears in the fog. His backup switches on his point-to-point radio and sends the message out, "Meet's done. Be advised, meet's done."

On top of the bridge, Brooklyn side, a tall man stands next to a black Lincoln Town Car leaning over a rusted railing peering through binoculars. It's Vic Ferris, Harlem drug lord, who followed Scalia. After observing for a few seconds, he mumbles to himself, "That fuck!"

Just yards from him, a homeless female is hobbling along the walkway with the aid of a crutch. Her shoeless right foot is wrapped with a dirty bandage, some of which drags on the blacktop as she slowly moves forward. The frigid wind blows across the bridge as the woman comes to a stop and with her free hand adjusts a red wool scarf wrapped tightly around her face. A frayed black coat, multiple sizes too large, is buttoned up to her neck as she raises her head staring directly at Ferris. While one hand rests on the crutch, the other slides down into a deep side pocket where it wraps around a semi-auto pistol.

The woman begins a burst of loud nonsensical words annoying enough for listeners, including Ferris, but not coherent enough to warrant a threat.

Ferris, grasping the commotion, lowers his binoculars and gazes over at the female believing it's just another slice of NY crazy. His driver and another bodyguard think differently making a quick exit from the car and head towards the intruder. With a swift motion, the two six-footers pull open their jackets and expose .357 magnums. One hood hollers out to her, "That's close enough, witch! Get lost!."

She pauses, weighing the odds, then sneers, but ultimately obliges the demand, turning and heading in the opposite direction.

Ferris climbs back into his car and reaches for the car phone. "It's as I suspected, Mr. G. I swear this mother fucker is a cop........Yeah, yeah. What's he doing under the Brooklyn Bridge then?.......You tell me!.......Fine, alright." Call ends. He orders his driver, "Let's get out of here." They drive off.

A minute later a dark van with no side or rear windows pulls up. The front passenger door opens from the inside and the woman makes a quick entry. They're gone in seconds.

---

Giadana is on the phone dictating to all his underlings in thick, Sicilian slang. "Watch Scalia. Our primo' drug pimp, Ferris, believes he's a rat. Maybe even a cop, which I find hard to believe. But, he's one of mine, so I'll take responsibility for him. For now, keep him alive and where he is on the inside with the families. We'll use him to our advantage. If it's true, I'll kill him myself. If not, I want Ferris removed. *Morte! Capisce?*"

## CHAPTER 12

# NARC FALLOUT AND GOODWILL

Early morning, just before dawn, uniformed police from the 35th are summoned to one of Harlem's largest drug dens. Radio transmissions blare back and forth from Central to a radio car.

The message crackles over the air. "Units be advised. We have one male and one female unresponsive at 160-West 141st Street, Apt. 4G."

The two-man patrol car responds. "Three-Five George, Central. On our way."

They park and walk up four flights of broken stairs in a partially burnt-out building. The two responding cops step over large slabs of broken plaster walls and piles of discarded food that rats feed on after dark. They comment to each other about the smell within the structure, knowing all too well what it is.

"Looks like we got some ripe ones, Tim."

There is no mistaking the stench of rotting flesh from junkies, mixed in with the feces and urine. They push the apartment door open. The able users have already absconded. Those remaining are the sickest, the usual addicts lying out on badly stained and torn mattresses strewn across broken floors. Amongst them are two dead bodies, lives snuffed by 'H.' One young, Hispanic male, and one middle-aged, White nurse proficient with syringes and still in her scrubs.

"Three-Five George to Central."

"Go ahead, George."

"Central, be advised, we got two apparent OD's, both DOA here on West 141st Street, Apartment 4G. Notify the Patrol Sergeant and squad to respond, Central."

"Central, 10-4."

A crime scene is set up, and the area is taped off. More uniformed police, Detectives, and a medical examiner with two black body bags arrive. Onlookers, mostly fellow junkies, begin filling the street. The two bodies are placed inside the bags, zipped up, and carried out to the morgue wagon parked out front. It's a sad, cold scene, highlighting the reality of two wasted lives being cast aside like road kill. The patrol cops assist the paramedics in bringing out the remaining drug users down into a waiting ambulance for transport to the Harlem Hospital Rehab Center. Sergeant Pasano appears on the scene.

One of the older patrol cops comments to him, "Ya' know, Sarge, this is a piece of hell on earth."

Pasano quietly responds, "We will end this, Richie. Notify Housing Preservation and Development. Let's clean out the rest of the building and get this place sealed up."

"Will do, Sarge."

Outside, as the two body bags are loaded onto the morgue wagon, the families of the victims are seen crying and begging God to reverse what lies before them. A father is seen on his knees with head down, sobbing over the loss of his 18-year-old son. Another man reaches out and unzips one of the bags to affirm his worst fears, praying maybe it's not his wife. The morbidity of the visual comes to an end, as one of the morgue's M.E. attendants rezips the open body bag and closes the corpse into darkness.

Just as everyone is pulling off the block, Pasano is summoned by two remaining patrol cops on the third floor.

One of the 'uniforms' confides to him, "Sarge, this sick addict has been asking for you. Says he knows about you and your program. You don't have to bother with him, I just thought I'd tell you."

Pasano responds, "Thanks, you did right. I'll check on him," as he goes into the burnt-out apartment and sees a few remaining druggies lying out on dirty mattresses. He steps over used syringes and lit candles on the floor and calls out, "Who's asking for me?"

A weak voice resonates from one of the dark corners, "Me, over here."

Pasano walks over and kneels next to him.

"Sarge, Ms. Jons said I can get help if I need to. She talked about you, told me you're straight up. I need some help. I'm screwed up. I did this to myself. I was somebody once. My name is Daniel Carter, and I'm a Korean War Vet. Got myself shot up a bit. They put me on morphine and sent me back home. Couldn't shake it. Been on 'smack' for over twenty years. Got some medals here in this old box."

Pasano grabs it, looks inside, and sees two tarnished medals; a Purple Heart and a Bronze Star.

"Hey, Daniel, you were someone and still are. Thank you for your service. You're headed to Harlem Hospital, pronto, okay, pal?"

With a weak grip from a swollen hand, Daniel grabs Pasano's arm. "Thank you, Sarge."

Pasano tells the patrol cops standing nearby, "Get another ambulance here forthwith, and keep me posted."

The two cops are somewhat surprised, thinking this Sergeant is not just beat-em' up, lock-em' up as they've heard, but in fact, he does care.

The next evening, in the midst of their ongoing anti-drug war, the unit finds a few moments of downtime that provide for some goodwill to those in need. The 35th Precinct Community Council sponsors the annual outing for Central Harlem's disadvantaged youth in conjunction with the Police Athletic League. Renee Jons chairs the charitable event. Sergeant Pasano and his team members chaperone and tackle the physical component. Everyone donates their time for the cause. Special needs children, orphans, and the poverty-stricken are treated to a special night. It's the Annual NYPD and FDNY Ice Hockey Game at the Nassau Coliseum. It's rivalry in the first degree between the Finest and the Bravest.

The cops, community residents, and children are picked up at the precinct, along with wheelchairs, crutches, and whatever the children need to get around. The kids are ecstatic, and the officers feel an attachment. It's rinkside, center ice, glass front row seating, compliments of the Coliseum.

Raider Gary Ritone, former high school and college hockey star, stands tall, strong, and tough as nails, and is part of the NYPD's team playing right wing. He's watched by his other narc team members, including their boss. It doesn't take long for the wisecracks and light banter to begin.

As soon as Ritone skates over to where the team is sitting, Will hollers out, "Hey, Gar', where are the 'brothers' out there? I see nothing but Wonder Bread slices skatin' around."

Rico cuts in, "Hey, what about some reps' from PR, man?"

The Sarge mumbles to himself, "Oh, no. This ain't right."

People listening might catch the wrong idea, but the cops and the raucous feet stomping crowd burst out in laughter and applaud the high jinks.

"Hey, you guys dominate every other sport," Ritone yells out. "Let us have this one."

John Calvoy chimes in, "Okay, Ritone. You and your buddies can have hockey and skiing. Too damn cold!"

More chuckles from the kids as Gary taunts JK, "Hey, 'Cool Breeze,' come out on the ice and let's see how you do."

Tough guy Kellig retorts, "Hey, Ritone, if I come out there, I'll force feed you that stick."

"You'll never catch me," Gary snaps back.

"Oh, yeah? I got something in my pocket that'll find your butt anywhere in the rink."

Gary gets banged up a bit, and the FD outscores the PD by a goal. But it's all for a good cause, the Police and Fire Widows and Orphans Charitable Organization. It is an excellent photo-op of Gary in his hockey uniform on skates, with Pasano and guys slipping and sliding on the ice in their Nikes. The kids find the display hilarious. For just a short time, there is no shop-talk, at least not for Pasano's guys.

In response to underground rumblings of personal threats against the Three-Five 'Narcs,' the NYPD and DEA begin their investigations and surveillance.

Working alone, a slender, well-dressed, armed woman, sporting sunglasses, sits just two rows behind Pasano and his guys. A spectator of sorts. Her head swivels in all directions, not following the hockey puck, but scanning the audience for assassins who would do harm to her law enforcement counterparts.

In the rear of the uppermost level of the arena, two men in suits stand behind a glass petition, look down, and make observations. One of them issues a series of commands to their subordinate Detectives of the Threat Assessment Team who wear NYPD and FDNY hockey jerseys and are spread out amongst the large crowd.

"Base to all units. Be advised, event is over. Keep eyes on our MOS. Unit 2 and 4, follow them out to their vehicles and advise of their departure."

"Unit 2, 10-4, base."

"Unit 4, copy that, base."

## CHAPTER 13

# VENDETTAS

For others, there is no break. Nick Scalia does not realize he's in grave danger. He is attending a birthday party for one of Giadana's lieutenants, Ralph Patasini, appropriately nicknamed by his associates, 'The Crazy One.' The gala is up in the Bronx at Marina Belle. Most of East Harlem's Mafiosos are in attendance.

---

Scalia has a long history of entanglements with the underworld. Over thirty years before, his father owned and worked a tailor shop in East Harlem, where a young Scalia grew up. It was a different neighborhood then, dominated by old Italians refusing to participate in the 'White Flight.'

His father paid his weekly allotment to organized crime for decades, until he began to fall behind and was ultimately assassinated in front of his boy for a mere seventy-five dollar missed payment. He was killed by a young, up and coming hot-headed mobster, Enrico Seteola, who also shot a responding uniformed cop in cold blood.

Seteola was forced by his elders to leave New York and hide in Sicily, where he worked his way back into favor within the Inzarita family. He was then promoted to oversee the poppy fields in Turkey. It was he and his murderous behavior that converted the hundreds of acres to bloodfields. Enrico Seteola was the epitome of the work or die mythology. Nick Scalia is well aware of the history of his father's demise. It was this chain of events that pointed him towards a law enforcement career. His knowledge of mob life and Italian language got him a spot in the prestigious Drug Enforcement Agency as an undercover. He blended easily as one of their own purporting to be an ally of organized crime. After 'hanging out' for a few years, Scalia became a staple in the Italian section of lower East Harlem. He played the part of a wannabe hood and was one of the youngest loyalists to the mob. He was personally recruited for induction into the cartel by Carlos Giadana himself.

---

A few years before, at the stroke of midnight on a warm summer's eve, down in the basement of the Italian club, Nick Scalia was formally issued the right of Sicilian passage into the organization. As the alliance of already 'made' men sat around a candlelit table, the police undercover took an oath of allegiance to his enemy. A small cut was sliced into his finger, allowing droplets of blood to fall upon a religious photo of a saint. The picture was held by him and burned as he spoke sworn words of loyalty and silence, *fidelta and omerta,* that have become a ritual and repeated for over 150 years by members of the Cosa Nostra. *'May my flesh, bone, and blood, be consumed by fire if I am ever disloyal to our Mafioso family of honor.'*

---

In the catering hall, Italian food is plentiful and drinks flow heavy, as does the braggadocio coming from the mouths of over a hundred of Giadana's extended family. Wives, girlfriends, and 'comares' are flaunted in gaudy style. Cash is flung around like marbles on waxed floors. Scalia approaches his underworld nemesis, Patasini, and wishes him well on his birthday.

"Today and one hundred more, paisan."

"Thank you. Thank you."

Scalia came alone. No women or other friends, but he's a good socializer. His thick, black hair is slicked back and his two thousand dollar Canali suit hangs well on a tall, defined physique. After four hours of partying, rows of Giadana's black limos, with bodyguards, pull up in front of the club as the mass of mobsters gets ready to leave.

Just as Nick Scalia is entering his limo, Carlos Giadana puts his arm around him and tells him, "Come. Go with me." Scalia and Giadana leave in the longest of the limos.

Patasini is the last to depart. As he's just about to enter his limo, two quick, silenced rifle shots, sniper type, are heard. *'Pang! Pang!'* A head crumbles to pieces. Patasini's. Remaining bodyguards, including some armed waiters and staff, draw their weapons and canvass the grounds. Silence follows for thirty seconds. The sounds of the NYPD's response with lights and sirens fill the late night airway. 'Uniforms' and Detectives flood the area. A crime scene is set up; however, there will be no arrests here. No retaliation, just another body. Patasini, 'The Crazy One,' is eliminated. The NYPD doesn't give a damn. It's just killers killing killers.

––––––––––––

In the back of Giadana's limo, the capo leads the conversation in Italian. "My young friend, how have you been? No women in your life? You know, a good woman teaches you loyalty. I tell all the young men, commitment to your family is a priority for survival and a good life. Understand?"

"Yes, Mr. G," Scalia, playing his role, says respectfully.

"Now go find a good woman. Make a family. And, let me ask you, who was your father? I don't remember him."

"He was just another tailor," Scalia tells him. "His name was Tony Scalia. He died of a heart attack when I was little."

Giadana says in a firmer tone, "Yes, yes. Listen, you remember your father, right? Well, I'm sure he was a righteous man. You be like him. *Capisce?*"

"Yes, Mr. G."

The car phone rings and the driver picks it up……..."O.K. I'll tell him." He turns to Giadana. "Sir, Ralph Patasini was just shot. He's dead. Do you want me to turn around?"

Giadana bangs his fist and says, "No. We can't bring back the dead. You'll notify his family and make arrangements. Use Monciti. He owes us. Have someone go back to the club, pick up his 'goomar,' give her five large, and send her away. Deliver fifty large to his wife and family. *Capisce?*"

The driver complies, "Yes, sir."

Scalia, nervous and thinking to himself, *'I hope Pasano didn't go all 'crazy cop' and whack Patasini.'*

———————————

The next morning, Sergeant Pasano enters the Three-Five and stops at the main desk.

The Lieutenant gives him two slips of paper and says, "Two messages came in for you overnight, Paul."

"Thanks, Lieu'."

Pasano begins his walk to his office and reads the two messages. First from Narc Intel, *'Sergeant Pasano, just a heads up. Ralph Patasini was killed in the Bronx last night.'* A second message from an unknown female caller, *'Sometimes people do get what they deserve.'*

The Sarge, elated and relieved over Patasini's demise, ponders the various scenarios. Did his comrade, Scalia, put an end to Patasini? Who was the female caller, and how'd she know about the killing?

## CHAPTER 14

# CASUALTY OF WAR

It's prime drug hunting season and another hot mid-summer day. Pasano and the team already have perps piled in the prison van parked on the street. One more hit to go, the corner of West 142 and Edgecomb, always a hot spot. They swiftly pull on to the block. Surprise is always their best weapon. They jump from their unmarked cars. The sellers, buyers, and armed overseers are caught off guard. They all scramble. Don Sels and Gary Ritone take off to cover the sides. Will Fennar and Pasano pursue the main group inside.

The duo runs through the building shouting, "Police! Freeze!"

The perps run faster, crashing through the rubble of a semi-demolished building. The police must be alert for trap-floor holes, purposely covered, hoping a cop would fall through down into the basement. As they near the back of the building, one of the perps jumps out of an old, broken-down doorway into the garbage-filled alleyway below. He falls hard. He scrambles to his feet, and emerges, gun in hand. Instinctively, Will moves across in front of Pasano with his body protecting him. As he's about to leap out of the doorway onto the guy, the perp opens fire, four rounds, point blank. Will retaliates, pushing off five of his own shots from his revolver. Light flashes from both gun barrels. Will remains full-bodied in the doorway opening. Pasano can't get off any clear shots.

To the cops, this whole encounter seems to be in slow motion. The plaster walls and ceiling begin coming apart from the rounds hitting inside the building where they're standing. A snowy dust storm comes down on them.

Pasano grabs Will and yells, "Are you hit?"

"No. Let's get this mother fucker!"

The perp turns and runs. Unbelievably, he wasn't hit either. It is like he and Will were shooting blanks, a few feet apart, muzzle to muzzle.

The perp moves like a rabbit, down through the alleyway to the street. He leaps over sinks, tubs, and garbage, the remains of what was once an inhabited row of buildings. Will is by far the fastest guy on the team. He races right after him. The Sarge manages to keep pace just a few feet behind.

Will is pissed, yelling, "Freeze, mother fucker, or you're dead!"

The perp runs through an open schoolyard carrying his gun, dodging through young kids at summer play. The children scream. He makes a turn-up West 140th Street towards 8th Avenue, with Will right on his tail. Pasano sees his chance to make up some time and head off the perp, running up West 141st Street and praying to get to 8th Avenue ahead of them. He does. Will is about ten feet behind the perp and tries to reload while he is running. He can't do it. He knows he is either out or low on ammo. The perp knows it, too. As he comes to the corner of West 140th and 8th Avenue, the perp quickly stops in his tracks and catches Will off guard, just a few feet behind.

The perp turns and points his gun at Will's head, point blank, and yells, "Your time to die, pig mother fucker!"

Sergeant Pasano is just off to the perp's right, crouched, combat stance, with a tight two-handed grip. His heart pounds as he squeezes off four quick rounds at the perp. One catches him in the right shoulder. It knocks him to the ground. Gun flash and smoke block his vision for a couple of seconds. As it clears, Pasano realizes he paid Will back for saving his life just a minute before. He returned the honor of keeping one of the most decorated and heroic cops in the NYPD alive.

The two high five, but seconds later, become distraught after learning via radio transmission that Officer Gary Ritone, long-standing friend and teammate, was shot in the alleyway during the raid. Pasano and Will race back to the target location and attempt to save Ritone's life. They kneel beside his body, holding Gary's head, as blood pours from the fresh bullet wounds. The street is flocked with police and ambulance personnel. There are frantic attempts by all first responders to save Gary's life. All in vain.

---

A couple of hours later, a somber sight inside Columbia Presbyterian Hospital E/R, where Sergeant Pasano is consoling the crying wife and young daughter of Officer Gary Ritone. There are scores of cops, uniformed, plainclothes, and Detectives. It was a brutal shooting, and there is no way to understand it.

Pasano, covered in the officer's blood, says to Gary's widow, "You know, Diana, there are no words to express how much Gary was loved by all. He lived as a hero every day and died the same." He turns to Gary's daughter and holds her hand. "Catherine, your daddy was a good friend and will never be forgotten. He will be in our prayers, and I will be your friend forever."

The three are joined by the entire team and hug as a group. Don Sels says in a comforting voice, "Let's pray together."

---

The Mayor holds a press conference outside the emergency room to a waiting public to explain what has happened. New York City is in mourning. Three days later an Inspector's Police Funeral for Officer Gary Ritone takes place. Over five thousand police officers are lined up. The team carries Gary's coffin in and out of St. Mary's in upstate New York. Bagpipers play, helicopters fly overhead, and there are many solemn speeches. The Harlem Raiders suffer their first casualty.

---

That evening following the services, Paul's wife, Rachel, engages him in quiet conversation after their two children are put to bed. The young ones are unaware of the violence that has taken their dad's comrade. "Paul, I'm sorry about Gary. I know what he meant to you."

"He was a loyal friend, Rach'. Irreplaceable."

"Are you sure you're not pushing too hard against such dangerous people?"

"The danger factor is what it is. I have to deal with it."

"It's just that you've gotten yourself in so deep with the Harlem community. You and your men have gone way beyond what anyone expected of you. When I talk with my mother and father, they can't seem to comprehend why you're so involved on a personal level, and, sometimes, neither can I."

Paul stares down at the floor for a few seconds, then raises his head. "Let me tell you something. Please sit down, Rach'. When I was seven years old, me and my friend Jeff, were playing around a small pond alongside the neighborhood park. It was hot, and I told my buddy I bet I could swim to a floating log out about twenty feet. He dared me. Of course, he couldn't swim, not even a stroke. I held my breath, jumped in with my shorts and sneakers on, swam out about ten feet and sank like a rock. As I was heading down, I remember looking up through the murky water and seeing the bright sun glistening through the splash and bubbles I created as I gasped for a breath and took in a batch of water. The more I flailed my arms, the further I sank. Funny, the only sound I heard was my friend yelling for help. It was only seconds, but it seemed like minutes. There were small cottages scattered around the pond. Somebody must have heard, but nobody came for me, Rach'. It was a weird feeling. I began to relax. I guess I gave up. I was just sort of floating, under the water, of course." Paul smiles as he glances over at Rachel who has a horrified look on her face.

"All of a sudden, I felt something grab me around my chest from behind. It began pulling and dragging me. My eyes were blurry, but as I strained and twisted my neck, I got a glimpse of a dark shadow of a huge guy who picked me up and body slammed me on the outside grassy area of the pond. This guy flipped me over on my stomach and began slapping my upper back, hard. Water poured out of my mouth like a faucet."

"I heard him saying, 'small breaths, small breaths.' "

"He rolled me back over and yanked me up by my tank top to a sitting position, stood up, and stared at me. He was the biggest guy I ever saw. I was more scared of him than of drowning. He only said a few more words before he walked away."

"You gave up. Why'd you do that? You never give up."

"Me and my friend ran home. I was dripping wet."

"My mother said, 'What the heck happened to you?' "

"I told her me and Jeff were playing by the pond and I fell in but never mentioned about the guy who yanked me out."

Paul stops to gain his thoughts, as Rachel cuts in. "Paul, what a horrible story."

"No, it's a good story, about one man making a difference and not giving up."

"Did you ever see him again?"

"All the time. He was a homeless guy who hung around the neighborhood. A Black guy who nobody gave a crap about. Whenever I saw him around, he would just give me a wink and never say a word."

"About a year later, my dad was reading the newspaper and I heard him telling my mother, 'Hey, you know that bum who hung around here? Well, it says he was found dead in an alley. Got beat up.' "

" 'Oh my God, that's awful,' " my Mom replied.

"My dad just said, 'I guess shit happens.' As he kept on reading he remarked, 'Wait, wait. I take that all back. It says here he was a Navy Vet, a World War II hero. Saved a bunch of sailors after their ship was sunk. How about that?' "

"I never said a word to them about what happened. Only you and Jeffrey know, and he got run over by a milk truck when he was twelve."

"Jesus, Paul."

Paul stands up and reaches out to Rachel's hand. "I can't give up. Let's go to bed."

In the middle of the night, while sleeping, Paul experiences his latest bout of nightmares. He suddenly jumps up, drenched in his own sweat, and shouts out. He breathes heavy, pulse racing. Rachel does her best to calm him, knowing full well the stress that's been put upon her husband. She hides her feelings well and gets no sleep, as she understands her husband narrowly escaped death. This time.

## CHAPTER 15

# THREATS AND HONOR

The next morning, Sergeant Pasano is sitting in the office with CO Victor Deteo. The inspector tells Pasano two members of the NYPD Intelligence Division are on their way from Headquarters to discuss a serious matter. As Pasano inquires as to the substance of the visit from Downtown, the two Detectives arrive.

The first Detective explains the visit. "Sergeant, your accomplishments in running the Harlem anti-narc operation have the Commissioner and the Mayor's office all abuzz. We have important information for you. There have been recent credible threats on your life. They are being retrieved from planted, confidential informants and undercover 'Narcs' via the intelligence division. Our Threat Assessment Team has done a complete work-up and will begin a formal program of safety protocols. As you know, our job is to not only conduct investigations as to threat sources, but to provide protection for yourself, your family, and team members."

Pasano is taken aback by the threat and cuts in on the Detective. "Look, I've been threatened before. I can't allow these people to derail our program. We started something and we have to finish it. I'll take more precautions."

The Detective continues, "There's something more serious. The Giadanas have put an open contract out on you and Renee Jons,

$50,000 each. If both of you are taken out, an extra $100,000 for the killer. This might extend to your families."

Pasano stands up, takes a deep breath, and leans over the CO's desk. His face contorts with rage as he vehemently declares, "Now I'll hit fuckin' harder. Thanks for your help, but I can handle myself on the streets. Please put checks on my family and Renee's, but understand this, we're on the right side here."

The Detective responds, "Fine, Sarge. Watch yourself out there. We can't follow you and get in your way while you're working, but we can set up special attention by the Suffolk County PD for your family. The NYPD will do the same for Ms. Jons, and we will collect and disseminate any new threats directly to you."

"Thanks," Pasano answers respectfully. "I appreciate your help. If I back down or lose focus, I lose everything. Harlem loses. I can't let that happen."

---

Later that evening, Sergeant Pasano and his teammates finish processing felons they had just picked up. The cops are heading downtown to Central Booking for their final step before the prisoners are lodged into the Manhattan holding cells. They'll be in court first thing in the morning. Arresting officers remain on the clock with minimal rest. After court, they return to the 35th and do it all over again. Collar-up, followed by court arraignments. The endless cycle continues. This evening, everyone is gone, and Pasano is upstairs alone in his office finishing mounds of paperwork. The phone rings.

While logging in the visitor standing before him, the desk officer tells Pasano, "There's a fellow down here who says he's the son of Daniel Carter, and he'd like to come up and see you."

"Thanks, Lieu'. Have him escorted up if you can."

"He's on his way."

"Thanks, boss."

A young man, maybe eighteen years of age, taps on the office door frame. He's carrying a wooden box. Pasano recognizes it.

The Sarge says, "Come in."

The young man responds, "Hello, Sergeant Pasano. My name is Sean Carter. My dad is Daniel Carter. I wanted to come see you on behalf of my dad and thank you for all you did for him. He passed away this morning at Harlem Hospital. I was with him to the end. One of the last things he said was how you and a lady named Ms. Jons helped him, so he wanted you to have these."

Pasano reaches out for the old wooden box, opens it, and pulls out the two war medals and one faded photo of Daniel Carter in his army uniform. There are silence and pause in the small office.

Pasano speaks just above a whisper, "I'm sorry for your loss, Sean. Thank you. I'm gonna' place these right here on my desk as a reminder of why we're out there on the streets."

The two shake hands, and as the young man exits the office, Pasano calls out to him. "Sean, listen, if you ever decide to enter law enforcement, give me a call. I'll do a letter of recommendation for you. With your dad's military background, the NYPD will be glad to have you, son."

"Thank you, sir," says the young man, as Pasano walks him to the door.

## CHAPTER 16

# MISSION COMPROMISED BUT SAVED BY A FRIEND

Early morning in a large conference room, Sergeant Pasano is going over plans to hit another location. His team and a well-armed contingent of backups are present. Careful instructions are given by the young leader on how the entire block at West 140th Street between 7th and 8th Avenues will be sealed off and drug dealers, users, and gun carriers will be targeted.

Pasano issues the final instructions, knowing there's always apprehension amongst the troops right before these types of raids. "Remember, safety first, remain calm and focused. Strike time will be at 0900 hours. All involved will be in their vehicles and ready to push out."

---

The Special Narcotics Enforcement Unit is concealed within an observation post in an unoccupied apartment midway up, two blocks away, peering down on the target street with high-powered binoculars and cameras. Point-to-point radio transmissions are constant.

The observation post officer dictates the scene.

"OP-1 to all units. Buyers and sellers—both sides of the street. Move in!"

The caravan of twelve marked and unmarked units with fifty highly trained cops are en route. Two large patrol wagons are along for prisoner transportation. Within one minute, the lead units seal off the corners, pulling a few moving civilian vehicles through and off the block. Done. The block is sealed and the combat units cram through the small corner openings and plant themselves in front of their assigned target buildings.

Pasano orders, "Work your way in. Stay on your radios. Hit your targets."

A few minutes past 0900, a phone call comes in to the DEA Covert Unit Headquarters.

A DEA undercover calls in. "It's Yono. I'm in the field with an emergency message."

"Proceed."

"Abort the mission in the Three-Five. Abort the mission. Alert the Narc Task Force forthwith!"

"Copy that Yono, stand by.....................Too late. They're already on scene."

"Shit!"

Without warning, cinder blocks and bricks begin raining down on the dozens of cops below. There has been a security breach. A serious one. A tip-off. Members of the service are sustaining serious injuries. Patrol cars are being totaled. Roofs, windshields, trunks, and hoods, collapsed. Cops charge into doorways for cover. EMTs standing by in ambulances are helpless. This mission has gone awry.

Pasano sets off an emergency message to all units.

"We've been set up! Take cover inside the buildings. Look for the throwers!"

There were over a hundred people; civilians, cops, and construction workers within the station house during the early morning planning and briefing session. It is possible any one of them could have picked up a piece of info and put the word out on the street. One phone call could have set this whole mess in motion. Pasano is responsible for the injured cops, damaged department property, and the operation failure. He's on the scene unhurt, but furious. The cops who are still capable, scramble up to the rooftops. Most of the brick and block throwers disappear. A few are found and rounded up. The roof edges are lined with leftover bricks and tiles ready for future use. There are frantic radio transmissions signaling the location and severity of the injured cops.

John Calvoy hollers out, "We got some guys down, Sarge!"

There is also one concerning message of a teenage hurler jumping from one of the rooftops to his death.

Quietly on his radio, Raider Don Sels relays a message. "Hey, Boss, we got one jumper during the pursuit. Looks like a DOA."

Pasano says calmly. "Got it, Don. Finish up. We'll worry about him later."

Over the decades, these types of incidents always lead to skepticism. Jumped or thrown? More Internal Affairs investigations and allegations. More DA's involvement, negative press fallout, and lawsuits lie ahead. Overall, this is an awful day in the drug war.

---

The narc team is gathered around the Sarge, sitting in a semi-circle for a late evening meeting. Just above a whisper, Pasano issues instructions in a serious manner.

"Look, prepare yourselves for some shit. They'll be looking for an internal rat who tipped off our operation. They'll also be crawling up our asses over that fucking jumper. I'm sure the DA, lawyers, and the press will be on their missions. Keep your answers simple. The mope ran, we lost sight of him, next thing he's lying in the alley, DOA. As usual, stay consistent and keep your cool. Got it?"

Pasano closes the meeting. "Arresting officers get your perps down to Central Booking. Everyone else get home to your families."

---

It's another late night ride home for Paul as he heads back to Suffolk County, Long Island at 3 AM. It was a long, exhausting day, which accomplished nothing but 'bad.' There are a number of injured cops with broken shoulders, arms, and head wounds. The start of Internal Affairs and DA investigations involving a perp's jump or push to his death adds to the stress. Pasano, like most cops, tries to never bring his job home. Don't bring the filth into your family's lives. It's a cardinal rule in law enforcement. It's too much for civilians, especially family members, to comprehend.

Paul leaves his VW at the top of the long driveway. As always, Rachel is at the door. The sound of the car's engine lets her know her husband is home safe and sound. No words spoken, no words needed. A quick shower for him and four hours of bad sleep. Then up again and a ride back into a city amidst turmoil.

The day ahead comes with a lot of scrutiny and Monday morning quarterbacking. 'Why didn't you do this or that?' Or, 'You're headed for some fallout.' With a hint of corruption in the air, the meat-eaters from Downtown, smelling blood, will surely swarm the precinct. Pasano knows the game and how to handle it; thick skin, no fear, and keep pushing ahead. He knows there's no turning back.

---

Pasano parks his 'bug' out front and walks in the station house.

Just steps inside, and the older, Black Desk Lieutenant who always looks out for Pasano, tells him, "Paul, they're waiting for you in the Inspector's office. Stand tall."

In a respectful return, Pasano says, "Thanks, Lieutenant. How are the injured guys doing?"

"Better. Everyone's stable."

After Pasano washes up in the men's room and takes a deep breath, he knocks and enters the CO's office. He makes quick notice of a lot of senior cops in suits. He knows these people are not his friends.

The Sarge stands just inside the office doorway when one of the 'suits' stands up and greets him. "Good morning, Sergeant Pasano. I'm Deputy Chief Colin Felicer, Internal Affairs. I'm here on direct orders of the Commissioner. Have a seat. We'd like to ask you a few questions about yesterday's failed operation. You personally are not the target of any pending investigation, but we have to find out if there was an internal leak. That's part one. Part two is the death of one of the fleeing perps who reportedly jumped from the roof. We have to clear any allegations that he might have been pushed by any officers. Bottom line, Sergeant, we will begin our interviews in a couple of days. All involved will be entitled to union representation. Do you understand?"

Pasano pauses and gives his answer, "Chief, I understand completely. I appreciate you being candid. I'll explain to all the responding officers, including my personal team members. But, if I may, Chief, with all due respect, respond to your point about me not being the target of any of these investigations. These are all my people, team members and other 35th precinct cops. On operation day, I was in charge. I planned it and carried out those plans. If it should turn out that any of those police officers were involved in any wrongdoing, I would ultimately be responsible. Each one of us puts our lives in the hands of one another. Living or dying is the consequence of our actions. I staked my life and career on the work ethics and bravery of every cop selected for that mission. I stand by that today."

With a scowl on his face, the IAD Chief tells this young supervisor, "Okay, Sarge. You're coming in loud and clear, and you're right. If it does turn out that one of your officers working with you that day is involved in wrongdoing, you're history. Your anti-drug campaign is over. If you keep your job, you'll surely be transferred. Understood?"

"I understand completely."

Chief Felicer looks at Pasano in anger. "So, your operation is on hold until all the interviews are done and we make a preliminary determination."

"Got it, Chief. I'm sure everything will work itself out." Thinking to himself, '*we're all going down in flames.*'

Inspector Deteo interjects, "Chief, if I may for the record. I fully support this Sergeant and all the men at the Three-Five."

"You should, Inspector, 'cause you know if things do go sideways, you're gone as well. Is everyone clear on the issues? If so, this meeting's over. We'll be in touch."

The Chief and associates head out of the office, leaving Sergeant Pasano and Inspector Deteo behind.

"Paul, close the door," the Inspector says in a serious tone. "Look, my career's over anyway. I'm way past my time on the job. I can put my papers in any time, but you're a young guy with a bright future. Don't get yourself tangled too tight. Protect yourself, son."

"Hey boss, neither one of us is going anywhere. I'm no fuckin' quitter. I started something and I intend to finish it. I've got a couple of calls to make. Maybe I can smooth things over with Downtown."

"Keep me posted, Paul."

Pasano leaves the CO's office and heads upstairs to his office where his guys are waiting for an answer on the outcome of the interview with Internal Affairs. He walks in and they can read his face.

Will Fennar jumps right in, "Hey, Sarge. It's over, right? We're screwed."

"Not yet. You hang out here. I'm going to see a friend."

The team nods in the affirmative.

"Got it, boss," says Fennar.

Pasano heads off in his unmarked car. It is damaged from the prior day's botched raid but is still drivable. He makes only one stop, Renee

Jons' apartment. He heads up and raps lightly on her door. The younger of her two sons, Cavon, answers and gives the Sarge a hardy handshake and an invite in. There are hugs with Renee's children and a longer one with Renee.

Paul says to the family, "I'd like to talk to your mom alone for a couple of minutes."

Without hesitation, they head for the living room, leaving Paul and Renee alone in the kitchen.

"Sit down, Paul. Your expression has that look of trouble."

"You'd be right Renee. Don't know if you heard about the large operation on West 140th Street that went sour yesterday. Cops hurt, lots of department property damaged, and one person dead under suspicious circumstances. All in all, a crappy day's work. To top it off, our entire operation is on hold and might ultimately be canned. That's the reason I'm here, Renee. I need some pushback Downtown. There are some who would love to see us fail. They don't understand the consequences."

Renee cuts in, "Paul, we've come so far. We've made great progress. Do you think for one second that I intend to allow anyone at Police Headquarters to stop our plans to build a new Harlem? To free thousands of people from the wrath of narcotics? Not while I'm alive. You go back and tell your teammates to give me just a little time to try and get this rectified. We've talked about this before. It's what's in your heart that matters. Even if things go wrong, the righteous will prevail."

Pasano has regained some lost confidence, even though he understands Renee's push might not be enough to put the narc operation back on track.

———————

Early the next morning at Police Headquarters, Internal Affairs Chief Felicer is throwing papers and forms across his desk. He's hollering full throttle at a couple of Captains and anyone standing within blast range.

"Who's responsible for this? Who gave these orders?"

One of his assistants, Captain Giafrono, meekly responds, "I think it came down late last night from the PC's office."

The Chief shouts out with more fire, "Get the Commissioner on the phone, now!"

"Yes, sir."

Felicer is muttering and cursing to himself. Thirty seconds later the Captain comes back in his office. "Commissioner's on line one, Chief."

He grunts and picks up the phone, "Yes, sir........Yes, Commissioner........yes, sir......I understand, sir."

The Chief hangs up the red phone. "Fuck! It came from the Mayor's office directly. It's that community leader from Harlem. Apparently, she's running the entire Goddamn department, not the PC."

––––––––––––––

At 8 AM, Pasano pulls up to his station house. Right in front, are three new, unmarked Fords. Next to those are four more new marked RMPs. There's a small gathering of cops outside gawking and laughing at what lays before them. This is Central Harlem. The bottom of the equipment chain. It's highly unusual for a precinct like this in a 'combat zone' to get such treatment. Pasano exits his car and is greeted by his teammates and other Three-Five cops.

"Hey, Sarge," John Calvoy shouts out. "Look, new 'rides.' There's even one for me. I never had a new 'ride' like this before," laughing with every word. "And guess what? We're back in business, boss. Operation's on again. Knew you would come through for us, Paul," as he grabs for his friend and boss.

"Thanks for the kind words, John, but believe me, this wasn't my doin'. This came from Downtown HQ via West 154th Street, if you know what I mean. I guess some people have more 'juice' than others."

"Inspector's waiting for you inside, Paul."

The Sarge hand-slaps his teammates on the way and walks into the Inspector's office.

The Inspector has a shit-eating grin on his face. "Hey, Paul, you owe someone a thank you. I'm sure you heard the operation is up and running again. Remember, all the investigations are still pending. I'm sure they'll be coming after you from HQ. Now you'll be fighting drug gangs and the PD. Good luck with that," as he smiles. "In all seriousness, work carefully. Tell your men the same. Use caution. We're all being watched. I don't want any of you dropping your guard out there and getting killed. I'll have to explain to your families the why of it all. I don't want to do that, my friend. One final note, you begin on West 140th Street. You've got some unfinished business there."

"I hear ya', and thanks for all your support, boss. I've got some calls to make."

The Sarge goes up the stairs to his office, grabs the phone, and makes two calls. One to Rachel, telling her all that has transpired, and one to Renee. Rachel is happy but inwardly concerned for her husband's safety as operations would continue again.

Paul, speaking to Renee, simply and quietly says, "Thank you."

Renee responds, "You're welcome, Paul."

---

The next morning, the unit and about fifteen backup members pay a return visit to West 140th Street. This time, no fanfare. No large-scale plans. Just jump in and hit five buildings and the street, sweeping up clusters of buyers, sellers, money, and gun holders. No kid gloves on this sprint, just plenty of necessary force. This smaller scaled operation is a success. Just seven department cars and new ones at that. Block sealed and quick work of overtaking the wanted ones. Fifty-five arrests in all placed into arriving prisoner vans. Younger officers follow senior members in for final cleanup and prisoner handling. Before leaving the block, the rookie cops have to perform roof duty. They climb to the roofs, one building at a time, and throw loose blocks, bricks, and other debris off into the alleyway below. This takes about two hours but is necessary to prevent a redo of the prior day's raid. The Task Force is back in sync.

## CHAPTER 17

# COMMUNITY/POLICE - SENIOR CRIME

Renee is making an all-out effort. She's heading an evening meeting with the police and community in the basement of the local parish. It's a large, open storage area that was painted over with two shades of drab gray. Fluorescent lighting does a good job to brighten the windowless cellar. A picture of Pope John Paul hangs behind the podium and old, broken statues of various saints line the shelves along the sides. She is making a speech to another packed house of local Harlem residents about how they and the police have to partner up to rid their neighborhood of narcotics.

Renee hammers her point home. "This is Satan's brew! It's killing our children, our babies. Please work with the police. Your calls will be anonymous. Give any information to Sergeant Pasano. Do not be afraid! This is our neighborhood, our home. We must fight for ourselves. Now, I'd like to introduce the person leading the battle to take back our streets, Sergeant Pasano."

There is light applause for Pasano as he thanks everyone. He explains the impact his team will have on the neighborhood and his style of enforcement.

"We work tough. Tell your teenage children not to 'hang,' especially with known narc thugs. If they do, they're going to be scooped up with the bad element. If they are personally involved with any form of distribution, drug or cash holding, being a lookout, or anything else, I'm going to put them in jail. You've got a lot of cops and community people, especially people like Renee, risking their lives for you and your families. Renee and I want all of you to live, work, attend church, and enjoy your communities in tranquility. I need your help. I need your eyes and ears. Contact the 35th precinct anonymously and give the info to anyone on my team. Freedom will ring out in this neighborhood. I promise you."

There is loud applause. The meeting ends, and as they file out, a little girl wearing a blue and white flower dress runs over to Pasano. With her two long hair braids dangling effortlessly, she sings out, "Hi."

Pasano, always equipped, pulls out a lollipop from his jacket and hands it to her, saying, "Here ya' go, 'lollipop.' "

She smiles and says, "Thank you."

Her mother whispers a thank you as well.

Pasano delivers a strong handshake to Renee, jumps in his VW and heads home.

---

Two of the oldest residents, Mr. Carell and Mrs. Sherod, both 80 years plus and lifelong Harlem residents. They have seen the tragic transformation of their community. As they walk out of the meeting and head for their apartments, the two seniors, living right across the street from each other, walk home together. Mrs. Sherod is a bit hunched and the old gent walks with a shined up, wood carved cane. The two lock arms and steady each other as they negotiate a series of bumps and large crevices in the sidewalks. There is quiet yet poised conversation between them. She leans towards her friend and questions him, "Do you really think this community can be brought back to the way it was? I'm sure that Sergeant has good intentions, but sometimes I believe we are past the point of return."

Expressing a positive view, Mr. Carell responds in a firm voice, "Well, we have to believe in someone. I think that young fella' spoke from the heart. I hear he's a tough cop and has an emotional attachment to our community. Maybe God's pointing him in our direction. Besides, Ms. Renee believes in him, and that's good enough for me."

"I hope you're right."

"Hope is all we have left. Be careful here, these damn street lights never work." He pulls the old woman close.

Just before they reach their respective buildings, from out of the darkness, concealed within an open doorway to a semi-abandoned building, a small band of young thugs leaps out. They jump, and using brass knuckles, beat down the two seniors pummeling their faces swollen beyond recognition. Faint cries for mercy are heard but laughed at. One perp using a box cutter, slices open the old man's pocket and removes a wallet while another snatches the woman's pocketbook, and with a handful of grease, yanks off her wedding ring. Within seconds, the group disappears.

The two seniors are barely alive when a passing Three-Five radio car sees them lying in the roadway bleeding from their heads. An ambulance is summoned, and the two are taken to Harlem Hospital and rushed into surgery. A proficient and well-versed medical staff works feverishly to restore the two lives. They survive but will need extensive rehab during a long recovery period. Headquarters is notified. The media picks up on the attack.

––––––––––––––––

The desk officer at the 35th calls Pasano's home and leaves a message with Rachel for the Sarge to call the precinct forthwith. She gets nervous knowing that calls to the house are always serious.

As soon as he walks in the door, Paul gets the message and calls.

The Lieutenant says with concern, "Sorry to bother you at home, Sarge, but this incident is high priority."

As soon as he hears the news, Paul's blood pressure doubles. He responds, controlling his rage. "Okay, Lieu', would you please notify the Detective Squad, Senior Citizens Robbery Unit, and Duty Captain. Put out descriptions of the perps, and I'll work on it first thing in the morning."

———————

When he arrives at the precinct, Pasano conducts a small team meeting that also includes five Detectives from the 35th squad. He instructs them. "This senior citizen beating must be resolved." Uniformed cops head to the streets giving out flyers with composites of the perps. The noose tightens.

———————

Early morning, twenty-four hours later, Mrs. James, Renee's neighbor, sweeps the steps leading into her building. She moves the worn, bristled broom back and forth, a ritual practiced daily by the elder, interrupted only by fresh water from a garden hose she uses when bloodstains require it.

Coming up the block towards her, Corisa shuffles, one foot dragging, as she approaches the elder. She raises her head and mumbles a handful of words. "Can I come near you? I mean no harm. I have something for you, but I don't want anyone to see."

With fear and confusion, Mrs. James hesitates then responds, "I've seen you before but don't know your name."

"Forget my name."

Corisa puts her head down and slowly limps past the elder and up the steps. "Please follow me inside."

Mrs. James looks around, and with the broom in one hand and the other on the railing, she pulls herself up the steps and into the hallway where Corisa is leaning against the wall. Corisa scants around and reaches into her pocket, removes one of the 'wanted' sheets given out by the police and hands it to the old woman.

Corisa, whispering, but in a demanding tone, "On this paper are the names and location of the teenagers who beat up the two old folks. Put it away, then call the precinct Detectives and give them the information."

Corisa moves closer to her. "Do not meet or talk to them on the street. Do you understand me?" She points to the roadway. "Too many eyes out there. Now go upstairs."

With a sympathetic tone, Mrs. James says, "Dear, please, I can help you. I'll get you some food and water."

"Don't worry about me. Please do what I asked," as she walks down the steps and away from the entrance.

---

Following up on the lead supplied by Corisa via Mrs. James, a team of Detectives with a warrant, shotguns, and a battering ram in tow, cautiously make their way up a lopsided stairway to an abandoned apartment on W. 155th Street. Three DT's separate themselves, one landing apart, as they head for their target on the 3rd floor. Two others take the rear alley to lay in wait for runners.

Standing well off to the side in fear of gunfire coming through the door, one of the men stretches his arm across and knocks. No response. Thoughts of police assassination loom and hearts race as he knocks again. Pausing, he grasps the handle, turns and slowly pushes the unlocked door open as his partners peer in. One of the Detectives is quick to respond, "Well, will you look at this," as he steps in, shotgun readied and aimed at four youths, balls/ass nude sitting in a circle on the floor. They're back-to-back, gagged and bound to each other with rope and duct tape.

The sleuths separate and do a toss of the apartment. One radios the outside team. "Apartment is all clear, we got four live ones up here."

One of the outside Detectives responds, "10-4, on our way up."

The Detectives converge on the foursome who squirm and moan. Their faces are red and swollen and blood oozes from their chests as one cop reaches over for a closer look revealing inscriptions cut in with a razor or sharp knife. The teens are scribed across their chest with the same words embedded into their skin, *'I did it.'*

The tape is removed from their mouths, and an explanation of a remarkable event comes out from one of the young perps. "Some crazy bitch in a ski mask fucked us up, man. She beat us with a gun, cut and ripped off our clothes and tied us up. That cunt carved up our bodies and put bullet holes in the floor right next to us. This is fucked-up, man! You can't treat people like that!"

One of the older sleuths leans over them and remarks, slowly and clearly, "You're not people. After what you did to those two seniors, you're animals."

"We didn't do nothin', man."

"Of course not. You guys are just a bunch of model citizens. I should have brought my Goddamn camera."

The Detectives laugh as one gives some orders, "Call for transportation for these twits, and some clothes." He turns to the perps. "Don't worry guys, they'll have some nice prison suits waiting for you at Rikers."

---

When the Detectives bring the young hoods back to the Three-Five, Pasano is quick to spurt, "Hey, guys, I would have backed you up on this."

One tenured sleuth blurts back, "I know, Sarge. These mopes went easy. But thanks."

## CHAPTER 18

# HELP FOR ADDICTED BABIES AND A TRUTH REVEALED

As a social worker assigned to Harlem Hospital, Renee routinely assists heroin-addicted persons, caring and finding decent housing and health care for them and their children. It includes addicted newborns, which recently has become the most horrific fallout from the big 'H' epidemic.

Sergeant Pasano responds to a 911 call of a DOA infant in a 'shooting gallery' on West 150th Street just off 8th Avenue. It's another of the dwindling drug dens thanks to his strike team banging away and sealing them up. Renee, working that day at the hospital, hears the call and responds with the ambulance personnel to the location.

Pasano, following loud infant cries, walks up a stairway with missing steps and handrails. He enters a garbage-filled apartment not fit for humankind where rows of candles are scattered about supplying light, and the all-important cog in the heroin preparation, heat. Dozens of used, blood-soaked syringes lay about ready to suck up and release the liquid supplying the fix. Renee is in the rear of what was once a living room decades before, holding a sick newborn, a preemie. The sound and sight of this addicted infant going through withdrawal are unmistakable. She has all the symptoms; malnourished, frail, and covered in rashes. She is twitching and howling from pain.

Pasano is exposed to another sad vista within his drug world. He walks over to a weeping Renee. He spots the infant's mother lying in a fetal position on an old piece of dirty carpet. She's grabbing onto a dead newborn, the twin of the other. Her weeping and bleeding from an early home, self-delivery, is heart-wrenching. Her refusal to go to the hospital or let go of the dead child is problematic. There are one hundred questions, but no answers.

Pasano leans over to a tearful Renee and whispers, "Let them take the surviving child to the hospital, Renee. My people will do the paperwork. Let's persuade the mom to go. They'll take the deceased infant on board. There's nothing more you can do here."

Renee cries as she questions Paul, "Do you think we can resolve this? I'm running out of strength, you know."

"Please Renee, I need you. Stay with me here, we'll do it together."

"Okay. I'm just tired. Remember your promise."

With his arm around Renee, he answers, "Yes."

One of the responding 'uniforms,' a Black female, attempts to remove the dead infant from the addicted mom. The mother pulls the limp infant closer and tighter to her body and says in a grieving tone, "Please, no. I think she's just sleeping. Please let me be with her."

The female officer backs away and glances over at Pasano, Renee, and first responders. There is a light tap on the broken door frame and in walks Corisa.

Pasano sights her first and says, "You everywhere?"

Corisa quips back, "I should be asking you the same."

"I'm getting paid for this."

Corisa counters in a snappy tone, "Not everything has a cash value, Sergeant."

As she walks over to the young mother lying out on the bloody floor, she kneels down next to her and whispers, "Hi, Tisha. It's Corisa, sweetheart."

"Oh, Risa', what have I done?"

"You did fine. You have a beautiful baby, and once you both get well, they will find a home for the two of you. Okay? Now, Tish', let me take this angel and give her to the medics. Ms. Jons, would you come over and give Tisha her baby?"

As Renee walks over with the living twin, Corisa gently places her marred hands under the lifeless child, removes, and cradles it. A paramedic standing nearby quickly takes the child and places it on a small gurney. All are assured of its demise, but a last ditch effort to revive her is put forth, with negative results. Corisa steps away, and Renee moves forward, kneeling and presenting the young mother with the crying newborn.

Aside from the cries, all others remain silent.

Corisa, in a soothing voice, tells Tisha, "Now, honey, you go with these good folks and let them help you."

"Can I take my baby?"

Renee cuts in, "Of course, dear."

Corisa adds, "I'll check on you, okay, Tish'?"

"Thank you, Ris'. I'm sorry to everyone for this. It's all my fault."

Renee, raising her voice, "The hell it is, child!"

The paramedics reach in, pick up and carry the mother and her baby onto the gurney.

Corisa is walking out. As she passes by Pasano, she moves in and tells him, "Her name is Tisha Lenon, 114 West 138th Street, Apartment 6. She's 16. I know her mother, Helen. She's a good person. This kid just got swallowed up, Sergeant."

"Like you?" Pasano replies in a combative tone.

Corisa, snapping back, "No, not like me. Mine was choice, hers wasn't."

As she walks out the door, Pasano calls out to her, "See you around. Get some help."

"Don't worry, Pasano, you'll be seeing me. I live here, you don't."

Corisa exits the building. Out front, she encounters Renee Jons, who is just about to enter the ambulance.

Renee reaches out, touches her arm, and softly remarks, "My dear, thank you for the heads up with my Olivia."

Corisa, always the abrupt one, responds, "No big thing," and walks away.

———————

Late that evening, in a nondescript, hidden DEA office, a 30-year-old tall, trim, Black female, is sitting in a make-up chair under some portable, bright white lights and mirrors. The reflection shows an eye-catching brunette, with alluring features. Her handler, Brian Wallace, a 50-year-old male with a ponytail, is applying make-up to her face and limbs, transforming DEA Agent Yono into Corisa, local junkie. Tactics are also discussed. Yono's handler leads off with a wisecrack.

"You do understand, Yo', bringing someone with your looks down to looking like shit is no easy task."

Yono jokes, "Yeah, yeah. My mother used to tell me that same load of crap, but I still can't get a date."

"Oh, right, doing what you're involved in—good luck with that." The two laugh.

"I'm running late. Gotta' be back out there before morning. This cop, Pasano, runs tight. We have to make sure he stays on the rails and not get himself killed. He's also got a chip on his shoulder the size of a Goddamn tree."

"Look who's talking. There's no one more ballsy than you. You'd make a good pair. You better stay within the lines. You're being watched by our DEA bosses, don't forget."

"No way, sweetie. You know me, I'm a loner. Although he is kinda' cute. But, right now, I just want to do my job and take down some of those wannabe mobster punks."

Brian says, in a firm tone, "Hey, slow the hell down, kiddo. First off, they're not wannabes, they're the real fuckin' deal. They 'make' you and they'll cut your pretty little head off. Understand me? Don't underestimate any of them. They're killers."

"I'm a big girl."

"Yeah, but you're my responsibility. You die and I'll have to retire."

Yono cuts in, "Let's get some more dirt on me. Corisa's gotta' look good for her next date."

"Go......Bobby will drop you off."

As Yono gets up and walks towards the door, she glances in the mirror and remarks, "God, I do look like shit."

Bobby hurries her along. "Hey, we gotta' get you out of here, let's go."

Brian shouts out to her. "Remember, Yo', stay in character—no unnecessary conversation, and we can't do backups for you. You're on your own, girl."

## CHAPTER 19

# JUSTICE

The team is done processing a fresh batch of narc dealers and buyers. They're preparing to transport them down to Central Booking and arraignment. As they're loading them into a prisoner van parked out front, more perps are being led in the front door by the NYPD's Organized Crime Control Bureau.

These undercover cops have just finished a buy and bust operation a few blocks from the station house. They have been working with Pasano's team on and off for the past few weeks. They're led by Sergeant Ricky Menez, a tough, well built, tattooed undercover who has conducted hundreds of narc buys and follow-up arrests. It's a fast but highly dangerous operation. The undercover, usually playing the role of an addict, goes into a location unarmed and unvested, buys a quantity of drugs and walks out, hopefully unscathed. He or she will pay with marked and recorded serialized currency. If undercovers are 'made' as cops, they would likely be shot by drug overseers.

Within minutes, backup plainclothes and 'uniforms' hit the location and collar-up the seller and associates, confiscating drug 'stash' and evidentiary currency. Sergeant Menez greets Paul at the Three-Five entranceway. Hearty hand slaps lighten the mood.

"Paul, can I talk to you for a bit, in private?" Menez asks Pasano.

"Of course. Let me get these prisoners loaded up, and I'll meet you upstairs in my office."

Menez is waiting in Pasano's office. As Paul walks in, Menez delivers the good news.

"Paul, listen, one of the dealer's associates we just picked up had a New York City carpenter's ID in his pocket. Apparently, he's working on your station house renovation. He also had a slip of paper with what appears to be a list of your intended strike locations, including a few prior ones. Your West 140th Street raid was on that list. I think what we have here, Paul, is your leak." Menez continues, "This guy said he was working the morning you were making preparations for that raid that went sideways. Bottom line, we did a bit of 'field investigation' on his ass, and he reluctantly gave up that he tipped off his drug associates that morning in exchange for a bundle of dope. They were waiting for you, Paul. You were set up."

Pasano's face drops. "Where is he? I want to confront this fuck. He caused my guys some hurt and threatened the whole Goddamn operation."

Menez cuts right in, "Look, let it be. He's already been 'tuned-up.' As is, I have to take him to the hospital. If you or me wind up killing this fuck, it'll only make things worse. I got a confession from him. I'll call the DA and IAD and straighten everything out. You go ahead and finish what you're doing."

"Hey, Ricky, I owe you big time. You saved my ass. Thank you."

Menez replies, "We're all part of the same team, right?" The two do a strong handshake and part ways.

Pasano is relieved and thinks to himself, *'One Internal Affairs investigation will be closed, but the jump-push probe is still pending.'*

He's quick to grab his phone and deliver the news to his unit but also delivers a warning to them. "Yeah, Will, pass the word along to the team. OCCB just picked up a bunch. One of them is a New York City carpenter who was working on the station house the day we planned the 140th Street raid that got screwed up. This fuck overheard our strike plans for the day's hit and a few others as well. He tipped off the druggies. This should put the kibosh on the Downtown brass looking at us for the leak. And, listen, as you deliver the news, tell the guys not to mess with that mope. We have enough to worry about."

"No sweat. Got it, boss."

The Sarge, not one to take his own advice, is the personification of 'do as I say, not as I do.'

Later that evening, as things quiet down and his guys gone for the night, Paul walks downstairs from his office and heads into the 35th Precinct holding cells. A uniformed cop stands guard and maintains the intake log. Paul greets the young cop, "How are you, officer?" He continues, "Just checking the log and a few perps," as he scans down on the thick, typewritten book, searching for a name.

"Sure, Sarge," the officer answers, not questioning the boss's motives.

Paul walks passed him and remarks, "Just want to have a word with a couple of them."

"Fine with me, sir."

Entering a dimly lit and well-stenched corridor, Paul walks to his destination. Cell #6. Peering inside, he eyeballs his target lying on a bench. It's the middle-aged junkie, the mole who jeopardized the safety of a large unit of cops and nearly derailed the Sarge's entire Harlem operation. The skel's face is puffed-up and small droplets of blood trickle from his mouth. Pasano raps lightly on the rusted-over metal bars. Just a hint of gray paint manages to expose itself after decades of neglect. The prisoner immediately recognizes the cop standing before him, jumps to his feet, and begins to tremble and stammer, "I..I..I'm sorry, sir. Sorry, sir. I didn't mean no harm."

Out of sight of the guarding officer, Paul peers left and right, and stands nose to the cage. He draws his off-duty revolver from its holster and brings it eye level, and points it at the man inside the welded pen. Ranting in a whisper, "I'm not going to kill you tonight, but someday, when you get out, I'm gonna' look for you and put a bullet in your fuckin' head. Hear me well, scumbag. I see you on the street—you're a dead man."

"Yes, officer. Yes, officer," as his voice cracks in fear.

Paul holsters his weapon, turns, and walks away.

## CHAPTER 20

# TWO FAMILIES—TWO TRAGEDIES

Another average school day on Long Island for eight-year-old Andrew Pasano. Some outdoor playtime at recess eases the regular drone of a third-grade classroom. The best part of his day is the bus ride home with a couple dozen of his friends. It's late spring, and as the school year is coming to a close, there is always extra glee in the demeanor of all school kids. More laughter and louder voices.

Rachel, her dark hair held off her face with a pink headband, just finished her daily walk and is waiting at the bus stop. The school bus pulls up and Rachel sees her boy exit. Little Andrew is holding his school painting and runs with all his might just twenty feet from his mother's waiting hug.

A car speeds around from behind the school bus. A terrifying sound follows as a small body flies through the air, twisting and rolling, as the little boy's painting flutters in the wind. There is screaming, blood, and tears. The bus driver notifies his dispatch. Police and an ambulance respond. There is a poor description of the driver and the car. A dirt-covered vehicle with tinted windows and no license plates will make this investigation a difficult one. Rachel is on her knees alongside her boy. Other parents are present, attempting to console the young mom.

A phone message is simultaneously left at the Pasano household. The person speaks with an Italian accent and no emotion. "You play with fire and you get burned."

The message from the Giadanas has been sent. Another message must be given to the father.

---

Sergeant Pasano is at the precinct processing four drug dealers. One had a gun, and three others have robbery and murder warrants. It's all serious business for these 'Narcs,' but something else takes precedence.

The Inspector calls Pasano into his office, and in a solemn voice, lays out the horrific news. "Paul, you're done for the day. There's been an incident. Your boy's alive but hurt bad. He was intentionally hit by a car."

Paul's face drops, no tears, just pain, fury, and cursing. There is also a promise by this young boss of retaliation by death. There is silence from onlookers outside the CO's office. Pasano's teammates rush to his side.

---

Rachel and Paul are at the hospital, talking quietly with the local priest from St. Thomas. Last rites are administered. Immediate family is outside the room. There are tears, prayers, and the beeps from medical monitoring devices with the unmistakable sound of a ventilator. Pasano's team members are on their way.

A doctor calls the young couple into the hallway. He explains the seriousness of the injuries.

"I'm sorry. I wish I had better news. The brain damage and paralysis are severe. Right now, it's touch and go. I promise you we are doing our best. Everyone here is pulling for your son."

The young parents are in shock. No words are spoken.

A few minutes later, Rachel overhears two doctors whispering. There is discussion of disconnecting life support. It will be dismissed by the parents. Paul and Rachel are insistent they will not let go of their boy. God's Hands are mentioned. Pasano leaves everyone behind and walks out into the hallway. His narc team members are outside waiting.

In firm and vengeful tones, the Sarge relays his intentions to them. "I want all those responsible for this—dead!"

The teammates, finding it hard to say the right words, pledge their support. John Calvoy, however, steps back and appears hesitant.

Two Suffolk County Detectives who are part of the investigation, hear most of the conversation, but take it no further. They attribute it to a father who is about to lose his son.

———————

It's a three-day lapse in the drug war. A new victim. A little boy has been targeted as a warning to all in law enforcement that the Mafia will fight for their multi-million dollar empire using any means possible, even targeting children. Paul has been recommended to take some time off to spend with his family. He refuses. A Chaplain is brought in and does a one-on-one with him, with negative results. This young boss is on a rampage and hell-bent on revenge for the attempted murder of his son.

The NYPD forms an investigative team. The Narc Intelligence unit is involved. The Organized Crime Control Unit takes the lead. It's 'all in' to find the person or persons behind the incident.

Pasano's narc team holds a private meeting behind closed doors. Pasano wants to do his own thing. Team members try in vain to calm him. One of the most matured guys on the team, John Calvoy, takes his shot at a one-on-one and talks Paul down a couple of notches.

"Let the NYPD do their job, Sarge," as John puts a hand on his boss's shoulder. "Don't jeopardize your family and career, or ours. We'll work on it from our end, but let's not wander too far over the line. Why give more energy to Internal Affairs and the Civilian Complaint Review Board? Let's prove them wrong. Let's show them we're not lawless marauders using Gestapo tactics to accomplish our objectives." John gazes steadily at his boss before continuing. "Look, Paul, we've been friends and teammates for a long time. Let's stay on course. We know we're hurting Giadana's cartel. We've been delivering casualty after casualty right to their front door. Look at our arrest numbers. We've gone from hundreds to thousands. Robberies and homicides have been on a steady decline. Let's keep banging away at them, and we'll win this thing."

Pasano, conceding, "You're right, John. I'm sorry. It's just that I can't shake off the images of my son lying in the hospital. They're telling me he may never walk again and might have sustained brain damage. It's a lot for me to accept, especially all that's happened is part my doing. Fight the drug war, yes, but to what end? I sacrificed my own flesh and blood. Not mine, but my son's."

"I hear you," as John tries to console the Sarge. "I'm sure I couldn't deal with it. But remember our commitment, our promise."

"I do," says a calmer Pasano. "I can always count on you to keep things on an even keel. We'll begin again first thing in the morning. I'll need you to take the lead on the next few missions. Your head is a lot clearer than mine right now. I'm gonna' see if I can contact an undercover from the DEA. Maybe he can lend some assistance into my son's investigation. I just want to feel like I'm doing something."

"I understand completely, Paul. We'll get the people responsible. You know that, right?"

"Of course."

---

It's less than a week after Paul's son was run down, and it's still open season for shootings in 'Dodge City.' Part two of the mob's message is delivered. Late afternoon, the radio car providing special attention to the Jons' residence responds to a phony 911 call of shots fired three blocks away, just as her oldest son, Richard, comes home from his part-time, after-school job as an electrician's apprentice. Once on his street, he encounters a serious problem. He's lured into an incident set up by the Mafia cartel and paid assassins to send another message to Renee and all those who dare interfere with the lucrative flow and distribution of heroin on their Harlem streets.

After saying a quick hello to some of his neighborhood friends, Richard hears what is a staged altercation. It is between a local junkie paid for his performance and Richard's younger brother, Cavon, who is unwittingly involved. A few junkies hawking drugs in front of his family's apartment building use Cavon as bait by luring him into a confrontation. There are some shoves and threats as Cavon demands them to leave. This is certainly loud enough and timed perfectly for the arousal of his older brother.

It is well known the 'Black Sunday' gang is behind the drug selling and control of this street and is sending a message. Cavon is surrounded by dozens of junkies and thugs. A few of the local community residents stand back on the sidelines out of fear of deadly reprisal.

As Richard gets closer to the crowd and the center of the disturbance, he hears his younger brother's voice ring out with disdain over the local drug dealing where his sisters play every day. This is a place where days before, multiple shootings took place a few doors down from his residence. Without fear, amidst a large assembly of thugs, he confronts the junkie/dealer.

Cavon lets loose with a barrage of demands. "Hey, all you losers, take your shit, beat drugs, guns, and junkies off this block and out of the neighborhood. I've got family here, man."

One doper exclaims, "Fuck off, punk! You and your family. We're here makin' money."

Cavon comes back, "No. You druggies are killing yourselves and our own people."

Richard tries to break into the circle to aid his kid brother. Just to his side, standing and leaning against a white Cadillac, is the bull. He is the operation's overseer, enforcer, and gun toter. As Richard moves into the ambush which has been set up by 'Black Sunday' and funded by Giadana, the bull steps forward to confront him by blocking his path. Richard, knowing he has to rescue his brother, reaches back and with every ounce of strength his body could offer, lands a punch that sends the enforcer flying to the ground. Without warning, the overseer pulls out a .38 caliber revolver and lets off a round, striking Richard in his face. Bleeding erupts immediately as his younger brother, Cavon, becomes entangled deep within the mob of thugs, is thrown to the ground, kicked, punched, and left barely conscious. The shooter flees the scene, and Richard, holding his shredded face, begs for help. There is none. He runs to the corner hoping to flag down a cab. The drivers see him but pass him by. No cabby working up in Harlem would dare put himself in the middle of a gun battle with a Black youth bleeding from his head.

There is no choice. No one calls the police until valued minutes go by, and Richard Jons has to run nineteen blocks covered in his own blood until he reaches the E.R. at Harlem Hospital where he collapses.

Renee knows nothing of these events until she comes home and is met by her younger children crying for their brother, as Cavon, still dazed, tells her what happened.

Cavon, in fear, tells his Mom, "Richard's been shot! I think he's at the hospital."

She races there, fearing the worst. The nurses direct her to Richard's room. Renee runs to his side and stands vigilantly over her son who incurred a massive wound. The bullet entered through his mouth, broke up into fragments, and scattered throughout his head. With prayers and a dedicated surgical team, doctors worked feverishly to keep him alive. Richard Jons survives.

Pasano is summoned to Harlem Hospital. He meets with Renee and tells her with anger how they targeted both their sons. "I promise," he says, "We will get those responsible for the assaults on both our boys,"

Still in shock, Renee is trembling and crying. "Please, Paul, please. Put an end to all of this."

With his arm around Renee, Pasano walks her over to a chair. She sits, and Pasano looks down into her eyes, and quietly but assertively speaks, "We will. My commitment has not changed."

Renee grabs his arm and weeps. Pasano, thinking to himself, *'I hope to God, we can.'*

———————

Later that evening, Renee sits with her three remaining children. With Olivia gone and Richard in the hospital in critical condition, there is nothing left for the Jons family except prayer. They pray for Richard and Olivia. A Three-Five patrol car sits in front of their building under special orders to safeguard the remaining members of a broken family.

———————

Sergeant Pasano heads down to NYPD Headquarters first thing in the morning and asks to speak to the CO of the Narc Intelligence Unit. Paul is demanding some answers, wanting to know how the investigation is going. He walks into Captain Ritenish's office, sits down and gets right to the point. "Look, Cap', I just want some answers. I know and appreciate that a good line of protection has been afforded mine and Ms. Jons' families. But, I want in on the investigation." The Captain from the Intel Unit is careful not to give too much info to the hotheaded Harlem team leader.

The Sarge continues, "Also, if I can, I'd like to get a message to one of the DEA's undercovers, Nick Scalia. At this point, he's the only one that might supply the answers to the players who carried out the attempted hits ordered by Carlos Giadana."

Captain Ritenish makes no promises but gives the Sarge a go-ahead, as he hands him a pen and paper. "Put your request in writing, Paul."

Pasano writes down one word. *'Who?'*

The Captain looks at the note. "That's it, one word?"

"Yeah, boss. Believe me, he'll understand."

"Okay, it'll get to him. You have my word. As soon as I hear from Scalia, I'll notify you immediately."

"That's all I ask. Thank you."

As Pasano is on his way out, Captain Ritenish makes a plea to the overwrought Sergeant. "Paul, please keep your cool and let us do our job. The NYPD has a lot of resources. They'll find out who did this to yours and Ms. Jons' boys and bring them to justice."

"I appreciate your confidence, Captain. The kind of justice I'm looking for doesn't come from the NYPD. But, thank you."

Captain Ritenish's face turns flush, but he doesn't utter another word. Pasano leaves his office.

---

Later that day, Pasano spends some time at the hospital. He visits with his son, Andrew, where he finds Rachel and daughter Linda sitting in chairs next to the boy's bed. The little girl can't comprehend what has happened to her brother. Life support has just been removed. Andrew is breathing on his own. His brain functions and recog' have yet to return to normal. His arms have feeling, his legs don't. Rachel is inconsolable, and Paul is motionless.

A senior physician breathes some new life into the young couple. He makes a commitment to new healing methods. It makes a difference. The two accept any promises from anyone offering hope.

Paul pulls Rachel close to him and whispers, "We'll get through this. I'm heading to work. Please call me if there's any change whatsoever, okay, Rach'?"

In a cracking voice, she answers her husband, "Yes, Paul, of course."

The Sarge stoops over and kisses his boy's forehead, then Linda's, and finally Rachel's. He exits the room. Outside the door is a Suffolk County police officer on guard.

"Thank you, officer," Paul tells him.

---

The Sarge's next stop is Harlem Hospital. Renee Jons' teenage son is still in serious condition following his bullet wound to the head. Richard's still unidentified shooter is in the wind. There's a large team of Detectives actively working the case. Two 'uniforms' sit outside his room. Renee Jons is bedside, attempting to make some kind of contact with her son. Something, no matter how little. Doctors here make no promises. This is a hospital deluged with shooting victims. They're the best in patching people up and getting them back on their feet. Head wounds are different, more uncertain.

Pasano tries to console Renee. "I'm so sorry. I feel responsible."

Renee responds with kind words, "How's your boy, Paul? Is he improving?"

"We don't know yet, Renee. It's medicine and prayers at this point, mostly prayers."

Renee whispers, "My prayer beads are all worn away. I hope God is listening."

"I hope so," Paul says as he stands up. "I'm heading back to the precinct."

A worried Renee tells him, "Please be careful. We can't lose you as well."

The Sergeant reassures her. "Don't worry about that. They don't want me, they want everyone around me so I can watch it unfold and live with it. It means we're hurting them. They're becoming desperate. They fear their time has come. I'll just have to rush things along a bit," forcing a smile.

As he walks away, he tells Renee, "Stay close by your children."

—————————

Early evening, Pasano slumps in his office chair and buries his face in his palms. No tears, just whispers of vengeance come from a man on the edge. There are handwritten notes scattered across his desk. He shuffles through them and comes across his old Brooklyn partner's message:

*Paul,*

*I'm sorry. There are no other words for me to offer, except I'm here for you. Hang tough.*

*Bobby Stewart.*

## CHAPTER 21

# GOOD WORK—BAD NEWS

It's well past noon as Pasano walks into the 35th. His guys are vested-up and heavily armed. The team is revved up and ready to go. Paul grins at his welcome and at the aggressiveness shown by his comrades.

Capo Carlos Giadana is pushing harder than ever, realizing his drug volume is operating at one-third its peak level. His street and inside narc locations are faltering. People are being arrested in great numbers, the buyers are deterred, and sellers are awaiting trials. Finally, the Narc Task Force is making headway towards his empire's termination. Harlem is beginning to lose its designation as the drug capital of America.

Pasano is playing a dual role. On one hand, he's leading the charge to break the Mafia's grip on the historically Black community. His second challenge is to pay retribution to those who brought devastation to his and Renee Jons' families.

This day is planned and designated by his go-to guy, John Calvoy, as *Buyers Beware Day*. The goal is to arrest as many drug buyers in one twelve hour period as possible and to confiscate and voucher their personal property as related evidence. This includes their cars, the ones they drive in from New Jersey, Connecticut, and the New York City suburbs. If the vehicles are used to transport any felony weight narcotics to or from Harlem, they will be removed and held as evidence of illegal narc transportation.

Pasano always stretches the limits of the Manhattan DAs, but the Sarge's persistence almost always prevails. Pasano and Calvoy's goal is to send a loud and clear message to all those entering Harlem to buy or sell drugs, that they are not welcome, and are part and parcel to the problem of the drug proliferation throughout the community. They are also destroying their own lives and the lives of their loved ones. It's a dirty business, and dirty tactics must be used to retaliate.

By 8 PM, over forty arrests and eighteen cars are gathered up in the sweeps. Two large-scale dealers are picked up at day's end. These well-paid mopes were constantly loading up with fresh supplies all during the day from shipments brought in overnight from their cutting, mixing, and packing plants in the Bronx.

The good news for the Unit is DEA and the NYPD's Organized Crime Control Bureau undercover teams in nondescript cars were following the shipments back and forth to the hot locations. A list is kept. When the final take-down takes place, these targets will be the focus of the operation. But not yet. Pasano reaches out to Narc Intel and gets their approval on the wait. It will come soon. There's still more set-up to be done. Giadana must not get wind of this inside info. Word is channeled to Nick Scalia as Pasano is still waiting to hear from him through Downtown Headquarters.

———————

Late that evening, while the guys are processing perps and vouchering their property, the call comes in. The Desk Lieutenant calls the Sarge over and delivers the news, "Paul, important call for you on line two. Take it in the Administrative Lieutenant's room. Close the door after you. Big ears can collect bits and pieces."

Hustling into the private office, Pasano anxiously responds, "Thanks, boss."

He shuts the door, picks up the phone, and prays this is the info on the family attacks. It's not. It's disappointment.

Captain Ritenish delivers the bad news, "Paul, I'm sorry, but the word from Scalia is he's being carefully watched by Giadana's scumbags. He's barely hanging on himself. He might have to pull out. It's getting too dangerous for him to stay undercover. He is unable to get you the info you requested."

Pasano's face reddens. His fist clenches tighter on the phone. He does his best to maintain some composure while talking to his Downtown boss. He forces words out he doesn't want to say but does anyway, "Okay, Cap'. Thanks for trying. When you next speak with Scalia, thank him also. I don't want to be any part of him being 'made' more than he is already. I'm sure he has his own family to think about..........Right boss........I understand..........I will, sir..........You too, sir."

The call ends. Pasano slams his fist on the desk. The sound and vibration can be heard and felt outside the room. A couple of his teammates and the Lieutenant scurry into the office and over to him.

A concerned John Calvoy speaks first, "You okay, Paul?"

A pissed off Pasano snaps, "Actually not, John. But let's get the paperwork knocked out and the prisoners downtown for lodging."

"Right, boss."

They all leave the office except for the Sarge and one of his most loyal supporters, the old Lieutenant, Cameron Devoe. The six foot four, gray-haired boss speaks, "Paul, listen up for a couple of minutes."

Pasano, still irate, says, "Sure boss, what's up?"

Devoe speaks in a military tone, "Look, son, I'm worried about you. You're coming unhinged. You can't continue like this. You're going to get yourself or one of your teammates hurt. For sure, you'll wind up getting into some deep shit with the job. Either you settle down or take some time off. Am I getting through to you, Sarge?"

"I'm reading you loud and clear, Lieu'. I appreciate your concern, but what you see before you, is me. I always run tightly wound, especially when things pertain to my family. I'll back off, boss, you have my word. Thanks for your advice."

Pasano reaches out his hand and Devoe responds. For the moment, Pasano appears calm.

## CHAPTER 22

# WORKING GIRL

The sun squeezes itself between the long rows of four and five story dwellings as it brings an early sunrise to a volatile neighborhood. Corisa is beginning her daily ritual of wandering about from drug dens to key narc selling spots collecting bits and pieces of intel and passing it through the pipeline to the DEA. The word on the street is the all-out war between law enforcement and organized crime, leading to hit contracts and assassination attempts.

The female operative crosses the line, using tactics non-conforming to Agency guidelines. Just inside an entranceway to a drug site, Corisa approaches a well-known gun carrying enforcer as he protects a local selling operation on W. 132nd. It's a four block square generating millions in annual revenue.

Standing directly in front of him trying to gain some info, she's to the point. "Hey, Malik, you wanna' make some 'bread?' "

"Get lost you fuckin' whore. You know where the 'H' is. Take your sick ass across the street and 'juice' up."

Corisa stops her advance and with one hand reaches under her sweatshirt. Malik is quick, pulling out a 9', and issues an ultimatum, "Hold it, bitch. Hand out slow!"

She hesitates but complies. "Ease up cowboy, I have an offer," as she pulls out a packet of five one-hundred dollar bills.

"Where'd you get that?" Malik remarks.

"I worked for it."

"Whad'ya do, give out a hundred blowjobs?"

Smacking her lips, Corisa counters, "It's all yours, I want in on the contracts. I know people who can do the work for us, and we can split the 'scratch.' "

Malik delivers an icy stare. "Who the fuck do you know?"

"What do you care? You in or not?"

"Okay, slut, two 'hits,' pig Pasano and that cunt, Jons. You get it done, I collect and pass half to you. You fuck up and I'll 'cap' your ass."

Corisa hands him the bills, turns, walks away and delivers parting words, "Be ready to collect what's coming to you, Malik."

Smiling, he counts the cash and pockets it as he mumbles to himself, "You fuckin' beast."

---

Corisa takes a slow trek to the west side of upper Manhattan ducking in and out of hallways, scoping in all directions to be sure she's not followed. Her handler waits in a safe house within a busy apartment complex. She hangs out front for a couple of minutes trying to appear a couple of notches above a grimy bag lady before darting in and entering the first-floor rear apartment.

Inside, her associate wastes no time in pumping up the undercover. "What kept ya'?"

"Fuck you, Brian!"

"Relax, what are you drinking?"

"A green meanie."

He and another agent, a long-haired, male DEA backup, laugh as her handler fetches a can of diet soda from a nearby fridge. "Here, no sugar calories for you," as he tosses it over to her.

Corisa sneers, plops down on a well-used brown leather couch, opens the soda, takes a mouthful, and continues her snarky style. "Who's this?"

"One of us."

"Looks like a leftover hippie. You know I don't like more people involved. More ears and more mouths," as she stares at the new face. "Does he know my street name is Corisa?"

Her handler, Brian Wallace, cuts in. "Yon', give it a rest. I filled him in on everything."

The younger agent walks over to her and puts his arm forward. "Doug Gecoi."

Corisa extends hers, and the two shake hands.

"Forgive the dirt. I work for a living." She settles in on business. "Listen, Brian, those contracts on Pasano and Jons are reaching a fevered pitch. Pass the word along."

"Copy that. How are you holding up? I can arrange a break for you. Come out for a few days' rest."

"I can't, I've got some unfinished business to take care of."

"Fine, but don't overextend yourself. Stay on script."

"Hey, you want to switch assignments? Let's get me a ride back, at least halfway. I want to stop and pick up some fast food for a couple of the galleries. I also need some more drug-buy bucks."

Frowning, her handler cuts her off, "That's another thing. You're spending too much time in the drug dens, and you certainly shouldn't be sleeping there. We have enough safe houses for you to catch your breath in. The info you're picking up is not worth the personal risk."

Corisa slams back, "How do you know? That's the real crossroads in hell. It's where the truth lies."

"You keep telling yourself that line of bullshit. I'm not buying it. You're moving too far off target. Get back on track. The tip on the contract hits is a good piece of work. That's the kind of intel we need."

"Oh, so that's good? Please, let me make my own decisions out there. And by the way, you know Giadana is picking up the tab. That old dick won't step foot on the street."

"No, but he's got all the money and power and sits around a dinner table giving out orders."

Corisa motions with her hand as if firing a gun. "Uh-huh, maybe I can get close enough to 'off' him myself."

"Hey, right now that's not your job!"

"I know what my job is. Speaking of Giadana, how's my male counterpart, Scalia, doing?"

"Fine. He's carrying out his assignment."

"Do me a favor, watch out for him. He has a habit of getting himself in trouble."

"We know that, and he's just as thickheaded as you," as Brian taps his head.

"One other thing," Corisa says, "Vic Ferris is out there spreading his wings and you know he's a direct threat to Pasano."

"That's why we have you out there. Stay tight."

"Easier said than done. This cop is a wild character."

"And please remember, Yon', caution before valor."

"Rah-rah, which manual did you read that load of crap from?"

"God, it's like talking to my fuckin' kids," Brian answers in disgust.

Corisa gives him a slick comeback, "That's why we're doing all this, you forget?"

"I know, I know."

"Come on, Gecoi, give me a lift. And what kind of name is Geee - co - weee?"

"Italian, Calabrese."

"Thought so. You're not one of 'them,' are you?"

"Brian, help me here," the young Agent pleas.

Yono gets off the couch, grabs a wad of cash from her handler and walks out.

As Gecoi follows behind, Brian takes him off to the side. "See that she gets out there okay, and do me a favor. Watch out for her."

---

After being dropped off, Corisa hoofs the last ten blocks back to three of the major narc dens. She's carrying a bag full of burgers. It's not uncommon for users to skip food and drink for two or three days at a clip. As she enters the first one, it appears different. Much quieter than usual. A bunch of junkies are semi-conscious and past the nodding phase following a potent hit of dope.

Corisa begins an inquiry as she hands out some food. "What the fuck happened up here?"

Most of them don't answer, fearing reprisal. One old junkie responds, "We got half loads for free, man."

"Same spike?"

"What the fuck you think, woman?"

Corisa's face turns to a scowl. "Who shot you up?"

"Potek, he's always good for it at least once a week."

"Here, eat this if you want to live."

"Live for what girl, to look like you?"

"I'm diggin' my way out, bro'."

"Who the fuck are you anyway?"

"Risa'. You've seen me around." She makes sure the dozen or so users have a morsel and walks out mumbling to herself, 'I'll deal with that scumbag, Potek.'

In public, Corisa never hustles. It's stepping out of character and could be dangerous. Today is the exception as she leaves one gallery and scurries to another. This one is a priority. Inside, she discovers the same as in the first one. Sick addicts lay about, most of them unconscious. She crouches over each one rousting them from an intentional stupor. All but two awaken, one of them is Gina.

"Gina, Gina! Wake up, wake up, Gina!"

After lifting the youngster's eyelids and checking her neck for a pulse, Corisa makes a beeline for the stairs and runs next door to an occupied building. She bangs on the door of the ground floor apartment. A gray-haired elder answers as the frantic woman in front of him is firing off a quick volley of words. "Sir, please, we have people overdosed next door. Call 911 and ask for an ambulance."

"Of course, young lady. I'll call the police and an ambulance."

"No police, just an ambulance."

"Alright, alright," he answers as he moves a few feet back into the apartment and grabs his phone.

Within minutes, an overworked EMS crew arrives, jogs up the steps and immediately delivers the necessary aid to Gina and an older, male junkie. The two are revived but refuse to go to the hospital.

Corisa begs Gina, "Please, go with them."

"No, if I go, I'll lose my spot here."

"You can't stay here anymore," answers Corisa as she looks over at the two EMS workers.

"Sorry, ma'am. We can't force her or anyone else to go. We have more calls to make. If they change their minds, just call 911 again."

Losing her patience, Corisa answers. "Fine," as she turns to Gina. "You can't go on like this. You're going to die next time. Did that fuck Potek come up here and do this?"

Gina nods a yes. Corisa grits her teeth, grimaces, and makes a quick exit.

## CHAPTER 23

# PAYBACK

Most of the Raiders load up the prisoners and push off for night court. Pasano's three Black 'Narcs' take a huddle with their boss.

Pasano sounds off first, "We've been asked to send a message, off the cuff. Will has received a couple of hot tips about Giadana's mopes hanging out in a lower East Harlem bar shooting their mouths off to any flunkies who'll listen. It's Saturday, their night to party. I figure we'd go pay them a visit. You guys up for it?"

Will Fennar rushes a response, "Ready up, boss."

"Look, I always appreciate your support, but I don't like you risking yourselves this way. Let's be careful. You know we're being watched."

"Hey, boss," Will harps in. "We've been through this shit before. We come from these streets, remember?"

"He's right boss. Let us do our magic," Jim Kellig says as he grins.

"Fine." Pasano dictates, "We'll leave in thirty."

Will laughs sarcastically. "With you? Absolutely not. We don't want no White boys with us on this unauthorized mission. Especially Italians! You go home to your family. Let us step out a bit. We'll list it as a scouting trip."

Paul hesitates then responds, "Okay, but don't let me read about it in the morning papers."

"Nah', boss, we'll be under the radar, all the way. Just do our job, in and out," Calvoy answers, smiling.

They all laugh. The Sarge's laugh is a nervous one. Lieutenant Devoe, standing nearby, overhears the ongoings.

———————————

Giadana's club is plopped right in the middle of lower East Harlem. Italians only. It's been that way for over seventy years. A few 'connected' celebrity singers hung out here many years before. The mob was different then. No drugs, just gambling.

The windows are blacked out. Two oversized armed goons man the front door wearing all black; suits, shirts, and ties. Business meetings with the capos and 'uppers' are conducted in the basement which is locked with double steel, reinforced doors. 'Lowers' are not permitted. The basement's a fortress.

The three Raiders pull up and park out front. They get out and slowly walk to the main entrance.

One 'wiseguy' outside says to another, "Who the fuck are these 'Jimmy Jives?'"

The other shouts back, "Cops, man! Cops!"

They attempt to slam and lock the door. They're unsuccessful. Will smacks one in his face with the side of his military .45. Big John throats the other with one of his huge hands. Kellig slithers inside and holds the door open for his buddies.

The club exhibits the ornate look from the early 1920s. Stained glass alternates between oversized mirrors and wood trim. Heavy tables sit on worn planked floors. It's not that crowded, only a handful of connected people, or those who think they are, and a few well-used, over-dressed females. Well paid ones.

The place quiets to a hush. The basement door slams shut and cross bars go into place. A couple of Giadana's lieutenants are locked in. The trio of cops are not even thinking capos. They're here to send a message.

Jim Kellig speaks first, "Hey folks, chill! We're just here to have a little chat with your friend, Carlos. Once we do that, we'll be on our way."

One of the large Mafiosos in his black attire plants himself directly in front of Kellig, and in a strong, Italian accent, mumbles a balky response, "Your kind is not wanted here."

"And what kind is that?" Kellig answers defiantly.

"The black and blue kind."

Kellig, challenging, "That's two. Pick one."

"The kind that's about to catch a bea……."

He doesn't get to finish his final word and Kellig connects with a throat jab in a millisecond. The once standing big guy is flat out, holding his neck and gasping for air. The once low-key club is now amidst a melee. The local hangouts are big and rowdy but no match for people who do this daily for a living.

The place comes apart easy. It was never meant to withstand 200–300 pound people being tossed around like stuffed animals. A pool table collapses, and bar stools are thrown through mirrors. One hood gets rapped across his face with a pool cue. No guns are pulled. Giadana's enforcers are losing their wind and teeth. Four of them are down. Three others stand back. A few women are in shock. An imposing man slams the front door open and appears head on. He's got a mean and touch of crazy look to him. He's holding an older, well-used shotgun. An Ithaca pump. 'NYPD' is sprayed on the gun butt.

He shouts out in a loud, commanding voice, "Okay, that's it!"

All take notice after he pumps up his arsenal. The click overshadows the fight. He's donning a Lieutenant's shield hanging by a chain around his neck.

One of the oldest mobsters, still standing, says to a younger one, "Ease up, I know this fuck. It's Devoe. He was a killer decades ago."

Devoe yells out, "It's over!"

The place quiets. Lieutenant Devoe, in an authoritative voice, speaks again, "That's enough. My people—let's go. The rest of you, call your own ambulance."

Behind the Lieutenant are three teams of 'uniforms' who responded to a radio run of a bar fight.

Devoe is quick to take charge. "It's okay, men. Everything's under control. Resume patrol."

Even though it's not his precinct, the 'uniforms' respect rank and don't want to get involved. They leave.

He orders the 'Narcs,' "Pull out guys."

They brush themselves off and leave. The Lieutenant, with shotgun pointed to the bar, backs out last. The bulls are still down. Giadana's lieutenants remain in the basement.

From inside, one of the senior mobsters mouths off, "This isn't over, Devoe."

"It's never over. Come up and see me anytime."

Out front, an apologetic Kellig says, "Shit, Lieu'. We didn't mean to bring you into this. Just wanted to even things up a little."

"It's fine. You did what I would have done about twenty years ago."

An inquisitive Calvoy probes, "Hey boss, one of the older ones seemed to remember you."

"Guys, I used to own these streets, but not anymore. Now I just sign and push papers."

Kellig comes back with a quick reply, "Not tonight, boss."

## CHAPTER 24

# MORE FLACK

After Pasano spends Sunday with his family for their sake and his, first thing Monday morning, he has questions for his three mercenary cops about their visit to the mob bar. "How'd it go?"

"As planned boss," John Calvoy calmly answers. "Just a little pushing and shoving. We left a message."

"That's good," the team leader responds. "Let's get back to business. We're heading down to W. 127th Street in an hour."

This location is a boundary between precincts—the Three-Five, Two-Eight, and Two-Six. It's a stubborn pocket where police confusion over jurisdiction often occurs. Bad guy, James Sepps, controls the street and surrounding buildings. He's a killer who manages to elude long-term jail time. Short stints only. Good, well-paid lawyers do their job.

Pasano's planned raid is sidetracked as Inspector Deteo calls Pasano into his office.

Without mincing words, the Inspector tells Paul, "An anonymous civilian complaint came floating in, alleging some cops from this command 'did their own thing' at the East Harlem Italian social club on Saturday night. An old-fashioned donnybrook without arrests. A passerby made the allegation of a fight involving cops. 'Uniforms' responded and were ordered to leave and resume patrol. An NYPD Lieutenant was supposedly involved. Devoe's name was mentioned. Paul, every day

I come to work, it's another surprise. Unpleasant ones. The only saving Grace here is that there are no complainants. None of those Giadana lowlifes will step forward and file a formal complaint. There was an undercover in the fucking bar. Nick Scalia. He took a pool stick across his face. Broken nose. Treated and released at Columbia Pres'. However, to add more confusion to this mess, the DEA CO and Narc Intel left a message for you from Scalia. '*Thanks. I'm back in.*'"

Pasano nods. Deteo continues, " I don't get it and neither do they. In the future, Paul, I certainly would appreciate being kept in the loop. The word I got from the Chief of Patrol Downtown is they're a couple of heartbeats away from shutting down this whole Goddamn place. They'll just transfer you, me, and everyone else the hell out of here. Please, Paul, if you know who was involved, I don't want to know. Just send the word out that your little Pasano Police Department has to end. Understand?"

"Yes, sir. If my guys did have any part in this, I am sorry. Is that all, sir?"

"Yeah. That's it, Sergeant. That's enough. I need a fuckin' drink."

Pasano leaves and walks over to his waiting teammates. He grins and in a low voice tells them, "Well done. Undercover Scalia says thanks."

As he walks past the main station house desk, he smiles at Lt. Devoe and does a quick, low key thumbs up. Lieutenant Devoe returns with only a wink and puts his head back into his paperwork. Inspector Deteo, past his prime, maybe, looks out and picks up on the antics, shakes his head, and closes his office door.

Then the team pushes out with a full unit and some backups to deal with James Sepps on West 127th Street.

On their way out, Will Fennar says to the Sarge, "You know, Paul, we'll probably have to kill this mother fucker to remove him."

Paul's response in an adrenaline moment, "Fine with me, Will."

Pasano gets in an unmarked cruiser and leads the crew downtown.

He transmits on a point-to-point radio, checking reception amongst the small teams.

Pasano orders, "All's positive, and the raid is a go."

The Sarge initiates another transmission, "Central, be advised, we have multiple plainclothes members operating within the 35th, 28th, and 26th precincts at the borders. Members of Service, including male Blacks and Hispanics, are wearing color of the day."

"Central, 10-4. 'Uniforms' notified."

It's a short journey from the precinct to West 127th Street. Pasano's car takes center. One car blocks the corner of 7th Avenue, another does 8th Avenue. Two uniform units enter the street next. A few grab up the local street dealers that have been targeted and photo'd by the Special Narcotics teams from the 35th and 28th precincts. It's specific, and the right people must be taken. High priced criminal lawyers using court challenges can get the cases thrown out if the arrest teams make mistakes. Two blocks away, at least fifteen buyers are apprehended. Two large-scale street dealers are quickly overtaken, searched, cuffed, and placed into waiting patrol cars. Large 'stashes' of dime and quarter size glassines and bundles of cash are confiscated. It will be meticulous work later this evening.

Now the challenge, banging out the seven inside selling locations amongst two buildings side-by-side. Pasano and his team use backup 'uniforms,' spread them out, and attempt to make quick work of it. There's an issue. Two shots ring out within one of the buildings. All take cover; police, civilians, buyers, and sellers. Confusion always comes into play when shots are fired. It disrupts the raid. That's the overseer's, James Sepps, escape plan. For more 'flight' insurance, he shoots one of the buyers in the head in the hallway and flees the scene after stashing his gun within a loose cinder block. In seconds, he's down in the basement crawling through cement and dirt tunnels dug out between the buildings to facilitate escape. He's picked up on West 126th Street by Harlem Kingpin, Vic Ferris, and swiftly driven away. He eludes the Raiders. By the time the dust settles, Pasano and company must pause to lend aid to the seriously wounded addict and search the buildings, high and low, for the shooter.

---

James Sepps is amongst the missing, along with most of the large-scale sellers inside the target apartments. Two dealers are arrested, five others abscond. In addition, when *'shots fired'* came over the division radio, it was transmitted to emergency and response units city-wide. The brass at Headquarters is also alerted, and a Chief is en route. The climate in Harlem is already a hotbed of controversy. The underlying problem with Pasano's raid is the mortally wounded buyer. No shooter found. No gun found. Did one of Pasano's guys kill him? That's the first thing the Downtown brass will be thinking. The Sarge is thinking, *'More paperwork and another internal probe.'*

After a couple of hours of crime scene photos and investigation by the befuddled and overworked Duty Captain, everyone returns to the Three-Five. Prisoners are lodged in temporary holding cells at the station house. To add to the mess, the shooting incident and the raid take place on the boundary line between the 35th and 28th, making both precincts territorially involved.

The Chief orders, "Pasano, in the CO's office now! Inspector, you stay out. I want a word with your Sergeant."

Inspector Deteo says respectfully, "Yes, sir," and leaves his office.

Pasano enters. When he's in the midst of his work, he's pumped and maintains an 'I don't give a fuck attitude.' Here in this situation though, better to make nice. Pasano's no fool. Careers are at stake.

The Chief speaks straightforward, "Okay, Sarge, do you want your union rep?"

"No, sir."

"Fine. I have one question for you. Did you or any of your people kill the guy?"

"Definitely not, sir."

"Good." He hollers out the office door, "Inspector, Captain, both of you, get in here!"

The two hustle in and respond in unison, "Yes sir."

"Okay, listen up," the Chief says in an autocratic tone. "Make sure all the cops and bosses involved have union reps' present. Do short 'one-on-ones.' I mean short! Check their weapons and make sure they weren't fired. After that, let them finish processing their prisoners. Then get those good officers the fuck out of here and home to their families. Where's the Detective Lieutenant in charge?"

Inspector Deteo responds, "He's right outside my office, Chief."

"Bring him in here now."

Deteo calls in the Detective Squad Commander, Lt. Retell.

Continuing, the Chief says, "Lieutenant, your father, Don Retell?"

"Yes, sir?"

"He still alive?"

"No, sir, died two years ago, lung cancer."

"Sorry about that, son. He was a good man. Now go get your Detectives out from their office upstairs, get them out on West 127th Street, canvass the whole fucking neighborhood, and find the real shooter. And the Goddamn gun. Don't come back to this station house until you do. Understand?"

Lieutenant Retell respectfully answers, "Yes, sir."

"And all of you, don't forget, this was somebody's son. You're all dismissed. I'm going back home to my grandkids."

The Sarge humbly mutters, "Thank you, sir."

"No, thank you for your work here. I did it twenty-five years ago when you were probably in grammar school. Best years on the job. You should be at home with your wife. Your boy's still in the hospital, right?"

"Yes, Sir."

"Go home."

The old Chief walks out. The remaining bluecoats are stunned.

"Holy shit," Pasano says quietly. "Who was that old guy?"

The Detective Lieutenant murmurs, "His son OD'd on 'H' twelve years ago."

The cops remain silent.

A Detective holding some paperwork walks in the front station house door and approaches the Chief. "Sir, I just received word on the victim's ID. Brady McRudden, nephew of former Senator McRudden."

The Chief blurts out, "Fuck! Send out for coffees, I'll be spending the night with you people. Call the CO of Department of Public Information. No leaks to the press. Make sure notifications to the Senator's family are handled with care. You guys better come up with a collar."

Ferris, in a blacked-out SUV, drives Sepps to a safe house in the Bronx.

He gives him strict orders, "Stay put, you're too hot right now."

---

The morning comes. Media coverage of the Senator's nephew being gunned down while copping dope in Harlem, hits big. A phone call comes in from Giadana to Ferris. The capo is pissed.

Ranting in English with a Sicilian slant, "What the fuck did that crazy idiot do? Turn on the Goddamn news. Sepps' face is plastered all over the place. The whole damn police department is looking for him. He's a liability. If they nail him, he'll flip and take everyone down with him. Waste him! If you don't do it as soon as we hang up, I'll come over and whack both of you, understand?"

"Yes, Mr. Giadana. I will," Ferris answers with trepidation.

The call ends. Ferris looks over at Sepps, who breaks out in a sweat.

Ferris hands Sepps $500 and tells him, "Mr. G. wants you out of town, now! Let's go."

Sepps gets off the couch with the cash and heads for the door. Ferris pulls his 9mm wrapped in a shirt and lets off two rounds to the back of Sepps' neck. The bullets exit from his throat with a large spray of blood. He collapses to the floor. Ferris bends down, rolls Sepps over, and snatches the $500 from his hand. Ferris is in the market for a new downtown Harlem overseer.

## CHAPTER 25

# PAYOFF AND CONSEQUENCES

Early evening, after telling his wife he needs a stretch after dinner, Assistant DA James Horith walks out of his house in Queens, New York. One block from his home, a black limo with darkened windows pulls alongside. A door opens. Like a planned event, Horith gets in and they pull away. Inside the limo, two Italian mobsters speak in broken English to the ADA.

One mobster questions him. "Where's the list?"

Horith passes a sheet of paper over to him. The 'wiseguy' hands Horith a large envelope with a packet of currency inside.

Horith breathes deep. "Please, like you said, as long as nobody gets hurt."

"You should have thought about that first," the hood counters. "But, I promise you this, if these drug locations are bogus, you and your family will be the ones to get hurt, understand?"

"Yes," a nervous Horith tells the mobster.

"Get out," the hood orders.

---

Two days later, communication ensues inside a Special Narcotics Enforcement Unit observation post. An abandoned, dust-covered apartment within a low rise, transforms into a lookout and surveillance headquarters for this narc team. It's bleak and simple. Camera stand, two chairs, and a clean spot on an otherwise dirty window. They take hundreds of photos of narcotic transactions down below on West 154th Street, the last uptown gang holdout scrambling for survival.

On information supplied to the Giadanas by the corrupt ADA, James Horith, an assassination takes place at this observation post just past noon on Wednesday before Thanksgiving. Two officers, one cop filming and one backup, are in the OP as four paid assassins kick in the bolted apartment door. They spray the room with a hail of .45 cal' bullets from Mac-10 submachine guns firing off over 50 rounds. The two young Special Narcotics Enforcement Unit officers don't stand a chance.

Another police funeral is generated within the confines of the 35th at the hands of the mob. Pasano's close association with the SNEU team places more strain on him. All narc members know it's a numbers game. You today, who tomorrow? Me? It eats away at this young boss. Everyone's shaken but more driven. Giadana continues doing what no mobster before him has done, kill police officers. SNEU tactics are questioned. More backup and reinforced security within OPs become mandatory. Locations are on a need to know basis only.

A Homicide Task Force is immediately formed comprised of the most seasoned Detectives on the job. They band together whenever a cop is killed in the line of duty. Their clearance rate in these types of cases runs near 100%. The killers will be found.

––––––––––––––

The sun rises early the next day, and after a sleepless night, James Horith is at home reading the news headlines of two officers gunned down in Harlem. With head in hands, the young ADA quietly weeps as he realizes the consequences of his greed.

Later that morning, chirping birds begin filling the silence. Loud female screams and a child's cry take over, as Horith's wife and young daughter discover his body outside hanging from the little girl's swing set with the chain wrapped around his neck.

---

Homicide Detectives are quick to glue the case together and make the connection between the DA's office and the Giadana crime syndicate. Red flags fly. The Manhattan Special Narcotics DA's Office comes under scrutiny. Prior court cases, including major traffickers, are in jeopardy. The hope is, this young ADA was acting on his own, and the entirety of the prosecutor's office is not involved. Narcotics enforcement is rocked. The NYPD's Internal Affairs Unit goes into high gear, believing that if the mob can get to a district attorney, they could also manipulate cops. Sergeant Pasano and teammates are well warned by Inspector Deteo at a unit meeting.

"Listen. You will be watched closer than ever. If they don't get you on flat-out corruption, they'll nail you on smaller complaints; brutality, overtime abuses, or even slanted court testimony. Be on guard."

"Will do, Inspector," Pasano responds.

The others nod in acceptance.

As the Raiders leave the CO's office, Will Fennar catches up to Pasano and says, "Shit, Sarge, O.T. abuse, maybe, prejudiced court testimony, possible, but brutality? We'd each owe them 50 years at least."

John Calvoy is quick to chime in, "Hell, I'm done beatin' and shootin' bad guys."

Jim Kellig sounds off, "Hey, let those cheese-balls from Headquarters try to come up here and take these mutts off the streets."

Rico Lorez, usually the quiet one, interjects, "All you guys do is talk. Your pullback will last all of about five seconds into your next collar.

You get smacked once or twice and we'll see how you react. Don't talk nonsense. We do our jobs. We do what we've been sworn to do. May he rest in peace, but you remember what our team brother, Gary, used to say, *it's what's in your heart that matters.*"

Pasano takes over the banter. "Prep up. We move out in thirty."

## CHAPTER 26

# TOUGH COMPASSION

The Sarge vests up and loads his personal shotgun. Before he heads downstairs to meet his guys, his office phone rings. It's a Lieutenant from the Narc Intel Unit.

The Lieutenant proceeds. "Sergeant Pasano, we received a call about a possible sexual assault being committed at 108 West 142nd Street. The female complainant requests assistance but did not want it put over to 911. It's classified as a sensitive assignment."

Pasano thought this notification was odd but did not take time to question it. He pulls his unit and races over to the location in a couple of nondescript cars.

---

In an abandoned building, Corisa is being sexually abused by two drug dealers, Tyler Jamol and Ray Potek. Her shirt is ripped off, exposing a large double heart tattoo with the words, *'not me,'* inscribed across her left shoulder. Her jeans are pulled open. Jamol has Corisa's right arm pinned against the wall with one hand while choking her with his other. Potek has her other arm slammed back against the wall as he rips her pants down. Blood pours from her nose and mouth. Her right eye is swollen shut as she begins to lose consciousness. Jamol and Potek are also bleeding from their face from Corisa fighting back.

Jamol yells in her face, "Do me or die, bitch!"

A gun clicks. Pasano has the barrel of his revolver pressed against the back of Jamol's head.

He whispers in his ear, "Do her and you die, dick."

As Jamol loosens his grip on Corisa's throat, Pasano slams his gun into the side of Jamol's face. Blood spurts out as the lowlife collapses to the floor. Potek receives similar treatment from Pasano's teammates. Both are cuffed and dragged down the front stoop and into the street.

Back in the hallway of the abandoned building, the Sarge is attending to a roughed-up Corisa.

As she puts her shirt back on, he quietly tells her, "You better get yourself straightened out and outta' here."

Corisa snaps back, "Thanks for your help, but don't feel sorry for me, Sergeant Pasano. You look out for your own self. If you want to do me solid, just let those fucks go on my behalf, otherwise, it'll be worse for me next time."

Pasano, pissed and disgusted, quips, "I have no time for this bullshit. If that's what you want, fine with me."

Pasano walks down the hallway, out of the building, and jumps in his unmarked car with John Calvoy and the two dealers. The two police vehicles leave. About ten blocks away, in an alley at West 151st Street, some persuasion and threats take place.

The unmarked car comes to an abrupt stop. Calvoy slams the shift into park, pulls his gun, leans over the seat, and points it at the head of Jamol. Pasano quickly draws his gun, points it at Potek, and delivers rapid, threatening words.

"You talk—you live. You don't—you die. Who's your street overseer?"

Potek spews, "Vic Ferris."

"Who's running the operation and where's the drop off point?"

"Giadana," Potek says.

Jamol spits out, "The 'smack' is brought in and dropped off at Webster Avenue, Bronx, overnight."

John Calvoy cuts in, "Fine. You live for another day, 'cause that woman you fucked with back there doesn't want to push the issue."

Pasano threatens, "You fuck with her again—you will die—that's a promise. Hear me?"

Together, Potek and Jamol reluctantly exclaim, "Yeah."

The two are uncuffed, dragged out from the car and thrown to the ground amongst the other garbage in the alley. Pasano and his team drive away.

The Sarge turns to John Calvoy. "Hey, John, that 'no brutality' commitment you made didn't last too long, did it?"

"Hey, Sarge, no disrespect, but go fuck yourself."

The two break out in laughter.

Jamol and Potek are lying in the alleyway. The two dope pushers murmur to each other.

"I'm gonna' kill those pigs," Potek says.

In his office, Pasano is on the phone feeding information back to the NYPD's Narc Intel Unit. Sergeant Tim Mulrey is on the other end.

"Yeah, Tim. Giadana's other headquarters, East Harlem, with product shipment entry points and cutting mills in the South Bronx. I'll send a full report to you by day's end."

"Thanks, Paul. I'll push what I have through channels and await the rest."

## CHAPTER 27

# CLUBBING

Social or after-hour clubs used as 'covers' by dealers have become problematic for law enforcement. Some of these heavyweight drug locations are built like fortresses. They mix their operations with dozens of well-dressed people to thwart off police.

Carlos Giadana talks about his most productive wholesalers to a group of his underlings at a late night meeting. Area rep' Scalia and first lieutenant Tiafona are amongst them sitting around a large table with the usual, oversized dishes of pasta and glasses of red wine laid on a white linen tablecloth.

In broken English, Giadana brings up the Third Planet, a club selling liquor in Central Harlem that has operated for decades and now has Turkish 'H' featured on its menu. After taking a sip of wine, he explains, "The local small-time dealers are good, especially when there are many, but our largest earners are these social clubs scattered across upper Manhattan that are becoming a trend. They are not much different than our coffee shops in Italy, except, Americans prefer a stronger dose of 'wake-up.' "

Smiling and looking over at Tiafona, he emphasizes the sales. "This location has brought in over one million dollars this week selling in bulk to large-scale dealers who peddle outside the city. This expansion is exactly what we need to re-energize the business."

Tiafona concurring, "I agree. We should look for more of these types of selling spots," as he taps on the arm of Scalia who nods and adds his opinion.

"Yes, but if we do this, there is no place for the dealers to escape. Once word leaks out to the police, they could easily surround the location and arrest everyone."

Tiafona abruptly shuts him down. "Not if the places are structurally sound and used by many. Private members only would access it to buy the product at specific times, by appointment only. Other than that, the place will have no drugs inside, only liquor."

Scalia, conforming, says, "I'll see what I can do."

Giadana turns to his right. "Vincenzo, I want you to personally have our people in the South Bronx increase their packaging volume. Tell them to hire more 'Ricans.' If necessary, give out bonuses. But, bottom line, we need more sellable product. This is your division, handle it pronto. *Capisce?*"

"Si, Carlos."

As Vito Tiafona looks around the table, he backs up his boss. "You others do the same. More locations, dealers, and product. Now go do your jobs."

The attendees nod and quietly affirm their first lieutenant. However, Tiafona is not satisfied and slaps the table shaking the glassware. "You sound like lambs, speak up!"

The subordinates, in a loud clear voice, pledge their allegiance, "Si, Vito, si, Vito!"

Giadana smiles at the obedience shown before him, while Scalia remains stoic as he contemplates his next move.

———————

The 'Planet' is flourishing, and Scalia believes enough time has passed for a law enforcement intervention. He reaches out to the one person who can counter Giadana's 'primo' marketplace.

———————

The paperwork is done, and the 'Narcs' and their catch for the day are at central booking. Paul is on his way out of the station house, and the Desk Lieutenant stops him. "Sarge, one of ours, a boss, is waiting for you across the street—dark blue unmarked. I verified him."

"Copy that. Thanks, Lieu', have a safe night."

He walks out and eyeballs a clean Crown Victoria, engine running, parking lights on. The vehicle lights flicker on-off once. Paul crosses the street and enters. Captain Ritenish is behind the wheel and leads off.

"How's your boy?"

"Same."

"Again, I'm sorry. I wish I had more for you. We received a contact from Scalia." He hands Pasano a sealed envelope. "You can open it now."

Paul reads, *'High priority—'Third Planet.' Fruit is ripe and ready for picking. Bulk orders by appointment only. Bronx packing plant increasing production. NS'*

"Got it, Cap'. You want this back?"

"Yes, I'll see that it gets filed. It's a special request, Paul. If you can't do it, I'll pass the word along."

The Sarge pauses as he looks over at Ritenish. "You kidding me or what, boss?"

"Sorry, I should have known better. Listen, I didn't forget about you and your family. The NYPD hasn't either. Work safe."

"Night, Cap'," Pasano tells him as he exits and walks away.

---

Early the next morning messages sail back and forth from narc-buy specialist, Sergeant Ricky Menez, and Pasano. Plans are formulated. Menez will do what he has done for almost two decades, role-play alone. This time he poses as an Atlantic City hood looking to score a hefty load of 'H,' twenty-thousand dollars' worth.

---

Some connected braggadocio and currency flashing get Menez into the Planet four days later. It's a nighttime operation. He's in and out in less than two minutes, jumps in a limo with a gym bag full of dope and speeds away. He meets Pasano and company and about thirty heavily armed NYPD backups in an underground parking garage. As he exits the limo, he approaches Pasano. " 'Fini,' Paul. I got the drugs, my marked currency is left inside, hundred dollar bills, two hundred of them. Our spotters are on adjacent rooftops. You're up, bud. It's all yours."

Pasano immediately radios the SNEU observation team, "Narc Sarge to OP-1."

"OP-1 standing by."

"Raiders are ready up."

"Copy that, Sarge. Planet is sealed tight, no movement in or out."

"10-4. We're en route. ETA two minutes."

"Copy that, boss, standing by."

Unit members arrive on the scene and surround the club with back-ups armed with shotguns, sledgehammers, and battering rams. Emergency Service vehicle lights flood the area as they begin banging away at the fortress. Within seconds, there is a realization that entry is more difficult than planned. The Sarge signals to the driver of the prisoner van parked a couple of hundred feet away. The van pulls up and backs onto the sidewalk stopping just feet from the main entrance. The rear doors open and a couple of vested-up ESU cops come out with large chains and wrap them around the handles of the club doors. The other end is locked around the van's bumper. Pasano gives the signal.

The van races forward as the two steel doors are yanked from the building along with the frame and cement blocks around them. The doors are dragged down the street, giving off sparks as the crowd of onlookers, both residents and druggies, stare with their mouths wide open. This is a seventies version of police work, and NYPD members smile. Dust and debris are everywhere. The team makes entry, quickly overtaking about fifty people inside, including a few well-dressed men and women mixed in with scuzzballs. It's a typical after-hours club setting with a large open area for the gathering of weed, cocaine, and heroin users.

A large safe is found secreted behind a twenty-five-foot bar between a sink and small fridge. ESU cops look over at Pasano for instructions. Without hesitation, the Sarge is loud and clear.

"Rip it up!"

The safe is torn from the wood floor using long crowbars. A gas powered, hard-bladed saw smokes and chatters, as the hinges are sliced off the heavy steel container. Bundles of Sergeant Menez's buy money and some coke and dope are found along with multiple guns. Weapons are unloaded and safeguarded. Cemented windows are smashed out with the sledgehammer. The bar, pool table, and couches are destroyed. It's demolition in the first degree without a bulldozer. The Third Planet is gone.

All perps are cuffed with daisy chains, put on prison vans, and taken away. A garbage truck passes by, and four unit cops pick up the massive doors and throw them on board. Pasano picks up a piece of broken ceiling tile and writes, '*closed for alterations*,' and leans it against the building.

Paul pulls two of his guys, Viega and Lorez, aside. "You guys prepared?"

"We're good to go, boss."

"Okay, we'll handle all the arrests here. As planned, you guys head to your old stomping grounds in the South Bronx tonight."

Paul gives explicit instructions. "Look, you'll blend as hangouts. Follow the leads to track down the exact location of the 'H' factories, including the hours of operation and shipments to and from. This will be vital for the final phase of the takedown."

In a more serious tone, Paul says, "Remember, caution before valor. You go under, get the info, and return. We'll route everything you get to the DEA and NYPD Narc Intel."

"10-4, boss."

"Don't worry, Sarge, It'll be like a vacation for us," Rico answers calmly.

---

The two get started in the late evening. Most of the weighing, mixing, and packaging into dime and quarter bags is done overnight. The fresh shipments are readied for delivery in generic 'rides' before dawn. Rico and Al grew up in this neighborhood. It went from good to bad in one decade. It's made up of mostly Hispanic inhabitants, who are woven amongst a physically devastated community set afire by its own people in defiance of everything. Rico and Al now live with their families upstate but know every inch of the streets and buildings in the South Bronx. They know who and how to ask for info. Cash buys all, especially info, and druggies are always hungry for cash.

---

The 'Narcs' blend as drug loiterers. They spread $20 bills up and down the streets, and by midnight already have a bite. One of the local junkies gives up some info.

"Stay away from Webster Avenue, just off East 166th Street. You hang there, you die."

For Al and Rico, that's their destination. Within minutes, they're wandering through. They see a four-story, semi-abandoned building. Two overseers out front. Street empty. Another is on the roof sitting in a chair near the ledge with a clear street overview. Rico and Al separate. They play their roles.

Al's a junkie, Rico's a homeless pushing a food basket with a car battery inside concealing a remote camera. Their clothes are torn and disheveled. They loiter, one on each side of the street in front of the target. One gun holder greets Al and merely pulls his jacket open and exposes a .357 mag'. He then wanders over to Rico who walks away. Lights are on in the upper two floors inside the building. The two disperse and meet up two blocks away. They head back as a team in a nondescript car with photo layout and diagram in hand. Assignment complete. The info will be forwarded to the DEA and NYPD Narc Intel.

On their return trip to the Three-Five, Viega makes a snide comment, "Hey, Rico, you miss our old neighborhood?"

Rico, countering, "You miss the plague?"

The two laugh but suddenly stop.

Rico continues, "Hey, bud, it's a thin line, right? *Allí pero para la gracia de Dios vaya nosotros.*" ("There but for the Grace of God go us.")

A sarcastic Viega finishes, "God? God left this place ten years ago and never looked back."

## CHAPTER 28

# COLLATERAL DAMAGE TO THE INNOCENT

Medical changes are taking place for the Pasano's and Jons' families. The Sarge's little boy has been placed in a rehab center. Prognosis is still unknown. Brain function and spinal restoration by a team of top specialists are speculative. Paul takes the latest development poorly. Each visit adds more trauma and his judgment is clouded by the need for vengeance. Rachel is more grounded and has been making most of the medical decisions. There are more sleepless nights for the young couple. Their marriage, once solid, is strained. Pasano's unit members are supportive but stand at a distance when any mention of Andrew comes about.

---

With all that has happened to them, Paul and Rachel make a visit to their local Parish Priest. They ask for a mass to pray for Andrew. Afterward, they go to confession.

In a dimly lit confessional booth at St. Thomas, Sergeant Pasano is confessing to an elder priest. "Father, as a police officer, I have maimed and killed other human beings. I have put people in harm's way who have been seriously injured or killed. I believe in my heart that I'm doing this for the greater good and for the decent people whom I have sworn to protect and serve. Is there hope for me, Father? Have I gone too far? What is God thinking about me? Is my little boy paying for my sins?"

The old Priest pauses and responds. "You have chosen your path freely. You have to examine your heart. Clear your mind of evil thoughts of hatred and vengeance. Even Jesus at one point said, '*Pick up two swords.*' Son, police officers and military people have been dealing with this dilemma for centuries. If you are living and fighting for good over evil, then you are defending the Kingdom of God."

Paul is given his penance in multiple prayers and recites the Act of Contrition.

"Thank you, Father."

Pasano walks out of the confessional booth and kneels alongside Rachel in one of the long, wooden pews, completing his penance with prayer. As he sits back and raises his head, Rachel leans in close and pulls him towards her, whispering, "God is here, Paul. He sees us. He's listening to us. I'm sure He'll come to help Andrew."

After a few seconds of quiet pause, he responds, "I hope so, Rach'. You know these past couple of years I've lost so much faith."

"Honey, hope and faith are all we have. Please, let's not lose that."

Paul abruptly stands. "C'mon. Let's go visit our son." The two walk hand in hand down the old church's center aisle and exit through the elaborate doors.

———————

The Jons family is trying to cope with Richard's return to Harlem Hospital's Intensive Care Unit. His brain is swelling from bullet fragments that were unable to be removed. This is his third return trip to neurology. Renee is beside herself. Working, taking care of several children, and involving herself with the anti-drug campaign have proven too overwhelming. She's drawn and tired. There is no one to reach out to besides Pasano, who deals with other people's problems better than his own.

Renee turns to God for strength. *"Please, Dear Lord, help my boy and help me."*

There is more collateral damage in the war on drugs. Following a morning raid, the team is loading up a prisoner van with about fifteen perps from a narc parlor at the corner of West 144th Street and Bradhurst Avenue. A volley of gunshots rings out.

Survival mode takes front and center, as the Sarge issues a series of loud commands. "Hit the deck! Down low, take cover!" He radios to Central, "Shots fired, 144 and Edgecomb!"

"Central to all units. Be advised. Shots fired, 144 and Edgecomb. Plainclothes members on the scene. All units use caution."

The gunfire lasts for about ten seconds as the team dives for cover behind parked cars, light poles, and hydrants. The Narc Unit finds itself in the middle of a battle over turf up in the northwest corner of the precinct, as two small rival narc gangs are engaged in a firefight over the control of a busy drug shop disguised as a bodega.

Just as the team scrambles for cover, so does an entire three blocks of pedestrians. Pasano and company unglue themselves from the pavement, look up to the corner of West 145th Street and Bradhurst Avenue and see the problem. About eight to ten dirtbags brandishing heavy automatic weapons standing in the middle of the intersection are blasting away at each other. As quickly as the team members recognize them, the perps recognize the undercovers as cops and suddenly change their targets. A new barrage of bullets begins hurling towards team members, ricocheting off cars, sidewalks, and smashing through store windows.

Caught in the middle of combat, Pasano fires off the first couple of rounds, followed by a volley from his team. Between the cops' and the perps' gunfire, it's like the last thirty seconds of a Fourth of July fireworks display, with multiple loud bangs, gun-flashes, and smoke.

As it ends, there are foot pursuits and radio calls for assistance. Pasano's fastest runner, Don Sels, is right on the heels of one of the shooters. Within two blocks, Sels grabs the scumbag by his throat and throws him against the wall, yanking a .45-caliber handgun from inside the perp's jacket. All this chaos and only one arrest. Despite creating a perimeter and search area with a slew of Three-Five backup units conducting an exhaustive hunt, the other perps get away.

When the dust settles and the team spreads out still hunting for perps, Jim Kellig calls in a radio transmission, "Sarge, you on the air?"

Pasano responds, "Affirmative."

"Sarge, we got somebody down on the corner of West 145th Street and 8th Avenue, no perp, and no member of the service. A civilian, Sarge. Need an ambulance forthwith."

"10-4, Jimmy.............Central—be advised we need an ambulance at W. 145th and 8th Avenue."

Sadly, an innocent bystander has been shot and seriously wounded. A young woman pushing her baby in a stroller has been struck. She's hit just below her hip, breaking the large femur bone in half. She survives but will be permanently disabled. Pasano later learns her name is Tamerine Jonasin, a mother out shopping for groceries. That changes things and pulls the rug out from under the team, turning a good crime interruption into a disaster. This young lady has been caught in the crossfire over two blocks from the scene.

Pasano is stunned, but that's only the beginning of the problems to come with lawsuits and civilian complaints. Eventually, the team will probably be indemnified by the City for this young girl's injury, and will receive awards and medals for ending a drug shooting and saving community residents' lives. In the eyes of the NYPD, the Narc Team did good. Regardless, the guys are sickened by the incident. They're just months from completing their goal and working on the last segment of the precinct, the Northwest division. The team knows it. Giadana knows it.

These types of incidents are a double-edged sword. One side leads to more internal investigations put upon the unit. The other, shrinks the selling turf available to Giadana and associates. Nonetheless, this incident leaves a permanent scar. A couple of days later, the unit sends flowers to the young mother.

Against advice from the NYPD and union attorneys, Pasano makes a hospital visit and attempts to confront the mishap straight on.

He walks down the long polished corridor with his shield dangling from his neck chain, and his overgrown black hair and beard liken him more to a lumberjack than a cop. He observes a group of the victim's family members standing just outside her room. Her mother and father are amongst them. Her husband, a New York City bus driver, is working a late shift.

Paul overhears some murmuring as the family looks his way and recognizes him from photos plastered across the TV news channels. He hears them say, "That's one of the cops who put Tamerine here."

Pasano walks up to them and politely remarks, "Excuse me, folks." They part for the intimidating figure as he walks passed them and into the room.

The young mother immediately recognizes him and fires off some quick, combative words. "Did you come to finish off the job, officer?"

Pasano, looking scruffy and miffed, responds, "Hey, look, this was unfortunate, but it was nobody's fault."

"I know all about you, Sergeant Pasano. What did ya' think, I was a drug dealer pushing a baby stroller? Is that why you shot me?"

"Of course, not. If we had thought that, you'd be dead."

"Well, two lawyers were already here and said I can sue you, your men, and the City."

"I don't care. Get in line. You're a casualty of battle. Let the City pay. You deserve some restitution." Pasano takes her hand, and in a softer tone tells her, "I'm sorry."

It gets a smile from her as he starts to leave. Tamarine, still weak and on meds, tells him, "Hey, Sarge, thanks for the flowers, but I'm suin'."

Paul laughs and walks outside the room, tells her family, "Sorry, folks," and walks down the hallway.

## CHAPTER 29

# 'NONNO'

Mid-afternoon, Giadana and his associates have completed their daily business meetings for the day. The group of mobsters, including Scalia, head up the stairway to the bar, then march single file out the main entrance onto the sidewalk. There's some hesitation as two of them begin peering left, right, and straight on, looking for a potential hit by rival Mafia factions or law enforcement.

The coast is clear and hand signals are given as the mostly overweight middle-aged entourage re-assembles alongside a handful of town cars lined up at the curb. Vincenzo Deluci, loyal henchman, brings up the rear with his arm shouldering Giadana who is leaning over and whispering to Scalia, "You and I have a family thing at the airport."

Scalia's knees wobble for a second, but the undercover specialist rises to the moment. "Of course, boss, anything you want," as he enters the rear of a midnight blue Lincoln.

Deluci sits up front and delivers a single word command to a burly driver, "Kennedy."

Scalia's composure falters as he leads an induced inquiry, "Kennedy, boss? What's up?"

Before answering, Giadana pauses, sensing some jitters from his underling and knowing these short drives to the airport are frequently reserved for body dumping.

"Relax, Niccolo, my grandchildren are coming from Sicily, and we're going to meet and follow them back to the Plaza. I haven't seen them in over a year. They are already teenagers, and it's time to show them the city."

The driver cuts in on the private conversation commenting to the carload of hoods, "Hey, Mr. Giadana, why don't you bring them up to Harlem and show them the animals? They'd get a kick out of it."

Giadana's jaw clenches and his teeth grind as he counters his most ignorant follower. "You fuckin' asshole! If it weren't for those animals, you'd be out of a job sitting on a curb next to your half-witted sister. Both of you would be eating out of a shoebox full of donated food from the rear of my restaurant. Now drive, don't fuckin' talk!"

"Sorry, boss."

Giadana turns to Scalia. "A smart mouth is not necessarily the sign of a wise man, you understand?"

Still skeptical, Scalia responds, "Yes, sir," contemplating having to kill the man sitting no more than two feet from him, followed by one bullet each to the heads of the mobsters in the front.

Across the street, four stories up in a broken-down tenement, two DEA backups are surveilling the line of luxury sedans, focusing their attention on one in particular. It's the last to pull away containing two pieces of valuable cargo. First, one of their own, Scalia, and second, their nemesis, Capo Giadana.

Unsure of the ongoings, an emergency message is delivered to DEA New York Headquarters, "Be advised, NS in the rear of a blue town car, sitting next to Capo-1 engaged in conversation. Two additional Mafia 'soldiers' in the front. Plate number 'George-Robert-Paul 3061.' They're pulling out now, Central, southbound, unknown destination."

"10-4, unit, we'll pick them up in a few."

----

Within minutes, a clean, four-door white sedan with a New York City Housing Preservation sticker on the door heads down W. 151st Street. It stops in front of an abandoned building where Corisa sits on the steps taking in breaths of air not contaminated by the stench of junkies.

The driver, a younger male in business attire, slides out, carrying a clipboard and pen. Making no eye contact with Corisa, he looks around as if inspecting what's left of the dwelling. Passing by the undercover, he parts with some coded words, "Forthwith, corner of 7 and 151." He mimics writing, enters the car, and pulls away. A half minute later, Corisa stands up and walks to her pick-up point where she enters the white sedan and is brought up to speed. "Your services are required. NS might be heading for a hit. Giadana's got him in a dark blue town car with two other bulls."

Corisa mumbles under her breath, "Fuck!"

"They're ahead of us by five minutes, hang on. Guns are in the lockbox on the floor. A change of clothes is in the duffel bag. I'm not sure what they want you to do."

"I know what I have to do. Just get me to their car."

Without hesitation, the junior agent conforms. "Yes, ma'am," picking up his walkie-talkie. "Central, do you have a location on the subjects?"

"Central, stand by........affirmative, East River Drive heading through the Battery Tunnel to the Belt Parkway."

Corisa, overhearing the communication, tells the driver, "Shit, they're heading towards the airport. Step on it!"

"Copy that," says the agent, as he floors the accelerator.

---

In the rear of the Lincoln, Giadana pursues the truth from Scalia. "I've been watching you mature. I need your loyalty now more than ever. Do I have that loyalty?"

"Yes, sir."

"Good. When we get to the airport, you'll stay close by me when we pick up the youngsters."

"Of course, Mr. G," thinking it's the final Mafia kiss of death.

Corisa puts on a clean, black, lightweight jacket covering a .45 cal' Colt military special, scanning ahead for the dark blue car.

Central cuts in on radio communication, "All units be advised. Subjects one mile west of the airport, right lane, slow speed."

Corisa raises her voice mixed with concern, "There they are! Stay on them, three cars back." Giadana's car enters the exit lane heading into JFK with the Agents following but laying back a safe distance not to be 'made.'

Reaching down into the weapons container again, Corisa pulls out an M-16 rifle and exclaims, "What the fuck is this guy up to now?"

The young agent responds, "Good question."

"Listen, if I tell you, pull in front of them, cut them off, let me out, and take cover. Can you handle that?"

"I can."

---

The mobsters, with Nick on board, pull into a spot in front of the International Terminal behind a long black limo with its engine running. Giadana says, "That's the car waiting for my grandchildren. Pull up close and wait." Giadana turns towards Nick and pats his arm. "Come, we go."

"Yes, sir."

"Vincenzo, stay with the car. We'll be right out."

"Yes, Mr. G."

---

"Stay behind them," Corisa tells the driver. "They're not gonna' kill Scalia right here out in the open. I hope not anyway."

"What's your move?"

"Stay put. I'm following them in," as she lays down the assault rifle.

"Alone?"

"I was born alone. If this is a bust, I'll be right out and you can take me back where you found me. If not and you hear shots fired, call for an ambulance and notify our base."

"Copy that."

Shoulder-to-shoulder, Giadana and Scalia head for the roped off area where customs opens up into the reception zone.

Corisa follows but then walks ahead a safe distance and does a turn-around heading back towards the capo and Scalia. As she passes them, she makes eye contact with her fellow DEA Agent, bumps him, and continues. Three young teens run towards Giadana shouting, "Nonno, Nonno!" They gather around and hug the old man as Scalia turns and looks for his female comrade. He spots her leaning against a water fountain nearby. The two nod to each other.

Wasting no time, Corisa hustles back to her car and jumps in. "Take me back to my nest. Nick lives for another day, Giadana, too. If it was up to me, I would have killed that old fuck right there and ended this whole fucking charade." She peels off her jacket, puts away the handgun, leans back, and grasps for a few stress-free moments.

Realizing his passenger is more than a handful, the driver, a novice Agent, refuses to add fuel to this fire and keeps it short, "Copy that."

## CHAPTER 30

# IT'S PERSONAL

There's a light tap on the outside door frame of Paul Pasano's office.

Jim Kellig says shyly, "Hey, boss. Got a minute?"

"For you, Jimbo, I got a lot more than a minute. Sit down. What's shakin'?"

Kellig sits in a chair next to the Sergeant's desk. He pauses, takes a deep breath, and opens up. "My fifteen-year-old daughter is being bullied at school by some older high schoolers and a couple of dropouts. She's being pushed into holding weed for local dealers during their selling binges at about 3 PM each day. You know the score, boss. The drug dealers are using my daughter to handle the transactions while the older ones oversee the operation and carry the guns.

"Her age means if caught, a juvenile delinquency, JD designation would accompany her arrest and thus lighten the hit, putting her right back on the street for them."

Kellig continues, "These are school kids, boss, but the sellers are not. They are forcing her because they can't get young people to volunteer. They threatened her until she had enough and came home and told me and my wife about it."

"Fuck, Jimmy! Did you tell the school about this? How about the local precinct?"

"Of course. Me and my wife made two stops. First to the principal's office informing him of the ongoings in and around the school. Second, to the CO of the local Queens precinct to explain and request enforcement. Both visits were met with sympathy and concern. The principal's answer, *'We have to tread carefully with school kids. We'll look into it.'* The precinct's answer was, *'It's a low-level marijuana operation. We'll have school security check it out and respond.'* And that was one week ago, and the situation still exists."

Pasano pauses for thought. He can read Jim's eyes and hear it in his voice. His fear is JK will go wipe out a gang of young druggies because he is a father.

"Hold it, Jim. Let's bring the team in on this. Maybe we can straighten things out for your daughter." Pasano calls out his office door. "Hey, guys. Come in here for a second."

The Raiders, large and imposing, squeeze into the tiny office and stand at the ready.

John speaks first, "What's up, boss?"

"Close the door. Jim needs some personal help. A small pack of smoke pushers is forcing his daughter into working for them at her high school. I figured we go pay a visit. You know our response will be outside the lines. You up for it?"

Most of the teammates nod in the affirmative. Calvoy's response, "Ready up, Sarge."

Then Will Fennar gives his okay. "Shit, yeah, boss."

Pasano pauses, picks up the phone, and calls the Queens precinct. He speaks with the Sergeant in charge of the Street Conditions Unit, a team that handles quality of life issues.

Pasano says deceptively, "Yeah, Sarge, that's correct. We'll be working around the Queens Annex High School on behalf of the Borough Commander. We'll be there to assist your unit in picking up a few of the local dealers and associates around the school."

Skeptical, the Queens Conditions Sergeant responds, "Of course. I can't believe they called in your entire Harlem Narcotics Unit to handle something this trivial. But, we'll be glad to have you."

Pasano concludes, "Fine. See you 1300 hours. We'll be in plainclothes, and you can do the uniformed backup and pick up all arrests."

Pasano hangs up and looks over to his guys. "Okay. It's a go. Am I fucked-up or what?"

They all nod. Calvoy gives him a hardy comeback, "Yeah! You're fucked-up boss, but so are we."

"I agree."

They all break out in boisterous laughter as Paul thinks to himself, *'We'll all wind up getting fired.'*

---

The next day comes quick enough. Everyone's pumped and ready to move out. It's personal. It's for Jim.

Pasano issues the final orders. "We go to the Queens precinct and meet with the Conditions Team. We go first and do our thing. We make some observations, take a couple of photos, and pick up a few sellers, money holders, and hopefully a gun carrier. Maybe two. We hand them over to the Queens Conditions Unit. No shotguns, it'll be overkill. Causes too much attention, which is exactly what we want to avoid. We're in and out. Clear?"

This Queens North precinct is considered a low crime area. Police officers here are well groomed and deliver a high level of community service to residents. Police work here is more geared towards service and less to enforcement. More help, fewer arrests. Harlem policing is different, especially with plainclothes and undercover teams, which includes the Raiders. Their focus is 'collars,' and their distinction is long hair, scruffy beards, dress down appearance, and of course, swagger. Lots of it.

---

Pasano and his crew park their 'unmarks' in front of the station house, and with shields hanging from chains around their necks, stroll in passed a gathering of 'uniforms' congregating out front.

When out-of-command cops infiltrate a precinct, there's always a bit of rivalry that leads to sarcasm and once in a while, line crossing. It happens here as the Sarge and guys pass through the small group of Queens 'uniforms.' A few derogatory words are flung about.

One of the 'clean-cuts' mouths under his breath, "Hey, check out this menagerie. Looks like some of the animals escaped from the circus."

Jim's head snaps in their direction.

Another, younger, White cop in a louder tone lets loose a piece of racial slang, "These guys must be lost. The gorilla cages are ten miles north-west."

It's a quick reaction as Will Fennar reaches out across the outdoor steps' handrail and grabs for the cop's throat.

Jim hops over the railing and joins in, "Say it again, punk, and I'll yank your fuckin' teeth out with my fingers."

Paul is quick to jump between and separate them. He grabs Will and Jim by their arms, pulling them inside, and in an authoritative voice says, "C'mon guys, don't lower yourselves. We're here to work. Let's go. Everybody inside!"

Once inside the station house, cooler heads prevail. The team meets with the Queens unit and discusses the operation. Thirty minutes later, they push out.

Calvoy and Viega are on top of an old abandoned, flat roof garage with binoculars, a Nikon, and point-to-point radios. A bell goes off, and within two minutes, the students are dismissed. There's a quick convergence around a gang dealer in the corner of the mostly black-top and broken concrete schoolyard. The kids gather. Quick sales are made.

Viega puts scripts' across the radio. "Dealer, male/Black, black vest over a white tee, dungs and white Nikes. Money holder, male/Hispanic, blue tee, dungs, Keds. Two young, White female lookouts/pink shirt, dungs, the other, floral shirt, black capris."

Kellig and Fennar move in with hoodies up, mope walk, sneakers open, pants low. Sels and McTerren, lacrosse sticks in hand, enter the set. The little weed operation goes down quick and easy. The backup Queens uniform Conditions Unit drives onto the school grounds. The four are picked up. No hitches. A few pounds of weed recovered, and three buyers picked up by the Conditions responding 'uniforms.' Good operation, but no gun. Not yet.

Pasano takes the dealer off to the side, grabs him by his throat and assures him, "We're here only for guns. Give em' to us and you all walk! Deal?"

The young weeder questions, "You swear?"

Pasano responds, "My word. I don't lie."

The dealer gives it up. "Under the garbage bin."

Fennar hustles over and removes the gun and holster. "Got it, boss."

Pasano finishes, "Okay, guys, good work. Let's help them escort all these mopes to the Queens station house."

The one dealer yells out, "Hey, you swore!"

Pasano counters, "I lied."

A grateful Conditions Sergeant says, "Thank you. Appreciate your help."

"No problem. It was fun out here in the 'burbs.' "

Jim Kellig walks over to the Sarge and shakes his hand. "Hey, boss, thanks."

Pasano brazenly remarks, "Your daughter's going back to school if I have to walk her to her fuckin' classes."

They laugh. They're more than teammates. More than friends. It's the unspoken brotherhood in blue. It's all for one. The small caravan of Queens patrol cars and Harlem 'unmarks' moves out.

At the Queens station house, the Sarge tells his men, "Wait out here. Stay in the cars. We'll be right back."

Will and Paul walk in with the Queens team, stop at the front desk, and log in the prisoners.

It's the change of shifts. The day tour squad of 'uniforms' is finishing as the 4 x 12's are just taking their posts. Paul grabs one of the Queens cops and asks, "Hey pal, where's the locker room?"

The young officer points. "Right back there, boss."

"Thanks."

Pasano walks over, puts his finger on Will's chest and quietly says, "You wait here. No matter what, stay put." He continues in a dictatorial tone, "You understand?"

Will pauses, and in a nervous voice says, "You don't have to do this, Sarge."

Paul retorts, "Yes, I do," and walks into the locker room.

The day tour cops are changing out of their uniforms and into their 'civies.' Pasano walks up and down the rows of cops and their respective lockers until he arrives at his destination. He spots his target, the two bigmouths that spouted some racial bullshit on the station house steps to him and his guys. The two cops make eye contact with Pasano. The Sarge has that look in his eyes, the one he has just before he beat or killed someone.

A murmured, simultaneous, "Aw, fuck," from the duo.

Other bystander cops see the unfolding trouble about to take place. They start drifting away.

Pasano orders, "Get out—you, you, and you," pointing to three cops.

It's a prompt, "Yes, sir," from them and they disappear in seconds, leaving his two remaining.

Removing his gun, Pasano walks towards the two half-dressed, White cops. They freeze. Paul is fast. Within a split second, his semiauto is propped against the first one's forehead while he has the other's Adam's apple clenched in his left hand.

The Sarge spews forth just a few words, "If I ever hear about you two slinging any racial slurs against any cops, or anyone else for that matter, I'll come back here and beat the fucking shit out of both of you."

The two reply respectively, "Yes, sir—Yes, Sarge."

Paul holsters his gun and taps on their chests. "Now you go home to your families like the men you are. We are all brothers in blue, right?"

"Yes, sir."

Paul walks out of the locker room and tells Will who was listening at the doorway, "Okay, let's go."

"Sure, boss."

They walk out front and Sarge hollers out, "Mount up and back home we go. Harlem, USA.

All the cops out front, including the Queens cops, laugh.

## CHAPTER 31

# UNLIKELY SUPPORT

The NYPD can only allow so much, even from the 'Sarge,' a Harlem street boss who is doing what nobody else wants any part of. After being ordered to Police Headquarters, Pasano arrives with his union attorney who gives him some instruction. "Sarge, you'll be questioned by Chief of Patrol, Tom Pavonel, the Manhattan Borough Commander, and two Captains, one from Internal Affairs Division and the other from the Civilian Complaint Review Board. You ready for it?"

"Definitely."

"And listen, if I cut you off at any point, go along."

"Fine."

They enter the Chief's office where a long, high polished table and thick leather chairs rest on dark red carpeting. Pasano thinks to himself, *'Where are we, the Waldorf?'* A small group of brass is waiting. Pasano and his lawyer find their place at two empty seats. Chief Pavonel is sitting at the head and commences.

"Sergeant Pasano, first of all, let me say I'm sorry for what your family has endured."

Pasano, respectfully answers, "Thank you, Chief."

"Second, this is not a disciplinary hearing, just a fact-finding inquiry. It is not protocol, in fact, it's highly irregular because corruption allegations go directly to Internal Affairs and brutality complaints go to the Civilian Review Board. But, in this case, with the importance of your mission and the number of complaints coming in, I wanted to get personally involved and hear from you directly." The Chief pauses and looks at Pasano. "Do you understand, Sergeant?"

"Yes, sir."

"We know you are leading the Harlem Narcotics Task Force and that it's backed by the Police Commissioner and Mayor's office. Everyone is behind you in the mission. However, there have been large numbers of serious allegations against you and your team members. Complaints are coming in every day of brutality, corruption, and entering and taking apart buildings and businesses using sledgehammers instead of warrants. The most serious was an innocent civilian caught in crossfire. None of us here, with all the years of experience, have ever seen anything like it. At first, I thought somebody was playing a joke. I didn't know what to make of it. I know you are represented by counsel. With his approval, we would like to hear from you regarding these allegations."

Paul looks over at his attorney, who nods in the affirmative.

"Good. Please make note, Sergeant Pasano's representative has acknowledged. Now, I'll give you a few minutes to justify your enforcement tactics to this group."

The Sarge begins at a slow pace. "Sure, Chief, I think I can clear this up. First, we started this unit and the program at the request of the Mayor, Police Commissioner, and the Harlem community. Innocent people are dying from heroin overdoses every day. People are murdering each other. Children are being maimed and killed. Cops are being shot. Harlem has turned into the murder and drug capital of America. Thus far, we are up around five-thousand arrests. These 'collars' haven't come easy."

The Civilian Complaint Review Board Captain cuts him off. "Because these thousands of arrests haven't come easy, Sergeant, does that justify you abusing your authority? And what about the warrant-less searches?"

Pasano grimaces, trying his best to hold back his temper. Just as he's about to unleash some disdainful words, his lawyer puts his hand on Paul's forearm and jumps ahead of him. "Captain, that's a loaded question and a negative assumption on your part."

Before anyone else says another word, a pissed off Pasano gets back in the conversation. "Sir, the fact is, we never abused our authority. You mention warrants, which are not needed when we are entering vacant or abandoned city-owned buildings deemed as narcotic prone locations. It comes under the jurisdiction of the New York City Housing and Preservation Authority. This gives us the right to enter, plain and simple."

Staring at the Captain, he continues, "And, sir, the type of police work we're doing, besides the personal risk factor, also leads to other fallout; allegations of brutality, denial of civil rights, and corruption complaints coming in from all directions. Not only are the drug dealers sending them through the NYPD, but every liberal from New York City is waving their flag chanting that we're molesting an entire community. They all think we're easy targets. They refuse to believe that we can remove such a vast number of people from the streets without denying somebody's civil rights. But, Captain, our paperwork is solid, and our court testimony precise. I understand, after receiving this many complaints, the NYPD has to check things out for themselves and verify that we are on the up and up. That's always the way with the department."

"Exactly, Sergeant," the Captain from CCRB interrupts, "and that's why you're here."

The Captain from Internal Affairs cuts in, "Then how can you justify all these allegations? After a long career in this department, I've found where there's smoke, there's fire."

The Chief of Patrol cuts them off. "Wait a second, both of you. I thought we were going to hear this officer out. So let him finish, unless either one of you would rather take his place, go up to Harlem and finish the job."

A hush comes over the room, as the two Captains sit red-faced.

The Chief continues, "Go ahead, Sergeant."

Pasano is getting pumped. "Look, from one side of the NYPD, it's go get 'em tigers, and from the other, "easy does it now." If things get screwed up, everyone runs to the corner of Headquarters and simultaneously hollers out, 'We never told you to do that!'"

His lawyer bangs Pasano's leg under the table with his fist.

Paul ignores it and continues his rant, "We're not rookies. We know the score. What we're doing is for the community, for our self-worth, and for the NYPD. But every cop has to account for every action or inaction he's involved in. Chief, at least once a week our integrity is tested by IAD. They send undercovers posing as junkies, dealers, or money-holders to see if we're abusing our authority by lifting some drugs, cash, or weapons from our perps, or doctoring arrest paperwork. Large amounts of cash and weapons are marked and secreted away in abandoned apartment buildings that are monitored by Internal Affairs. We're called to answer out narc complaints at specific locations, and the department scrutinizes our confiscation of this planted property. We all know the drill."

The Patrol Chief's face turns from generic to a scowl. His two hands resting on the table convert to clenched fists as he interjects. "Hold it, hold it! Is this true? Are these cops being subjected to integrity tests? If so, they stop forthwith! Understand?" He looks over at both Captains and gives them a stern look. "You two see me after the meeting."

Pasano pauses then continues, "Chief, as far as my people are concerned, they're all beyond reproach. In fact, I believe they are all heroes. These guys live it and sometimes the department has a bit of a problem absorbing that fact. They're just good cops doing work nobody from HQ dares think about, let alone get involved in. So, boss, I apologize if I'm coming across as disrespectful, but I won't apologize for our work. Please, come up and spend some time with us. See for yourself what we're doing. Even go out with our arrest teams. See how it is to lock up killers and dope pushers, and what force is necessary to overtake them."

The Chief cuts in, "Okay, Sergeant. I've heard enough. Captains, I'll give you one week. Finish up your investigations."

They nod and respond, "Yes, sir."

The Chief lectures Pasano, "Sergeant, first off, do you think I got here by shuffling papers for thirty years? I know these streets, so I'm giving you the benefit of the doubt. I'll back you up, but know this, you're in a fishbowl. Be straight up. This meeting's over. Everyone's dismissed. Get back to your assignments."

Everyone walks out in silence. The Captains from IAD and CCRB lag behind.

On their way down in the elevator by themselves, the union attorney whispers to Pasano, "Jesus Christ, Paul, I was trying to stop you. I thought they were going to throw a fucking net over you and take your gun and shield right there on the spot. Was that bullshit about the warrants true?"

Sarge mumbles sarcastically, "Some of it."

"Goddamn, Paul. Now please, listen to what I'm telling you. These people are not your friends. Don't trust them. They'll look to fire your ass in a heartbeat and then look to put you and your guys in fucking jail. Warn your team. Get your stories straight."

"Got it."

## CHAPTER 32

# MOB RUMBLINGS— UNDERCOVER HAZARDS

Plummeting heroin street sales and diminishing demand for product creates disharmony amongst the three Mafioso families. The Seteolas are backed-up with an over-supply of raw poppy discharge. Tons of bundled tar are in Turkey, stacked in large, wooden storage sheds, awaiting shipment to Inzarita's labs in Palermo. Inzarita is the impatient one of the three capos. His constant challenges to his cousin, Carlos Giadana, in New York, have rocked the business partnership within the trio.

At a small gathering within his farmhouse, smothered by the smell of Sicilian cigars and anisette, Sonny Inzarita spits out some venom to Seteola, "I've just about had it. My lab workers are not getting paid. Mixing material and cutting tools are not being used. Our profits for the two families living and working abroad have diminished to the point that I know my cousin Carlos' replacement has been discussed. As pissed as I am, I refuse to go along with any proposed 'coup' ousting him."

Enrico Seteola feels differently, and after the meeting with his counterpart, Inzarita, he decides amongst his personal family heads to have henchmen in place ready to forcibly remove Giadana and his associates from their New York throne. In the mob and narc business, failure means elimination.

Nick Scalia has picked-up on the negative rumblings within the Cosa Nostra families. He knows he's being watched and followed twenty-four-seven. He can avoid detection and death, pull out, and call it a semi-successful mission. Or, he can stay under and risk his life a little longer, gathering vital info for Giadana's final takedown. There is no supervision here. An undercover makes his own decisions. Scalia chooses to stay put, gathering bits and pieces of narc info and passing it along to the DEA and NYPD Narc Intelligence Units.

Carlos Giadana has been giving him less and less responsibility as liaison between the Harlem streets' overseer, Vic Ferris, and the Mafioso's first lieutenant, Vito Tiafona. Neither Ferris nor Tiafona has relied on Scalia to render any decisions about the ongoings of the street trade. Any menial assignment the undercover is given, is immediately reported to Giadana. The capo is playing it safe, using Scalia for 'busy work' and keeping him close enough to discover any ties back to law enforcement.

Scalia feels like he's trapped in a box, eating scraps. His workplace is out of the basement of the Italian social club in East Harlem. His personal apartment is modest. A 500 square foot refurbished rental on Mulberry Street in downtown Little Italy, which from the outside has a ratty appearance, with darkened brick and mortar derived from a century of city smog. The inside is not great, either, with a few coats of cheap paint and a layer of chocolate brown indoor/outdoor carpeting placed over crooked oak floors. There are three other Giadana slugs living in the same building. Their job is to travel with Scalia to and from the Harlem Headquarters and keep an eye on him when they're not working.

---

One late evening, the foursome is hanging out and exits a private bar just off Mulberry Street. It's a typical 'Italians Only' club with blacked-out windows and limited seating inside. Clientele is mostly Sicilians, with a splash of Neapolitans and Calabrese.

As they exit, Scalia, knowing he has a scheduled meet with a DEA operative, makes a suggestion, "Hey, let's jump to the whore house."

One of the Mafiosos responds, "Sounds good to me, let's go."

They're all a bit buzzed and head for a quick visit to a local pros' upstairs from the bar.

She's a middle-aged Puerto Rican who works out of a lacey parlor which is decked out in shades of red, with a small, private room to conduct her personal business. They drop over four bills at the bar, and now another eight with the high priced hooker. It's all part of the job, and Scalia blends in easily and is the last to leave. On his way out, Scalia's DEA backup, posing as the lady of the night's bodyguard, completes the scheduled meet by placing a slip of paper into Scalia's jacket pocket.

The four men barely make it back to their rooms, but Scalia's night is not over. After entering his apartment, he pulls out the secreted piece of paper. On it is written, *Ful' Fish, slip 22, 0400, white truck, C.O.D.-Green.*

It's a cold and rainy night, but this undercover has work to do. Police work. It must be done before 8 AM when the four head back uptown and report to Tiafona for their day's illicit assignments. Scalia trades his multi-thousand-dollar Canali threads for a black turtleneck, black jeans, dark green skull cap, and boots.

The young undercover uses his oversized hands to force open the bedroom window and climb down a rusted fire escape, dropping the last eight feet to the alleyway below between the buildings. In his wharf worker's garb, he heads to the lower East Side's Fulton Fish Market to scout for a shipment of Sicilian Turkish 'H.' The former Seal handles it with ease. He cabs his way to the market, where the hustle and bustle of fish deliveries crowd the docks. Addicted hookers dot the fringes, hoping to pick up some chump change. Scalia hustles to Dock 20, close enough for viewing Dock 22, but safe enough not to get 'made' by the underworld. This market is rife with gangland deals. Fish is only part of it. It's also another location on the police corruption list. If not on official business, it means stay away.

Hired guns in suits clutter the wharf. Dock workers in black garb, push and load barrels, bins, and carts. After two hours of observations from a planted pickup truck, Scalia recognizes a familiar face. Tiafona—Dock 22, passing a thick envelope to a large, scruffy, fishing boat Captain. Some of the workers begin rolling sealed bins over to a blacked-out, dark-colored van. Four bins are rolled up a portable ramp and into the back, followed by two armed hoods.

The doors close. Tiafona and a driver get in the front. The van pulls away. It's followed by another decoy van, not with dope, but packed with four, armed Giadana goons. Scalia photos the entire sequence of events with a small Nikon fit with a night lens. His work here is done. Vital evidence has been gathered, and an entry point for future shipments is found.

The undercover leaves the camera under the seat, exits, and locks the doors to the truck. He starts walking two blocks west for a cab. It's a dark, remote portion of roadway under the highway above. A car pulls in front of his path. Two men in suits exit. It's two of the Giadana 'grunts' that Scalia had been partying with earlier. They were assigned to watch and follow Scalia while the third slept. Semi-autos are drawn. Within a second, they're pressed against the Agent. One to his back and one to his right temple.

The taller one instructs Scalia, "You move, you're dead." He removes Scalia's gun and orders, "Now walk slowly. Get in. We're going for a ride."

"Whack him right fuckin' here. Then we'll take his body up to the boss. Easier that way," the short, stocky one adds.

The taller thug concedes, "I like your idea better than mine."

Scalia realizes he must make his move or perish without a fight. He takes a deep breath, tightly clenches his fists, and is about to make a combat move, but in a split second is showered in blood. The two hoods collapse to the pavement. Scalia's stunned. He pauses, looks around. A large, nondescript, white box truck pulls up rapidly and screeches to a stop. Six vested up DEA Agents jump out, grab the bodies of the two mobsters, and flip them into the back of the truck like sacks of fertilizer.

Scalia gets a glimpse within the back of the truck and sees two other Agents, one male, one female, both holding scoped sniper rifles, dragging the two corpses forward as pools of blood, mixed with brain tissue and skull fragments, blend into long streaks. Scalia wipes some of the blood splatter from his eyes and calls out to the Agents who saved his life without a split second to spare. "Hey, guys, I owe you!"

The male merely nods. The female has a few words to offer. "Hey, tough guy. You're playing it a bit too close, no?"

"Nah'. I knew you'd be hanging around nearby, Yono. You've always had a soft spot for me."

"In your dreams."

Scalia and Yono do a quick tap on their chests with the peace sign, as the gangster's car is driven up the ramp and into the truck. The doors close.

One agent slaps Scalia on his back, hands him a towel and says, "Here, clean yourself off and cab it back." He returns his gun to him. "You want out, say the word."

"Copy that."

The Agents pile in and the truck pulls away. The pickup truck follows behind. Scalia continues his walk. Two blocks west, he hops into a cab. He's relieved to be alive, but his mind races for story-time at 8 AM.

---

Nothing has changed with the distrust the DEA has for Pasano. They believe the Sarge is a loose cannon and liable to 'go rogue,' killing anyone in connection with the personal assaults on his and Renee Jons' families. As such, orders are given by the DEA to Nick Scalia not to give any pertinent info regarding the person or persons responsible for those attacks.

Scalia has been ad-libbing for years. It has been his main source for survival. It's all part of the undercover process. He works alone. When under, he makes his own decisions. However, he's always being monitored and even tailed by other agents. When told not to do something, he might do it anyway. That applies here in his association with Pasano. Scalia remembers all too well what the Mafiosos did to his own father decades before. He harbors the vengeance in his heart and can understand Pasano's rage towards the Giadana clan. Scalia also understands what will ultimately come. Some people will die. Maybe Pasano, maybe Giadana or his associates. But, someone will pay for what was done to his, the Jons, and Pasano families.

## CHAPTER 33

# FRIENDS RISE TO THE OCCASION

Late night, paperwork complete, his men are downtown with a fresh batch of perps, and the Sarge is done. The 35th's rundown holding cells are emptied and cleaned, although the leftover stench never recedes. Pasano heads for his car parked just down the street. There are two uniformed cops walking security on the block 24-7. This is for everyone's protection; cops, visitors, and civilians. It's an easy place for a police assassination or bomb plant. This precinct was plagued with cop killings just a few years before.

Paul Pasano has worked right through the cop murder era. First, he battled the Black Liberation Army, and now he encounters a new and more deadly wave, the Cosa Nostra.

On and off duty, he carries two guns. He takes a PD portable walkie-talkie to and from work. His and other police families are being guarded. The officers constantly look over their shoulders. Never stand in a group. Split up, stay alert.

He takes a couple of hundred steps to his 'ride.' He gets the feeling. All good street cops can sense it. He's being watched. Two Con Ed employees, wearing hardhats, are working in a lighted corralled area set up over an open manhole. Paul always looks for gun bulges, a walking hitch, lean, or a weapon adjustment.

He's twenty-five feet away and spots it. Both of them armed under their utility company's orange vests. It's a quick draw and his revolver is in his hand under his jacket. He's close to the duo. He can't turn around and lose sight or attention. The block security cops are gone. The two see his one hand is secreted and get nervous.

One worker, without hesitation, offers up, "The C.O.D. is orange. Lighten up. We have a message from a friend. Unauthorized."

The area light is turned off. Pasano holsters his weapon. The other male walks over to him with hands well exposed.

"Hey, Paul, a message from Nick."

In the darkness, he moves his arm forward to shake his hand. Paul responds in kind. A small note is passed. Pasano pockets it, nods, heads for his car, and pulls away. He looks back in his rear view mirror. The two undercover workers are already packed up. Tape, barriers, and lights are thrown in back of the truck. By the time the Sarge gets one block, the Con Ed truck disappears.

Paul pulls over, reaches into his jacket pocket and pulls out the note. Written, *'Richard Jons' shooter, Leon Galven, Brooklyn South area……….. Driver of car who ran down Andrew Pasano, Giadana's 2nd lieutenant, Antonio Palatzi, Belmont Raceway, Thursday 1 PM.'*

The Sarge's hands quiver. He reads the message three times. He takes the car's cigarette lighter, lights up the note, and places it in the ashtray.

He pauses and mouths, *"They're dead."*

Paul Pasano's first order of business is to come up with a plan to do away with the two perps responsible. He must not let his personal vendetta get in the way of good, old-fashioned police work. Get too sloppy and people get hurt, or he'll get himself killed and not be able to finish the unit's objectives.

---

Pasano reaches outside his team for help. If things go sour, he'll suffer the consequences alone. He's well past the point of formal investigations, grand juries, and court-ordered arrest warrants.

The Sarge calls a friend. His old Brooklyn South partner, Bobby Stewart, who left the precinct after he did. With Stewart's military background, job accomplishments, and balls, he landed in one of the NYPD's most deadly units, the Stake-Out Squad. It was a small, specially trained unit of men who secreted themselves inside stores that have been plagued with armed robberies. Usually one cop with a shotgun. Armed robber comes in and sticks the place up. On his way out, he's blown away.

The unit's success rate was astounding. The kill numbers were off the charts. A major New York City newspaper got ahold of it and bang! The unit was abolished. Too cruel, too violent. Rights violated. Bobby Stewart was one of the best in the unit. Most takeouts. Got him his Detective shield and a transfer to Brooklyn Homicide. A good fit for him. A good find for Pasano, who reaches out to this seasoned Detective.

The two meet at a Brooklyn cop's bar off Snyder Avenue. It's a large, open, club-like setting, stocked with off-duty officers and top shelf liquor. On occasion, it's sprinkled with a few on-duty cops sliding in for a quick shot. The two friends sit at the far end, on two bar stools, out of earshot of other patrons.

"Paul, it's been too long. How's Rachel holding up?"

Paul shakes his head in the negative.

Stewart says quietly, "I'm sorry for what you've been put through. How can I help?"

"Bobby, I've read about what you've done. Congrats are in order. I'm here to ask a favor."

"Anything, anywhere, anytime."

Pasano looks around and brings the conversation down to a whisper. "I need your tracking expertise to find a scumbag, Leon Galven, the one who shot down my community associate's son and tore her whole family apart. He's supposed to be in Brooklyn. This guy's being sponsored by Carlos Giadana, who I'll deal with later. Right now, I have a promise to keep. So, Bobby, please, I don't want you too deeply involved. Just gimme' his location, and I'll handle the rest."

"Listen, Paul," Stewart lectures, "We're friends, right? Then let me talk to you like a friend. First, you're running too far over the line. You're probably battle fatigued and letting your personal hatred guide you down a path to self-destruction. You'll lose your job and family."

"Bobby, you don't know what these fucks have done."

"I know exactly what they've done. That's why you should gather yourself up and get back on track before it's too late."

The Sarge lowers his head. It's hard for him to accept, but he realizes he's too far removed from the right side of the law.

Stewart continues, "So here's my offer. I will help you find this scumbag. But, my way, on my terms. Deal?"

"Yeah. Thank you, Bobby. You were always the level-headed one."

"First, we go to my office and do the paperwork," says a more upbeat Stewart. "Everything legit. This way, I can go out and canvas the local hangouts and talk to my CI's. I'll spread a few bucks around, make some inquiries, and rattle some cages. If this guy's in Brooklyn, I'll find him. Now drink up. To better days."

"To better days, bud, 'cause they can't be worse." The two swig down shots of Dewars.

---

In the Brooklyn South Homicide squad room, Stewart introduces Pasano to some of his partners. All rough looking characters, who somehow fit in perfectly with an office about five years over-do for a paint job. First up amongst the squad of 'D's' is a burly, crew-cut Irishman, with a brogue that could cut through ice. Behind him are a couple of tenured Italians with Raging Bull 'mitts,' finished off with a big, linebacker-size,

Black sleuth with a shaved head, whose neck overwhelms his collar, and a hand that envelops Pasano's right hand like an adult to a child. He sits behind a normal size office desk and looks like a parent sitting behind a first grader's desk at a PTA meeting.

Paul thinks to himself, *'Man, I could use a few of these guys back up in Harlem. Wouldn't have to fire a shot. The bad guys would just surrender out of fear.'*

Most Brooklyn cops have always been different. A guy who was born and raised in Brooklyn, who becomes a New York cop and ends up working here, has mannerisms that set him apart from other cops around the city. He accepts little bullshit and lacks patience and tolerance. He takes no guff and hits or shoots rather than talks. Bobby Stewart fits right in here.

"This place has character, Bobby."

"Doesn't it?"

Pasano remarks, "And you look good in that suit and tie sitting behind the desk."

"Hey, with your background, they'd give you your own squad tomorrow."

"Me, nah'. I've been a street grunt my entire career. I'd be bouncing off these walls. I can't do 'inside.' Never could. You know that."

"Yeah, I guess you're right."

"The Harlem streets are like my second home. Maybe a little more broken, though."

Stewart, joking, "Ya' think?" Two buddies laugh. "Now listen, put everything you have in the '61.' I'll have my Lieutenant sign off on it, and I can begin tonight. These old guys will back me up. I promise you, I'll toss the entire fucking borough if I have to."

"Great. And, please, all I ask is that you call me as soon as you have something on this guy. Anything. You pinpoint his location, and I'll join you in the takedown."

The two cops spend an hour and complete the reports.

"Safe home, Bob."

"You as well. I'll call you."

Pasano walks out past the squad of well-seasoned Detectives who, with bone breaking grips, shake his hand once again. The Sarge drives his unmarked back to the 35th and feels some relief. These personal involvements drain his energy.

---

He heads home to Rachel and Linda and thinks about Andrew, whose progress has plateaued. It's a late dinner, some hand-holding, and prayers for their son. A hot shower and rest follow, interrupted with the ever-present bad dreams. 6 AM and he kisses his family an early morning goodbye. The embraces between Paul and Rachel have lasted longer over the passing weeks. There is always that fear of the final one.

Just as Paul is walking out the door, the phone rings. He answers. At this time of the morning, calls are usually downers. This one's different, and confusing.

"Hello."

"Hello, Paul. Bobby Stewart here. Listen, I got the info you wanted."

"God, fast work, Bobby, thanks. Where is he? We'll meet and take him together."

"451 Clarkson Avenue."

"That's the address of the Brooklyn morgue."

"And you'd be right. That's where he is, buried. About two hours ago. He didn't want to give up. All done, okay, my friend?"

Pasano pauses. "Damn, Bob. I owe you and your partners big time. Thank you. Can I ask how it went down?"

"No. Like I told you, Paul, this is Brooklyn. You know we do things a bit differently. Paperwork is on its way to you. My best to Rachel and family. Stay tough."

Pasano hangs up and takes a deep breath. Rachel awaits his next words.

Paul, quietly and slowly says, "You remember my old partner from Brooklyn, Bobby Stewart? He took care of Renee's son's shooter."

Rachel begins to cry. "My God, Paul. So much violence. Will it ever end?"

Paul attempts to calm his wife. "It will, I promise you, it will," as he gives Rachel another hug. His mind always racing and thinking ahead, a day at Belmont coming up. Palatzi's on the race card.

---

It's Tuesday, Pasano and his men are swamped with court time. They do their best to put most of their cases on for the same day. Pasano gives instructions. "Here's our schedule for the next few days. Let's knock out all our pending court cases today and tomorrow. Remember, simple and concise with your testimony. I'll be in and out of court for each of the cases. I've got a doc's appointment for Andrew on Thursday. I'll be taking the day off. You back-fill with the Special Narcotics Team. Everyone on the same page?"

There is a scheduled appointment with another neurologist, but Pasano will not be going. Rachel will go it alone. So will Paul. They'll be about twenty miles apart with completely different agendas. One will be to save a life and the other will be to remove one.

## CHAPTER 34

# A DAY AT THE TRACK AND A PRESIDENTIAL COMMITMENT

Since opening in 1905, Belmont Raceway has always been a collecting ground for organized crime. Family meetings and heavy-weight betting on the ponies have always gone hand-in-hand. Speculation over fixed races runs wild, especially ones that were set up by the mob where they could reap the benefits. This Thursday would be no different. Bundles of cash, flashy suits, alcohol, and hookers galore.

Belmont is a large track with a massive seating area. The weekday crowds are only a fraction of what shows up on weekends. This makes it more conducive for the Mafioso families to enjoy the afternoon and conduct their business meetings undisturbed. The big crowds would make for an easier blend. Fewer people mean more exposure, although less collateral damage if it turns out to be a bloodbath. The Sarge takes what he can get.

Pasano is blinded by rage over someone harming his family, especially little Andrew. He wouldn't mind losing his job or even his life to settle the score with Giadana. He loads up heavy, packing a .45 cal' military, two clips, and a .38 snub-nose backup. Hollow point rounds are used for more damage. Both pieces are silenced. He parks outside the raceway on the streets of Elmont, pulls and tightens the Velcro straps on his Kevlar, and buttons up his white shirt. The white collar lays over the dark blue sports jacket lapels. No tie. A large gold chain with a horn hangs around his neck. Sunglasses are in place just below a NY Yankees dark blue cap. For this outing, Pasano has to get to the clubhouse area on the upper floor and wait for his opportunity.

This private area is reserved for people who pay a few extra bucks, are dressed properly, and are usually big bettors. Paul flashes some cash and places a couple of bets. He mixes in with a few private business people and engages in small talk. Bettors, mostly men, are eating and drinking. Track security personnel are thinly scattered.

Paul eyeballs his target. Antonio Palatzi leaves his table, places his bets, turns and walks to the men's room. There are no doors, just side entry into a large, open area that leads into the bathroom. Pasano waits about ten seconds and follows behind. Just as he's about to enter the long hallway to the men's room, a raceway cleaner, a tall, Black man with a beard, is working a mop back and forth on a wet floor. Two orange cones are blocking the hallway and Pasano's path. This does not bode well for the Sarge. With a hand under his jacket on the .45, he continues walking forward. He nears the cleaner. A hooded person with their head down walking at a fast clip leaves the bathroom and passes by him. Pasano pushes forward.

The cleaner puts his arm up in front of Pasano, blocking his path. "An accident in there, sir, you can't go in until I clean up."

Paul pushes his arm away. "I have to go, pal, step aside."

The cleaner steps in front of Paul and says, "The color is blue. Go home to your family."

Pasano is stunned. He pauses. Three armed security guards rush down the hallway past him and the cleaner. The cleaner puts his mop against the wall, grabs the Sarge's arm, and leads him away. The sound of police sirens fills the airway outside the raceway as he lets loose of Pasano's arm and in a confiding tone says, "You're not working alone," and walks away.

The Sarge, caught off guard, pauses and heads towards the escalators. Unbeknownst to him, just seconds apart, the mobsters are heading down on the same set of escalators. Amongst them is Carlos Giadana, surrounded by several of his armed enforcers, including his first lieutenant, Rick Tiafona.

Heavily armed police personnel swarm the entrance out front. Pasano casually walks past the large assembly of cops. He overhears one say to the other, "Yeah, one of those mob fucks, Antonio Palatzi, took a hit. That's one less scumbag we'll have to worry about."

Pasano murmurs to himself, *'My sentiments exactly.'*

He heads for his car thinking, *'My two worst enemies are gone, without me firing a shot.'* He'll bring the news to the Jons family and home to Rachel. Vengeance has been done. Most of it anyway.

---

On Pasano's return trip back home, he shakes off the two nemeses' killings. Coming into focus is his son and his visit with the neurologist. As he walks in the door, he hears Rachel crying and walks over to the kitchen table where she's sitting. This is the same place where not too long ago, laughter was abundant, and family stories and dinners were shared. Rachel immediately stands up and embraces her husband. The sobbing doesn't stop.

"The news is that bad, Rach'?"

"Yes, Paul. They said we should prepare for the worst. Andrew may never regain his mental and physical faculties. What is now, might be forever. Oh, Paul, what are we going to do?"

Responding softly, "We will get through this, Rachel. The people responsible are dead."

Rachel's face turns red, she bites her lower lip and stands up to Paul. "I don't care about all your killings! Don't you understand that? I want my son back the way he was. I want our little boy to run and play like other children. You can't do that for me, Paul. All you can do is take people's lives. That doesn't help our family."

Paul says in a stronger voice, "No, Rachel. What I've done, what I do every day, won't help us. But, it will help thousands of other families so they won't have to go through what we are going through now. Can you understand that?"

"Yes, but it's hard for me to accept."

Paul puts his arm around his wife. "I know."

---

It's an early start for Pasano the following morning. First, a call and a stop at Renee Jons' apartment to see her and the children. They're all sitting around the breakfast table which appears empty without Richard, who's back in the hospital, Cavon already in school, and Olivia, away. The younger ones won't understand the news. Paul asks to speak to the mom alone.

"How's Richard?"

Renee shakes her head, no, as she tells the girls, "Go get dressed for school."

She looks drawn and tired. When alone at the table, the Sarge unleashes the words this single mother of five has been waiting for.

"Richard's shooter has been found and taken care of."

Renee sighs with relief. "Paul, he's in jail? How? Did you arrest him?"

"No, he's dead. My old Brooklyn partner had to kill him."

Renee's face goes sullen as she responds, "Thank you, and thank your friend. He must be troubled by what he had to do."

"Trust me, he's not."

There is more silence and confusion from Renee, as he continues. "In addition, someone killed the driver of the car that ran down my boy. I don't know who or why. I just know he's dead as well. The two people who took parts of our families away from us are gone, Renee."

"You know Paul, I'm a religious woman. I don't condone killing of any kind, but I'm glad it's over."

Renee catches her breath, changes the subject, and speaks with a bit of hope, "I finally have some good news. I just received a response from someone I thought didn't even know I, or Harlem for that matter, existed. And now, she's coming up from Washington to attend an anti-drug community meeting at the high school next month."

Paul questions her with interest. "Who is it?"

Renee proudly states, "The President's wife."

"Are you kidding me or what? How the heck did you manage this?"

"I'm serious. I sent a letter to her explaining the devastation in our community that has been overrun with drugs. I told her of all the violence, senseless killing, and the suffering incurred by our seniors and children. I wrote, have we become the forgotten people? I made a plea for help, Paul." With trembling hands, she shows the First Lady's letter to the Sarge.

> *Dear Mrs. Jons, As you know, I am well beyond the years of a younger person. In all those years, I have never read a letter from someone who has and is experiencing what you are going through. I commit, that because of you and others like you who are enduring the ramifications of drug use, I will title my personal campaign, 'Say No To Drugs.' If you wish, I would be honored to attend your community meeting. In addition, I personally put your letter into the hands of the President. He would like to add his own words.*

> *Mrs. Jons, I am sorry for the devastation that has befallen your community, your people, and your family. Please understand, I serve at the behest of those very people. Across America, I have seen what the residuals of narcotic*

*use have done to our fellow citizens, especially the children.*
*I will see that enforcement measures and proper financing*
*are undertaken in your community. I will have my staff*
*consult with the NYPD and DEA to monitor progress.*
*Please be assured, Ms. Jons, I, for one, have not forgotten*
*you. May God be with you today and forever.*

"Jesus, Renee, for the first time in my life, I'm speechless."

"On top of that, Paul, because she's coming to the meeting, so are the Governor, Mayor, and our local Congressmen. We're doing something right. People are starting to listen. They know we're struggling. They're coming to help. I want you there. I want you to speak to them. I want them to hear from the person who's leading the fight right here on our streets. Will you do that for me?"

Paul is quick to joke. "Of course. I'll even get a haircut for the First Lady. I hear she likes cops."

Renee smiles. "And listen, Paul, I'm thinking of asking Corisa to come. Being addicted, she would be an example of the kind of people we are helping."

"Junkie Corisa?"

"Stop it, Paul. She's a human being and has a good heart. Don't lose sight of why we're doing this."

Pasano grins and stands up. "Keep it simple when you tell your children about what has just transpired about Richard's shooter. I've got a full day's work ahead of me and a lot of news to bring to my team and the 35th. Renee, you know that yours and the children's lives are still at risk. Be on guard. The precinct is still on watch. The more progress we make, the more desperate Giadana and his associates will get."

Pasano touches her shoulder and goes to leave. Renee's younger ones enter the room.

The Sarge tells them, "Take care of your mom."

One of the youngest, Aretha, shouts out, "The President's coming to our house!"

Pasano laughs, puts his hands on his head, and walks out. On his way down the stairway, he thinks to himself, *'The President's wife. Wait til' the guys get a load of this. Wait until the NYPD, Police Commissioner, and the Chief of Patrol find out. They're not invited. But I am. Me and Corisa.'* He laughs even harder than before.

Laughter is rare in crime fighting, but Pasano grabs for the moment. It's mostly cynical comedy or a splash of craziness. Probably a blend of both. Battle fatigue enters the mix as well. Alcohol softens the anxiety for some, but it never worked for Paul. Immersing himself within the chaos seems to be the Sarge's best source for stabilization. But, he's far from being an even-keeled guy. If he was, he would never be where he is or do what he's doing.

## CHAPTER 35

# DISTRAUGHT COPS AND CAPO

Narc enforcement continues with an afternoon raid on West 154th Street. These locations, if not hit every day, pop back up like stubborn weeds. Pasano and his Raiders are positioned on Saint Nicholas Avenue, two blocks west of the target. They sit with nine uniformed backups on two, long wooden benches bolted to the floor within the rear of a generic box truck. They wait for Organized Crime Control members to finish making a number of undercover buys.

In a 4th floor vacant apartment, east of the hot zone, the Special Narcotics Enforcement Unit, (SNEU), zooms in with their cameras and snaps away at buyers entering and exiting the building. The junkies are of all races and ages. Some walk and some come by car. They'll all be picked up by the arrest teams down on the street a few blocks from the location. The further away the better, so the sellers aren't spooked.

The drug-buy operation and SNEU work are complete. Pasano and company are given the go-ahead to sweep the building and come up with the wholesaler, money, and gun holders.

From within the observation post, the photo tech rattles off a message, "Narc Sarge on the air?"

"On the air."

"OP 1, Sarge. Photos and buys completed. OCCB undercovers have the names and locations of our two targets........Number one, Angel

Ramin—black hoodie, gray pants, and number two, Jerod Spunel, green jacket. Both remain with others on the second floor, 458 W. 154th Street, apartments 2B, 2C. Receive?"

Pasano calmly transmits, "10-4, received, OP 1. Two targets, black hoodie, green jacket, second floor, 458 W. 154th Street, apartments 2B, 2C. We're en route, ETA 1 minute."

The 'Narcs' begin a slow trek towards the target, pulling up in front of, as the rear doors are opened from the inside. The contingent of men bails out with shotguns, rams, and sledgehammers. The 'uniforms' split up in teams of three, covering the back and two sides of the building.

The Sarge and his teammates head for the main entrance, take the stairway to the second floor, and begin their encounters. The heavy-weight, John Calvoy, wields the sledge, and Kellig uses a ram. A few swings by each and they bust through the two, second-floor apartment doors. The element of surprise works well with minimal resistance.

Sellers, money holders, and bulls are arrested. Amongst those apprehended is Angel Ramin. Absconding is Spunel, running up the steps attempting to get to the third floor. He is chased down by Pasano, who grabs him by his ankles, turns him over, and punches him multiple times in the face and ribs. He's still conscious but is quickly rolled again and cuffed. The two 'Black Sunday' wanted perps are finally collared up. The operation total, 30 arrests, and over a thousand dime and quarter bags of 'H' confiscated. By all accounts, a successful strike.

Under the Rockefeller Law, the dealers will be looking at life. Pasano should be content, but he's not. He finds large amounts of heroin and cash, but no guns. Guns mean death to police officers, creating funerals, orphans, and widows.

He grabs Spunel, the known weapon holder, by his throat, and places a gun to his head. "Okay, mother fucker, where's the gun?" Spunel is too tough and cunning. No response. Pasano drags him by his shirt to a broken staircase, leans him over the railing, and gives him an ultimatum. "No gun and you fly. Got it, prick?"

Still no response. Pasano pushes him over. Spunel falls one flight landing on his face. Blood pours from his head. The Sarge runs down, props him up, and drags the bloodied Spunel outside to the awaiting uniformed backups who put him in their RMP and take him to Harlem Hospital for treatment. The other perps are put on a prisoner van and taken to the Three-Five for processing.

---

Two blocks away at a traffic light, the injured Spunel is sitting in the rear of the patrol car. He quietly swings the cuffs from behind his back and over his legs. In one continuous motion, he reaches over the front seat, grabs one of the rookie's guns, and shoots both cops in seconds. One is struck in the jaw, the other in his shoulder. The car lunges forward and strikes the rear of a postal truck.

He kicks out the rear window of the radio car, climbs out, and flees down the street, still cuffed, but hands now in the front, and heads for an abandoned building, gun in hand.

One of the injured officers shouts into his radio, "Central, signal 10-13! My partner and I have been shot, 152 and St. Nick. Perp on the loose, male Black, green jacket. Unknown direction. Armed!"

Central dispatches the emergency message, "All units, be advised. Signal 10-13. 152 and St. Nick. Two officers shot. Armed perp, one male Black, green jacket, fled, unknown direction."

Pasano hears the message, and his head spins in fury. He exclaims, "Fuck!" He realizes he should have killed Spunel when he had the chance and will have to track him down again and do it.

---

Paul is running for multiple days without sleep. His stress level has peaked. In addition, the NYPD has not let up on their IAD and CCRB investigations. Open allegations still remain. Pasano knows he's operating way over the line. It's too late to turn back. The violent scenarios bring equally violent cop-mares. While asleep, cops are involved in shootouts, pulling the trigger, and nothing happens. It's a common occurrence. Pasano is all too familiar. Nightmares okay, but being at home and leaping out of bed in his Fruit of the Looms brandishing a gun at 3 AM is not normal. And it was ongoing.

He's been unloading his off-duty gun each night and separating the gun and bullets in different rooms of the house. This is out of fear of pulling off some kind of a family massacre during one of the episodes. It's combat fatigue, first degree. If he says anything about it to the NYPD, it's over, and they'll just stamp his personnel folder, *fucked in the head—remove all guns.'* Just dismiss it and move on. His teammates are experiencing the same. Pasano knows it's his fault but refuses to let up. The finish line is ahead. So he thinks.

The next morning he holds a team meeting with the 35th precinct Detectives. A Borough Task Force is formed. Spunel will be hunted. Paul has his own tactics in mind.

---

The NYPD and Pasano are not the only people holding regular meetings. A distraught Carlos Giadana does the same.

Hines, the older Black waiter, serves his last round of Sambuca and espressos to the mobsters. He leaves the large meeting room and walks up the dark stairway to the restaurant above.

Capo Giadana slams his fist down on an old wooden table in the basement of the Italian club surrounded by all the usuals, including Nick Scalia. With highly trained and experienced hands, Scalia conducts a quick sweeping motion and affixes a 'bug' under the long table. It goes undetected.

His federal comrades are listening in and recording every breath. First lieutenant, Vito Tiafona, is present and catching most of the 'fire' from his boss. Giadana's second lieutenant is dead. Belmont Raceway, the mob's playground, is off limits. The Feds and the NYPD have it monitored.

Giadana is ranting in his Sicilian dialect, "How did we let someone kill one of our own? I want to know who and why. If we allow this, we lose our only advantage, fear. I want the name of the person responsible. Do you fucking hear me?"

Tiafona, in a low voice, mentions the name, "Pasano."

Two other mobsters utter the same, "Pasano."

An enraged Giadana's eyes bulge and a vein in his neck swells as if he's being strangled. He looks around, glares at each of his subordinates and shouts, "Goddamn it! How is that fucking cop still alive? Raise the bounty to 250G's. Everyone out except Tiafona!"

The crew leaves in silence and closes the steel door behind them.

Giadana, in no more than a low, raspy voice, speaks in Italian. "I'm embarrassed. Enrico Seteola and my cousin, Sonny Inzarita, want me removed. I won't have that. This is my town. My business. Seteola wants his brother from Palermo sent here to replace me. They say I'm too soft. It's different for us. We are in sales. They are in manufacturing. We can't just kill our own salespeople. We have the police and Feds to deal with, they don't. If I go, you go. I'm counting on you to take care of this cop."

Tiafona says quietly, "It will be done."

"You know, in Sicily years back people wanted to be led," Giadana continues. "My father used to tell me your friends and neighbors are like sheep. Without a shepherd, they would wander off and die. Families fought one another and the strongest would prevail and control the others. It was a simpler time and place." He continues, "They told me go to America, land of opportunity, where the weak are waiting for your strength. Nobody counted on resistance, but here we are. We must fight to our death to salvage our honor. "

Giadana speaks in just above a whisper, "Now I'm confiding in you. A large shipment is coming in on the 23rd of next month to the

market downtown. Dock 22, 5 AM. Let the Montoriffi brothers oversee the transaction. They'll die for me if need be. You stay back with
Scalia and the others. If we can't move this product to market, we're
done. Understand?"

"*Capisco.*"

"Then go to work."

---

The DEA is way ahead of these Mafioso's when it comes to technol-
ogy. The planted receptor feeds the vital info back to a trailer located
on Randall's Island. There, a team of Narcotics Task Force members is
recording the capo's plans to do away with the Harlem Sergeant and
bring in hundreds of millions of dollars of raw heroin ready for cutting, packaging, and distribution. They hear not only the viciousness
in Giadana's voice, but also the sounds of a desperate man. This killer
doesn't fear death. He fears failure, not wanting his legacy to be one of
defeat at the hands of the Americans.

## CHAPTER 36

# UNAUTHORIZED BEHAVIOR— BOUNTY'S UP

A couple of hours later, Giadana's dark, damp meeting room empties out. Carmella, the olive-skinned, Hispanic cleaning girl, begins her work. This is her daily chore each evening after the capo meetings. Her second assignment is to service Nick Scalia. She's smitten with him and vice versa. The unmarried undercover maintains this one flaw. It is neither known about or condoned by DEA brass.

First, Carmella removes all the glassware and utensils. She sweeps the meeting room floor, followed by a mopping of the same. The odor of heavy cleaners floods the basement. Her final chore is to spray polish the well-marked, wooden table.

As she wipes the underneath where Scalia was sitting, a small round object falls to the floor. The bugging device has come loose. Carmella bends down beneath the table and quickly picks it up. She's examining it and not sure what she's holding. Standing out in the hallway, looking into the room is Hines, the waiter. He walks in the dimly lit room and approaches her. He reaches in his pocket, pulls out a hundred dollar bill, hands it to her and puts his index finger up to his lips motioning her to be silent about what she's found. With his other hand, he politely removes the small device from her palm and pockets it.

He tells her in a commanding voice, "You have a nice quiet night, Carmella."

"Yes sir, Mr. Hines."

The restaurant and bar empty out. Scalia stays behind as he's done on numerous other nights. A heavily armed enforcer remains for the midnight shift to protect the Mafioso premises and walks into a private office leaving the bartender behind. Hines leaves the meeting room and heads back upstairs to the club. He puts his topcoat over his waiter's outfit and begins walking past the bar stool where Scalia is seated.

Scalia calls out to the bartender, "Please, another shot of vodka on the rocks."

As Hines passes by the bar, he says, "Goodnight, Mr. Scalia, sir."

He reaches out to the undercover to shake hands. Scalia reaches his right hand forward and the two shake. The 'bug' is passed from Hines to Scalia, whose face flushes as he can feel the tiny device knowing full well what it is and its ramifications.

Hines walks out of the club. Just the bartender and Scalia remain at the bar. Carmella walks up the staircase to the bar and sees her beau. Scalia slowly walks over to her and simultaneously pockets the 'bug,' as the two begin to leave, arm-in-arm.

As they pass the bar, Scalia tosses back his last bit of drink, lays out a hundred dollar bill to the bartender, and says, "Good night."

"Good night, Mr. Scalia. Drive safely."

Just outside the club entrance, the slick undercover looks around to survey the street and adjoining sidewalk. He pauses long enough to give a good stare across the roadway to assure safety, a trait shared by cops and mobsters alike. He escorts Carmella to his black, flashy Caddy. They leave, heading down to the Waldorf for an overnight rendezvous.

---

Nick parks out front. A young valet takes the keys and a twenty-dollar bill and parks his 'ride.'

Once inside, Carmella remains in place while Scalia heads over to the tall reception desk. His steps are muffled by the plush red and gold leaf carpeting spread across the lobby. With no words spoken, he signs the register for his usual room. A porter comes out to assist. Scalia recognizes him immediately. He walks the couple over to the elevator and Scalia hands out another twenty. Inside the folded bill is the 'bug.'

The porter, a fellow agent, politely says, "Thank you, and good night, sir."

In the elevator going up to the eighth floor, Carmella tries to be amorous, but Nick does not respond. They enter a posh room done-up in various shades of purple with white marble accessories where they undress and slip into bed. But the silk sheets and mirrored ceiling do not enhance the mood.

Carmella whispers to Nick, "I found something tonight. A small, round piece of something. I don't know what it was. Hines took it."

"That's fine. However, you will never mention it to anyone ever again. Okay?"

"Yes, Nick. Why so serious?"

"I just had a rough day."

"I like rough, Nicholas," as she laughs.

Scalia does not laugh in return. He has some important issues to deal with in the morning. First and foremost, he must get a notification to Pasano about the rise in bounty for his death. At '250 large,' bullets and claims of job completion will be coming in from every low-life within Giadana's long reach.

Second, he must absorb some intense heat about the botched bugging and his unauthorized tryst with a bystander caught up in his undercover op'. The Feds are always quick to acknowledge good work but even faster to personally condemn any rogue or sloppy activity.

It's by the book or you're out. Scalia is saved because of what he has accomplished to date, and at this point, any change would jeopardize the operation.

There is discussion by the supervising agents of what to do about Carmella. The idea of her being forcibly removed and sent away, probably to Arizona or New Mexico, is floated but discarded. For now, she stays. Nick's got a girlfriend whether he likes it or not. When the mission is completed or terminated, she's history. If he refuses to go along, he's gone as well. No games here. Lives hang in the balance. Scalia knows this full well and has no say in the matter.

---

The same morning finds the Sarge in his office reviewing battle plans with his men for the day's challenge. Street sweeps at a few prime narc locations are on the agenda. These are stops, jumps, and collars, with minimal legal justification that usually net remarkable results. Pasano speaks in measured terms, "Remember, we spot a group and pull up carefully. Rob, Don, and Al, go long. Me and Will do the middle. John, Jim, Rico, take the rear. Box them in and approach slow. When we toss them, our first priority is guns, then drugs. Watch their hands. Don't get led away by runners. Stay tight, no separation. Any questions?"

---

Plans for the day change in a hurry, as a male Black wearing a dark green hoodie and baggy pants is stopped by a young PD officer out front of the Three-Five. These are dangerous times. A pipe bomb blew out this entranceway only three years prior. One senior cop was blinded.

"State your business," the cop says in an official tone.

The male snaps back, "You're staring right at my business, officer. The color is green. Bring me to Lieutenant Devoe."

The young cop motions to another officer standing nearby. "Kyle, watch this one. I'm going in to see the Desk Lieutenant."

"Sure, go ahead. I got him."

The hooded man smacks his lips in impatient disgust. The young officer goes inside and behind the desk with Lt. Devoe's permission. He whispers to Devoe.

The senior Lieutenant responds, "Bring him in the 124 Room. It's empty for the moment."

"Yes, sir," the officer says and escorts the male into the clerical office.

Devoe walks in and is quick to declare safety procedures, "You armed?"

"No, I'm not! Here, this is for Pasano." He hands him a small folded note, turns, walks out and away from the building.

Devoe says to the young officer, "Watch the desk for me, I'll be right back." He walks up the stairs to the Sarge's office, taps the outside frame, steps in and palms the note to Pasano.

A young, Black male left this for you. He knew the day's color."

"Thanks, Lieu'."

Devoe leaves.

Pasano unfolds and reads the note. *Bounty's up to 250. Stay in. Too hot today. Tomorrow cooler weather.*

Pasano's office phone rings. He picks it up and ID's himself, "Sergeant Pasano."

A male caller speaks, "Yeah, Sarge, color's green, you got the message?"

"I did."

"Consider yourself notified."

Pasano's guys overhear and ask him, "What's up?"

"A warning, they're up to 250."

"Fuck it, boss," Will Fennar says. "What's the plan?"

Trying to hide his concern, the Sarge states with authority, "Stay focused. We do paperwork today. Tonight we prowl. At least we still own the night. Tomorrow, sun up, we hunt again and do our jumps."

# HELP FOR THE SICK AND A SEARCH FOR CORISA

It's a Saturday filled with sunshine. Harlem shares in the rays. It almost looks like a normal American neighborhood. Although anxiety runs through Pasano and company, this morning brings a brighter spot for Renee Jons. She's working an early shift at Harlem Hospital organizing her list of addicted men, women, children, and infants. Her social worker status allows her to reach out to those who are most affected.

There has to be a priority list. There's just too many, and not enough meds and beds. Nurses and aids cry when the daily quota is reached. The cutoff is painful. It's mothers, children, and infants first. Men here come last, depending on their disease progression. There is a common feeling that outside of veterans, many of who came back as addicts, that men caused this epidemic. Most don't even know who Carlos Giadana and the Mafia are. That's Godfather movie stuff. But, there was some truth there, 'Keep it with the dark ones.' It came to be, but the side effect was delivered to the tens of thousands of middle-class White youngsters living in the suburbs.

Just past 10 AM, Renee is summoned to the Hospital Administrator's office.

Her first thought, *'What went wrong now?'*

The truth is, what finally went right.

Longtime Administrator, Molloy Thomas, tells her the good news.

"Renee, the Mayor's rep' from the Health and Hospital Corporation called. The US Department of Health and Human Services just loosened up funds for our drug outreach expansion. It's a grant, Renee. When up and running, we'll be able to handle more than double the amount of people."

Renee is overwhelmed with the news. She sits in disbelief. With a trembling voice, she answers, "Oh my God, Molloy, we did it!"

"No, I didn't do this, Renee, you did. Apparently, you have a friend at the White House. They said something about the First Lady, whose exact words were, '*Hope this helps. See you shortly.*' Molloy is puzzled. "How the heck did you pull this off, girl?"

"I begged. I begged on behalf of the children."

"Well, it worked. Speaking of work, you're now running the whole division. This is yours, Renee. You earned it."

Renee, feeling tired, says, "I hope I have the strength."

The two stand, shake hands, and hug.

Renee cries, then silently prays. '*Thank you, Dear God. Thank you.*'

Renee leaves the hospital at noon. She's on cloud nine with the funding news and says to herself, '*People do care.*' It's a quick stop to pick up the younger girls at Mrs. James' apartment and give explicit instructions to Cavon to watch his sisters while she leaves on her own personal mission.

She's canvassing all the old drug haunts for Corisa. Renee, the ever-caring woman, thinks of everyone, especially the poorest and sickest. In her mind, Corisa easily tops that list. Most of the 'shooting galleries' are closed up thanks to Pasano and his wrecking crew.

The last surviving addicts have crammed themselves into a couple of the remaining abandoned buildings that have yet to be sealed. Conditions inside are worse than they've ever been. A solid 'H' fix has become harder to find. Outsiders, particularly suburban, White buyers, have diminished. This is good for the overall war on drugs, however, for the leftovers, the true Harlem 'fiends,' it means no 'hits,' which usually transforms into a slow death if not treated properly. Rotting bodies are discovered day and night. It's the end of days for this neighborhood. The dark before dawn is a sad vista of this disregarded society.

Hope is near, but there's a lot of work yet to be accomplished. Renee and Pasano realize this. She is the giver, and now her goal is to physically search these dilapidated buildings for as many living addicts as she can find and transport them to her hospital facility. Renee believes if she can save Corisa, the worst of them, then her legacy base will be set. Two hours of searching prove negative.

Unfortunately, there are others searching for Corisa. Two on that list are Tyler Jamol and Ray Potek, the 'Black Sunday' dealers who are barely surviving on minimal street sales. Their desire to find Corisa extends to a different level. 'Black Sunday' is the last hope for their overseer, Vic Ferris, who has been threatened with replacement by Giadana's first lieutenant.

The plan is to make a huge push by flooding the market with a fresh supply of a super strain of undiluted 'H' by using the pending shipment into the Fulton Fish Market. There's talk of price reduction which goes against all principles of the narcotics business. The decision by Seteola, Inzarita, and Giadana, is to lower the price and spread the distribution outside Harlem to other parts of New York City and into the surrounding suburbs. Middle and upper-class Whites have more money with less in-fighting. Why let them come to Harlem? Start in Harlem and deliver directly out to them. White dealers and overseers will be recruited, and a whole new network will open up.

The Narc Task Force and DEA are well aware of the capo's agenda despite Nick Scalia's limited access to inside info because of the mob's suspicion of his police connection. But, he's gathering enough for law enforcement to counter with their own plans. Pasano has a strategy of his own but will go along with the established method of law enforcement. His personal goal, however, is to kill all those connected with the drug trade before it's too late.

Renee is exhausted after driving and walking over thirty blocks and three avenues in her search for Corisa. She questions dozens of still existing addicts. Now she's worried about the safety of this young woman.

Jamol and Potek have a better network with which to locate someone. They are part of the underworld. They find Corisa tending to Gina and a few of the remaining addicts in a candle-lit room. The two overtake Corisa from behind. One yokes her by her neck and the other jams the splintered handle of a coal shovel into her rib cage. There are bone-breaking sounds as the young woman collapses to the floor. Her face falls in old piles of defecation. It mixes with her blood.

The sick junkies observe and scatter with hardly a whisper except for Gina, who intervenes, lunging forward attempting to tackle Potek, who grabs her throat and body slams her against the plaster wall. The youngster slides down but remains conscious. Jamol swings the metal end of the shovel, smacking her across the side of the face. She's dazed but manages to crawl to her mattress, collapsing face down.

Corisa is dragged by her hair to another room and now belongs to 'Black Sunday.' A payback ritual for what Pasano had done to these two is just about to begin.

Potek rolls her over and yells in her face, "Junkie bitch, where's your boyfriend, Pasano, now?"

Jamol stomps her head into the floor. Full loads of undiluted 'H' are injected up and down her arms and neck. She's unconscious. If she awakens, she'll receive more. One of the junkies, an old man who knows and was helped by Renee, hobbles out of the building. Renee is slowly driving down the street looking into each abandoned structure. The old addict spots Renee and flags her down. She pulls over and exits the car. He looks back over his shoulder and up and down the street to make sure no one sees him talking to her.

He blurts, "They have Corisa upstairs, third floor, 3C. They're killing her!"

Renee's face goes sullen. She paces up and back on the crumbled concrete sidewalk in front of the building. A traffic control cop, Cal Gifil, driving solo after finishing his tour at a school crossing, is coming down the street on his way back to the station house.

Renee flags him down and runs to him. "Please, it's an emergency."

She explains the circumstances. The cop, like all Three-Five men and women, knows Renee.

He quickly responds, "Yes, ma'am. I'll call Sergeant Pasano."

The Sarge is at the lower end of the precinct, gathering up the remaining addicts, the residuals of the team's narc enforcement efforts, when he hears the radio transmission. Four units with team members on board, respond in less than a minute. Blocks before, the lights and sirens are turned off as not to alert the perps. It's a screeching, sliding halt five buildings ahead of the target. Renee is standing by in front, visually upset. The eight are vested-up with guns drawn, and exit their 'unmarks.'

The traffic officer quickly approaches and relays the info. "I didn't want to go up without backup, Sarge. Apartment 3-C, assault on a female."

Pasano, assures him. "You did right."

Across the street on a rooftop, five stories up overlooking the activity below, the wanted 'gun bull,' Jerod Spunel, acting on planned vengeance and the two hundred fifty thousand dollar open contract for Pasano's death, peers over a broken cement ledge. He's looking down through the scope of a .30-06 rifle. With hatred and money on his mind, he grips the weapon tightly and jams it against his right shoulder as he sites in the forehead of the Sarge. Pasano is just about to give orders to his guys when Spunel begins squeezing off multiple, quick-fire rounds in a final act of retribution. Loud, crisp rifle shots ring out as the armor piercing bullets spin their way down onto the street in a millisecond, missing Pasano and his crew by inches. They ricochet off the old brick and mortar building facades. The guys jump from the street into the building. On his way, Pasano grabs Renee by her jacket and pulls her inside.

He hollers to her, "Stay down!"

Frantically, the team scans the rooftops and upper floor windows for the source of the gunfire. More shots ring out, but none from the second volley come towards them.

Pasano immediately transmits, "Central, Three-Five Narc Sarge, be advised, we have sniper fire from above at 154 and St. Nick. Send no units onto the location. That's no units directly to the location. Unknown shooter, exact location, or direction of flight. Be advised, Black undercovers on the scene."

Central rattles off, "10-4. Be advised all units 10-85 forthwith, shots fired, 154 and St. Nick. All units enter at perimeter only and use caution. Unknown shooter, unknown direction. Narcotics on the scene conducting operations. All units be alert to the day's color."

Pasano, advising, "Central, we'll be inside at the location and on adjacent rooftops for a perp search."

"Central, 10-4."

Pasano begins issuing orders, "John, Jim, do the rooftop search across the street. Rico and Al, search the lower level. Rob, you and Don stay down here and cover them. Watch the rooftops and upper windows. Make sure they get across safely. Will, me and you head upstairs and finish what we started. Renee, stay out of the way against the wall. Cal, you stay with her."

Potek and Jamol are upstairs and hear the commotion.

Potek rants, "Those fucking cops are dead-meat, man! Give that cunt some more 'juice!' "

Sarge and Fennar walk quietly and slowly up to the third floor. Apartment 3C is the target. With one on each side of the door, the two Raiders are at the ready. Pasano motions to his teammate and kicks the door in. Half the frame goes with it. Corisa lies tied up hog-style, bleeding, mouth gagged, and semiconscious. The lethal heroin shots are lingering.

The two dealers begin pulling their semi-autos. They're too slow. It's quick. Within a couple of seconds, the two cops find their marks. The gunshots echo throughout the street. Jamol and Potek are down. Both are moaning, rolling, and bleeding out from neck and chest wounds. Their guns are removed. Pasano wastes no time. He scoops up Corisa and carries her down the broken stairway. Fennar follows behind. He and Will pass their teammates on the first floor.

Pasano tells his guys, "Cover us."

He says to the traffic officer, "Cal, let's go to your car."

Turning around to Sels and McTerren, he shouts, "Go upstairs and finish it!"

The former special forces duo nods in the affirmative and hustles up the steps.

Renee overhears the direct order given and speaks in angst, "Paul, no. Please!"

Pasano carries Corisa in his arms, her head, arms, and legs dangle lifelessly. As he passes Renee, he murmurs, "I should have taken care of them a long time ago. Today it's done."

Two more shots ring out from the upstairs apartment. Renee puts both her hands over her mouth in shock. This is a new side of her friend. This is Harlem narcotics enforcement. This is war against organized crime.

Cal pulls his marked RMP up in front and Pasano slides Corisa in the back seat. He tells Renee to get in the back and go to the hospital with her. This personalized service is usually reserved for fellow cops or children. Corisa is the exception. Cal drives, lights and sirens, to Harlem Hospital. The shooting scene is flooded with backups.

Investigators and upper brass will trickle in. The medical examiner is a late show-up before the bodies are removed. Witnesses—none.

## CHAPTER 38

# LOST CHILD

For a moment, the scene turns quiet. Then come loud female screams and sobbing from the adjacent empty lot. Pasano and Will run out and around the building to investigate. Before them is a woman kneeling over the body of a little girl in a white dress. It's Monica, the lollipop girl. Sorrow fills the air. The child has been shot through her chest by a massive bullet. She lies lifeless. Pasano attempts to stop the bleeding, while Will transmits on the radio for an ambulance.

Pasano picks up the little one and instructs Will, "Bring the car over. We'll take her."

While he's waiting with the child in his arms, the old addict who flagged down Renee, walks over to Paul and whispers, "There were three. Two upstairs and a third one, Spunel, left the building before you came."

Paul thanks the old man, and just moments later, he and Will escort the mother and child to the hospital.

The Sarge delivers an emergency message, "Central, be advised we have a mother and a shot child en route to Harlem Hospital. Alert the ER. We'll be there in two minutes."

"10-4, Sarge. Alerting them now."

---

Renee is at the emergency room standing outside in a waiting area. A team of doctors and nurses work to x-ray, patch up, clean and detox a broken young lady. When asked for personal info about her, Renee tells them, "Corisa is all I know. She lives on the streets and in abandoned buildings. She is a user."

An unmarked car, lights and sirens blaring, pulls up in front of the ER. Pasano carries out Monica and places her on a waiting gurney with a doc' and two nurses standing by. The child whisked into the ER. Renee sees and hears the commotion. She spots Pasano and Will Fennar. She sees the lifeless girl and senses the anguish.

It's quiet in the waiting area, but behind the glass, two blood-soaked gurneys lie side-by-side separated by a curtain. Two medical teams work feverishly to save two lives. There are long moments of silence interrupted by the sounds of a crying mother who has just been told her little girl is deceased. Renee and Paul walk over to the young woman, hoping to console her.

A sympathetic Pasano tells her, "I am so sorry."

Moments later, a doctor informs them that Corisa is critical but should recover.

Renee is overwhelmed with the unfolding tragedy but still shocked over Pasano's actions at the shooting scene. She was disconcerted by his team members' use of deadly force.

Renee speaks in a hushed voice. "Paul, why?"

"Why what?"

"Why did you and your men have to do that. Take two people's lives. Just shooting them the first time wasn't enough? You had to send your officers back up again?"

The Sarge takes Renee off to the side. "First of all, you didn't belong there. I let those 'Black Sunday' dealers live the first time they attacked Corisa. That was my fault. So what did they go and do? They did it again. This time, worse. Look into that room. Look at Corisa in there.

If she lives, ask her how she feels. Ask her if she would question what I did. Then go ask the mother of that little girl. So please, don't be surprised at my actions. It's what I do. It comes with the job. I let them live, they recover. They go through the system, make bail, and disappear. Then they go after our families, killing them. Our children, Renee. So don't feel sorry for them. The two low-life dealers are eliminated."

The Sarge continues. "Listen, you stay with Corisa if you wish. I have to get back to the shooting scene. I've got a hundred questions to answer and mounds of paperwork to complete. And congratulations. I heard about your new position and the funds coming your way for the narc rehab center. It'll be good. You know where to find me."

Pasano starts to walk away. Renee grabs his arm and puts her face close to his.

Tears fall from her as she whispers, "I'm just so tired, Paul. Tired of all the hurt, all the killing. I'm sorry."

"Hey, don't quit on me now," an exhausted Sarge tells her. "We're almost there." He grabs her arm in return.

Both loosen their grip. Sergeant Pasano tries to wipe Corisa's and the little girl's blood from his clothes, unsuccessfully. Police work is ugly.

The shooting scene is swamped with bluecoats and upper bosses. A lot of the old brass hasn't been to Harlem in decades. They're visibly uncomfortable and shaken by the mess left behind by the 'Narcs.'

Pasano arrives back on location. He's immediately approached by one of the PC's puppets. "Where were you? You left an active crime scene. A shooting in which you were involved."

Pasano snaps back, "I was at Harlem Hospital saving lives. The dead perps upstairs were not going anywhere. My concern is with the living, not the dead. Besides the woman who was taken to the hospital, I had to take a seriously wounded child there as well."

The boss continues his admonishment. "Shake the fucking attitude, Pasano. If you fucked-up here, you're done."

"Those words have a familiar ring to it, Chief. But all that aside, this isn't as complicated as it seems. Capo Carlos Giadana's flunkies tried to set us up for a hit. They lured us on to West 154th Street by kidnapping and assaulting a young female addict well known on the streets. Two armed perps had her concealed within a 'shooting gallery' inside this abandoned building. We were alerted by community activist, Ms. Renee Jons, and traffic officer, Cal Gifil.

"My team responded with lights and sirens and were met by a sniper on that rooftop across the street who fired two volleys of multiple rounds, probably from a scoped rifle. The first volley was targeted at us, missing its mark. The second went astray. I alerted Central and all responding units of the condition. I sent some of my guys to search that building across the street. I went upstairs with Officer Fennar to overtake the perps holding the female. We entered the apartment and they reached for their semi-autos. We had to use deadly force, shooting the two perps. I carried the injured female down and sent her to Harlem Hospital with Officer Cal Gifil. We were then alerted by the mother of an eight-year-old girl who was struck by that second volley of rifle fire. The child was struck in her chest by at least one round. Me and Officer Fennar brought her to the ER. Those on the scene with responding backup from Emergency Service, led by Captain Powers of ESU, searched for the sniper with negative results. The young female might survive. The child is dead. Story done. I'll put it all on paper for you, Chief."

"You always have the answers, Sergeant, don't you? One day you'll step on your dick, I'm sure of it."

Pasano says with attitude, "Hey, Chief. I'm Italian. I've done that many times already. And I wouldn't stand too close to me, boss. They're trying to kill me, you know. Bounty's up to '250 large,' " as he slowly glances up at the rooftops. It takes about two or three seconds. When he looks back, the old Chief is gone.

The Sarge hollers to his guys, "C'mon, let's clean up. Help them get those two pieces of trash upstairs out of here, and do another toss for Spunel."

The Raiders are physically exhausted and mentally drained. Every shooting incident brings hours of investigation and pounds of paperwork, this one in particular. If the perps are DOA, Grand Jury testimony may still be required. The firearms control board takes the lead when it comes to justification of deadly force. IAD follows suit. It's never-ending, especially when multiple incidents are involved and unauthorized weapons used. It's a tap dance.

Pasano's guys are good, not only on the street but also when it comes to testifying. This leads to frustration by the Downtown brass, who on one hand wants to hang the team out to dry, but on the other, has to answer to the PC and Mayor's office when it comes to the war on narcotics and organized crime. Ultimately, the powers-to-be want the 'Narcs' to stay put and finish their campaign. Their tactics are certainly not condoned, but their results are remarkable.

––––––––––

After a two-hour search for Spunel, the rooftop sniper, Pasano and guys meet later that evening in his office. They sweep the room for bugging devices, in, under, and on old metal cabinets, desks, and shelves. Ceiling tiles, especially the cracked ones, are pushed up and inspected, and bulletin boards removed and rehung. The unit uses different tactics, and the NYPD does the same. Info is kept tight. Stories must jive. Paperwork and subsequent interviews have to align. Sunday will be a day of rest for his guys, but not for the Sarge.

––––––––––

It's a fast trip back to Long Island for Paul to spend some non-quality sleep time with Rachel. As he enters his driveway, he notices a Suffolk

County cop car parked out front. It's a quick wave of acknowledgment as he pulls in. SCPD is doing a good job of giving special attention to his family. There is little explanation at home, only another load of bloodstained clothes and an apology to his wife.

With their six-year-old daughter, Linda, fast asleep, Sarge and Rachel share a midnight dinner. She's afraid to put forth any verbal resistance to whatever her husband has to say.

She proceeds carefully, "Paul, are you okay? There are so many things they are saying about the violence in Harlem."

"I know. But I'm fine."

A more serious Rachel continues, "I worry about you and our family. I don't want to lose you. I need you to help me with Linda and especially, Andrew. You haven't been to the rehab center in days. I look into his eyes and I see emptiness. When I say the word, 'daddy,' his face brightens. Dr. Talbert says that's a good sign. Your son needs attention from you."

Paul, running tight, raises his voice and unwinds. "Don't you think I know that, Rachel? Why do you think I'm doing all this? It's for Andrew."

Rachel counters, "It won't cure him. All the violence will not return our boy to us."

"Rachel, please, this is all I have left. Making the people responsible pay."

"Paul, it's not all you have. You have us."

Pasano gets up and walks over to the other side of the kitchen table, and hugs his wife who just doesn't understand. Nobody understands, especially the NYPD.

"Let me try to get some rest. I'm going in for just a couple of hours in the morning. Some paperwork and a stop at Harlem Hospital. I'll be back before noon, and we can go together to see Andrew. Is that okay?"

"Yes, I love you."

"And I love you. Please be patient, Rachel. Have faith in me. I will resolve this."

Paul puts his arm around Rachel, and they head for Linda's room first. They glance inside, pause for a moment, and then walk to their bedroom.

## CHAPTER 39

# HOSPITAL VISIT

It's just past 8 AM, and Pasano is already at Harlem Hospital. Corisa has been moved to a private room, thanks to Renee's influence. Most of the machinery and tubes have been removed. She's awake and being served some soft food and liquids by an older, Black female nurse. Corisa's entire face is bruised and swollen, one eye partially opened and bloodied, the other completely shut. Her ribs are taped and bandaged, and her arms and neck are dotted with a colored antiseptic liquid covering the needle puncture wounds delivered by Potek and Jamol. Her heroin detox is apparently working. After observing for a few moments, Pasano taps on the doorframe and asks permission from the nurse to enter.

The soft-spoken nurse leans over to Corisa. "There's someone here to see you, dear. I won't forget about that teenager you asked about."

Corisa turns her head towards the doorway, sees the Sarge, gives a depressed look, but nods in the affirmative.

The nurse touches Corisa's hand gently and smiles at her. "I'll be right outside, honey."

Pasano enters and begins some light banter, "Hey, kiddo, you look good."

Corisa forces a slight smile. "Yeah, right."

Pasano ensues. "You're making a habit of this now. That's twice I saved your butt."

"I didn't ask you to."

"Regardless, this time I had to carry you down three flights of stairs. Maybe on this liquid diet, you'll shake a few pounds."

"Fuck you, Pasano!"

The senior nurse overhears and calls from the doorway, "Sir, can I see you over here for a second?"

Pasano turns and walks over to her. "What's up?"

Spewing anger, she states, "I know you. You're Sergeant Pasano from the Three-Five. Well, let me tell you something, officer. This girl has been severely traumatized. When you talk to her, you keep a civil tongue in your mouth. You hear me?"

The Sarge is taken aback. Nobody in his thirty plus years has ever talked to him that way and remained standing. Either they were knocked or shot down.

Pasano, replies, "Yes, ma'am."

The nurse turns and walks away.

Paul walks back to Corisa, who almost gives a full smile and quips sarcastically, "What's the matter, Sarge, you afraid of a woman?"

"That one—yes. You—no."

"Shit, you think you're all that, Pasano."

"Listen, the two guys who roughed you up a couple of times, Potek and Jamol, well they won't bother you anymore."

Corisa's partially opened eye wells up, and in a whisper, she says, "Thank you."

A few moments later, Renee arrives, carrying two boxes.

"Hey guys, how's the patient?"

"Good morning, Renee. You got Corisa a great room. I'll leave you two to hang out. I have to get back to the Three-Five."

He looks down at Corisa and says, "You take it easy, girlie."

Just as Paul gets ready to leave, Corisa reaches out, grabs his arm, and squeezes it tight. Pasano is puzzled. He stares at her. She turns her face to the side into the pillow. Pasano pauses again but turns and leaves. Renee sees the exchange but says nothing. She walks over to Corisa bearing gifts.

"How are you feeling, young lady?"

Corisa looks up at Renee and wipes tears from her cheek.

With compassion, Renee remarks, "I understand this is a rough time for you sweetheart, but you will get through it."

Corisa answers in a cracking voice, "I know."

"I have something here for you," Renee goes on. "The President's wife is coming to my Harlem community meeting. I want you there also. It's two weeks away. I'm sure you'll be up and out of here by then. They're also going to get decent housing for you outside the neighborhood. This will help you to get back on your feet and attend the outreach treatment program."

Corisa doesn't respond.

Renee begins opening the two white gift boxes and continues, "I want you to wear this green dress, which goes with your eyes, and these shoes. They're Olivia's. I want to show you off, Corisa. I want them all to see how you fought, survived, and are getting help."

Corisa responds quietly, "Thank you, but I don't think it's my place. Nobody wants to see someone like me."

"Yes they do," Renee says assuredly. "You're a beautiful young woman who has a whole, wonderful life ahead of her."

Corisa, speaking again in a broken voice, "I might have to leave. My cousin said I can stay with her for a while in South Carolina. She's going to come up and drive me down."

"That's good news, dear, but maybe you can go down South after the meeting. Wouldn't that be something for your cousin to see, the First Lady of America?"

"Yeah, I guess it would. We'll see, Renee, we'll see."

The nurse taps on the door frame and walks in. "Okay, visiting hours are over, folks."

Corisa turns to Renee. "Thanks for coming and the presents."

Renee leans over and kisses her lightly on the forehead, and as she leaves, says, "I'll come visit again."

The nurse hesitates then steps closer, picks up a visitor's chair and sits alongside Corisa. She affectionately holds her hand, and in a sympathetic tone, parts with carefully guarded words. "Sweetheart, you were asking about Gina, the girl you were with when you got hurt."

"Yes, is she okay?"

As she squeezes Corisa's hand tighter, she tells her, "I'm so sorry, honey, but she was brought in by ambulance early this morning—deceased."

"Oh my God, no." Corisa begins to sob uncontrollably, turning her face into the pillow.

In a voice just above a whisper, the nurse says, "She must have been a good friend."

Through her tears, Corisa forces out her words, "She was my baby sister."

The nurse remains silent. She stoops over Corisa, wraps her arms around her, and hugs her patient.

"I'm sure your sister knew you loved her."

"She didn't know I was her sister. I left home when she was little and could never tell her the truth."

Tearing up, the elder nurse attempts to bring closure. "God has already explained everything to her. Now let's get you some rest, okay, honey?"

"Yes, ma'am."

## CHAPTER 40

# SUICIDE AND BACKLASH

Pasano heads down West 145th Street to his precinct. As he enters the block, he comes to a stop. Traffic is backed up. Ahead of the line of cars are five RMPs with lights spinning and flickering. Two ambulances are parked out front with their flashers on.

Paul mutters to himself, *'What the fuck happened now?'*

He pulls his car onto the sidewalk and trots down to the station house.

He's met outside by Lt. Devoe who puts his hand up to stop him. "Paul, listen, Cal Gifil is down in the basement in front of his locker. He's dead. Suicide. Ate his gun. He left a note apologizing to you and all the guys. He said he didn't mean for anybody to get hurt. Apparently, Giadana got to him. Cal took a few dollars to pay for his wife's cancer treatments. The day of the shooting, he was waiting on the street to call you onto the block to set you up for a hit. It's bad Paul, real bad. Don't let those cheese-eating bosses inside get to you. You did your job. You did good. Keep pushing ahead. Understand me, son?"

Pasano's lost for words but recoups. "Yeah, boss. Thanks."

He heads into the Three-Five and is greeted by a red-faced CO, Inspector Deteo, surrounded by an army of 'suits' and brass from Downtown.

Deteo commands, "In my office, Sarge."

"Yes, sir."

The two are followed in by the higher-ups.

Pasano and the others sit in vinyl chairs. The Chief sits behind the CO's large metal desk and begins. "Short story, Sergeant Pasano. You and your guys will be off patrol for a few days. You'll be assigned Downtown to the Chief of Detectives' office during the pending investigation starting first thing in the morning. Call your guys and make the formal notifications. IAD has to give this a long look, Sergeant. Understand me?"

"Yes, sir."

The Chief commands, "You're dismissed."

Paul turns and walks out, dumbfounded.

He hears one of the bosses say, "Send a car to Officer Gifil's house to inform his family of his death. Keep it clean. Careful with the children. Not a word to the media until his family is notified. Understand?"

Inspector Deteo replies, "Yes, sir."

The Chief, dictating policy, says, "Keep it general. Investigation pending. Cast a net. If no one else is involved, end it. It'll just be a suicide by a distraught officer over his wife's illness. It stays within the NYPD. I want this whole thing in writing within two hours so I can present it to the Commissioner."

Deteo responds respectfully, "Yes, Chief."

"And find out about his wife's medical care. The Patrolman's Benevolent Association will make sure it gets taken care of. Also, call Officer Gifil's union rep."

All other bosses respond in unison, "Yes, sir."

Pasano is back in his office and makes a round of phone calls. The first is to Rachel. It's another apology. This Sunday, the day he promised to spend with his family, is not going to happen. Rachel, once again, has to bear the burden of Andrew alone.

He calls his team members explaining what has transpired. They take it hard. It makes their mission, which is near completion, more difficult.

Monday morning the Raiders are off the streets. With two ringleaders out, a big chunk of 'Black Sunday' has been removed. Score one for law enforcement. The team off the streets, point - Giadana.

---

There's an immediate and fierce reaction to the murder of seven-year-old Monica Taylor. The media brings attention to Pasano's team, the work they're doing, and the alleged corruption in the Three-Five. This type of attention is not wanted by the Sarge. Investigators will only get in his way.

---

There is fallout amongst the mobsters. At a dinner table in the East Harlem Italian restaurant, Nick Scalia is breaking bread with Carlos Giadana, his first lieutenant Tiafona, and two underlings. The family head is pissed off at Scalia for his improper handling and control of one of the most vicious drug enforcers, Jerod Spunel.

The fire-faced Giadana is opening up on him, "Do you watch the news and read the newspapers? They'll be bringing in the fucking Feds again. This one is on your turf. He's one of yours. He's stupido! He kills a child instead of Pasano. We don't need this. Do you understand?" He points a bent finger at Scalia sitting across the table. "Handle this and pronto!"

Scalia nods in agreement. The obviously perplexed undercover is caught in the middle. Disappear and kill the operation, or fulfill Giadana's orders and eliminate Spunel.

---

Scalia is not the only one caught in the middle over the serious blunder committed by Jerod Spunel. Pasano and his guys are down at One Police Plaza, NYPD's Headquarters, to answer questions delivered by a series of investigative units.

The Patrolmen's Benevolent Association and the Sergeants Benevolent Association attorneys are walking side-by-side with the 'Narcs.' The team is in uniform as required during internal investigations. The Sergeant's attorney tries to lighten the mood. "Hey, guys, doesn't it seem like we were just here?"

The PBA rep chimes in, "You people should think about renting a room in this building. It would certainly shorten your travel time."

Pasano cuts in on the conversation, "Glad you guys are having fun. If we wind up getting shit-canned, you guys will be out of a job."

In a small conference room, Internal Affairs Chief Felicer lays out the objectives of the probe to the department's upper echelon and a team of investigators. "I want to know the depth of the payoffs that went to officer Cal Gifil. Did it go beyond him to other members of the department, the Three-Five, or Pasano's team? The Police Commissioner and Mayor are demanding a completed preliminary investigation within 72 hours." Felicer, the team's nemesis, forces out the next stream of words, "If there's not enough evidence to pull Pasano's unit, we'll let them get back to work. Agreed?"

The bosses in the room sound off in the affirmative.

For two days, the Raiders are sequestered at Headquarters with their attorneys, going over allegations and evidence that ultimately led to the suicide of the rogue cop. One-on-one interrogations are conducted with each of the members, including Pasano.

On day three, the IA Captain, who did most of the grunt work, looks down at his notes and explains the results of his investigation. "There is nothing on the Raiders beyond Cal Gifil, a traffic officer, acting on his own, being enticed by Giadana's first lieutenant, Vito Tiafona. It started small; some free dinners, drinks, and show tickets to overlook some parking indiscretions around the mobsters' club in lower East Harlem. Some weird friendships were born when Gifil's wife became ill and his family was buried in medical bills. The young officer found himself trapped. Small talk progressed to an offer to help defray the costs. Once hooked, threats of exposure followed if Gifil didn't go along. Finally, a one-time offer was made. Distract Pasano from his narc operations, and he'd be a free man with more than enough cash to care for his ailing wife and quit the job.

"The Commissioner refuses to have Gifil's wife interviewed by IAD." The Captain pauses….. "Bottom line, I'm recommending an end to this inquiry and an additional recommendation that Sergeant Pasano and his Narc Task Force members resume their regular duties."

Sitting across the table, his IA boss, Chief Felicer, gulps for a breath. His disdain for Pasano has never been a secret as he spews anger, "Despite the results of this inquiry, I still believe the Sergeant's participation in the demise of the Mafioso runs astray of sound police principles and rules and regulations maintained by the Department." Thinking to himself, *'I swear Pasano and his men are working outside the law.'*

The CO of the Organized Crime Control Bureau, Chief Eric Stein, being of equal rank as Felicer and with more job tenure, counters as he looks over at the Manhattan Borough Commander, Chief of Detectives, and the PC's Deputy Commissioner, who will render the final decision.

"First of all, I talk with my people every day. I've also been on the phone daily with the DEA to monitor the progress. They report to me that Sergeant Pasano and his unit working with the associated Agencies, including community leader, Renee Jons, have done more to dismantle and destroy the Giadana cartel than any weapon we can put forth.

"Secondly, it has been made clear to me and to the Mayor's office, that the removal of Sergeant Pasano would overturn years of work that everyone, including his team, has put in. This includes his ten thousand arrests. It is my opinion that we stop wasting time and get this Sergeant back uptown where he belongs, doing what he does best, locking up drug dealers and murderers. If they resist, he uses necessary force. So be it.

"I tell you now, if you lose this cop, we're done. You will never find anyone who can replace him and do what nobody here even thinks about, let alone going out with a handful of men and actually doing it. Now, here's a copy of what has transpired to date in these folders." He drops two large file boxes onto the table. "It's over 5000 pages of narc enforcement tactics and achievements since this war in Harlem has begun. At your leisure, please read it.

"If you have any questions, I'll be in my office on the 5th floor of this building. If you do not believe what I'm telling you, or if you want to misrepresent what I talked about here today to the Commissioner, fine. Because after this is over, I'm pulling the pin. Thirty-five years of working with people like you have been more than enough. Have a good morning, gentlemen."

All the brass gathered are red-faced. IAD Chief Felicer grinds his teeth.

Chief Stein gets up and walks out of the large room, leaving behind embarrassed brass pawns. As he leaves, he notices a row of cops in uniform sitting on a long, wooden bench just outside. He observes the serious and drawn look of exhaustion on their faces. He catches a glimpse of the racks of medals above their shields and Pasano's name tag. These are the Harlem Raiders.

He barks a direct order towards them, "Stand up, gentlemen."

The team of Black, White, and Hispanic cops jumps to their feet.

"I'm Chief Stein from OCCB. You guys have been working with my people over the past couple of years. I've never met you personally, but I wanted to congratulate and thank you for what you have accomplished under trying circumstances."

The Chief shakes their hands one at a time, starting with Rico Lorez, and moving up the line to the Sarge, where he pauses and grips both his hands around Paul's one.

"I know what you have sacrificed; your family and your comrades. You have the admiration from this old cop. Go finish what we started and don't make a liar out of me."

"Yes, sir."

The Chief walks down the hallway to the elevator, pushes a button and leaves. The guys look left and right at each other in silence. Another Chief comes out and tells Pasano to come in. The Sarge stands before the brass.

The PC's Deputy Commissioner sums up, "Sergeant, we just heard from Chief Stein who swears by what you're doing. That's enough for me. Go back to work and stay safe. You're dismissed."

"Yes, sir."

Sarge walks out and gathers with his men.

Paul, with a stunned look on his face, shrugs his shoulders and quietly says, "We're back to work forthwith."

The 'Narcs' smile in relief.

The PBA and SBA lawyers, standing by, look at each other.

The SBA rep remarks, "You fucking kidding me or what?"

The PBA rep responds in kind, "You know they'll be watching you, right guys? If Felicer can't get you removed, he may just shoot you!"

When everyone leaves the conference room, an angered IAD Chief Felicer and his assistant remain.

The Chief orders, "I want them all tailed, phones tapped, on and off duty."

"Yes, Sir," the Captain answers.

## CHAPTER 41

# ANGEL TO REST—MORE REVENGE

A better night's sleep for the team. The next morning, there's a funeral mass for Monica Taylor, age seven, the youngest victim of the Harlem drug wars. The intimate church with vaulted ceilings and stained glass windows is overcrowded with hundreds of local community residents, political dignitaries, and police officials. Pasano and his team are present, dressed in uniform with white gloves. There is open weeping by many.

Father Ingal speaks from the pulpit, "It is a sad day in Harlem. It is a sad day in American history. We have lost an angel on earth. The Lord said, *Blessed are the children for the kingdom of heaven is theirs.* On this day, it is Monica's."

Hundreds of people pass by and put roses on the tiny, white casket in front of the altar. As Pasano passes the casket, with one hand he places a single rose, but with a lollipop attached. The other hand is a tightly clenched fist.

---

The unit is back at the Three-Five following the church service changing out of their uniforms. They're done for the day but hold a team meeting down in the basement coffee room. It's a dusty, unpainted room, damp and cold. Most of the guys don't bother with it. That's fine with Pasano, who has things to tell his guys that are not shareable with non-team members.

Sarge is dictating some policy to the Raiders.

He speaks quietly, yet with an autocratic tone, "Look, this prick, Spunel, aside from shooting a few 35th Precinct cops, he tried to kill us and murdered an innocent child in cold blood. And God knows who else he killed or injured. We can't let this go. We find Spunel and we kill him. No questions asked. We've got no time for court, trials, or Homicide Detectives tracking him down.

"Spunel knows he fucked-up and is being hunted. He's backed into a corner. If we don't get to him first, he'll come after us, or I should say, me. That will be his only redemption with Giadana. It's easy. If I'm dead, he lives. Now, if anyone wants out, just say so."

The small group nods without hesitation.

Will Fennar, concurs, "We're with you, boss."

"Okay. Listen up. We go about our business as usual. Put the word out to your non-reg' informants. Everyone we 'collar' gets grilled. It'll be cash up, even if we have to use our slush fund. Someone out there knows where this fuck is holed up."

Ten days later, Jimmy Kellig gets a hit and the plan gets launched. Pasano's Raiders gather in one of the precinct's darkened basement hallways.

Paul lays out the plan, muffling his voice, "We go tonight. One of Jim's CI's is meeting us in Queens on Jamaica Avenue. He's got word that Spunel has been laying low for a few days. We use our own cars and meet up at 160th Street and Broadway at midnight."

The informal meeting comes to an end. Pasano huddles up with JK, alone. "Did your guy make the call?"

"He did, boss. He put a phony IAD complaint against us for tonight. He told them he heard we're meeting up with some of Giadana's guys to accept some 'bread' down on the Lower East Side at the Seaport."

"Good. That should occupy Internal Affairs for a few hours while we work. You know, we only have one shot at this, right?"

"Got it, boss."

"See you tonight," Sarge reaffirms.

---

There's a light drizzle, 1 AM, on 166th Street and Jamaica Avenue. The Raiders meet up with Jim Kellig's CI, a 36-year-old male with a long history of drug arrests. At present, he claims to be thriving on methadone from alternating walk-in clinics. Needle marks are well hidden by long sleeve sweats. Heavy users who buy from multiple dealers know everyone in the business. They hear rumors. This tip goes beyond hearsay. He stakes his reputation as a non-registered CI in pointing to Spunel.

He's approached by Kellig who is dressed-down in druggie clothes. The two chat for a few seconds and walk over to JK's car and get in. $100 cash is transferred. A slip with an address is given in return. The CI exits the car and walks away into the darkness.

Jim pulls alongside the Sarge's car. Some quick conversation and JK leads the way, followed by five private cars. They pull up on Jamaica Avenue. The street lights are out. It's almost pitch dark. JK exits and surveys the area. The rest of the guys exit and confer. Jackets concealing bulletproof vests are zipped up tight. 9mms, .45s, and a couple of .38s are eased from their waistband holsters and tucked inside their jackets. The guys are on their own. Shields will not be shown on this trip. It's life and job threatening.

Kellig leads the way into a dimly lit and smelly hallway. The target apartment, 2nd floor, 2D.

Pasano, speaking just above a whisper, "I go up with Jim and Will. Rico and Al go up to the third-floor landing and stand by. Don, Rob, John, stay down. Nobody in or out."

Jim and Will pull their military .45s from their jackets and quick fix their silencers. Pasano does the same with his 9mm, and gestures to

Rico and Al to go up first and take their places. They climb as silently as possible on creaky steps. Will, Jim, and Sarge follow behind and peel off onto the 2nd floor.

The apartment is just a few feet from the landing. A quick glance exposes a broken door latch with candlelight glowing from inside. A TV is on low volume. The Sarge enters first, followed by his two comrades. As always, guns pointed forward, two-handed grip, they walk slowly and cautiously under the sound of the television. First, an empty, dirty, disheveled bedroom on the right, and one on the left. A few more steps and they enter the kitchen.

The gas stove is lit for heat and simmering spoonfuls of heroin. JK makes the first noteworthy observation, thumps his chest and points. The body of a forty-something male lies face down on a roach infested, cracked linoleum floor. He's sprawled out in a large puddle of old, semi-dried, dark blood. Most of it is coming from his head. Flies and maggots have already found a home.

Pasano orders, "I stay. You guys toss the rest of the apartment. No prints behind."

Within seconds, they return as the Sarge is rolling the body over. No doubt. It's Jerod Spunel meeting a fitting demise. Monica Taylor has been avenged. Two large caliber rounds delivered, one in each eye exposing two quarter sized holes the devil once looked out from. The back of his head is blown apart like a smashed pumpkin. Large pieces of scalp with hair attached and brain tissue are scattered beneath. His mouth is wide open. Pasano sees something inside. He takes his small mag light and shines it close up. He crouches over and looks inside. Jammed almost completely down his throat is a long, live, .30-06 round. In the corner, standing against the rusty fridge, is the scoped rifle used in the sniper attack on the team and the murder of Monica Taylor.

Paul says to his guys, "Fuck him," and rolls him back over to his original position. "This is not our work. Giadana beat us to it. He's not going anywhere. We don't belong here. I'll have an anonymous dime dropped in the morning. Go up and get Al and Rico. Head out two at a time. Leave well apart. Go home. Tomorrow we resume at the Three-Five, 0800 hours."

Jim Kellig and Sarge are last to leave.

Paul grabs JK's arm. "Jimmy, thanks, bud. You did well. Make sure you thank your CI. He was right on the mark."

Jim Kellig detaches his silencer, pockets it, and holsters his .45 as he responds, "Hey boss, this was no big deal. One big team, right?" He grins and walks away.

Paul remains for a few seconds, thinking to himself and hoping this wasn't Jim's work. It won't be mentioned again as the Sarge knows, he himself, is the poster child for unmitigated violence.

---

The sun hasn't come up yet. With three hours rest, Pasano is on his way in and takes a detour as he passes through Queens. He pulls up in front of a beverage house off Queens Boulevard. It's an old, refurbished warehouse with faded paint. It looks worthless, but people apparently make a living here. The employees haven't shown up yet, but the owner is in his office. Paul enters through a broken side door holding a couple of cups of coffee and is greeted by ex-cop, Billy McCardel.

It's cold. McCardel looks like a bum, unshaven with tattered clothes. The two came on the job together. There's a strong handshake and the traditional shoulder hug amongst fellow cops. It's been a few years, and McCardel has packed on the pounds. Idleness, depression, who knows. McCardel was dismissed from the job a couple of years back. He separated a husband and wife up in Harlem during a dispute. The drunk husband sucker punched him. Billy cold-cocked him with his blackjack. The guy dies. Bad luck. It happens. Billy's got a new career. Selling booze and soda. It's different. Paul asks a favor.

"Billy, I need a dime drop. A phone call reporting a shooting at Jamaica Avenue."

Billy responds without hesitation, "Consider it done, Paul."

---

Sitting in his office just before noon, Pasano gets a call from a Homicide Task Force Detective on the hunt for the cop shooters. "Sarge, Detective Galiss, Homicide. Listen, we were closing in on your boy, Spunel. We connected him, not only to the two SNEU cops shot up in the OP, but also the shooting of Monica Taylor, not to mention him trying to take you out. Couple that with the two 'uniforms' shot from the back of the radio car, made him a treacherous scumbag. I wish it were us, but somebody beat us to it. He was found shot, DOA, up in a Queens apartment just an hour ago. We don't know who or why and don't particularly care. So, bottom line, boss, this cop shooter's case is closed."

"That's another fuck out of the way," Paul responds. "Thanks for keeping me in the loop."

"Be safe, Sarge."

"You too."

They hang up. Paul pauses and breathes deep.

---

Word leaks back to Carlos Giadana and his first lieutenant, Vito Tiafona, about the killing of Spunel in Queens. Within minutes, Giadana arranges a meeting where he singles-out underling Nick Scalia for the hit. He's overplaying the accomplishment, trying to put a positive spin on a menial task. The Italians around the table sense it, but no one would ever question anything this Don has to offer up. Regardless, he is trying to maintain leadership amongst his subordinates.

Giadana commends Scalia, "Well done with Spunel's removal. Now, I want you to work together and remove that scumbag cop, Pasano.

Spread more dollars around. Do it locally. Find an opening and get it done."

Scalia looks around the room as all attendees nod in the affirmative over his quick takeout of the rogue bull. He accepts all the accolades but internally remains confused.

Scalia thinks to himself, *'Somebody did everybody a favor, but that somebody wasn't me.'*

Before closing out the meeting, Giadana orders his people to extend sales, "Reach out and recruit younger people to push dope around schools. Generate new business. *Capisce?*"

Once again, his associates agree, although with some reluctance. More desperation is showing.

———

There is also concern within the Palermo farmhouse. Sonny Inzarita, the man responsible for the endless supply of heroin to New York, is on the phone throwing a tantrum. He's berating his New York cousin, Carlos Giadana, for his failure to kill the cops and community meddlers who are disrupting his entire drug empire operation. "How is it you can't eliminate those people? Do I have to come to New York and do it myself? You should be ashamed. Your family's name is at stake. I have a multi-million dollar shipment pulling out from the port of Sicily heading to America. I'm counting on you to move the product."

Inzarita doesn't trust his first cousin to get the job done, so after hanging up, he curses and points to his henchmen. With a fierce look on his face, he gives orders in Italian, "Get on a plane, head to New York and meet with my cousin, and eliminate those community punks and that cop, Pasano. Finish them off, all of them! *Morte!*"

In Sicily, orders are carried out in a more dictatorial fashion as compared to that in America, especially when they come from Capo Inzarita. Failure means family banishment or death.

Within two days, the four Inzarita assassins land in New York and meet with the Giadana cartel members. They're driven by limo into an abandoned airplane hangar and given bulletproof vests and submachine guns with oversized clips. This foursome speaks no English and are known in Sicily as 'Zips.' They know little about American life, but they know how to kill. The direct descendants from the Sicilian Mafioso are an undisciplined clique who has no qualms about murdering people considered off limits by the American Mafia, such as police officers, judges, women, and children. They're known for blowing up their targets with bombs without concern for innocent bystanders. Point out the intended target, and they do the rest. Their rate of success is high.

The leader of the small group speaks a slice of Sicilian dialogue that is incoherent to people of any other region of Italy. It is a firestorm of few words delivered to Giandana's underlings by a hulk of a man with bloodshot eyes and a scarred mouth drooped on one side. "Take me on a tour. I want to see exactly where these people live and work. Then I never want to see any of you again. Me and my associates will do what has to be done and return to Palermo. Is this clear? No more talk, now we go."

This last breath of retaliation by the Sonny Inzarita enforcers is a gift to his cousin, Carlos Giadana. It's meant as a token of loyalty to a family member in time of need. In the ruthless world of organized crime, it is accomplished through the bloodletting of the member's enemy. In this case, it's to destroy Renee Jons' family and kill Paul Pasano.

## CHAPTER 42

# FEDS TRY

Pissed off Internal Affairs Chief Felicer continues his vendetta against the Raiders. He plays another angle and brings in the Feds, hoping they can do what he has been unable to do, bang Pasano and his guys on Federal Civil Rights violations.

Paul is pushing paperwork upstairs in his office, a room that contains multiple maps with stickpins denoting Harlem narc prone and murder locations. Filing cabinets contain the mounds of paperwork. The four beige walls are covered with Polaroid photos of over five thousand arrested perps organized by area. The photos are edge-to-edge. They resemble wallpaper from ceiling to floor. It is both impressive and eerie. Two Homicide Detectives are scanning the walls trying to match-up a few of the photos to a couple of their wanted murderers.

One Detective says to Pasano, "Jesus, Sarge. I've heard about you, your work, and all these photos. But now that I see this display in person, I'm friggin' standing in awe with the amount of work you guys put in. I've never seen anything like this. We just want to take a picture of a few of these and bring them back to our office for viewing by some of our witnesses."

"Fine with me, guys, help yourselves."

Two men in black suits enter the Three-Five. They stop at the main desk, standing before Lt. Cam Devoe. The towering former marine, with thirty years on the job, dressed in a white shirt with medals up to his chin, asks them to state their business. They identify themselves as FBI Agents and request to see Sergeant Pasano. He gives the okay, and they head up to his office.

The Desk Lieutenant calls Pasano. "Two Feds are on their way up to see you, Paul."

"Thank you, Lieu'."

Paul hangs up, and his face turns flushed.

'Oh fuck!' He says to himself. 'How the hell could these guys have gotten word about Spunel already? Are they here to collar me up?'

The two Detectives are snapping away picture after picture. In a couple of minutes, the two FBI Agents arrive at the office and introduce themselves before entering. They ask to speak to Pasano in private, and the detectives realize this is their cue to leave. On the way out, one of the old sleuths grabs Pasano by his arm and whispers in his ear, "Be cautious with these two."

The Agents congratulate Pasano on his team's accomplishments. Within thirty seconds, the conversation turns to questions about some of the more violent arrests and the shooting of the innocent bystander, the young woman, Tamerine Jonasin. Pasano realizes he's in the midst of a Fed investigation without warning and no reps'. This isn't going to fly. One of the Agents, clean-cut, tall, donning a well-cut suit, gets to the 'meat' of it. "So, Sarge, we'd like to go down this list of about ten arrests. Go over them and check your tactics, ya' know, to make sure all your ducks are in a row and everything is on the up-and-up, which I'm sure it is."

The now well-seasoned street Sergeant cuts them off. "Okay, guys, I see where we're headed here. Let's cut to the chase. File your paperwork with the NYPD's Internal Affairs and the Manhattan DA's office. With the proper subpoenas, they'll be able to pull my paperwork from Downtown; arrest reports, incident reports, shootings, and all that stuff. But as far as me talking with you here and now, well, it's not gonna' happen."

The Agents seem huffed and taken aback.

One says, "You know, Sergeant Pasano, this situation can be serious."

Pasano snaps back, "Not can be, Agent, this is serious—deadly serious. You guys come up here to Harlem, look to make a name for yourself, and Monday morning quarterback everything me and my guys have done. Well, we're alive. That's the priority. Killers and dope pushers are in jail." Paul stands up. "We're done here. You all have a good day. I see you are not wearing vests. If you need an escort out of Harlem, I could arrange that. If not, be careful driving through the streets with those shiny cars."

Suddenly, filling in the doorway is Lt. Devoe, always the imposing figure. He cuts right in on the conversation, "Hey Sarge, is there a problem here?"

Silence, then Pasano answers, "No boss, I think these gentlemen were just leaving."

"Okay then. Why don't I just escort them out? Let's go, guys," the Lieutenant says firmly. He follows them down and out of the building.

With his job tenure and street experience, Devoe understands the internal workings of the NYPD better than most anyone on the job. He double-times back up to Pasano's office and sits the young Sergeant down for a one-on-one. "Paul, listen, son. I'm telling you like a friend, not a boss. Someone Downtown is out to get your ass, one way or another. Those Feds didn't come here on their own. They were sent. My guess, by some piece of shit brass from Headquarters."

"Hey, Lieu', you think I don't realize that? I know exactly who sent them. It's that fuck, Felicer. He won't let it go."

Devoe looks down and grunts in disgust. "I know that prick. He tried to jam me up a decade ago. He almost had me on some bullshit department charges, but I challenged him on it. Felicer told me to put my papers in and enjoy an early retirement, or else. I lost my cool and almost my job. I told him to go fuck himself and reached across the table to strangle the little dick. His sissy-cunt assistant, a Captain no-balls, overheard the conversation and stepped between us. Long story short, I'm on the desk sliding papers back and forth."

Pasano bursts out laughing. "Shit, boss. We're that much alike, you and me?"

Devoe pauses at the answer his subordinate just delivered to him. "Hey, man. No joke. Think about your family. You need this job. Now listen. Try to fix the wrongdoings, and you and your guys should operate on the straight and narrow for a while."

The Sarge stares at the roughly etched face of his Lieutenant and quietly puts an end to the conversation. "It's too late for me, boss. I'm too far over the line, and I've taken my cops with me."

## CHAPTER 43

# GIRL GONE

It's been some time since Renee made a visit to Corisa in the hospital. Family matters and her social work have her putting in twelve-hour days. Her recent fatigue has become more noticeable. She tries to keep it to herself. This will be her final attempt to convince Corisa to attend the upcoming community meeting.

Renee walks down the long, white, antiseptic hallway of the women's ward and stops at the nurse's station holding a bunch of assorted flowers she bought from the gift shop.

She asks, "I'm looking for Corisa Doe. Can you help me?"

Because Corisa refused to give her last name and had no ID at time of admittance, the generic surname was given. During this drug epidemic, names mean nothing. Drug addicts receive little investigation into their background. No dependent children at home? You're a Jane or John Doe.

The nurse checks her patient records. She pauses.

"Yes, ma'am," The nurse says in a quiet tone. "Would you please wait while I get the head nurse on duty."

Renee nods in agreement.

Some anxiety overcomes Renee. Did Corisa die? Did she walk out? The mysterious young woman was always surrounded by drama. Within minutes, the head nurse comes and asks Renee to step into a private office. Renee fears the worst. The two women stand face to face. The nurse hesitates and expresses some confusion but manages to part with some carefully guarded words.

"I was working the late shift a couple of nights ago just beginning my double. 1 AM—everyone's asleep. Two, well-dressed people come to the nurses' station. A man and a woman. They show their Federal badges. Their names—Willard Cordova and Evelyn James. I questioned them. They showed me a warrant with Corisa's name on it. Corisa Tekil. I called down to the Administrator's office immediately to verify. It was quick. The woman helped Corisa get dressed. She was handcuffed and walked out between the two law enforcement people. She was stoic. On her way down the hallway, she handed me this sealed envelope and told me to give it to you. I tried to reach you, but your phone just kept ringing."

The nurse hands Renee the note and says, "I'm sorry, but there was nothing I could do to stop them from taking her."

"Thank you. I appreciate it," says Renee, as she accepts the envelope.

Renee hands the nurse the flowers and walks away. Midway down the hallway, she sits in a visitor's chair.

She catches her breath as she opens the envelope and reads a hand-written note. *'Renee, I'm sorry for what I have put you through. Thank you for all you do and everything you have done to help me and so many others. And be sure to tell Pasano, he ain't all that. God Bless you and your family. Risa.'*

---

Late that same evening, Yono, A/K/A Corisa, fights for her continued personal involvement in the Harlem/Sicilian connected drug war. It's just before midnight as an exhausted and injured Yono sits alongside her handler, DEA Agent Brian Wallace. The two are being interviewed at a covert location by their Agency superiors who are emphatic about pulling the agent out of her undercover role as the addict, Corisa. Her latest serious injuries pushed the US Drug Enforcement Agency well past the point of removing her from the assignment. The overweight DEA Manhattan head supervisor, Adam Mason, monotones the devastating words.

"Agent Yono Ferrara, we're pulling you out. First off, you've gone beyond what we have intended for you. Secondly, you've exposed yourself to an unnecessary and unauthorized risk of serious injury or death. Apparently, you've done this of free will. I have to ask you, did anybody in this room ask or coerce you to do this?"

"No, sir," Yono answers.

Mason looks over at her handler and continues, "Did you ask or coerce Agent Ferrara to partake in these activities?"

Agent Wallace responds, "No, sir."

Another DEA brass in dictatorial fashion joins in. "Then it's settled." He slides a form across the long table in front of her. "Sign it. You'll be temporarily relieved of active duty and placed on disability for the time being. I am sure when all this shakes out and the entire operation is completed, you'll be put in for Agency valor and recognition for what you have accomplished and contributed to the assignment."

He hands her a pen.

Yono pauses. She softly lays the pen back on the table, takes a breath, and in typical Yono style, answers. "No. I won't sign."

The superior retorts, "You have to sign. That's an order. Look at yourself. You are in no mental or physical condition to continue."

Yono responds in anger, "I don't care what you do to me. Fire me if you want, but I'm not signing that form."

Staring directly at the high-brass agents, Yono grimaces and continues her tirade. "Sir, I have people out there depending on me; fellow agents, NYPD officers, and community residents. These people have been through a series of unfathomable events. I'm helping them, not quitting on them. Maybe you believe I'm not needed out there, but I know they need me."

The supervising Agent steps in. "You and Wallace wait outside a second."

Without another word, Yono pushes her chair back, walks alongside her handler, and out the door.

Outside in the hallway, Brian tries to calm her down. "Look, Yon', go easy here. Don't push these old guys in a corner."

Yono raises her voice. "I don't give a Goddamn, Brian. They're not pushing me out. If I was a fuckin' guy, they wouldn't pull this shit. You and I both know they didn't want me out there from the 'get-go' until they found out I was good at my job."

Wallace cuts her short. "Is that why you're doing all this crazy shit out there? A vendetta against the Agency?"

Yono slams back, "What? What am I doing out there, Brian?"

Brian lowers his volume. "This discussion's over."

Yono, unrelenting, says, "Nothing's over."

The door opens and one of the agents waves them back into the room. The two enter and stand before their superiors, as Agent Mason issues the orders. "Okay, Agent Ferrara. Here's the deal. You'll be put back out in character after you take a few days to recoup and after a good review by Agency doctors. Furthermore, you will not put yourself at any further risk or compromise the operation. You'll report in daily along with your handler. You'll continue your focus on your original assignment as it relates to Sergeant Paul Pasano of the NYPD. Is all this understood?"

Yono answers with respect, "Yes, sir."

Mason continues, "And look, even though you're an experienced Agent, we are responsible for you and make the final decisions. We need you for two upcoming assignments, and they're more important than what you're doing now. If you become disabled, it could jeopardize the entire scope of the mission. Think about that when you're out there." He turns away and speaks to Yono over her shoulder, "Don't let me regret this, Agent Ferrara. Dismissed."

## CHAPTER 44

# PRESIDENTIAL VISIT AND A SON LOST

After weeks of planning, Renee Jons' community meeting is just twelve hours away. The area surrounding the high school is swarming with Secret Service Agents. First Lady, Governor, Mayor, and local Congressmen will be here. The drug dealers and buyers won't. Not for a day anyway. This is the beginning platform for the First Lady to launch her 'say no to drugs' campaign. It will be her legacy. What better place than ground zero, the world's heroin market. Renee will be honored for her work to date, along with the Sarge. It's an evening event. Renee is emotionally drained handling the preparations.

---

The morning of the community meeting, Renee is at the intensive care unit of Harlem Hospital. Her son, Richard, was brought in for the fourth time in two months. Brain swelling again.

Surgery is scheduled the next day to offer relief. No guarantees. Bullet fragments, even small ones, cause their intended havoc.

As he lies in an induced coma, Renee stands bedside praying. She left her other children at home with the always dependable neighbor, Mrs. James. This was supposed to be an uplifting time in her life. It is not. There is another consult with a top member of the surgical staff, who does not sugarcoat the details. "Mrs. Jons, honestly, we just don't know. Surgery at this point is our only chance to relieve the pressure, clean the wounds again, and take another look. I wish I could give you better news, but I can't. I promise you this, we'll have a full staff of surgeons available."

The single mother kisses her oldest son on his forehead and cheek, as tears flow from a mom that has endured an abundance of tragedies. A soft hand-to-hand touch and Renee leaves her boy behind.

------

Central Harlem High School is surrounded by uniformed police from multiple precincts. Metal detectors are arranged just inside the entrance. Bomb-sniffing dogs scout inside and out. Temporary Headquarters within trailers are staggered over a five-block square. Spotlighting is produced by generators. Police helicopters fly overhead within a civilian no-fly zone. Police and Secret Service portable radios squawk overlapping messages. The First Lady is at the Waldorf with her husband. The President is scheduled to be downstairs at a benefit dinner for handicapped children as his wife is preparing her speech.

While they're waiting for the prestigious and influential guest of honor to arrive, Renee engages Paul in conversation that includes the removal of Corisa. As always, she gets right to the point. "Paul, Corisa was taken by Federal authorities from the hospital late at night. Nobody knows why. She was just handcuffed and taken away."

After a couple of seconds, Pasano delivers a cold response to her. "I knew that girl was trouble from the beginning. She was born a mystery. Anyway, you've got enough on your plate to worry about. Think about yourself tonight, just this once, Renee. Corisa's a tough broad. She'll survive."

Renee snaps back, "Paul, please, I know you have more compassion than that."

8 PM, and the auditorium is packed with community residents. Pasano, in dress uniform, sits on the dais on a stage four feet above the audience. The Governor, Mayor, and Harlem Congressmen sit up front. There's a seat reserved for the President's wife—center stage. Behind the podium, Renee stands nervously at the ready. Thoughts of her son are constant.

NYPD motorcycles lead the way onto the street in front of the school. A long row of black limos with bulletproof panels and windows pulls up. In between, are Feds with assault weapons exposed.

The First Lady pulls in front of the school and is whisked inside to a warm welcome from those who seek her support. As she walks in, a standing ovation is put forth by a crowd who dispels politics when it comes to a First Lady, especially a gracious one who vows assistance.

Renee is a natural. Her college education comes through as she begins her introductions, thanking the audience, her personal family members, and dignitaries, including the First Lady, who receives another round of applause. The Governor and Mayor speak first, giving short speeches, each solidifying their support of the police and community as a partnership.

Then Renee begins her speech. She minces no words and excuses no one. She places the blame on a community that allowed some of their children to become pawns for organized crime. She criticizes a police department that, up until a couple of years ago, isolated and labeled Harlem as beyond help.

Renee goes on in an inspiring tone, "I am not here only to cast negativity. Tonight, I wish to acknowledge and thank the community for rising up and working with the New York City Police Department in overcoming the underworld of narcotics. When I speak of the NYPD, I must single out someone who has become my best friend and has put his life and that of his family's in harm's way. Sergeant Paul Pasano of the 35th Precinct is here, up on this stage. His men, along with Inspector Victor Deteo, are seated in the front row. Some others have been seriously injured or killed. They must always be remembered in our prayers. If it were not for them and so many of you in the audience, we would not be near the finish line. Together, we are taking back our streets and our homes. We are close but not there yet. We still have more work to do. I would like Sergeant Pasano to say a few words."

The overflowing crowd stands and applauds. Pasano has become a fixture within this community. He signals to his teammates, a cross-section of American heroes, to stand and face the audience. The applause gets louder. The First Lady is surprised at the support of the community for its local police. Paul stands at the podium. He is not a shy man but is humbled by the overwhelming reception from the crowd. He begins speaking in a calm voice. It's something he doesn't regularly do.

"I want to thank the First Lady, all the dignitaries on the dais, and everyone else present. I want to thank Inspector Victor Deteo for allowing me the opportunity to work for all of you, and for his support. I want to extend a thank-you to my teammates who put their lives on the line for me and each of you, so that you may one day be able to walk freely through your community, to live, work, and worship in peace, without the fear and threat of violence. Your children and grandchildren will once again be able to play outdoors. I still need your help. Please, report the wrongdoers. Call my office. All calls remain confidential. We will win. You have my word. Thank you."

Renee reintroduces the First Lady of the United States and thanks her for the improvements to the addiction rehab center at Harlem Hospital. There is another a round of applause.

The First Lady speaks in quiet tones, "Mrs. Jons and these police officers have sacrificed themselves and their families. I urge you to stand behind them. Help them to achieve their objectives. Remove the evil from your neighborhood."

She ends softly. "I hear you. My husband hears you. America is behind you. I have never seen a blend of community and police band together for such an important common cause. The President sent me here to tell you that he will work tirelessly to help bestow freedom to your community. Tonight, I will commence my mission to alert children of all ages to 'just say no to drugs.' God Bless you all, and thank you for having me."

She steps away from the podium and begins shaking hands with all the dignitaries on stage. Pasano, his guys, and finally Renee, are reserved for last. Applause is continuous. Renee steps up and thanks everyone for attending and for their support in the fight against the proliferation of narcotics in this historic community.

In the rear of the auditorium is a female figure in a green dress. She stands between two men dressed in dark suits. The trio, unnoticed, turns and walks out.

Of the dignitaries, the President's wife leaves first. She's driven away in her motorcade in less than thirty seconds. Next, The Governor and Mayor exit with their bodyguards. Finally, the audience files out.

After ten minutes, the only remaining people are Renee, her children, Pasano, and his teammates. Some congratulatory small talk lingers. Inspector Deteo enters and makes eye contact with the Sarge. He has a serious look on his face. He gestures to Paul with his hand to come over. They talk quietly in the corner for a minute. Both men project solemn looks. Inspector Deteo remains in place, while Paul walks over to Renee. He guides her off to the side. His eyes well up.

He leans in closer to her, finding it difficult to push forth some unwanted words.

"Renee, I'm sorry, Richard passed away just fifteen minutes ago."

Renee falls into Pasano's arms and begins to sob. "Paul, my baby is gone? Why did God want my son, and tonight of all nights?"

Sarge answers in a consoling voice, "There are no answers. I'll drive you to the hospital." He turns to his men and says, "Would you please take the children home and make sure Mrs. James, Renee's neighbor, is with them? I'll see you all in the morning."

The guys all nod in the affirmative to their boss, and as they leave, give their personal condolences to Renee.

The auditorium empties. A janitor begins sweeping up. Outside, the sounds of police sirens, once again, take their place within a struggling community.

A funeral Mass is set for 9 AM on Tuesday morning at St. Bartholomew's. Father Ingal will once again preside. Monica Taylor was the youngest victim. The latest, Richard Jons, was just a teenager. Both cut down by bullets from drug dealers. This Mass will celebrate the life and untimely death of Renee Jons' son. It has impacted an entire community. The media picks it up. Adult casualties are accepted. Children's are not. Fear and empathy spread throughout the entire city.

———————

A clear, crisp morning and the Raiders once again don their dress uniforms. They file in the second row with Rachel and the other team members' wives who vow support for their husbands, Renee Jons, and her family. The first row is occupied by Renee and her three younger children. Olivia is saved from the pain by absence. The Jons family must now overcome an unfathomable loss.

The small church is overflowing with community folks, dignitaries, and police brass. They also line the sidewalks out front where an amplified speaker is placed.

Father Ingal begins his eulogy, "No family should experience what the Jons' family has recently endured. Richard was a young hero living amongst us. He shouldered the responsibility that we adults have shied away from for decades. He sacrificed his own life so that we may survive. *Greater love hath no man than this, that a man lay down his life for his friends.*"

Tears fall freely within the Chapel.

The Harlem Boys' Choir sings a series of solemn hymns befitting the service, *How Great Thou Art and Amazing Grace.*

Renee can be heard crying as Father Ingal concludes, "Now I tell you, today this teenager is a man in the eyes of God. Richard shall see Him in all his Glory. Tomorrow evening there will be a solidarity candlelight vigil in honor of Richard Jons and Monica Taylor. Let us show the city, America, and the world, that we will not be a forgotten people."

The diverse gathering of those paying homage, stand, pray, and weep, as the teenager's dark blue casket is slowly rolled down the center aisle of the church to a waiting hearse. Renee and her children follow behind. Cavon, her only surviving son, steadies his mom. His face is one of pain and anger. He knows he will one day avenge his brother. The service has ended. They're on their way to the cemetery, where an open grave awaits.

## CHAPTER 45

# KARMA

Early Wednesday morning, Pasano and company are laying out plans for the day. They'll be doing a double. Narc work first and then the candlelight vigil. The daylight hours will be used to target a couple of remaining dope locations. Most of them are off the street. They're usually secreted in the hallways adjacent to abandoned apartments. Drugs, cash, and guns can be secured in the flats, while 'smack' transactions are completed rapidly in the darkened halls. It's fast and profitable. Lookouts point roaming buyers to the spots. Lines of junkies are not visible from the street, making it more difficult for photos and planned buy and bust ops'. Locations change day-to-day, sometimes, hour-to-hour. Supply and demand dictate the amount distributed to local dealers.

Kellig and Calvoy blend as potential buyers traveling up and down the side streets in an old beater used by undercovers. These jalopies are rotated from precinct to precinct each week to avoid being 'made' by local drug hacks. The two teammates are able to identify a hot spot. A quick communication is delivered to Pasano, and the guys are en route to a noon raid.

Three nondescript 'unmarks' enter West 153rd Street. One team goes long, one takes the middle, and one short. Hopefully, it contains the buyers and sellers inside the building. It works well. Fourteen buyers rounded up. Pasano and Fennar race into the hallway, and at gunpoint, overtake the seller, who attempts to run into a first-floor apartment. Within a minute, backup 'uniforms' join in, and the apartment is dismantled. Bundles of currency and glassines are recovered. A loaded .357 is found in a broken fridge.

Out front, JK is holding a young, White buyer, who drops two dime bags to the sidewalk. Jim picks them up. They're stamped, 'double play.'

An angered JK exclaims, "What the fuck you doing?"

He slams the young junkie's head into the side of the building.

The buyer holds his head and winces in pain. He claims, "That's not mine, sir."

"Well, what are they gonna' believe, my eyes or your mouth?"

He cuffs him facing the wall and asks a fast question. "Any needles in your pockets? I get stuck, you get beat!"

The tall, twenty-something replies, "Yes, sir. I have a syringe in my front pocket."

"Okay—then don't move!"

With his leather gloves on, Kellig carefully removes a capped hypo and two more dime bags of 'H.' "This is no biggie, kid—a misdemeanor hit. You got any warrants?"

"No, sir."

"We'll check on that. If you got no hits you'll get a Desk Appearance ticket, and you'll be out by late afternoon."

"Yes, sir."

"What's your name?"

No answer.

"You hear me, son? What's your name?"

No answer.

JK goes deep into the druggie's back pocket and comes out with a small ID wallet. A driver's license and an NYPD courtesy card, embossed with a Chief's shield, are inside.

On the front of the license, JK reads the name and murmurs to himself, *'Aron Felicer. Fuck, you shittin' me or what?'*

JK thinks to himself. *'Either it's found or stolen, or we got some mystery.'*

He sends a 'uniform' inside to get Pasano and continues his interrogation, "Your father NYPD?"

"Yes, sir."

"What's his name?"

"Chief Colin Felicer, sir."

Sarge comes out and goes over to JK. "What's up, Jim?"

Kellig doesn't say a word. He just hands Pasano the small ID wallet containing the Chief's courtesy card and the kid's license.

Pasano, unfazed, remarks, "What's he holding?"

JK hands him the four glassines and an empty hypo. "He had two on him and dropped two to the ground."

Pasano grabs JK's arm and pulls him aside. "Your call, partner. He's cut loose, and we keep the card and voucher the 'skag' and hypo as found property, or we take him through the system. One way we get satisfaction, and the other, we get an upper hand."

JK, with a rapid response, "For me boss—easy choice. We cut him loose and mail the courtesy card back to his father. When he gets it, he'll know his son was picked up. We need some leverage. He'll owe us one."

"Fine. This is all on me, Jim, understand?"

Kellig nods.

"You process the others, and I'll walk this one away." Pasano heads down the street with Felicer's son cuffed and puts him in his car. He pulls around the corner, leans over the seat, and removes the cuffs.

Pasano questions, "How much you using?"

"Two bags a day, sir."

"Your father know?"

"No, sir."

"You live at home?"

"Yes, sir."

"Go to college?"

"Yes, sir."

"Let me see your arms."

Felicer moves them forward. Pasano pushes up his sleeves displaying rows of spike marks.

"Okay. You're a fuckin' junkie. I'm letting you slide today. You live in Westchester. Tonight you tell your father you need help. Tomorrow morning, first thing, you sign yourself into a walk-in rehab center up there. Every hospital has one. I'll follow up to see that you checked in. I'm not going to personally tell your father. You don't have to either. I'm just showing him the respect that he never gave me. But that's okay. Get it, kid?"

"Yes, sir. Thank you."

"Okay, go do what I told you."

The young man leaves and walks away. Pasano drives back to the drug spot. Prisoners are placed in the wagon and taken to the Three-Five for processing. Only two felons. The sellers are headed downtown. The others are issued Desk Appearance tickets. No warrants.

At the station house, Pasano goes over to JK and shows him a note and a department envelope. On the note, "You're welcome," envelope addressed to Chief Colin Felicer, IAD, NYPD/HQ. He places the note and NYPD courtesy card in the envelope and drops it in the department mail bin for evening pick up. Felicer will know in the morning.

Pasano states, "Okay guys, listen up. Don Sels, junior team member, goes downtown with the two perps, and everyone else, get in uniform. We've got to motorcade the vigil tonight. Clean up, we gotta' look good. We'll be on TV."

The guys laugh. It lightens the seriousness of the upcoming event.

## CHAPTER 46

# VIGIL AND A PROMISE

7:30 PM—the candlelight vigil honoring Richard Jons and Monica Taylor begins on the street in front of Renee Jons' residence. Over one thousand people are present, spreading over four blocks. Pasano and his teammates head the march with a motorcade. Plenty of Downtown brass, with dozens of uniformed patrols, walk alongside. Traffic teams block streets, allowing the procession to go uninhibited from uptown Harlem to downtown, ending at Carlos Giadana's club. Candles are distributed and lit.

Renee leads the throngs of people down Frederick Douglass Boulevard. It will be a two-hour walk. Along the way, large masses of supporters join the crowd. They're from all parts of New York City and surrounding suburbs. Whites, Blacks, Asians, and Hispanics walk arm-in-arm. Midway, there are over three thousand marchers. Traffic is tied up. The media is following the crowd. New Yorkers are watching along with America as it makes world news. Two hours later, they arrive in front of the Mafioso's club. Lights are off inside. No one guards the front door. It's surrounded by police behind barricades.

An incident is not wanted. The large crowd begins to chant as they raise their signs high in the air. The collaborative voices reach a deafening pitch. The slogans are varied. Most of them demand Giadana's Mafia exit their community and take their poison with them. "*Mafia leave,*" and "*Stop killing our children.*" There's some pushing against the police barricades as the NYPD doubles up on the manpower to keep the throngs of Harlemites from rushing through and destroying the mobsters' NY Headquarters.

Cops comment amongst themselves, "Let em' wreck this place. It'll make things easier for us."

One declares, "I'm on the wrong side of the barricades."

Another remarks, "I hope people are watching, especially Giadana and his goons."

The point is made, and a message has been sent. The children have been memorialized, and Renee is exhausted. Pasano exits his marked RMP and watches her closely. He sees her resting her arms on a police barricade, slumped over. Within seconds, she faints and falls back into the crowd. Paul and Will Fennar waste no time. They hustle over to her as she comes to. They lift Renee, gently, and see the distress on the middle-aged woman's face. It's an expression of pain and fatigue.

Sarge dictates in his usual autocratic voice, "Renee, you did your part. You paid tribute to little Monica and honored your son. You did enough. Let's get you home. My car's right over here."

Renee answers in a voice engulfed in pain, "Thank you, Paul. I won't be going home tonight."

Paul, confused, questions her, "What are you talking about?"

"It's time for me, Paul. Please take me to the hospital. Cavon will come with me. Please look out for my children."

Silence overcomes the three. The two Raiders, almost carrying Renee, escort her to their RMP. She's carefully put in. It's a slow start to get through the massive crowd, then lights and sirens to the hospital.

The ER is packed as usual. Renee is looked at by a team of nurses and a young ER doc who recognizes her. A battery of x-rays and lab tests are ordered. She's admitted. Pasano makes arrangements for her children. The timing is terrible.

Pasano can't stay. He gives instructions to Cavon.

"I'll be at the Three-Five for another two hours at least. I'll check on your little sisters at home with your neighbor, Mrs. James. Call me with an update on your mom. You got all that?"

"Yes, sir."

"Take care of your mother."

---

11 PM, and Pasano is about to leave for the night. Renee's 13-year-old son does what he promised. The office phone rings, and Paul picks it up.

"Sergeant Pasano? It's Cavon Jons. Sir, I just wanted to let you know my mom is resting. They gave her some sleep and pain medication. They took a lot of tests and will know more by tomorrow."

A tired Sarge replies, "Thank you for keeping me informed. You need a lift home?"

"No, sir, one of the nurses, a friend of my mom's, is giving me a ride."

"Fine. I'll talk to you tomorrow. You look after your little sisters, okay?"

"Yes, sir."

The next day, Pasano and guys finally have some time off. Paul, Rachel, and Linda spend the entire day at the rehab center with Andrew. Teammates are home with their families. Rachel is kept in the loop about Renee's stay at Harlem Hospital. Sarge heads to the phone booth just off the main hallway and places a call.

"Renee, how are you doing?"

"Much better. They've still got me on some mild pain meds. I feel like one of our local addicts."

"Hey, don't laugh, you can get hooked on those pills."

Renee laughs a bit and thanks him for calling. "Paul, listen, thanks for everything, and I mean it. The doc says I'll be taking another battery of tests today, and I can leave first thing tomorrow morning. He thinks exhaustion is a major part of my discomfort. You be sure to give my regards to Rachel and Linda and a big kiss to Andrew. They're your priority, ya know."

"Yes, I do. Talk to you again."

Paul hangs up realizing everyone is just plain exhausted, as he thinks to himself, *'We all could use a day of rest.'*

One person not getting any rest is Carlos Giadana, who has vowed to counter the community vigil with expansion. His intention is to spread heroin by delivering it directly to the outer suburbs. He will send recruiters to outlying neighborhoods to reel in dealers in mostly White neighborhoods.

Local police receive word from their CIs. Rumors spread quickly. A new, fierce pushback results with suburban community residents voicing their opinion, *'Don't bring it here!'* Giadana has no choice. Harlem, once fertile territory, is drying up. America is a big country. Lots of cities and towns. He'll use the large incoming shipment to spread the product. It's his last resort.

---

Hope and prayer prevail within Renee's mind as she is signed out of the hospital. She's still tired and experiencing sporadic pain. Her doctor asks to see her in his office. As she enters, he asks her to please sit. He has a somber look on his face. Renee's been around long enough to know. Her doctor delivers the upsetting news of her condition. It's quick, to the point, and devastating. Cancer. Pancreatic. Terminal. Six months—maybe.

Dr. Tilof, the most senior oncologist, holds Renee's hand. It's a friendship and trust that have developed over years while both working at Harlem Hospital. He says, "Your symptoms and pain will worsen. I can control most of it with medication. Think about making arrangements for your family, Renee."

Tears flow as she speaks in a monotone, "It's not for me but for my children. They're so young. I've also not completed my task. Why would God take me now? Maybe I've angered him."

"Renee, after twenty years in this field, I've delivered this type of diagnosis to hundreds of people, the good, bad, and indifferent. You, Renee, are one of the Angels. Now, let's choose a plan to help you get through this. New trial medications are arriving every day. You'll overcome this disease for the same people you've just mentioned. Promise me, you will fight for yourself as you've been fighting for everyone else. I'm not giving up. Don't you."

"I will not give up, Doctor. You know me, I won't go easy," Renee says, as she forces a smile.

―――――――――

Pasano's team has completed their last strike for the day. They're at the 35th, booking prisoners, getting them ready for overnight incarceration. Sergeant Pasano is in his office with the Lieutenant Detective Commander of the Manhattan North Homicide Squad. Two of the Narc Team's catches for the day are wanted for a double murder down in the 27th precinct. It's a solid day's work for the Raiders with excellent results. No injuries. For some, one day is good. For others—not, as dismal news arrives.

Pasano's phone rings. It's Renee Jons speaking in a broken voice asking to meet. "Paul, please, I would never bother you, especially last minute, but can I come see you for just a few seconds? It's a personal issue."

"Of course, Renee. I'll be in my office."

"Paul, I'm only here a few minutes, and I already see you've got your hands full," the Detective Lieutenant comments. "You're burning that candle. Ease up, pal. Set your priorities and avoid burnout and worse yet, mistakes. But, I thank you for the two perps you collared for us. Helps with our clearance rate."

"Thanks, boss, and for your advice also. I'll sign the paperwork downstairs for prisoner transfer over to your squad."

The two shake hands. The Lieutenant leaves Pasano's office. Five minutes later, Renee arrives. She walks in with a concerned look. Pasano tells her to sit and gets her a fresh cup of water from the fountain.

"What gives, Renee?"

"Paul, I'm sorry to take up your valuable work time, but I was at the doctor's today. He says I'm sick, cancer. I have nobody to turn to. Nobody I can trust. Only you. If anything happens to me from all those evil people in organized crime, or I can't take care of the kids anymore, I need you to do me a special favor. Please bring my daughter, Olivia, home from Antigua, along with my Aunt Bay. She'll take care of my family and make arrangements. Here's an envelope with all the personal information you'll need. Also, tell Olivia I've always loved her."

The Sarge is stunned, and after a few seconds of hesitation, speaks in a soft voice. "Say no more. You have my word, my promise. But, please, don't count yourself out. I need you. Your family needs you. I'll do everything I can to keep you safe. Can you understand that?"

"Of course. But just in case."

He gets up from his chair, goes over to Renee, and puts his arms around her. She is weeping. Her fear and pain are exposed. Paul is upset but must maintain his focus. Mission completion is at hand, and this woman deserves to see it through.

---

On a Sicilian waterfront, another mission is running simultaneously. It's the middle of the night, drizzling and foggy, as Sonny Inzarita and accomplices are at the Port of Palermo, Italy. His crew is loading thousands of kilos of refined heroin onto a red and yellow, rusted-out ocean freighter. It's owned by the family. It transports olive oil and dope, two of their most profitable commodities. Waiting on the other end in New York to accept delivery are Giadana's workers with trucks of their own.

All have a schedule to keep. For the Mafiosos, a successful eight-day voyage is imperative for survival. For law enforcement, it is the interdiction of the heroin and the collapsing of the Seteola, Inzarita, and Giadana organized crime empire.

Plans are coming to fruition as strike day is imminent. Personnel changes are ongoing to assure the safeguarding of street operatives. Priority one is Corisa, who has gone beyond what anyone expected. She's in her usual gallery, sleeping, sprawled out on a mattress covered with a makeshift blanket of old coats.

Realizing the Giadana regime might be nearing an end, Ferris sends Malik, his toughest street enforcer, to hit all the local drug dens scavenging up the cash by robbing the junkies. He knows exactly where to begin.

It's the middle of the night, and Malik rummages his way through the personal belongings of local addicts at Corisa's den. His scores are minimal as the remaining users have little or no cash and are surviving on clinic-issued methadone.

When Malik nears Corisa, he has other ideas besides robbing her. He always hated this woman's attitude and her constant meddling. Payback is imminent, as he removes a large serrated edged hunting knife from his waistband and quietly kneels next to the exhausted female. He raises the knife over his head and grips it tightly with two hands. He is about to complete the downward stroke when a forearm comes from behind grabbing him around his neck, closing off his airway, and a hand grabs the knife and plunges it into his chest. Malik collapses, falling over onto Corisa who pushes him off and jumps to her feet. She's dazed but is fast to consume the episode.

"Fuck! Holy shit, Gecoi?"

The long-haired undercover agent barely breaking a sweat, responds, "They sent me to bring you in. They're changing your assignment."

Corisa, catching her breath, exclaims, "What about him?"

"Fuck him, let's go," as he grabs her arm.

She looks over at Gecoi, thinking to herself, '*he is a tough guy*,' as she stops short and looks back at the other addicts who are fast asleep.

Sensing her angst, Agent Gecoi attempts to soften her concern. "Don't worry, they're beginning a final sweep tomorrow, canvassing all the galleries and removing the addicts by force, if necessary, and placing them into the new rehab center."

Corisa is quick to chime in, "Just a little too late."

"What are you talking about?"

"Forget it, let's go, and thanks, Doug, I owe you."

"That's Geee - co - weee," spreading his name out, forcing Corisa to smile as they rush out.

## CHAPTER 47

# OPERATION FREEDOM

The entire street in front of the 35th precinct has been cordoned off. Parking spaces are reserved for the attendees of a large Narcotics Task Force meeting. DEA and NYPD brass are present, along with corresponding team leaders from both Agencies.

The mission is 'Operation Freedom.' The goal is the final collapsing of the Mafioso's drug empire. Captain Bill Rainer of Narc Intel is outlining the plan in detail to the assemblage of law enforcement. "Before we begin, I just want to thank everyone here for their work over the past twenty-four months. All of you, especially Sergeant Paul Pasano and his Narc Task Force, have sacrificed themselves and their families. It's been a long road to completion. Now, let's finish it.

"Okay guys, please listen carefully. Friday morning, pre-dawn strikes will go as follows; DEA Agents, NYPD's Organized Crime Control Bureau, and Emergency Service SWAT Teams will intercept the Fulton Market drug shipment scheduled for two days out. Sergeant Pasano's unit will take out Carlos Giadana's headquarters in lower East Harlem and his remaining street overseers. Precinct Anti-Crime teams will assist. The Special Narcotics Unit will hit the cutting and packaging lab in the South Bronx, with ESU taking point. Communication and timing are a priority to prevent tip-offs and ambush. We'll have approximately one hundred uniform backups using point-to-point radios programmed for this mission only.

"Expect pushback. Color of the day will be issued at the time of the operation as will arrest and search warrants. I will say this only once. Not a word of what we discussed here leaves the room. Not even to family. We meet here at 2000 hours, Thursday night. We suit up, review final tactics, and move out. I will be on the streets with you every step of the way."

———————————

Early Thursday evening, the Zarita Shipping and Freight Company has its largest vessel anchored twenty-five miles off the coast of Southwestern Long Island. With calm seas and just a slice of moonlight, the ship remains anonymous under the near pitch-black skies. A well-paid crew of freight workers scurries to transfer the valued cargo onto a much smaller fishing boat alongside. Swing control arms with winches and ropes carefully guide the sealed containers down onto the ship's deck. Well-positioned spotlights illuminate the process. Within two hours, the task is complete. Multiple bundles of cash are moved back and forth between the two boats' operators, so that all workers may be well compensated. This is a lucrative business, albeit a dangerous one.

———————————

Word comes into Operation Headquarters from a Coast Guard cutter sitting with lights and engines off. They're anchored five miles from Inzarita's freighter. The Coast Guard observation team records the drug cargo transfer, but they will not overtake and board the vessel until well past the raid at the market in the morning. For legal and safety concerns, the exchange of undiluted heroin must take place on shore. The transaction will be videoed and scribed for future court testimonies.

It's 2000 hours and the 35th is bustling with a wide variety of police agencies intermingling and exchanging operation details. Sergeant

Pasano and his team are standing-by, preparing to overtake Giadana's club at dawn. Hopefully, the market takedown will have evolved. Once accomplished, they'll push out to collar-up the last remaining street drug overseers.

Word from Nick Scalia, through his handler, is a 7 AM meeting with all of the capo's associates at the club. A mad push of Mafia tactics will be enacted during the morning hours. The four Inzarita Sicilian 'Zips' will begin a personal mission. Once again, Scalia fears for his life as he will be examined up and down after any law enforcement strikes.

Within thirty minutes, the first phase unit pushes off for its assignment, positioning themselves at the Manhattan waterfront. DEA and PD undercovers filter in slowly, assuming their various, well-disguised roles. They are scattered around the entire Fulton Market, blending as dock workers, fish wholesalers, truck drivers, and homeless. Trucks are evenly spread. In the rear, heavily armed SWAT Teams are ready to go. Before midnight, everyone is in place. Captain Rainer is on the scene in charge. They wait.

Within a few hours, the Fulton Fish Market comes alive. The dark skies are illuminated by glaring spotlights placed along the dozens of boat slips. Union dock workers are pulling, pushing, and carrying oversized bins overflowing with fresh catch. Hundreds of pounds of ice are strewn across the top layers of the dozens of species of ocean life. The air is filled with the strong scent of raw fish. The loud shouts from workers giving and taking unloading instructions, do not overshadow the roar of the metal conveyor belt rollers. The blacktop surrounding the entire street and pathways is drenched in wet droppings. Puddles form in minutes. The bustle is constant. On slip #22, for the moment, things are more quiet and unassuming.

———————

The ships detach themselves, and the fishing vessel, loaded with a full day's catch plus hundreds of millions of dollars in heroin, slowly motors its way into the channels of New York City. The currents are flowing, overlapping, and swirling. Low speed is mandatory. Well before dawn, the vessel idles into a berth for its final destination. It rests at dock slip #22. Giadana's men are awaiting delivery. These guys are strong and protective enough to easily handle the two products. Eight, well-armed Mafia enforcers man the delivery trucks.

The boat is rapidly tied to cleats and pilings. Roller ramps are locked into place, as clanking of metal fills the night air. Thousands of pounds of fish and dope begin their journey. The mixed cargo will be separated. One will be put on sale at the market in the morning, and the other will be trucked to the Bronx for a different, but more profitable market preparation. That's if all goes as planned.

The Feds and the NYPD have their own idea. The first phase of Operation Freedom is about to unfold. Finally, 0515 hours, and the orders that dozens of law enforcement personnel have been waiting for come from two men assigned to an observation post across the street in a warehouse facing the waterfront. "Go! Operation Freedom, go! Operation Freedom, go!"

The multitude of well-armed and vested-up cops, some with NYPD and others with DEA lettering across their dark jumpsuits, exit from the four, nondescript box trucks parked nearby. Within thirty seconds, their presence is announced by those well-known phrases, "Police! Hands up over your heads. Don't move! You move—you're dead!"

The small army of men is armed with assault weapons, shotguns, .45 and 9mm semi-autos. Only two of Giadana's thugs responsible for overseeing the heroin unloading and delivery operation act in defiance. They reach for their Mac-10s. Captain Rainer's response team makes a decision. Multiple shots from ESU marksmen using high-powered guns ring out. It's loud and quick. The gun flash is brief, but the smoke lingers. Chest and head shots bring the 'perps' down immediately. There's no movement.

The Montoriffi brothers, the most loyal soldiers to Carlos Giadana, are dead. The dozens of others are instructed to drop to their knees, hands clasped behind their heads, fingers interlocked. Giadana's subordinates are swarmed, searched, and cuffed. Weapons are removed. Two bloodied bodies remain unattended until one of the NYPD's ESU officers runs over and removes their weapons as well.

Captain Rainer is quick to radio Operation Headquarters at the Three-Five. "First phase done. Two perps down, twenty-one others apprehended. The product is safeguarded."

———

A message is sent from HQ to the Coast Guard and DEA to overtake the freighter en route back to Italy. The cutter pulls alongside and fires multiple warning shots from a mounted, high-powered machine gun across the bow of the freighter. It's a quick surrender.

There'll be an entire day of counting and vouchering. Prisoners will be interrogated and sent through the system. The boats will be confiscated and held as evidence. Sonny Inzarita is at his well-fortified farmhouse in Palermo. When he learns what the Americans did, he will be a distraught mobster.

———

There's a sigh of relief from Operation Headquarters and a quick burst of loud conversation. Phase Two is kicking off. The Special Narcotics Enforcement Unit loads up and heads to the Bronx to take out the cutting and packaging factory. Sergeant Pasano and his Raiders, well stacked with 'nines' and 'pumps,' move out for Giadana's club. The two strikes will be well-timed and coordinated. Even though they are at different locations, both have the same intent, to dismantle the Giadana, Inzarita, and Seteola empire.

It's a pre-dawn quiet at the target in the South Bronx at East 166th

Street and Webster Avenue. A cool breeze with filtered moonlight hovers over a section of streets that have been plagued with deadly violence for two decades. The precinct, nicknamed 'Fort Apache,' encompasses a major piece of the surrounding real estate. Most of it has been condemned, boarded up, or occupied by felons, addicts, or innocent people, who have been forced to live trapped within invisible boundaries by a host of social and economic barriers. Adults and children are swallowed up daily by the lingering effects of neglect by a society that shies away from the truth about narcotics abuse. For this South Bronx community, the beginning of change and freedom are moments away.

The upper two floors of the 'H' mill appear benign from the street and rear alleyway. Just a glow of dim lighting peeks through windows sprayed over with several coats of black paint. Inside, the adjoining apartment walls have been knocked through to create factory settings on both floors. Rows of long, metal tables and chairs cover almost every inch of the old, cracked, brown vinyl flooring.

Aside from the makeshift bathroom and kitchen facilities, there is nothing but armed overseers and enforcers standing in each corner. Seated on the folding chairs are local, young men and women dressed down to a minimum to prevent narc skimming. Most of the employees are Puerto Rican who speak broken English. They each net about $100 per shift. They're hard at work, weighing, scooping, and mixing blends of a lactose powder with pure Turkish opiate. Glassines from one to two-inch sizes are carefully filled with exact amounts in each. Satisfied junkies are a priority. Repeat business is essential for increased profit.

The squad of heavily armed Emergency Service SWAT officers begins filtering into the hot zone from the surrounding streets. The SNEU team will go in just behind the SWAT Units to make the arrests and process the perps. Across the street and five buildings down from the target, in the pitch dark, two NYPD SWAT snipers are adjusting their night scopes affixed to kill rifles. Earphones are in place as conversation ensues between them. Their squad Lieutenant is positioned three buildings closer, looking through binoculars at the factory rooftop where two armed local bulls have AK-47's slung over their shoulders, engaged in small talk, unaware of the unfolding events. In the alleyway behind the factory building, communication between the contingent of ESU cops and SNEU members is ongoing.

On the top floor of the rear building are four ESU members with their canister guns at the ready, loaded with smoke and bang grenades. Then radio checks. Veteran Lieutenant Locasil gives the final command, "Greenlight—snipers."

There is barely a whisk of sound. The two armed bulls incur deadly head wounds and crumble to the tar and pebble roof. Immediately following, multiple canisters are sent crashing through the rear windows of the target apartments. A choking and eye-burning smog fills the factories on both floors. Repetitive electronic bull-horned commands in Spanish to disarm and come-out are delivered, as the squad of air-masked ESU and SNEU members wait in the hallways. Within thirty seconds, dozens of workers followed by the unarmed overseers file out.

The perps are overtaken, cuffed, and searched. A cascade of weapons and multi-millions of dollars of 'stash,' some packaged and some not, are confiscated. A Department of Corrections transport bus waits out front, as an assembly of backup 'uniforms' escorts the crew on board.

Radio communication is loud, clear, and fast, "Phase Two completed. Phase Two completed." Pasano's Raiders are up next for the Giadana Headquarters' take-down.

The mob's early AM meeting has just begun in the darkened, East Harlem basement. Pool table lighting hangs from the ceiling. Despite the time of year, it's damp and musty. Ten middle-aged mobsters are gathered around the well-shined, long, wooden table covered with cups of espresso. All are wearing suits or sports coats concealing their weapons. Nick Scalia is the last to arrive. He remains on shaky ground, believing this cartel has suspicions of his ties to law enforcement. He carries his signature shoulder holstered, nickel-plated .357 revolver loaded with six hollow point rounds. This morning, he also carries a backup piece, a .25 cal' semi-auto in an ankle holster. He believes he was given an erroneous starting time so they could begin discussions without him. On his way into the room, he sees Vito Tiafona whispering in the hallway to the four Inzarita henchmen. The 'Zips' and the first lieutenant are speaking in hushed Sicilian tones not meant for Scalia or anyone else. The four are well-armed, and within a minute, leave quietly, walk down the hallway, and up the steps.

Scalia walks up to Tiafona and asks, "What's up? Where's the boss?"

Tiafona, abruptly counters, "I'm the boss today. You take orders from me."

Nick replies submissively, "Sure."

"You're late."

"Nobody called me for the earlier start."

Tiafona orders again, "Get in the room with the others."

There are rumblings amongst the men. Rumors of failure of the expected drug shipment surface. Without Capo Giadana present, confusion takes over. His first lieutenant, Vito Tiafona, attempts to control the restless crew. Carlos Giadana, himself, is in the 'wind.'

Scalia is prepared for the worst, but his presence is essential. It's operation day, the conclusion of years of work put in by DEA and NYPD undercover Agents and a host of law enforcement people who gave their lives to get to this point. His absence could unravel the final mission. He will intermingle with the enemy, hopefully, for one last time. Two priorities, do his job and survive. Scalia knows the inner workings of this Giadana network better than anyone. He'll be documenting any last minute changes and decisions. He must be patient for just a bit longer. The Raiders are on their way.

The older waiter, Hines, enters, serves, and refills more cups of coffee. While he's in the dingy room, no discussions of any substance take place. As he pours, he lays down napkins in front of each of the members.

When he comes to Nick Scalia, it's the same, but on his napkin is written in small script, *'They know!'*

The waiter leaves the room. The veteran agent makes no moves. He resumes small talk but discloses nothing. After a couple of minutes, Tiafona closes the meeting, instructing everyone present to remain calm, reach out to their overseers, and keep moving the remaining product. As the men stand and begin filing out, Tiafona tells Scalia and three others to remain to discuss personal issues. Scalia's heart skips a couple of beats, and his face reddens.

Tiafona commands, "Sit, relax."

They do, as the bulk of the half-dozen others head down the hallway and up the cement stairway to the bar above. There's a quiet pause. Some scuffling and noise erupt from outside the room. Giadana's second lieutenant, Joe Capolla, is dragging a body by its hair into the room. It's a female, Nick's 'girl-pal,' Carmella. She's bloodied with a swollen face. Her mouth is open and blood and lip tissue pour out. Two front teeth are missing. The attending bulls, including Scalia, are stunned, and quickly push their chairs back and rise to their feet.

Tiafona slams the table with his fists and commands in a loud, deep voice, "Sit!" *"Intransitivo sedere!"*

The four slowly sit back down as Carmella is propped against the wall, peering through one, partially open eye. She mumbles as blood gurgles out, "I'm sorry, Nicholas."

Tiafona pulls his .45 and hollers out towards Scalia, "I trusted you with my life!"

Nick reaches under his jacket, pulls out his .357, and fires off four quick rounds striking Tiafona, who is only able to get off one wild shot of his own before falling face down on the table in a mass of blood. Three of the four massive hollow points found their mark—center chest. The two other Mafiosos, including Capolla, pull their 9's and attempt to get off their own shots at Scalia. They are cut down by Hines, an undercover narc, whose real name is Tony Delco. He stands alongside Paul Pasano, Jim Kellig, and Will Fennar, who light up the room with loud, rapid, multiple rounds from semi-autos. The smoke-filled room turns silent. Giadana's cohorts are all down. Their weapons removed.

Seconds later, loud shouts come from above as John Calvoy, Al, Rico, Sels, and McTerren beat down Giadana's other thugs who remained inside the bar. NYPD Emergency Service officers with assault rifles provide the incentive for a white flag. The club is no more. An immediate notification from point-to-point radios alerts the Temporary Headquarters. "Be advised," Sergeant Pasano, says, "Phase III, Giadana's club has been overtaken and secured. No injuries to any law enforcement personnel, multiple perps down, DOA. Others arrested."

A sigh of relief and a couple of high-fives as Scalia tells the law enforcement responders, "Hey Paul, Tony, and you guys," pointing to Kellig and Fennar, "Thank you."

Will is already carrying an unconscious Carmella up the stairs. An ambulance is summoned. It takes no time before the club is overrun with 'uniforms' and brass.

Scalia exclaims in a loud voice, "Paul, four henchmen left earlier. They're on a personal mission."

Tony cuts in, "I overheard. They didn't think I understood Italian, they'd be wrong. They're on their way to your community friend, Renee Jons, to carry out Giadana's and Inzarita's personal vendetta."

Paul doesn't utter a word, but double times upstairs, pulling Jim with him.

Once upstairs, he tells his guys, "The 'uniforms' can handle this for us. We're outta' here. Make sure you reload."

The team hustles out the door.

Pasano tells his fellow Raiders in a loud, clear voice, "Four assassins are on their way to Renee Jons at 154th Street. We go fast, guys. Stay with me."

Will and Pasano jump into the lead, unmarked, and the multiple, two-man units follow behind. Lights and sirens are instantaneous. Dust and taillights are visible in seconds.

Inzarita's four imported mercenaries drive onto Renee Jons' block and pull alongside a marked RMP with a young, female, uniformed Three-Five cop, sitting inside providing special attention to the Jons' family. Without a split second of hesitation, a Mac-10 appears out an open window of the assassin's car. A quick burst of .45 cal' rounds is let loose at the officer. Windows immediately shatter. One bullet grazes the officer's forehead, while the others impale themselves within her bulletproof vest. A light spray of blood dots the inside of the front windshield. She slumps over, unconscious, although miraculously incurs only a minor injury. The 'Zips' drive forward and pull in front of Renee's apartment house.

One bull remains with the car. Three others strategically place themselves within the building. Two Molotov cocktails are lobbed through her 3rd floor window facing the street. Explosion and fire blow out the living room windows as Renee, Cavon, and the twins are having breakfast. The sound is deafening. Glass shards and the oil and gas mixture engulf the entire apartment in seconds. Teenaged Cavon literally throws his two little sisters out the door of the apartment into the hallway. He goes back for his mom who has small pieces of hot glass impacted across her face, arms, and chest. She lies unconscious, face down on the floor. Cavon stoops over, picks her up, and carries her out. The two are out in the hallway. Her son holds her head off the floor and Renee comes to. Cavon attempts to wipe the blood from her face. More blood seeps from her eyes.

Renee expresses her first concern. "Where are the girls? Please, Cavon, get the girls."

Cavon lays her head back carefully and yells out, "Aretha! Kalin!"

There are no replies.

Out front on the street, screaming and crying seven-year-old twins are jammed between two 'Zips' in the back seat of a Town Car with blacked-out windows. It speeds away. Cavon, running out onto the street, falls to his knees, places his head in his palms, and weeps. It's early morning. The explosion and fire cause a crowd, as neighbors exit their buildings and run over to the boy.

Men, women, and children surround him in support. Renee struggles down the final steps and exits her burning apartment building. The remaining families all escape the fire and smoke. The street is in chaos. Renee, in shock, stands before the crowd, bleeding from dozens of small punctures. She sees her son sobbing.

She screams out, "Where are my babies?"

Police sirens are heard from the distance. The sounds become more potent and clear within seconds. Screeching tires from four 'unmarks' amplify an already tumultuous scene. Leaping from the lead vehicle while carrying an Ithaca pump is the frantic Sarge, realizing he's too late. The twins are gone. The wounded officer lies across the front seat of her RMP. An ambulance and two fire trucks file into the street. The EMT's begin treatment on Renee and the officer immediately. Within seconds, the cop is whisked away to the hospital. Renee must also go but refuses. She will not leave the streets that took her children.

Two local teenage junkies who witnessed the kidnapping approach Pasano and give him the details. Radio transmissions from the narc team flood the airways.

"Three-Five Narc Sarge to Central."

"Central, go, Sarge."

"Central, be advised. We have one wounded officer en route to Harlem Hospital. Notify the ER. We also have two female, Black, twin seven-year-olds, taken by force at W. 154th Street and 8th Avenue by four armed White males. Escaped in a black Lincoln, four-door Town Car—darkened windows—unknown direction."

"Central, 10-4 Sarge. Harlem Hospital notified of incoming officer. Central to all units, be advised, we have two female, Black, seven-year-olds, taken by force from W. 154th Street and 8th Avenue—perps escaped in a black Lincoln, unknown direction. White, male perps are armed. Repeat, perps are armed. All units use caution."

Within seconds, marked RMPs stocked with 'uniforms' swarm W. 154th Street to back up their 'Narcs.' A Duty Captain also responds, along with the Three-Five's well-seasoned Detective Squad.

Sarge issues orders to all present, "Okay, men, we split up. We do all the streets at rapid pace. Don't miss a one. 'Uniforms' do W. 130th Street to W. 150<sup>th</sup>. Plainclothes do 150th to 170th Street, East/West. They're here somewhere, trying to lure us in and take us out. You spot something—you radio it immediately. Do not go it alone."

All present acknowledge the order, and the bluecoats push out in a life or death search for the two youngsters.

Despite her condition and multiple requests for her to go to the hospital, an inconsolable Renee Jons stands amongst a crowd of her neighbors and begs their assistance.

"Please, please, help me find my girls!"

There is no hesitation. Over fifty men and women spread out on foot and begin a building-by-building search. Everyone is well aware that time is of the essence. Every minute lost means a greater likelihood that the girls will be murdered in typical retribution style used by the Mafiosos.

The NYPD is heavily armed. The local community folks are armed only with their allegiance to their sons and daughters. There is no looking away. The mob underestimates the will of Harlemites for the love of their children and families.

Multiple marked and unmarked units methodically move up and

down the streets and avenues. Dozens of people are stopped and questioned. Someone must have seen the Town Car. At 157th Street off of St. Nicholas Avenue, Pasano and Fennar spot a familiar 'want.'

Ferris, desperate to please his boss, is secreted in a doorway with two of his bodyguards to protect him. He's always been a loyal Giadana employee. When he was told to continue pushing the remaining supply of heroin, he followed orders. With the failure of new product proliferation and warrants issued for all the local players, it's unwise for him to be out.

Too late. He's been spotted. Sarge and Will bail from their car, and a foot pursuit ensues as Ferris and his two stooges abscond through the main floor hallway of the building and out the back through an abandoned apartment window. The three land in a debris-filled alleyway and get themselves sliced up falling on broken pieces of glass, old piping, and bricks. Will is fast, but Pasano is close behind.

One of the two Ferris bulls doubles back into the building and disappears. Will overtakes Ferris with a solid swing of his .45 to the back of his head. Pasano closes in on the second 'perp' who is running out of breath, as he attempts to re-enter an adjacent building through an open doorway off the alley. The low-level bull turns and pulls his 9mm and points it towards the oncoming Pasano. Sarge has no time for second-guessing. Two shots to the neck of the tired runner fells him. Pasano runs over to him as he's bleeding out and watches one more human's last gasp of life. He's hoping Will keeps Ferris alive to find out where the Inzarita 'Zips' are stashing the girls. He removes the dead man's gun and runs to Will and Ferris.

His first words to his teammate. "Don't fucking kill him! We gotta' find out where they're holding the kids."

"I'm workin' on that right now, Sarge," as he's got two inches of his gun pushed into Ferris' mouth as he questions him. "Okay, mother fucker. Do you live or die? Where are the kids?"

Ferris garbles out some sound, "162 and St. Nick, gray building, 4th floor."

The two 'Narcs' drag Ferris over to his dead associate and cuff them together.

"Stay put for a while," Pasano tells Ferris, "Or you'll wind up like your buddy here. Understand me? We'll be back for you later."

"Yeah," as Ferris is relieved to be breathing.

Will glances over at his boss. "You know this is fucked-up, Sarge."

"Tell me about it. We don't have time for the paperwork. If we still have a job or we're still fucking alive, we'll do it tonight."

"Fine with me, boss. You know I don't like paperwork anyway."

They hustle out front. The Sarge gives a quick signal to his teammates in the other cars. He does it carefully, not to alert the entire army of police on the search mission. Better to keep it amongst the team. Street justice is better served with fewer witnesses. He uses a radio code known only to his fellow 'Narcs.' Just a series of numbers put across the air with nothing else attached. It designates the street where the guys will meet. It almost always means, 'forthwith.' The numbers are a street designation in reverse. The Sarge is at 157th Street. He says only once and in rapid succession, "751." His guys, and no one else, pick up on it. The Raiders will be afforded an opportunity to rescue the twins and do what else must be done.

---

It begins to rain as the community folks continue their search for the two children. Renee has fallen behind. Her illness and injuries have been too much for her. The exhausted woman nearly collapses two blocks from her burnt-out apartment. Cavon supports her the best he can. He places her down to rest on the front steps of an old, Episcopal church. He removes his jacket and places it over her head and shoulders to keep her dry, and walks up the steps of St. Bartholomew's. He reaches out for the tarnished gothic door handles and pulls with all his might. The doors are locked. He frantically bangs on them with his fists and yells for help. No one answers.

He returns to his mother's side, puts his arm around her, and softly tells her, "Mom, please, let me take you back home. You're not well. You can't go on like this," as he wipes more, small droplets of blood mixing with rain from his mother's face with his wet jacket sleeve.

Renee answers with a shallow breath, "Oh, Cavon, you've become my man now. Honey, we have no home to go back to. We have to find your baby sisters."

A faded, blue livery cab pulls up and screeches to a halt. The driver, a burly male, remains behind the wheel as two armed Sicilians jump from the rear seat. One walks to Renee and grabs her with one of his massive hands, crushing her throat. He lifts her off the ground by her neck, as she gasps for a breath. Her feet dangle aimlessly for a couple of seconds. Just before she passes out, he drags her over to the cab and throws her across the back seat. More blood spatters from her face and mouth. Cavon attempts to intervene but is clubbed across his face with a 9mm. He bleeds and falls to the ground as the 'Zip' stomps on his face.

Renee hollers from the car, "Please, no! Please, no!"

The other enforcer takes a roll of duct tape, peels and tears off a piece and slaps it across her mouth. He does the same with her wrists, tying and wrapping them tightly. Renee is done. She's a woman physically and mentally conceding to numerous, violent acts of trauma. She sits slumped over between the two bulls in the back seat as the cab speeds away.

A boy is left unconscious, lying out on the sidewalk, bleeding and swollen, in front of a church displaying an old granite cornerstone engraved with the proverb, *'Trust in the Lord with all your heart and lean not on your own understanding.'*

---

The cab pulls in front of 162nd Street and comes to a halt. The two bruisers pull Renee out, and with one on each side of her, drag her up the steps to the 4th floor. It's a personification of a bittersweet moment when Renee awakens and finds herself tied to an old cast iron radiator in a broken up apartment next to her little girls, Aretha and Kalin, who are also bound and gagged with duct tape. She pushes herself over, stretches, and attempts to reach them. The mother and her two children weep.

———————

Three more 'unmarks,' loaded with six of Pasano's best, pull up right behind the Sarge's car on 157th. No lights, no sirens. The Raiders meet the boss and Will out front.

Pasano begins giving orders. "Okay, guys, we got a location—162nd and St. Nick, gray building, fourth floor. And in case I forget, remind me later, we got Ferris cuffed to a DOA here inside the building." Sarge continues, "Listen up. We go this alone. Stay off the radio. Less people, less confusion. We'll keep it as simple as possible. We park down the block. We go in quiet and quick. Kill all the mother fuckers, grab the girls, and pull out. I'll go up first with Will. John and Jim, you come in from the rear alley. Don and Rob, you follow me up one floor behind. Al and Rico, you head for the roof of the adjacent building to the West. Stay on tac 2, point-to-point radio comm'. Keep in mind, guys, one of the mopes got away from us over here. He might have left the area and went up and warned Giadana's scumbags. Either way, they're not gonna' go easy. Ready up?"

The small unit catches his energy. "Ready, boss."

Sarge gives the final go. "Let's move out and end this!"

———————

Pasano and Fennar pull slowly and quietly onto 162nd Street, one block east of the target. Three more 'unmarks' park behind. The guys exit, spread out, and file in. Two at a time, they walk tight to the buildings and take up their positions.

The Harlem team of streetfighters makes their way forward. They're also dealing with the onset of darkness. It would be nearly impossible to negotiate these dilapidated, abandoned buildings without some natural light. The incessant rain is a minor distraction but aids in the noise abatement of footsteps. They swiftly branch off for their assignments.

The Raiders repeated this ritual a hundred times before. Al and Rico slide into an abandoned building next door and jog four and a half floors to the roof. They're up in less than a minute. They quickly move across the adjoining tarred, flat roof, hop the two-foot brick border ledge, and meander around debris onto their hot zone. The metal roof door is ajar. Dark, but doable.

It's just a whisper into the point-to-point to their boss, "Top team, we're up and ready."

Sarge quietly replies, "10-4. Stand by."

John Calvoy and Jim Kellig slide through the thin, side alley and into the rear main alleyway behind the row of attached structures. It's knee deep in garbage. There's a couple of stray dogs wandering about. Besides using them for target practice, bodyguards use them as warning devices. Barking dogs are usually a sign of strangers. Strangers meaning '5-0s.' John picks up a piece of broken wood, delivers a quick flip, and the animals disperse.

Within seconds, JK signals, "We're out back, boss, all clear, standing by."

"10-4. Stand by."

All Raiders anxiously anticipate their boss's 'go' orders.

Pasano and Fennar make their way up, silently and cautiously, one floor at a time. The old, broken and worn marble steps are slippery from human and animal waste combining with rain. A quick search on each floor. Radios are on low volume.

Don and Rob follow behind. Shotguns, 9s facing down. Fingers at the ready but off the triggers. No safeties on. Live rounds in all chambers. Every cop here is either wet by rain or sweat from anxiety and fear. Fear is always present but dismissed. If any vet or cop says differently, they lie. People will die here.

Aside from the rain leaking down, it's quiet. Breaths are taken in short bursts. One floor to go. The duo pauses. Sarge taps his vested chest with his fist and does the same to Will's.

He nods to his 'brother' and gives the go signal quietly on his point-to-point. "All teams go. All teams go."

Sarge and Will lean tightly against the peeling plaster wall for the final flight. In ten seconds, they're up and peer around the corner of the staircase looking down the long hallways in both directions.

John and Jim come up a fire escape and enter behind the 4th floor stairwell and remain at the ready. McTerren and Sels come up one more flight and join them.

Sarge gives the order for a room-by-room search. "One team for each room and watch for crossfire and the girls."

Starting from the center, Sarge and Fennar, and Calvoy and Kellig take the row of apartments to the west. McTerren and Sels, and Viega and Lorez take the ones to the east. The unit begins moving carefully down the hallway hugging the walls across from each other. Before they get to the first door, a woman is pushed from one of the apartments down at the west end. It's Renee Jons, staggering and bleeding. Her hands and mouth are covered with tape as she shivers from the wet, cold, and illness. The entire team focuses on her. They go low into combat positions, guns pointed down towards her, but well to the sides.

Pasano hollers out, "Renee, come towards us, Renee! Come towards us!"

Within a couple of seconds, two of the henchmen jump out behind her, their assault weapons pointed at her back, using her as a human shield. Renee is sobbing. They each spray a full clip of Mac-10 rounds down the hallway at the 'Narcs' and duck back into the adjacent apartment. In these tight quarters, large caliber rounds sound like explosives, with flash and smoke to match. Ears immediately deafen, and vision is cut to nil. Calvoy is struck in his lower abdomen just below his vest. He's down, bleeding, but still manages to grab for his 9mm. Fennar takes one to his neck and is immediately dropped as blood flows from his mouth. Kellig crawls over to the two and protects them with his body. He and Pasano are not hit.

Renee, in shock, stands alone in the middle of the hallway. Paul runs to her, grabs her, and pulls her down against the wall as the two 'Zips' jump out from the apartment again and open fire. Renee, Sarge, and Kellig are hit straight on. Renee, a chest wound. Massive. Kellig takes one to his shoulder. Pasano, one into the vest, breaking his ribs, another into his thigh. He falls, pulls Renee close to him, and removes the tape from her mouth and hands.

In a split second, two more of the thugs jump from an apartment all the way down on the east end of the hallway behind the team and open fire, one with a 9mm and the other a Mac-10. It's more rapid, automatic, high caliber gunshots sliding and bouncing off the walls towards the other team members. The Raiders are caught off guard and pay for it dearly. It is a well-designed and executed trap. Al Viega and Don Sels go down with neck and arm hits. Lorez and McTerren spin around and fire their shotguns loaded with solid slugs, pumping off four rounds. One of the bulls struck goes down, but the other fires off the clip from his Mac and fells both Lorez and McTerren, one tagged in the lower stomach, the other, his thigh. Both are in pain but still holding tight to their weapons. The 'Zip' slams a fresh clip into his weapon and continues his walk towards the vulnerable 'Narcs' as the other two mobsters continue their march towards Renee and Sarge. Finality is at hand.

Renee is bleeding profusely. Pasano attempts to curtail it, unsuccessfully. He's unable to load a fresh clip into his nine or reach for his shotgun because of his injuries. Calvoy still lies bleeding but manages to let off another five rounds. On the sixth shot, his auto jams. Sarge puts his arm around Renee and pulls her closer to him. Her once vibrant, dark, oval eyes are dimming.

She whispers to her friend, "Paul, please don't forget your promise."

"Never," Pasano tells her solemnly.

The Harlem Raiders are down. They underestimated their enemy and overestimated their own power. They were never invincible, just human beings with a cause who acted as if they were.

The Mafiosos are ready and poised for the final kill. Guns are raised and aimed.

One calls out in Italian, *"Voi Americani, è il tuo turno per morire!"* ("You Americans, it is your turn to die!")

Suddenly, it's quiet, and to the bluecoats, everything appears in slow motion. A common occurrence during violent combat scenarios.

Then, instantaneously, there is shouting from the center hallway landing of the stairways to the roof and the lower floors. It is immediately followed by the unmistakable sounds of loud gunfire from automatic rifles and shotguns. The barrage of bullets from these assault weapons lasts for a few seconds. Muzzle flash and smoke fill the entire hallway end to end, from ceiling to floor. Through the fog, images of bodies being thrown about and collapsing in pools of blood present themselves in visions of unreality. Dozens of men and women double-time up and down the staircases, assuming combat positions awaiting further orders. They're dressed in dark-colored jumpsuits. As the smoke dissipates, lettering upon their front chest, bulletproof vests, and rear backs are exposed. Some have three large white letters, 'DEA' on them, others have 'NYPD.'

Leading one group of law enforcement personnel is Lieutenant

Abrams, in charge of The NYPD ESU SWAT Team. Along with him is his good friend, Cam DeVoe. The DEA SWAT Team is led by two people Sergeant Pasano and his 'Narcs' are all too familiar with. The first one is easily recognized as he begins walking over to the Sarge. It's Nick Scalia. A welcome sight. But just behind him is someone shouting out commands to all law enforcement personnel which causes Paul and his guys, who are all bleeding from gunshot wounds, to do a double take. It's Corisa, in tactical uniform, carrying an automatic rifle with a smoking barrel.

She takes charge in a loud, clear, and commanding voice, "Okay, let's move quickly, guys. Remove the weapons from the wounded and dead perps. Search and find the girls. Work careful, people. There still might be more of those dirt-bags in these vacant apartments. When the floor is secured, bring up EMS to attend to the wounded. And get the Three-Five narc team out of here."

Lieutenant DeVoe issues orders, "Okay, guys, you heard her. We'll take the east end. The DEA will take the west. One room at a time. Nobody gets hurt. We all go home tonight. Move out!"

The highly trained unit of bluecoats from the two agencies fan out into the apartments.

Within one-half minute, a shout erupts, "We got the girls!"

A sigh of relief overtakes the entire army of men and women. The twins are escorted out by two female NYPD officers. The children are covered and protected with a blanket over their heads so they will not see the carnage that lies before them. One in particular not to be seen is their mom, Renee. Time for that later.

As Scalia walks by Pasano, he comments, "Hey Paul, you did good, bud."

DeVoe comes over to him next. "Hey, I was worried about you."

Pasano forces a grin. "Hey, boss, how'd you know where we were?"

DeVoe sarcastically answers him, "You sort of left someone behind.

Some guy handcuffed to a body. He was screaming and calling for help. Very confusing. We negotiated a bit, and he told us you'd be here."

"Oh, shit. I forgot about Ferris."

"I'm sure, but we'll talk about all that later. Let me help mop up here."

Then Corisa moves in towards the Sarge.

Despite his injuries, he forces out words fitting the moment, "You got to be fucking kidding me!"

Corisa as always, delivers the snappy response, "Hey Pasano, what did ya' get yourself into here?"

Paul, bewildered, states, "I think I'm dead and having a vision."

Corisa lays down her weapon and leans over him checking his wounds. "You're fine, you'll live. You're a tough guy. And what's the matter, Pasano, you embarrassed being saved by a girl?"

"Oh shit, this is bad," he jokes.

Corisa tells him, "Look out. Let go of Renee, and let me check her." She kneels alongside the women who was a friend and savior to so many and checks her wrist and neck for a pulse then examines her eyes with a small flashlight.

Corisa leans back over to her street companion, and in hushed tones, whispers to him, "I'm sorry, Paul."

The Sarge's head lowers, and he responds, "It's okay. It's what she would have wanted, to go out this way. Just a few blocks from where she was born, and she helped save her daughters as well."

Corisa issues an order to one of the men, "Please have EMS take this woman out first. I don't want her lying out here."

"Yes, Ma'am."

"Okay, Pasano, let's get you up and out of here." The undercover DEA agent slings her assault rifle over her shoulder, puts an arm around Pasano's waist, and raises him to his feet. "Hey, Paul, you could afford to lose a few."

"I can't laugh. It fucking hurts."

"You men. You never could tolerate any pain. You able to walk or do you want me to carry you down?"

"God help me! And who cleaned you up anyway?"

Corisa snaps back, "You're a jerk, Pasano. That's why it was easy to fool your ass. You never realized how far a little make-up and dirt would go, did ya'? Things and people aren't always what they seem. Look deeper."

"Deeper, why, so I can be more disappointed?"

"You need more help than I thought. And when you get to the hospital, call Rachel before she hears of this mess on the news. Enough small talk. C'mon, Mr. Macho, let's go. I have work to do."

For the moment, the Sarge is silent as the two shuffle slowly out, leaving a bloodtrail.

Within minutes, the dual agencies shout out, "Floors all clear! All clear!"

EMT's swarm the area performing triage on the Raiders. Bleeding is stopped and IV's hooked up. The Harlem Hospital ER is notified of incoming. Investigators, Downtown brass, and Crime Scene Units begin their work. The dead mobsters are left in place for the ME. Renee is rechecked, respectfully lifted, placed on a gurney, and covered. Corisa and Sarge slowly make their way down. She assists two EMT's in getting him into one of the waiting ambulances. He's still bleeding and in pain but will not dare wince in front of his people.

As he's placed in the ambulance, he asks, "Hey girl, what's your real name anyway?"

"Yono, Sarge, Yono Ferrara."

"What kind of a name is that?"

"Black, with a splash of Spanish. I'm a real mutt. What's the matter, Pasano, you prejudiced?"

"Yeah, I hate everybody, especially Italians."

Yono laughs and snaps back, "Okay tough guy, you go with these good people, and let them fix you up. I'll visit you at the hospital."

Pasano says in a timid voice, "Hey, Yono, thanks."

She winks at him and closes the back doors to the ambulance.

The other members of the narc team are placed in the waiting ambulances and whisked away. Yono is out front, directing operations, consulting with her DEA team members, and the NYPD's response units.

She's approached by a young teenager with a swollen face and tears in his eyes. It's Cavon Jons, who speaks in a broken voice. "Ma'am, maybe you can please help me? I'm looking for my mother, Renee Jons. She was taken by a group of men earlier. I asked one of the officers, and he told me she might be here, and that my little sisters were taken to the hospital, but are okay."

Standing behind him is the family's neighbor, Mrs. James, who also appears distraught. She remains silent but makes eye contact with Agent Yono Ferrara, who shakes her head in a 'no' fashion. Mrs. James picks up on it, pulls out a handkerchief from her purse and blots her eyes. The boy does not recognize the tragic symbol.

Yono reaches out to Cavon, puts her arm around his shoulder, and walks him over to the side. She talks slowly, and in mellow tones, explains the loss of his mom.

Cavon breaks down and openly cries for his mother, "My mom is gone? What is my family going to do?"

He falls into the arms of the receptive warrior. Mrs. James pauses for a short period and intercedes, gently detaching the boy from Agent Ferrara.

Yono walks over to two Three-Five uniformed backups standing by their marked RMP.

"Guys, can you do me a favor and take these folks back to their residence. It's the son and the neighbor of Renee Jons."

One of the uniformed officers responds, "Of course."

As Yono assists the two into the car, she grabs the youngster's arm and whispers to him, "Cavon, your mom's in Heaven. I'll have your little sisters brought over to you tonight. I want you to look after them and Mrs. James."

She pulls him over to her and kisses his cheek, "I'll check on you tomorrow, first thing."

The radio car pulls away. For just a few seconds, Yono remains perfectly still with her eyes closed. She then opens them, takes a long, deep breath, and walks back inside the building to finish her assignment.

The rain stops just before the sun sets over the west end of Harlem as the delegation of law enforcement moves about fulfilling their duties.

---

Carlos Giadana is already on his way to Sicily by private jet. His failure in New York is only accepted by his first cousin, Sonny Inzarita, who will provide him safety. They will regroup and plan new strategies, but as of today, the Harlem-Sicilian connection is broken. The Inzarita, Giadana, and Seteola crime families no longer have a stranglehold on a community that lived in fear for over a decade. What is left behind are many broken community families that must rebuild their lives. In time, all that will be left are sad memories and the heroes that a neighborhood gave rise to.

## CHAPTER 48

# ON THE MEND

An open ward at Harlem Hospital is filled with injured cops. Gunshot wounds can have a delayed impact. Many of the rounds or fragments may not be removed until a later date after patient stabilization. So it is with the Three-Five unit. The team, minus Rob McTerren, who has been in and out of surgery since the shooting and remains critical, is laid out in hospital beds as a collection of machines beep and buzz. Docs and nurses come and go, delivering a wide variety of treatments. Two 'uniforms' stand guard out front of the specially assigned ward.

Visitors are carefully ID'd. Retaliation is never off the table. With organized crime, vendettas never dissolve. The mood of the men is good. Completion of the assignment was always first and foremost. They're alive. Banged up with career-ending injuries, maybe, but alive. The hardest news to swallow is the death of their community friend, ally, and number one supporter, Renee Jons. It is a heavy price to pay. Pasano feels responsible. A funeral will follow shortly, where the reality of a devastated family will be eulogized.

Immediate family members are making their visits. Rachel is one of them, along with the other wives. The women are happy to still have their loved ones. The stories shared amongst them are put into humorous context to ease the stress and concern. The Mayor, Police Commissioner, and other dignitaries make their way up to offer appreciation on behalf of a city that was besieged by a relentless and murderous family of Mafiosos. The media is exploiting the Freedom Operation but not granted any personal interviews.

The Three-Five CO, Inspector Vic Deteo, and Lieutenant Cam Devoe, walk in, escorted by Detectives and 'uniforms' well-known and supportive of the team. Light banter ensues, with some storytelling without revealing career destroying details. Jokes can turn to job dismissals on a dime. Inspector Deteo shakes the hands of all the teammates. "I'm glad you guys are alive," the Inspector says. "I could not face your families otherwise. I'll make sure Ms. Jons is properly represented by the NYPD, and before I retire, I'll be at the medal day ceremony for all of you. You did damn good. Now get back on your feet and home to your families. That's an order!"

He salutes the crew. It's respectively returned. They all leave, but Devoe stays behind. Always the cool man with a wit to match, he looks around to make sure no one is within earshot outside the ward. He speaks just above a whisper, "Goddamn guys, you sure know how to draw attention to yourselves."

The entire team nods in agreement.

"But, overall you did good. I'm proud of every one of you."

Pasano jumps in, "Hey boss, we got you back on the street, even for just a while."

"Oh yeah," DeVoe continues. "Believe it or not, because of that, they're putting me out in the field permanently. It's my last shot before I pack it in. I'll be heading up one of the NYPD's Emergency Service Units. I'm transferred as of tomorrow. I've come to say my goodbyes."

He gives another quick look around and continues in secretive tones, "Now listen to me, guys, and take my advice, especially you, Pasano. If you can, retire. With all your fucking bullet holes, it should be easy. Take your disability pensions and run."

The unit cracks up.

A more serious Devoe continues, "Hey, I'm not kidding. You come back and they'll be asking you a thousand questions about the whole shebang, especially your latest debacle. Ferris cuffed to your shooting victim. It's fucked-up, man! You'll either get some awards and accolades, or they'll put you in cuffs. If I were you, don't take that chance." He goes on with a cracking voice, "So it's been a pleasure. In my book, you're all heroes." He goes up and down the row of cops and shakes their hands, congratulating them one by one. When he comes to the Sarge, he says, "Especially you, Paul. You be safe."

"Hey, you're the one leading a SWAT Team. You be careful, boss."

Cam leaves and the guys begin their nonsense once again.

Paul declares in a loud voice, "Hey, what the fuck is the big deal about Ferris anyway? We let him live, didn't we? I knew we should have shot him too. Less bullshit."

The guys laugh.

Will Fennar cuts in, "Hey, I told you it was fucked-up."

"Yeah, I remember. But I told you to remind me about Ferris. You forgot!"

"Remind you? I had bullets sticking out of my ass. I wasn't thinking about that loser."

The entire team breaks out in hearty laughter.

JK, changing the subject, remarks, "Hey, you know that young nurse?"

The team rapidly responds, "Yeah, oh yeah."

"Well, she thought I was sleeping, and I caught her peeking under my sheet."

Rico, being sarcastic, says, "Here we go. This guy's always dreaming."

"Anybody hungry?" John Calvoy asks. " I could go for some grits."

Sels changes topics. "Nobody looked under my sheet."

Viega, chiming in, "I asked for rice and beans and they looked at me funny."

Sels, still talking food, "I could go for some Jell-O. There's always room for Jell-O."

Pasano, not believing the conversation, replies, "Rice, beans, and Jell-O? Shoot me now. I gotta' get outta' here. Where's my fucking gun?"

The team breaks out in loud laughter sprinkled with painful groans.

Fennar remarks, "I think they're gonna' get a rubber gun for you, boss."

"Okay, okay, that's enough. I need some rest. That's an order."

The young nurse comes in and declares, "Hey, hey! What's going on in here?" She dims the lights. "Visiting hours are over!"

———————

On day two of the team's hospital stay, the guys are becoming restless. After a hospital breakfast, the old nurse from the ER, well known to the Sarge, enters the room with some flare. "Listen up all you guys. You call yourself, 'Raiders?' I'll tell you who the real Raider is. The woman who saved your asses. She's on her way up now. You treat her right, or I'll put poison in your IV's! You hear me?"

The entire team's quick response, "Yes, ma'am."

On her way out, she says in softer tones, "I'm sorry about Renee. She was my friend too. This hospital will miss her."

In walk Yono and Nick Scalia. The neatly groomed couple appears different, as another side of the two DEA undercover Agents is revealed. Yono's long, black, ponytailed hair bounces softly over a tailored, black pants suit covering a white dress shirt. Semi-heels and makeup complete the fashionable, but professional look. Scalia sports a dark blue suit, white shirt, navy tie. His slicked back hair exchanged for a softer 'do.' The injured cops stare, mostly at the young woman who hid her natural beauty from the rough and tumble bluecoats for years.

A smiling Yono opens, "You guys decent or what?"

Pasano wisecracks first, "Uh-oh, here she comes, cover up."

Yono smacks back, "Don't worry, I'm not interested."

Jim Kellig quips, "That's what they all say. Then one day, you find yourself wearing a tux, being dragged down the aisle, standing in front of a priest."

The team laughs.

Yono, listening to the quibble, responds, "Didn't I tell you, John? These guys are trouble."

Sarge cuts in, "John? I thought it was Nick?"

John, clarifying, "No, Nick Scalia was my undercover name. You know, to protect my family. My real name is John Cafira, from Jersey City. How you doin', Sarge? I'm sorry to see you down on your back."

"Thanks, John. I'll be out of here in a couple of days. I have a promise to keep."

"I hear ya. I just wanted to come up and say thanks for savin' my butt back at Giadana's club."

Paul responds with gratitude, "Hey, I owe you and your partner for pulling me and my guys out of that uptown mess."

"Let's call it a wash."

"Deal," the Sarge agrees.

Yono, butting in, "Okay, enough of the lovey-dovey shit. I hear you guys are getting some sort of medals. For what, getting yourselves shot?"

Sarge comes back with sarcasm, "Where's my gun? Where's my fuckin' gun?"

Everyone breaks out in laughter, even Yono and John.

"Listen, in all seriousness," Yono remarks. "You guys did good. Get well and get home to your wives and girlfriends. Take some time off. You've got some decisions to make."

Paul, responding, "What about you guys? You deserve a long vacation."

"You're right," John agrees.

"We just have one more assignment," says Yono, "and then we'll also take a break. As a matter of fact, my partner here was even thinking of giving up on the Agency and going into a teaching career. Go figure."

Standing nearby, John shrugs his shoulders.

Delivering a line, Jim Kellig, A/K/A 'Cool Breeze,' "Hey girl, come down here and let me get a closer look at the one who pulled me out of a firefight."

Yono walks over to JK and challenges him. "I know you're married Kellig, so behave yourself or I'll send nurse Ratched back in."

Jim smiles. "Oh, well. Can't blame a guy for trying,"

Cafira walks back over to Paul for some one-on-one. "Okay, Paul, you take care of yourself. I'm sure we'll meet up again. Remember under the bridge? We'll all go out and do some beers."

"Hey, you're the one that better take care, bud. That was some shitty assignment."

"Hangin' with Giadana? Nah', piece of cake. The one with the tough assignment was Ferrara."

Paul, conceding, "Yeah, I guess you're right. Laying out, playing junkie for two years, and reporting back all the intel was beyond the worst."

Cafira leans in. "Hey, Sarge, that was only a small piece of her assignment. Her major task was to keep you alive. One way or another, using any tactics."

Rocked, Paul remains silent.

Cafira finishes, "Okay, my friends, take care. Yono, I'll meet you downstairs. I have to call the office."

"Go, I'll catch up with you. And you guys, hopefully not, but I'll probably see you back on the streets."

On her way out, she stops by Sarge's bedside. "Hey, Pasano, you take it easy and get back home to the suburbs. Your family needs you.

Anyway, thanks for saving my backside a couple of times. And you carried me no less. That was cool but embarrassing."

"You should get home to your family as well," Paul counters.

"I told you a long time ago Paul, this is my home."

"He pulls Yono to him and whispers, "I'm sorry about your sister. If I had known, I would have helped, you know that, right?"

"Of course."

"And John told me what you did for me," Paul says.

"I was just doing my job. Now go have some fun. You like playing the ponies, right?"

A staggered Sarge remarks, "You—Palatzi's takeout, hooded sweatshirt-Belmont?"

Leaning over, Yono whispers in his ear, "That was special. It was for your little boy."

Thinking for a moment, Paul continues, "Patasini and Spunel?"

Yono snaps back, "You saw my tat'. Remember what it said? 'Not Me.' Now, you know, a girl never tells," as she smiles.

Feeling dissed, the Sarge presses, "And I always wondered about those mopes who roughed up you and Olivia."

Yono cuts him off, "Hold it, Pasano," as she distorts her face into a weird shape and squints a crazy look to her eyes. She again leans in close to the Sarge's face, and in a snarly whisper, "What do you make me for, Paul, some kind of a psychopathic killer?" She taps his nose with her finger. "You better be a good boy," and laughs. "You know I can't admit to anything. Now, enough questions, Pasano. I gotta go. John's waiting for me. You know Giadana absconded. He's back in Italy."

"I know, don't remind me. It's part of my failure."

Yono immediately delivers a steely look as she again puts her face close to Pasano's and unleashes, "You never used that word before. If I ever hear it again, I'll put my thumbs in your bullet holes."

The two laugh as she punches his good leg. Pasano grabs her arm and squeezes it. Yono turns and starts walking out. She stops, does an about-face, and hustles back, giving Paul a hug.

Kellig remarks, "Hey, what's going on over there?" The guys laugh.

Yono releases the Sarge, looks toward the bed-ridden cops, flips them the bird, turns, and walks through the double doors.

Kellig retorts, "Now that's a tough broad!"

Entire team except for Pasano, responds, "Yeah."

The Sarge hesitates, and then says, "Yeah, she is."

---

A few hours later, doctors are out in the hallway talking with family members, Inspector Deteo, and a priest. A crying wife and young children can be heard through the swinging doors into the open ward where the unit lies. Pasano is in the bed closest to the entrance and can see through the two glass windows out into the hallway. He recognizes the young mother of three as the wife of the seriously injured Raider, Rob McTerren. The family is ushered to a private room by two female uniformed officers from the Three-Five. The guys hear the commotion.

Will asks, "What's all the noise, boss?"

Sarge says in a low voice, "It's Rob, prepare yourselves."

Two of the men speak in rapid succession, "Fuck."

Inspector Deteo enters escorted by the two policewomen. His face is drawn and flush. In a hushed tone, he tells them, "I'm sorry, fellas'. It's one of your guys. Rob died during another surgery. Just too much damage. He was a fighter."

John Calvoy exclaims, in a cracked voice, "Of course, Inspector, he was a Raider."

"Yes, he was, John," the CO says. "Listen up guys, I'll take care of all the arrangements. You get back on your feet."

Sarge interjects, "Hey, boss, I'm going to his funeral if I have to drag this Goddamn bed with me."

Two other teammates join in, "Amen to that." "I'm with you, boss."

Inspector Deteo, agreeing, "Okay, guys, we'll get you there one way or another. I have to get back," as he leaves the room.

An emotional Calvoy remarks, "Hey Sarge, sorry about Rob."

"Me too, John."

Sels cuts in and raises his arm and voice, "To Rob and team!"

The men chime in, "To Rob and team!"

Just before visiting hours end, a teenager knocks softly on the swinging doors to the ward. He enters with a shy expression across his face. The Sarge, sitting up, is first to respond, "Hey Cavon, I'm glad you came up to see these losers. Come over here, son, and let me look at you."

As soon as the youngster gets closer, Paul extends his right hand out to the boy. Cavon grabs it. Sarge pulls him in and Cavon leans over and gives his mom's best friend a long hug.

Paul whispers, "I'm sorry about your Mom, and I'm sorry that I can't be there for her funeral service. You explain to everyone why. Your Mom is at peace now, and you know she was loved by all and gave her life so you and your sisters will have a better one. Do you understand that, son?"

A tear rolls down the teen's face as he acknowledges the wounded cop, "I do, Mr. Pasano. I just wanted to thank you for everything you did for my family, especially my mother."

The other 'Narcs' start shouting out to Cavon, "Hey, come over here and shake hands with all of us."

JK remarks, "You know, the Sarge didn't do it all by himself. We helped just a bit," and laughs.

It forces a smile from the youth as he walks over to the unit members, shakes their hands, and thanks them one by one. He's well received.

On his way out, Sarge gets in the last words, "Make something of yourself, Cavon. On behalf of your mother, do good for other people like she did."

Cavon's fast response, "I will Sergeant Pasano, I promise."

---

With some prompting from the two impatient cops, doctors sign the release forms for the Sarge and Will Fennar. Their wounds were the least serious. With assistance, the duo is able to attend Detective McTerren's funeral along with ten-thousand other law enforcement personnel.

---

The following morning, it's home confinement and rehab for Paul who lives on a soft diet and pain pills. He's hunched and uses a cane to get around. He receives a phone call. A disturbing one.

Agent Cafira, speaking in a muted tone, "How are you, Paul? I hear you just got home."

"Yeah. It feels good to be out of the hospital."

"I bet," Cafira acknowledges. "I wanted to send you my best and give you an update. That final mission that Yono and I had to take care of was in Turkey and Sicily. We just completed it. We did receive some pushback, but my unit took care of Enrico Seteola and his cohorts and burned down the poppy crops across the bloodfields in Turkey. I finally settled an old score with Enrico. Before I took his life, I shoved $75 down his bloodied throat and told him I knew he killed my father. Yono's team removed Sonny Inzarita and Carlos Giadana and their small army of Mafiosos in Palermo. They didn't go easy, but they went, along with their farmhouse and lab. We're both back in the U.S., down in D.C."

Paul steps in, "Jesus, John, sounds like a big deal."

"It was. We did what we had to. You'll be glad to know that Giad-ana, Inzarita, and Seteola are fucking dust."

"That's great. I thank you for that. I wish I could have done it myself. Believe me, I tried."

"I know you did. But you handled your business, and we did ours. There's something else."

"There's always something else," the Sarge interjects.

"Like I said, we did what we were assigned to do and everything went as planned. But there was some fallout. A couple of our Agents were hit. One of our senior guys took a head shot. It doesn't look good. Also, a round sliced through a piece of Yono's spine, and she lost a lot of blood."

"How bad?"

"Serious. We won't know for a couple of days. They did the best they could for her and have her in an induced coma."

"Aw, hell."

"I'm sorry to deliver the bad news, Paul, but after what you did over the past few years earns you the right to be informed."

"Thanks, John. I'm heading on a short trip, and as soon as I get back, I'll call you. Our prayers will be with Yono and her teammate. God forbid the worse happens, please call the Three-Five. They'll know how to reach me."

## CHAPTER 49

# A PROMISE KEPT

Eighty degrees and sunny is the day's forecast for Antigua as the wheels of the 727 touch ground. On board, Paul, with Rachel by his side, is completing a commitment made to a dying woman. Renee's daughter and her Aunt Bay will be met. A story of the teenager's mom's valor will be told.

Over one hundred passengers walk down a long, multi-colored pathway after passing through Island customs to retrieve luggage. An even blend of vacationers, business people, and residents move quickly to begin their journeys. Moving more slowly, with Rachel's assistance, is the Sarge. A small crowd stands behind roped off barriers. Amongst them is a stately, silver-haired, elderly woman dressed in Caribbean garb. Alongside her is Olivia, strikingly beautiful as always. She is older and taller than remembered but well recognizable to Pasano. Her long, straight hair and dark eyes exude the image of Renee. The two groups of people make immediate eye contact. Only the youngest does the running. Olivia lands squarely into the waiting arms of a receptive cop. Tears flow from both parties. Onlookers join in without knowing the circumstances. Rachel hugs Renee's Aunt.

The family elder parts with some kind words. "Thank you for this."

Brief words come from a person who has taken many lives. But here, this day, is a compassionate man who simply declares to Olivia,

"It's time for you to come home. It's safe now. Your mom said to tell you, she loves you."

There is no immediate verbal response from the teenager, just crying. Then finally, she opens up, "Please take me home, Sergeant Pasano, please."

---

The last of the Task Force leaves Harlem Hospital. New lives begin, but with the injuries sustained, careers will end. Unit members spend their time equally divided between physical therapy, required court appearances, and rebuilding family relationships.

After helping to put the remainder of Renee Jons' family back together, Paul and Rachel are now concentrating on their own. They are renewing their efforts in getting new medical treatments for Andrew. Most of them offer little improvement. Acceptance of the boy's condition is difficult. Their youngest daughter, Linda, is their saving grace and offers them solace. With the devastation of so many lives over the past few years, any small semblance of hope is cherished.

---

A groggy, young woman sits up in a hospital bed. Agent Yono Ferrara is the recipient of a small miracle as she awakens after two weeks of weaving in and out consciousness. One of her DEA teammates was not as fortunate and died from bullet wounds incurred during the overseas operation. By her bedside is the always loyal, John Cafira, who has become close to her since her serious injury.

A phone call comes into the Pasano family from over two hundred miles away. It's some uplifting news. "Hello, Paul, John Cafira, D.C. I've got someone here who wants a word with you."

Yono starts the conversation in Corisa style. "Hey, Pasano, what's the good word back in New York?"

"Holy, shit. Yono, A/K/A Corisa, you back from the dead?"

"Yeah, I'm sorry to disappoint you."

"Nah, I actually put you in my prayer cycle along with two dozen other names."

"Don't make me laugh, Pasano. You know you're going to hell."

The Sarge laughs. "Hey, girlie, if I'm heading down, you'll be right there with me, even on a lower floor."

"It hurts to laugh Pasano, but you're right. Listen, I've got more calls to make. I just wanted to let you know, I'm still here."

"No more foolin', Ferrara, I'm happy for you guys. Take a vacation, both of you. And one other thing. Hang on to that Cafira guy. He's good people."

"Yeah, yeah, he's okay. But as soon as I'm outa' this bed, I'm taking two weeks in Aruba."

"Aruba sounds nice and warm. But you in a bikini? I don't know."

"Dream Pasano, dream," as she laughs.

Paul, countering, "As a matter of fact, I was thinking about a trip to Italy for me and Rachel."

Yono snaps, "Italy? Well, if you do, don't go to Sicily. I sort of messed it up."

"I heard."

"But don't worry, Pasano, when all is said and done, I'll be coming back to good old Harlem, USA. I'll see you then."

"I'll be here. I don't venture too far anymore. I walk with a cane now."

"Oh, God. You men are all the same. Wimps! Bye," *click.*

Two hours later, the Pasano phone rings again.

"Hello Paul, it's me, John. I wanted to give you the straight scoop about Yono."

"I figured there was more."

"Lots more Paul. As of today, they say she may never walk unassisted. She's got limited feeling in her lower body. The best they offer is years of therapy ahead. Probably spinal surgery. Sorry to bring you such bad news. And, Paul, please don't tell her I told you all this. You know she's got this macho thing going, especially with you."

Silence, then Paul speaks in a low, broken voice, "I understand. Take care of her."

"Always."

## CHAPTER 50

# FREEDOM RINGS

The day-by-day battle lasted for multiple years. It was a block-by-block, building-by-building struggle that netted over 10,000 arrests, millions of dollars of narcotics, and thousands of guns recovered. The Sicilian and Harlem heroin connection that took in hundreds of millions of dollars annually, was no more. It was a community and police partnership that prevailed.

By the end of 1983, there is a declaration of victory in the newly rebuilt and revitalized expanded Harlem. A community, once besieged by narcotics under the control of the European Mafiosos, is free to thrive. Bloodshed and murders are replaced by fully attended schools, churches, and parks. There is a new birth of people who stand up for the positive values of life itself.

---

On a chilly morning in April 1984, freedom rings out for the residents of Harlem. A large crowd is present for a day of triumph and celebration as a ribbon cutting ceremony unfolds at a newly constructed park just one block from the Jons' residence. It is a small patch of greenery dotted with colorful slides, swings, and fountains for the children. In the center, a brass plaque is placed on a coral granite stone. It reads, *Renee Jons' Memorial Park.*

In attendance are the Mayor, local Congressmen, community leaders, high-ranking police officials, the surviving members of the Narcotics Task Force and their families, including Sergeant Paul Pasano, and the DEA members, with Agents Yono Ferrara in a wheelchair, and John Cafira. Up front in the first row are the remaining children of Renee.

A series of community awards are given to all the team members from the NYPD and DEA. The gathering of people applauds as speeches are delivered. Sergeant Pasano's is last. It is short and speaks of friendships and lives sacrificed. He closes with words he himself proclaimed at every meeting that were converted to a plaque hung within the Three-Five station house lobby, *'There is no greater weapon for a police officer than the support of a community he has sworn to protect.'* As the audience claps, the church bells toll, and the children begin to play.

---

Later that year, members of the Raiders are also honored at the annual NYPD Medal Day Ceremony, where each is awarded a medal of honor. Det. Gary Ritone and Det. Rob McTerren are issued theirs posthumously. With family and friends on hand, it is a proud and uplifting moment, but also signifies the separation of all team members from the department. Retirement for these men doesn't come easy as symptoms of post-traumatic stress find their mark with the replaying of many violent scenarios encountered during their careers. Peer and professional counseling help counterbalance the effects as the journey to physical and mental healing is a long one. Most of the guys eventually assimilate into civilian life. Paul doesn't do as well. Life expectancy for police officers involved in combative situations falls far below the national average. This comes to pass for the team as Al Viega takes his own life on Christmas Day, 1985, leaving behind a wife and three children.

## CHAPTER 51

# 'FIDELIS AD MORTEM' (FAITHFUL UNTO DEATH)

It is present day in Central Harlem High School's auditorium as hundreds of students, faculty, and parents are standing and cheering the lone senior sitting before them on stage. Tears flow from the corners of both her eyes as the elder woman strains and attempts to pull herself out of the cushioned chair. The well-intentioned school principal standing nearby, Mr. Cafira, extends his arms to lend assistance.

She mutters to him, "I can do for myself," as she straightens her body perfectly upright, raising her chin in a confident manner and asks for silence. "Please, please, sit back down. My husband, John, thinks I'm helpless. I assure you, I'm not. I'm Yono."

Once again, the crowded assemblage rises to their feet applauding the couple who is holding hands.

The frail woman continues in a softer tone, "I want to thank you and Principal Cafira for inviting me here today and listening to my story of hope and freedom. Sadly, many of the good people involved are no longer with us. They gave their lives for all of you, so you may have one of peace and prosperity. Please don't waste it on drugs. Learn and become good American citizens. Stand up for yourselves and never let anyone or anything take away what the generations before you fought

327

for. Partner with your local police to combat any evil intenders who may do harm to your communities. May God be watching over your two classmates, Lina and Brianna, and bless all of you."

There is a final standing ovation. John puts one of his arms around Yono's waist and his other hand on the edge of her walker, and the two seniors move slowly off stage.

He bends over to his wife of many decades and whispers, "You did great. You feel alright?"

Despite the many passing years filled with memories of violence and trauma, the older woman's intuition and personality never waiver as she gives a concerned response, "No, I have a bad feeling. Something's wrong."

------

The same morning, a senior couple watches the TV news of the two teens who OD'd on a Harlem rooftop, including the memorial service for them at the high school. Appearing on the screen is a photo of the MS-13 drug lord, Ramone Alegez, covered in Mara Salvatrucha tattoos, wearing his traditional blue bandana.

The old woman remains stoic while the old gent stares intently at the television as a news commentator rattles off the details. "Wanted for questioning by police, Alegez is reportedly the community drug kingpin overseeing the distribution of heroin throughout the neighborhood. Police now believe it was a deadly mix of his 'loco' heroin and fentanyl that caused the two cheerleaders' deaths on W. 141st Street."

With a clenched fist, the old man slams the arm of the couch they're sitting on. "Now it's these Goddamn drug gangs! They might as well have shot them dead in the street," he says with anger. "Same result."

"Too much violence," his wife states calmly.

He looks over at her gesturing in agreement. His bride of over 50 years had sometimes provided a perspective, which brought a deeper truth. He knew he upset her, as a look of distress settles across the face of a once strong woman.

He hands her the remote and pats her knee. "You rest. I'm going to stop by and stay with Andrew for a while."

"You tell that boy to come in for lunch. He's late and still didn't do his homework." She was living in the past, not sure what year it was. Andrew hasn't done homework in over 30 years.

He manages to get off the couch and makes his way out of the living room. "I'm going to call Linda and ask her to come by," he says.

He is a tall, trim man with a shaved head and bushy mustache, wearing a single gold cross earring. He limps, leaning heavily on his cane as he makes his way down the hall. He has forgotten what it feels like to move without pain, though he says it isn't as bad as it had been. He supposes he gets around well for 73. He shuffles to the dresser and removes a small stack of papers from the top drawer.

He then pulls out the *Liberty Life Care and Rehabilitation Center and Admission Applications.*

He reads them again, for about the hundredth time. Picking up a pen, he slowly begins to sign the papers.

That was the easy part.

Limping over to the phone, he takes a deep breath, as his fingers find the numbers. Part of him wishing his daughter didn't answer, but that would only make things worse.

"Linda, it's Dad . . . No, everything's fine. I mean, the world's going to hell, but we're still here. Listen, I need you to come by and watch your Mom for me . . . Yes, honey, it's time. I just signed the papers . . . I know, but it's done. I appreciate everything you've done, sweetheart . . . Yes, I know, I know. I love ya' too."

He hangs up, pauses, and thinks to himself. *'Linda is such a good daughter.'*

He goes to the closet, opens the door, and sighs. Another thing not to look forward to. Propping up his cane in the corner, he bends down and crawls to the back, reaching for a large metal container. He slowly kneels, cursing as he attempts to open the dusty combination lock on the chest. He's successful on the second try.

Reaching inside, he grabs a 9mm semi-auto handgun with three clips wrapped in an oil cloth.

His experienced, yet trembling hands check a clip then slams it in. He lays the other two clips back in the container before locking it.

With some effort, the elder pulls himself to his feet and exudes a long series of troubling coughs, but manages to catch his breath before placing the pistol in the front pouch of a black hoodie sweatshirt he's wearing.

Cane in hand, he heads back out to the living room and sees his wife is asleep. He sits, wanting to spend a few more moments with her.

On the coffee table, an old, faded photo album lays open to a page displaying the beaming smiles of a little boy and his younger sister next to their mom and dad. The old man leans over, touching the portrait with his fingertip, wishing he could feel that happiness once again. His heart beats faster, as he removes the photo, and takes it with him.

He sits up, putting an arm around his wife, before giving her a kiss on the cheek. He whispers, "I love you."

Her lips are dry and cracked. Her hair is uncombed and gray, but she is still the most beautiful woman he's ever met.

He takes a tissue, dabbing at the corner of her mouth before getting up and pulling the old checkered wool blanket higher so she wouldn't chill.

Hearing his daughter's car pull up, he grabs his keys, hobbles over to the front door, and opens it for her. There are tight hugs, but no words exchanged, as he steps out into the pouring rain.

———————————

The old man pulls into the parking lot of the Liberty Life Care and Rehabilitation Center. He finds a spot and shuts off the engine. He sits for a few moments, considering what he was about to do. He has the papers, now it is just a matter of following through. With his sweatshirt hood up and drawstring tautly pulled, he exits the car and goes in with the aid of his cane.

Making his way down a long, polished hallway, he stops at the nurse's station. "Hello, Mr. Pasano, you're a little late today," one of the nurses says.

The old man nods. "Yeah, I had something to take care of this morning. Would you please process this for me?" He hands her his wife's admission papers.

"Sure, sir. We will forward these to administration. Your son is awake and just finished lunch."

"Thank you." Paul lowers his head, and he resumes his journey. He passes multi-colored rooms, in varying shades of green and yellow, until finally coming to his destination.

While standing quietly at a room entranceway, he gazes in on a forty-something male sitting in a wheelchair with head, back, and leg supports in place. They face each other, and the older man's eyes well up.

"Hello, Andrew."

There is no response from the paralyzed patient.

Pasano pulls up a black, vinyl chair, sitting right next to the wheelchair as tears roll down his face.

He reaches over, kissing the younger man on his cheek and forehead before whispering, "I'm so sorry I did this to you, my boy. I love you like no other."

Once again, there is no verbal response, although as he gains focus, the young man's eyes open wider. The father softly touches the top of Andrew's clenched hand, who opens it slightly in response.

After several minutes, he begins moving toward the door. He turns to get a final look at his son, bowing his head in silence.

Leaving the room, he walks down the long hallway. There is no one in sight as if everyone was hiding. The sound of his cane echoes through the hallway as he heads toward the exit.

Once outside, the rain on his face mixes with his tears. He enters the car, wipes his face, then takes a deep breath as he turns the key. The windshield wipers whip back and forth, pushing aside the pouring rain.

He turns on the radio and tunes in the news station. Within seconds, the radio host announces, *"This just in. Police report Ramone Alegez, Harlem's drug kingpin, has been found shot to death early this morning in a hallway at W. 141st Street. Wanted by police, Alegez was apparently the victim of a wild shootout, as witnesses reported hearing over a dozen gunshots. No further details. Detectives are on the scene."*

Turning off the radio, Pasano calmly reaches into his sweatshirt pouch removing his pistol and a bloodied, blue MS-13 bandana. He pauses, holding the gun, then hangs the bandana around the rearview mirror. Catching a glimpse of himself, he unties his hood and lowers it, exposing a deeply creviced face, scarred from decades of violence, and carefully removes a handkerchief covering a bullet wound on the side of his neck that is slowly oozing blood. The old man grunts and places the gun back in the front pouch, while grabbing the photo of his family. After taking a large gulp of air, he rests his head back and closes his eyes while tightly clutching the photo. Within seconds, his hand loosens as the photo drops to the seat, face up. On it is written—'*never give up.*'

---

The sun's rays glisten over a meadow of freshly cut grass, as the dancing clouds cast moving shadows across the hundreds of tombstones. Three figures stand arm-in-arm at a gravesite.

Yono, John Cafira, and Will Fennar, remain at attention with heads lowered in prayer. Will, the last surviving member of the Raiders, steps forward and gently places a bouquet of flowers at the base of a black granite stone. Engraved at the bottom, under the name *Paul Pasano*, are the words, *'The Sarge, Leader of the Harlem Raiders.'*

## THE END

HOUSE OF REPRESENTATIVES
WASHINGTON, D. C. 20515

MARIO BIAGGI
TENTH DISTRICT
NEW YORK

July 11, 1983

Lt. Peter J. Pranzo
NYPD

Dear Sgt. Pranzo:

Your extraordinary courage......

in the thick of hot battle......

with life and limb at peril......

has brought you one of the highest awards of the New York City Police Department, the Combat Cross. Congratulations Peter. You have the admiration of this former police officer.

Be thankful that you have survived the ordeal of that bitter experience. And enjoy the significance of that very cherished award.

You have created another chapter in the best of the tradition of New York's Finest. That chapter has become part of the legions of heroic performances. It is a tremendous credit to you personally and the Department.

My very best wishes for your future.

Sincerely,

MARIO BIAGGI, M.C.

Sgt. Peter Pranzo
NYPD
32nd Precinct
250 West 135th Street
New York, New York  10030

# SAVE A LIFE

**National Drug Helpline: 1-844-289-0879**
The National Drug Helpline offers 24/7 drug and alcohol help to those struggling with addiction. Call the national hotline for drug abuse today to receive information regarding treatment and recovery.

**SAMHSA Helpline: 1-800-662-4357**
The Administration Substance Abuse and Mental Health Services (SAMHSA) is the agency within the U.S. Department of Health and Human Services that leads public health efforts to advance the behavioral health of the nation. SAMHSA's mission is to reduce the impact of substance abuse and mental illness on America's communities.

**National Suicide Prevention Lifeline: 1-800-273-8255**
We can all help prevent suicide. The Lifeline provides 24/7, free and confidential support for people in distress, prevention and crisis resources for you or your loved ones, and best practices for professionals.

**COPLINE-An Officer's Lifeline: 1-800-267-5463**
The hotline is open to active and retired officers and their families who are dealing with the many stressors involved in police work, both on and off the job.

**CRISIS TEXT LINE: Text HOME to 741741**
Crisis Text Line is a global not-for-profit organization providing free crisis intervention via SMS message. The organization's services are available 24 hours a day every day, throughout the US.

CPSIA information can be obtained
at www.ICGtesting.com
Printed in the USA
LVHW090043070820
662472LV00002BA/170